True Heart of a Murderer

True Heart of a Murderer

Ryan Johnson

AuthorHouse™
1663 Liberty Drive
Bloomington, IN 47403
www.authorhouse.com
Phone: 1-800-839-8640

First published by AuthorHouse 6/16/2011

ISBN: 978-1-4634-1475-7 (sc)
ISBN: 978-1-4634-1474-0 (hc)
ISBN: 978-1-4634-1473-3 (e)

Library of Congress Control Number: 2011910111

Printed in the United States of America

1

I woke up on April 22, 2001. It was a school day and I wished I didn't have to go, since that's also my birthday. God, I didn't feel like going, but I remembered that my best friend Pricey needed me to do something for her. She wouldn't tell me what. I fell out of bed and slowly got off the floor starting toward the bathroom. I had taken my bath the night before and the only thing stopping me from getting dressed was brushing my teeth. I opened the door and almost shit my pants when I saw my mom in the tub just staring at me.

"God, you scared me," I told her.

I walked over to the sink and pulled my toothbrush out the medicine cabinet.

"Sorry Veronica. Where are you about to go so early?"

"School. I can't stay home and hang out with you today."

"I don't care. Your father doesn't want to be with me and now you're leaving me."

"Mom, you know I love you and I wish we could spend every day together, but if I don't pick up my grades I'm going to flunk. Come on. Get out of the tub, so I can make you some breakfast before I leave."

I reached for her hand, but snatched mine away when I noticed how cold the water was.

"How are you just sitting in that freezing-cold water?"

"I can't feel a thing, Veronica. I've been in here waiting on your father all night, but he hasn't been home." She made a face that said she knew he was with another woman last night.

"Mom, don't start. You know Bernard just been out on the block working."

"Don't ever let a man make a fool out of you," she said. "Veronica, don't ever fall in love."

"Mom, don't start this, okay? "I'm going to go get your medicine and start breakfast."

"No, just go. Just go to school and learn something, Veronica."

"Mom, promise me that you will get out of the tub, eat something, take your pills and relax. I don't plan on staying in school all day. When I get back we can go get some lunch."

"Veronica, come here."

I got up and sat on the end of the tub. My mom kissed my forehead and pulled me in the cold tub with her. I tried to jump out, but she held me tighter.

"Veronica I want you to know that I love you. I might not have it all upstairs, but I know what I have to do. I don't want this to be a sad day for you. I want today to be the day that you decide what you're going to do with your life. There have been so many times that I have made a decision in an instant, not thinking, and had to pay for it for a long time. This is *your* day."

"Mom I love you, too, but I'm cold as fuck. You're going to be okay, I'll be home in no time. The sooner I go, the sooner I can come back." I jumped out of the tub, angry.

"Veronica, remember what I said. I know you're your father's daughter, but it's never too late to set yourself free—to have what you want."

"I know."

I rolled my eyes and, finally, left the bathroom. If I had a nickel for every time my mother started talking crazy, I would be set for life. I slipped on some clothes that I'd laid out the other night and ran out of the house, fearing I would be late and couldn't get into class. I ran to school, but stopped when I saw Pricey. She ran up to me and gave me a hug.

"Veronica, I have great news! The best news ever!"

"Alright, let me get happy so I can take in all this good news," I replied.

"First, tell me what's wrong because, whatever it is, my news is going to lift you up."

"It's nothing, really, Pricey. My mom was just talking crazy before I left."

"About what?"

"My dad didn't come home last night. He still ain't home and she was just running her mouth. Telling me to free myself and shit."

"Yo mom thinking about leaving your dad?"

"I don't know, Pricey."

"I have never known anybody more in love or faithful than yo mom, Veronica. She not some whore, like my mom. Your mom not going nowhere. She has told everybody in the 'hood that she would kill herself before she left him."

We both fell silent for a moment and then, as if a ton of bricks hit us at the same time, we took off running back toward home. I was inside the building and two floors above Pricey, but she met me at the door because I couldn't unlock it. I was so nervous about what I might find behind it. Pricey took the key from me and opened the door. I ran past her and kicked the bathroom door open; I felt my legs get weak. I fought the urge to fall out. Instead, I jumped in the tub with my mom. Both of her wrists were slit and the water in the tub had turned a deep red. Pricey fell to the floor as I reached for towels to wrap my mom's wrists with. I yelled to Pricey to call 911 and she left the room. I kissed my mom in the back of the head and held her wrists tighter to try to stop the blood from leaking out of her. But she was so limp by the time the ambulance arrived that I knew they weren't needed. By the time they made it to the hospital I knew she would be dead. I never expected that today she would die when she had tried to kill herself more than ten times while I was growing up. Most times, I had to be the one who found her and held her until someone came to help. This time, when the hospital called and told me that my mom didn't make it, I just cleaned the bathroom. Pricey started making dinner and I changed my clothes. I sat at the table and Pricey sat with me. I gave her a weak smile because she was looking at me with worry in her eyes.

"So Pricey, what was that good news you had to tell me? As you can see, I need it right now."

"First, I want to tell you that I found this out the other night and the only reason I didn't tell you was because I didn't know how you would take it."

"This don't sound like any damn good news to me, Pricey," I said with a smile

"It's all in how you take it, Veronica. I'm your sister."

Pricey didn't say anything for a moment, then continued when she noticed I wasn't going to say anything.

"Veronica, I'm your older sister. It turns out that my mom is really our aunty from our dad. She told me that our parents gave me to her when I was born. So we are *real* sisters. We don't have to pretend anymore."

Pricey's face lit up, but my heart sank. She grabbed me and held me tight. I could feel her happiness run through my body and I was praying that she couldn't feel my pain. I held on to her and began to cry. Never had a tear dropped from my eyes, even when I was a baby. My mom told me I never cried. I never had a reason to. What I felt that day from my mom's death I didn't want to feel again, and with Pricey now as my blood sister? If anything ever happened to her I couldn't live with that pain again. I cried for two days straight, not sure of what to do. Pricey stayed by my side. She was a year older than me, but I had a very strong feeling to protect her. The third day after the news of having a new sister, I knew it would only be a matter of time before Pricey started asking me questions. I couldn't bear to think back on all the times I had spent with our mom, so I just handed her mom's diary. The words in that book belonging to Martha Peterson, plus her death, had affected us in very different ways. Pricey would choose one path and I'd choose another. But the one person who would help mold us both, down to the very last detail, didn't walk into the house until a week later.

2

Bernard came home late that night, smelling like weed and liquor. Pricey and I were sitting in the living room watching TV.

"Pricey, why is your mother calling me telling me she hasn't seen you in a week? Both of ya'll ain't been in school. What the fuck is going on?"

"Do you notice anything different, B?" I asked with anger in my voice

"It's a school night; you have company when yo ass should be in bed. Where is Martha, 'sleep?"

"Something like that, Bernard." I said with sarcasm in my every word. "You know how mom is always trying to kill herself?"

"Yeah, did she try that shit again?"

"Boy, did she, B! This time, she actually succeeded, and this all happened a week ago. Where the fuck were you!"

"Hold up, little girl, you need to cool down."

"Fuck you! Why the fuck you ain't tell me Pricey was my sister?"

"What? Who told you this?"

"My mom," Pricey said, speaking for the first time since B came in.

"What she say?"

"That you and Martha gave me to her."

"Aww, shit," Bernard said as he sat on the couch next to Pricey.

"Look: I am yo dad and Martha's yo mom. The reason we didn't keep you is because you were born in a time when I wasn't feeling the parent thing. So Gina took you off my hands and, by the time Veronica was born, I had no one to take her. And Martha swore she would die if she couldn't keep Veronica, so I let her. Nothing against you, Pricey, but I just figured it would be best if you didn't grow up around Martha's wildness. Gina was doing a good job of being a mother, so I just left you where you were."

"Gina, a good mother? She was a *real* good mother when she let her boyfriend rape me!"

"I took care of that nigga, didn't I? That bitch six feet under now. Look, ya'll not about to put all this shit on me! What's done is done! Pricey, you eat and you got clothes on your back just like Veronica. What more do you want?"

"Nothing! I don't want shit from you!" Pricey got up and ran out the door. I ran after her.

"Hold up, Pricey," I called. "Let me walk you home." We made our way out of the apartment and walked.

"Veronica, why he got to be like that? What did I do to him? I didn't ask to be born!" Pricey was trying to hold back her tears.

"Nobody ever does, Pricey. Don't let B get to you."

"How could he just give me away? And give me away to Gina, for that matter?"

"For all the hell you get from Gina, living with Bernard and Martha wasn't any better. B is an ass, he ain't never home, and I had to raise Martha like she was my child. I had to make sure she took her pills and I had to comfort her when B wasn't there. She was more like a friend than a mother, and that shit *sounds* nice, but trust me, it's not. Fuck Bernard and Martha. The best thing they've ever done was give you to me and me to you." Now, we stood outside her door.

I gave Pricey a hug and she went into the house. It was one in the morning and I was walking home by myself at the age of sixteen. When a car pulled up beside me I was ready to run all the way home, until the window rolled down and I saw it was Tyrese McKinney—the guy I had been in love with since the day I laid eyes on him two years earlier at a block party.

"Veronica, what you doing out here this late at night? I hope you not turning tricks."

"Naw, never that. I was just coming back from walking Pricey home."

"Get in. These streets are no place for you."

As much as I wanted to stand there and argue with Tyrese 'cause I didn't want him to think I was some helpless little girl, I just got in. I never knew how long it would be before my crush would just pop up on me again. He was riding in his Impala with the music turned down low, looking sexy as fuck. Tyrese was four years older than me and I knew that all he wanted was sex, if he was even interested in me at all. I was still a virgin and my mother always said that only sluts sleep around. My virginity was a gift that should only be given to my husband, she said, and I did agree. But Tyrese was too fine for me to turn down—if he ever asked for my "gift," I would give it to him. I lay back in my seat and wished that I didn't have to get out his car anytime soon, but my apartment building caught my eye when we were a block away. I took a deep breath and opened the car door.

"Thank you for the ride, Tyrese."

"No problem. If you're ever out on the street while I'm making my rounds, I'll pick you up any time."

"Cool. See you around, Tyrese. Be safe."

I went inside and Bernard was sitting on the couch in the living room. I was about to go to my room when he called me. I stood in front of him waiting to hear what he had to say.

"I made some calls and your mother's funeral is tomorrow, so call and let Pricey know."

"Yeah, whatever."

"Sounds like you have something to say to me, Veronica."

"Be real, B. Tell me the truth: Why did you give Pricey to Gina?"

"When she was born I was working for this guy named Bradford. I had been putting off paying him some money because I was buying things for Pricey. That's really how she got her name. Bradford paid me a visit one day asking for his money. When I told him I didn't have it, he just flipped. He told me to meet him later. When I went to see my sister Gina, she was in the middle of the floor bleeding to death. Bradford had stabbed her about five times, and he told me if I didn't want this to happen to Martha or my unborn child, I better have his money. Your aunty has a two-inch scar down her back, to this day. It haunts me every time I see her. I didn't want that to happen to anybody else that I loved. To be in the business that I am in, you can't have feelings and you can't have ties because it will only be used against you. Remember that, Veronica. You're coming to the age where you need to pick which road you go down."

"You know mom was saying the same thing right before she killed herself. So since we having this little daughter-father moment, can you please be honest with me? That was a nice story and all, but I know you. You lying, so just be real."

"You know you are the only person who can tell when I'm lying. I think you have been around me too long. Fine. The truth is Gina is not my sister. She was this chick I used to fuck with back in the day. Bradford did cut her up, which made it easy to break up with her because she bought the story about her being used against me. I really don't know if Pricey my child, but I take care of her any way, just in case she is. I've been meaning to get a paternity test, but it keeps slipping my mind."

"Did you care about my mom at all, or have you always been heartless?"

"Somehow I feel that you're going to pin all this on me anyway, so let me give it to you straight: Your mom was some broad that I met when I was down South. Her people were loaded and, while I stayed down there, she was cashing me out all the time. When her dad heard about me, he was happy and wanted me to take Martha off his hands, so we made a deal. I take Martha and get a check every month. I grew to care about Martha, but I never loved her or no shit like that. When she had you, I was like, 'Good, something to keep her busy.' I never wanted kids. Too much shit to deal with. Money, time, and worrying about your safety. I just didn't want to deal with it and I still don't."

"So what you saying? I can't live with you no more?"

"Naw, I'm not saying that. But I can't do shit for you. I don't want you to be used against me."

Bernard got up and left.

I couldn't believe that nigga, I take that back—yes I could. That bullshit excuse he was trying to feed me about me being used against him! The only reason he wasn't trying to do for me no more was because my mom wasn't here to make him. I went in my room and called Pricey to let her know what was up. She told me she would be over in the morning. I went to sleep and woke up the next morning with what B had said on my mind. Me being used against him. For me, that shit had some truth it. Unlike him, I had somebody living in this world that I loved and who I didn't want anything to happen to. What he said was sticking with me and as I sat in church, looking at my mother in her casket, with Pricey crying her eyes out, I knew what road I was going to go down. I looked over at Bernard and Gina all hugged up. I held Pricey's hand and broke the news to her about her parents. She looked over at them and then up at my mom.

"Well shit. Easy come, easy go," she said, wiping her eyes. She stopped crying completely. I couldn't help but to laugh at her.

"I wonder why your mom would lie about you not being her child," I said.

"The same reason why I tell everybody that I come in contact with that she my cousin and my parents died in a plane crash. Well, everybody except you."

"You ain't have to tell me shit 'cause we been around each other since forever."

"That's true. I can't get you to leave me the fuck alone." We both burst out laughing.

Pricey pointed out that Tyrese was in the back and I couldn't contain my smile. He looked even better in a suit, and he had a fresh haircut. I was happy that the funeral wasn't long, because I was ready to go. When they dropped the casket into the ground I felt the peace that my mother never had the chance to feel. She was finally going to be happy. As they started to put the dirt over her casket I was tapped on the shoulder by my father. Pricey and I turned around to see this fine-ass, light-skinned brotha. We both knew who he was, but we had never been introduced.

"Veronica and Pricey, I would like for you to meet Dorian James, my boss," B said. I shook his hand and smiled.

"It's very nice to meet you, Veronica. I'm sorry about your loss."

"Thank you for coming, Dorian."

"I want you to know, if you ever need anything, I would be happy to help. I only met your mother once, but she seemed like a wonderful person."

"She was," I said.

Dorian smiled at me and left. Tyrese walked over and gave me a hug. I damn near melted in his arms, he smelled so good. I reluctantly let him go and he walked off with Dorian. Pricey grabbed my hand and we got in the car with Bernard to go home. He dropped Pricey off first and I told her I would call her as soon as I got home. B stopped in front of our apartment and, as I got out the car, he pulled off. I could tell that my life after this was not going to be so great.

3

When B told me he was cutting me off, basically, he meant it. He left me in the house with only a day's worth of food and no money at all. Not wanting Pricey to see me like this, I had not taken her calls and I stopped going to school. But after a week of not eating, I had to swallow my pride and go see her. I was shaking like a crackhead. Without food to keep me balanced, I didn't care about anything else. I hadn't been able to match my clothes or do my hair. I really looked a mess. I thought I saw Tyrese's car when I got halfway to Pricey's house, so I ran the rest of the way. He was not going to see me like this. I made it to Pricey's and was so out of it, it took all I had to knock on her door. Pricey drug me in and closed the door behind me.

"Veronica, what's wrong? Say something!"

"Food. I need some damn food."

Pricey gave me a crazy look and made me a sandwich. I killed that shit. I got up and ran over to the kitchen for more. I opened the refrigerator. Nothing.

"Where is all the damn food, Pricey?"

"Veronica, you know Gina don't buy no groceries. You act like you ain't ever ate a day in your life."

"Try a week, Pricey. I haven't seen Bernard bitch ass since the funeral. He told me that he wasn't doing anything else for me."

"Girl, at least he ain't put you out like Gina try to do me all the damn time. So what are you going to do now?"

"What do you mean?"

"How are you going to live? Where are you going to get money from?"

"I don't know. What *can* I do?"

"Veronica, you got to find you a hustle if you want to survive out here. My mom has put me out plenty of times and I had nothing. No food, nowhere to stay, and I was walking the streets with only the clothes on my back. It didn't take me long to figure out I needed a backup plan if this were to ever happen to me again, which it did, but my time on the street became longer and longer."

Pricey got up to answer the door and I watched as Gina's long-term boyfriend walked in. I was about to say hi until I saw him kissing Pricey in the mouth.

"Mike, stop," she said. "Let me close the damn door first."

I stood up on my feet, shocked and ready to fight because I didn't know what was going on.

"Alright, but we got to hurry. I have to be at work in a half-hour," he said.

"No problem," Pricey replied. "Veronica, go ahead and eat my food. I'll be right back."

I couldn't get any words out, but my eyes followed them back into her room. What the fuck was going on? I couldn't focus on much because the Mexican food that Mike had brought for Pricey was calling out to me. I had eaten her food in less than five minutes and lay out on the couch on a high of fullness. I came back to earth when Pricey and Mike left her room. Mike gave her a kiss on the forehead and left. I sat there with my mouth open, shocked. Pricey sat next to me and looked into the empty container where her food had been.

"Why are you looking at me like that?" she asked.

"What did you just do with Mike?"

"We kissed a little and I gave him some oral."

"*What?* You do know that is your mother's boyfriend, right?"

"Yeah, Roni, and Mike's not her one and only. Like I said, you need to find a hustle. I did. Mike give me money and take me in when my mom puts me out."

"Do you realize that you are only seventeen? You had sex already, and you didn't tell me?"

"Not yet, but I can only hold Mike off with oral for so long."

"You really want to give your gift to Mike?" I asked. "Ain't he like thirty?"

"Look: This little gift in between our legs is a gold mine, okay? Now I'm not talking about being no trick and I'm fo' sho' not telling you to do what I do, but right now this all I got going for me. I'm the only person taking care of myself. I'm not doing this for clothes or no expensive shit. I need a roof over my head and food in my stomach so I'm gon' do what I have to do. Trust me, I don't like it no more than you, but hey, such is life. Anyway, it's this guy I've seen hanging around with Tyrese every now and then. His name is Trip and if I can become his main, I'll be set.

I see him flashing his money around and I don't think he have a girl, he seems real nice. I want to get with him, but you know it will take some time. As skilled as I am, I can have him by the end of the summer."

"Really. You have it all planned out now, don't you Pricey? What type of skills do you have?"

"Plenty, Roni. I have done so much research on sex that I could get a degree in it if I wanted to. Trust me, when that time do come, I'm gone put it on Trip."

"You sound real sure that you gone hook up with him."

"I know I will, just like I know that you will have Tyrese. I know that he know you want him, and all that curiosity gon' make him kill yo cat."

"Whatever, girl. Tyrese doesn't even know that I'm alive."

"You would be surprised, Roni, I've caught him looking at you the same way you look at him sometimes. So what you gon' do?"

"Well I have to warm up to the idea of messing around with some guy, but I'll figure out something. What *you* gon' do if Gina find out about you and Mike?"

"I'm not gon' do nothing. What she gon' do to me, kick me out? I'm not worried about Gina. I hope she do find out, in the worst way possible."

"Alright. As long as you know what you doing. But whatever you do, don't give Mike your gift, no matter what he does for you."

"Alright, Roni. I'll keep that in mind."

Pricey did my hair for me and I went home later that night. I sat in my room and thought about what I was going to do next. The only person who was running anything around here was Dorian. He was in charge of all the illegal jobs in Chicago and I knew he wouldn't let me get on because I was a girl. Another week passed and I was hungry again, Bernard was nowhere to be found, so one day I just got up and went to the store. I started just putting food in my shirt and down my pants. When I was able to walk out with no problems, I had found my new hustle. I just kept on stealing until I got better at it and moved up from food to clothes. I got so good that I could just go into the mall and get whatever I wanted. I was contemplating breaking into houses, but I wasn't sure if that's what I wanted to do. A month had passed and Bernard finally came back home acting like nothing had ever happened. Just when I started having a little money in my pocket, he wanted to show his ugly face. I hadn't talked to Pricey in a while and I wanted to take her out for dinner to show her I was doing alright. I called her house and there was no answer, so I called Mike. He told me he had just dropped her off and a bad feeling washed over me. I ran out of the apartment and straight to Pricey's house. The door was already opened and I could hear an ambulance coming in the distance. Before I could run into the house I spotted Pricey on the grass next door. I went over to her and she was slipping in and out of consciousness. There was so much blood that I could not tell where it was coming from. I kept asking her what happened, but all she could do was mumble. Gina stood in the front doorway yelling, calling Pricey a slut, so I figured out what had happened. The ambulance finally showed up and I got in with her. Pricey held my hand and I wouldn't let go of her, even when the doctors was working on her. Gina had beaten up on her so bad that her whole face was swollen and she needed stitches inside of her lip. There were bruises all over her body; Pricey just looked like a whole different person.

I stayed with her for the rest of the night and she was released the next morning. I called a cab and took her home with me. I made her some soup and let her sleep in my bed after doping her up with pain relievers and putting cream on her bruises so they could heal and not leave any scars. As Pricey sat there in my bedroom healing I got madder and madder, Gina was going to pay for this. One night I decided that I was ready to make my first break-in. I was low on money after taking care of Pricey and paying the rent when B did another disappearing act. It was three o'clock in the morning and I dressed up in my father's clothes and shoes. I didn't need anybody recognizing me tonight so I slipped on a hoody and made my way over to Gina's. I knew that she didn't own a gun so I wasn't worried about anything like that. I busted open the side door and could hear loud music from upstairs. I found Gina on the couch drunk out of her mind and still drinking. I slipped on my gloves and made my way to the kitchen, grabbing a knife. I walked into the living room with Gina and she fell off the couch in fear.

"Veronica, what you doing here?" she asked, getting back onto the couch.

"Why did you beat up Pricey?"

"'Cause she is a whore. Pricey was fucking Mike."

"She wasn't fucking Mike. She is still a virgin."

"Whatever! She a slut and I showed her who was running shit around here; I should have killed her stupid ass. Ain't no point to her life any way, Pricey just a fucking burden and I wish I never had her."

"I've heard enough, Gina," I said. "It's your time."

"What you mean, it's my time?"

I ran over to Gina and stabbed her in the throat, so she couldn't scream. I kept stabbing her until I heard a squishing sound in the couch. Her blood was soaked inside the sofa and she was dead, her eyes open and the look of shock on her face. Her expression of regret and pain made me laugh. Gina looked so stupid and pathetic, which made me happy. I had never laughed that hard or had such a good time. There was no point to Gina's life. When you do bad shit, bad shit happens to you. I took a deep breath and went searching for something I could get money for. Gina didn't have a lot. Hell, she really didn't have shit. She had a couple of dollars and some jewelry, but nothing good. I was just satisfied with what I had done to her, so I was ready to go home. Before I left, I took a moment to look at Gina. She was covered in blood and so still. I thought of my mother and all the times I had seen her covered in blood. Life and death ran hand in hand to me. I went out of my way to go as far from Gina's house and my apartment as I could to dump my clothes in a trash can and set them on fire. I didn't make it back to the house until the sun started to show. Pricey was still asleep in bed and I fell out on the floor on top of my pallet. I woke up to the sound of Pricey screaming at the top of her lungs, "Oh my God!" I ran into the living room and sat on the couch next to her.

"What are you doing up?"

"Roni, look!" she said, pointing to the TV. "Somebody killed Gina."

"What? That shit made the news?"

"Oh my god."

"Are you upset?" I asked, not even thinking that maybe Pricey would be upset if I killed her mom. Now I wondered if I should have done what I'd done.

"Roni, I honestly don't know. Give me a moment."

I sat back on the couch and waited for Pricey to give me an answer. I had no regrets, but if Pricey wasn't happy something was wrong. Should I have killed Gina? What would Pricey think of me if she found out? I got nervous the more I thought about what was going to happen. I was damn near about to shit myself waiting on what Pricey would say.

"Yes! That's what that bitch get, the fucking rat!"

"So you happy that somebody murdered your mother?"

"Hell yeah! I just wished I knew who did it so I could give them a hug."

"Well hug away, Pricey," I said with a half-smile, not knowing if she would feel the same way once she knew her sister killed her mother.

"Veronica, you did this? You killed Gina?"

"Uh, yeah. Look how she fucking treated you! Not only are you my best friend, but you my sister and ain't nobody gon' hurt you as long as I'm alive. Fuck Gina!" I said with anger. The more I thought on it, I really didn't give a damn.

Pricey stood up and looked at me, and then she sat back down on the couch. She stared out into space and then slowly turned to face me. It seemed like years had passed before Pricey spoke.

"Thank you, Veronica."

"Are you sure, Pricey? I mean I can't bring Gina back, but if you not cool with what I did, I'll, at least, say sorry."

"Believe me, I will never feel bad about the death of Gina. I'm just worried about what I'm going to do now. Mike not gon' let me live with him and not give it up."

“Fuck Mike! Stay here. Bernard don’t never be here and I can take care of the bills.”

“How? You ain’t got a job, Roni.”

“That don’t mean I don’t get what I need. Pricey, I’ve been stilling shit left and right. Don’t worry about anything.”

“I won’t, Roni. Between me and you, ain’t shit we can’t handle.”

“Damn right.”

So there it was. Me and Pricey together, making it the best way we could. I taught her how to steal. She would get the food and I would get clothes. I let Pricey have my room and I slept in B’s room. Everything was smooth sailing once the police stopped popping up asking questions. With Bernard being our alibi and us being his, we were good. And once I tipped them off about Mike messing around with Pricey, they jumped all over that. We were both still in school and when the end of the year showed its wonderful face, we were shocked to learn that we had passed our junior year of high school. Pricey woke me up one morning and drug me out of the apartment. When I opened my eyes Tyrese was looking down at me. I smiled thinking that this was one of my lovely dreams—until my big bunny slippers caught my eye and I realized I was outside in my pajamas standing in front of Tyrese with my hair all over my head and my breath on bump. I stepped back and tried my best to look as attractive as I could. Tyrese took his sunglasses off and smiled at me.

“Pricey didn’t tell me you were sleep. It’s the middle of the afternoon.”

“Well it is what it is. Can somebody tell me why, exactly, I’m out here?” I looked over at Pricey like I was ready to pounce on her.

“Tyrese, Roni is not a morning person. The reason you’re out here is because . . .”

“Because I wanted to see you Veronica,” he said.

“Why?” Everybody kinda looked at me like I was crazy.

“What do you mean ‘why,’ Roni? Tyrese and Trip want to take us out!”

"Oh, Trip." I turned around and looked over at Trip so I could wave. "Hey Trip, I didn't see you there. You know, with the way Pricey talk about you, I feel like I know you already. Hell, you family, damn near." Pricey pinched my arm.

"She didn't mean that, Trip. We'll be right back." I laughed all the way upstairs. Pricey pushed me into the bathroom.

"That shit was not funny, Veronica. I don't want Trip knowing that I think about him every second of the day like you do with Tyrese. Get ready and I'll pick out your outfit."

"That's what you get for pushing me up in Tyrese's face while I'm looking a mess. I probably have dried up spit on my face."

"He don't care. Tyrese is feeling you. Trip said he wouldn't go out with me if I didn't get you to go out with Tyrese. You know they cousins. Trip just got him an apartment."

"So you're going to make your move soon?"

"Not yet, Roni, but like I said—by the end of the summer, hopefully, he will be mine."

I turned up my face.

"Why you say it like that, Pricey? Like I'm not taking care of you."

"You know I love you, Roni, but sometime in the near future you knew I might find guys attractive. I can't be your love slave forever." She smiled at me.

"Pricey, why not? I thought we would be together forever." We both laughed our asses off until we were in tears. I brushed my teeth and put my hair in a ponytail.

"Here go your clothes," Pricey said. "Come on. I'm ready to go." I grabbed my stuff from her and closed the bathroom door.

"Boy, are we excited. Chill. We both know that you have Trip right where you want him."

"I hope. Come on!"

I put on my white jeans and a white halter top. Pricey was wearing a white baby doll dress. We both looked way older then we actually were. I hadn't even hit puberty yet. I had the body, but my "friend" still hadn't come to visit me. I wasn't sure if that was a good thing! We finally made our way downstairs and Trip was sitting on the car. Tyrese was selling weed to some guy. I walked over to him and he smiled at me again.

"So Tyrese, what are we supposed to be doing today?"

"Me and Trip are about to go to play some ball."

"And what are me and Pricey supposed to do, just sit there?"

"That's what most people do when they not playing ball."

"Get the fuck out of here. I'm not about to just sit around and watch ya'll play ball while the sun burns me to death!" I didn't like how Tyrese was trying to play me off like I was nothing. I'm no one's groupie.

"Suit yourself, Veronica. Trip, let's roll."

"See you, Pricey. Maybe we can do this next time," Trip said.

"Next time? What you mean 'next time?' Fuck that, we doing this shit today! Roni, don't start this shit."

"Don't start what shit? What the fuck I look like sitting around watching these niggas play ball. Bitch, it's summer time, it's fucking hot and I'm not going for this shit today. I could have stayed sleep for this shit."

"Come on, Roni," Pricey pleaded. "You not doing nothing else today. Come roll with us. For me."

"Get in the damn car so we can go," I said, disgusted.

Pricey hopped in the back seat with Trip, damn near sitting in his lap. I had to sit up front with Tyrese. I had already made up my mind that I didn't like him anymore. How he gon' try to play me like this? Wanting to see me just so I can watch him play ball with the hot-ass sun over my sexy-ass body! Tyrese smiled at me again with this stupid look on his face. Pricey was lucky. She already knew I would give her the world if she wanted it. I loved my sister, so what was a couple hours of my time? We made it to the park in a matter of minutes. Pricey and me went to go sit on the bleachers. There were more people than I expected, and when we made it on the court, I could see why.

Dorian was there and he was suited up, ready to play ball. Pricey picked some seats in the front. Tyrese and Trip took it upon themselves to leave their bags with us. The game had started soon after and, already, the sun was bugging me. I spotted some seats all the way at the top of the bleachers where there was some shade, so I tapped Pricey on the shoulder.

"Come on. There are some seats up there. We can get this sun off our backs."

"Naw, I'm cool. I want to watch the game up close. I know Trip gon' take his shirt off any minute now."

"Whatever. I'll be up there."

"Aren't you going to take Tyrese's bag with you?"

"Fuck Tyrese bag! If it's so damn important, he should be watching it."

Pricey was pissing me the fuck off. I didn't like how she was playing herself all over Trip like that. So far, from what I could tell, he wasn't about shit. Pricey was going about this all wrong. Ain't no sense in getting with a guy if he don't respect you. I put my shades on and tried to get into the game, but I couldn't. I wanted to carry my ass home and go to sleep. About half-hour into this game, I noticed some girls approaching Pricey. I got up and made my way down the bleachers to see what was going on, 'cause we didn't associate with females at all. I got closer and I could see some super-skinny bitch pointing to Trip's bag.

"Bitch, what you doing with my man's bag?"

"I think you better get yo ass out my face, 'cause I'm not hearing nothing you saying," Pricey replied.

"Look ya'll! This little bitch trying to be tough," the girl said to her crew. "Since you a groupie, I'll spare you the ass-kicking and just take my man's things."

"Bitch, you can touch this bag if you want to, and get fucked up."

By this time, I had heard everything and I was waiting on these bitches to make a move. I grabbed two empty 40-ounce bottles and walked into the group that was in front of Pricey. There were only three girls and they were older than us, but fuck it—I was about to even the odds for Pricey. This was about to be a one-on-one fight. As soon as I saw one chick slap Pricey I walked up behind the other two bitches and broke the two bottles over their heads. They both fell out on the floor and all the attention shifted from the game to us. I looked at Pricey: "Handle yo shit."

I stepped back and watched Pricey go to town on this skinny bitch that, just a second ago, had enough mouth for everybody in Chicago. One of the girls that I had knocked out got up and was running at me. I just smiled and punched her in the face. Blood gushed from her nose. Didn't these hoes know that we loved to fight? I walked over to Pricey who was now on top of big mouth, still giving it to her.

"Pricey, that's enough; let's get the fuck out of here." Pricey stood up and spat on the girl. Before we left, Trip came running over to us.

"Where you going, baby?" he asked Pricey.

"Baby? Nigga, you got me fucked up! Call that skinny bitch yo baby! Got me out here fighting bitches over you, like yo ass somebody! You must take me for some type of fool!"

"Why you trippin'? She ain't shit to me. I'm trying to be with you."

"You done already fucked that over."

Pricey and me walked back home. She sat on the couch and I got her a glass of water.

"Here, drink this."

"Girl, I *need* some water. That nigga got me heated."

"So I heard, Pricey. For a minute there, I thought Trip had you open."

"Open? Roni, that's just a role I play for these niggas. I'm just so tired of not having money in my pocket, you know. I see all these niggas out here flashing they money around, spending it on bullshit, and it pisses me off. I want to make some money, get me a place and a car. Be able to go over to New York and buy up some shit I can barely pronounce," she said with a smile.

"Shit, I feel you on that, Pricey, but you have to know these niggas ain't out here trying to give you the world. They want to control yo ass and get a nut. They don't give a fuck about us. Look at how B got us living."

"I see. Look at us talking like we some old-ass women. Fuck, I'm still in high school. I shouldn't have to deal with this shit."

"You right, but this is our life right now and we got to make the best out of it. What you expect? We are raising ourselves. No time to be a kid. That part of our lives is over."

"As long as I got you, Roni, life for me is alright."

"Same here."

4

Pricey ran around the apartment day in and day out, trying to come up with a hustle that would bring in more money. She was so mad that her plan had fallen through with Trip, or had it? I knew that she was still fucking with Trip. A week after the court incident, Trip called Pricey on her cell phone at two in the morning and she meet him outside. The rat didn't come back until the next night. Since then, they had been seeing each other for two straight weeks. Word was that Pricey had Trip hooked, but who knew how he would react to her once she gave up her gift? I found new lingerie in Pricey's room, shit that had been bought from Victoria's Secret. Yeah, it was about to go down real soon. A week later, I caught Pricey trying to sneak out the apartment with an overnight bag. I came out of my room and scared the shit out of her.

"Where the fuck are you going?"

"Hey, Roni! What you doing up, girl?"

"Answer my question, Pricey."

"Nowhere, really. I met this guy and he supposed to be taking me out."

"Could this guy be Trip? The same nigga you been seeing for damn near a month?"

"How did you know?"

"Bitch, we live together. How could I not notice? All I want to know is why didn't you tell me ya'll hooked back up?"

"And make myself look like a fool after all the shit I talked about Trip, how he this and that? How could I face you and tell you I was seeing him again?"

"What you do is yo business. Just don't try to keep shit from me, Pricey. We better than that."

"You right, Roni."

"So Trip the one? You about to give him yo gift?"

"Yeah, and so?"

"I just can't believe that you giving yourself to Trip. How you know you ain't gon' end up like that girl you beat up at the park?"

"One, I don't care that much. If Trip want to mess around with other bitches, I could care less. As long as I'm taken care of, he can do what he damn well please. Two, I can beat any bitch ass that step up to me, and three, after tonight, Trip won't be able to live without me."

"Be a fool if you want to and give Trip yo gift. See what happens. He gon' toss you to the side once he get tired of you."

"You know what, Veronica? You really need to get off this 'gift' shit. Every bitch got a pussy and yours isn't no different than the next bitch. What make anything special is who you give it to and how many times you give it away. All you got going for you is that thing in between yo legs." Pricey was pissing me off, acting like every female in this world was only good for a nut and couldn't maintain without a nigga. I had to lay into her ass and correct some shit.

"Maybe that's all you got going for you, Pricey. Once Trip get his fill of it, he'll be done with you. Then you gon' move to the next guy and the same shit gon' happen over and over again."

"Whatever, Veronica. I'll see you when I see you."

Just like that, Pricey was gone. I sat on the couch mad as hell. Where had Pricey picked up her way of thinking? All that shit she had pushed out her mouth was bullshit. She would see. Trip didn't deserve her, and he wouldn't appreciate her. Pricey would be back, it was just a matter of time. I just hoped I didn't have to kill somebody else over her ass, even though I could use another good laugh. I went back to bed and went to sleep. Soon another week passed and Pricey hadn't been home since that night when we got into it. I walked around asking people if they had seen her, but everybody said no. I didn't start getting upset until another week went by, and still there was no word from Pricey. I didn't even seen Trip or Tyrese around the 'hood any more. This was turning out to be one shitty summer; all I did now was worry and sit up in the house. Early one morning when I heard a knock at the door, I just knew it was Pricey. Boy was I wrong. As soon as I opened the door, in walked Tyrese. He didn't say anything, just pushed past me and came into my house. He sat on the couch and I stood in front of him.

"What do you want, Tyrese?"

"Don't act like you not happy to see me, Veronica."

"Happy to see yo ass for what? You act like we got some type of history."

"Oh, but we do, Veronica. Remember the basketball court?"

"Yes, I remember you being a asshole and wasting my time, but I would hardly call that history."

"Don't put on a front, Veronica, I know you want me."

"I *wanted* you. Very much past tense, Tyrese."

"Whatever, Veronica. I didn't come here to have this conversation. Word is that you've been around asking for Pricey, like the girl missing."

"She is missing. I haven't talked to her."

"Just because someone doesn't want to see you and talk to you don't mean they missing. Pricey is living with Trip now, something she told me you said couldn't be done."

"Well you tell her to, at least, come pick up her shit, since she so certain that's going to be her place of residence forever."

"Why do you think all guys ain't shit? Trip is feeling Pricey and what they got not gon' end no time soon."

"What they got? All they got is sex. There is no way you're going to get me to think any different. Trip is twenty and Pricey seventeen. Not only is that sick that they're even sleeping together, but the fact that they're over there playing house is almost about to make me vomit on myself."

"So now that you're not feeling me anymore, any girl that is dating a older guy, their relationship is sick?" he asked.

I sat down next to Tyrese.

"I'm just saying, why set yourself up for the downfall? Trip only wants one thing. It's not like dude about to marry Pricey or some shit."

"You never know how their story might end, Veronica. Not everybody is cold-hearted like yourself."

"Cold-hearted? You really think I'm cold hearted?"

"Hell yeah, you didn't even cry at your own mother's funeral."

"Not that it is any of your business, but what reason do I have to cry for my mother? She got exactly what she wanted, death. She had been trying for so many years that the whole thing doesn't seem very real to me."

"Pricey said that ya'll found her body and you held onto her until the ambulance came."

"I did."

"How did that make you feel, holding her until she died?"

"It didn't really make me feel like shit. I mean I'm gon' miss her, but I look at it like this: I'd much rather die from my own hands than from another's. Everybody is promised death when they are born and I'd much rather go when I feel like it than for it just to someday pop up on me when I least expect it."

"There he is! Everybody in the 'hood say they see B in you, and there he was, pouring out yo mouth like ya'll one person."

"My mom said I was my father's daughter and maybe she was right."

"So Veronica, what made you stop taking a interest in me?"

"When you show interest in me, Tyrese, I'll show interest in you."

"Really? So where is B anyway?"

"Hell if I know. He don't be here like that. Good thing 'cause he would not be going for me and you sitting up in here like some shit about to pop off."

"Don't insult me, Veronica, I'm a gentleman. The last thing on my mind is having sex with you."

"Shiiiiit."

We both fell out laughing, and then we sat there and talked for most of the day. That became our little thing we did, sit and talk when Tyrese had the time. With Pricey paying me no mind, I was almost happy that I had Tyrese to keep me sane in the days that came. I wasn't really mad at Pricey for not calling. The summer was almost over and everything she said would happen had happened. Trip had let her move in and he was hooked on her bad. He wouldn't even entertain the thought of talking to another girl. I saw with my own eyes how he would damn near push girls out of his face. I just wished Tyrese would do the same sometimes. No, we weren't together like a couple or anything, but we did start going out. I saw him every day. Sometimes he would take me to the movies and out to eat, but that was it. We never did anything physical, maybe a hug and a kiss on the cheek every now and then. Tyrese wasn't disrespectful about seeing other girls. When we were out he would give me his full attention and he never accepted phone numbers. He did tell me about the girls he hooked up with, what they let him do to them and how they were all hoes 'cause they let him hit it so quick. Now I would never put myself in the position to fall in love, 'cause I felt like that was my mom's last, dying wish for me not to, but I felt it was all right to love Tyrese. He made me feel like I was more than what I really was. Like I was a queen or something. Like what I said mattered, and I loved all of that.

The end of summer was damn near right around the corner and every day that I spent with Tyrese got better and better. I knew that I was going to give Tyrese my gift, but I needed some questions answered. I caught the bus over to Trip's apartment one night, happy that he wasn't home. But Pricey was. I knocked on the door and she let me in without saying a word. I looked around the living room.

"Don't be scared, Veronica, have a seat."

"Look, Pricey. I'm gon' get to the point: All the shit I said to you that night you left was wrong. I just felt like you could do better than Trip and I didn't want to see you get hurt. I was being too over-protective and I was just plain wrong."

Pricey came over to me and gave me a hug.

"You don't know how bad I missed your stank ass, Roni."

"*My* stank ass? You don't know how bad I missed you, trick."

"Missed me so bad that you made Tyrese yo new best friend."

"Damn near. I got to talk to *somebody*. So how has life been treating you, Pricey?"

"Good. Real good. Trip gone most of the time, but he always leave me with plenty of money, in case I get bored."

"I hear that. So Pricey, did it hurt when ya'll first had sex?"

"Like hell, Roni! That pain was so severe that I thought I would die for the first couple of minutes. Once I got used to it, though, girl, I think I'm hooked! Every time I see Trip I want to jump his ass and just take it. I think I might be addicted to that nigga dick."

"What? Trip got it like that?"

"Veronica, sometimes we be in bed together and I will wake up in the middle of the night and his dick will be calling to me. It be like, 'Pricey. Pricey, come to me. Suck on me. Ride me, Pricey.'" I couldn't help but to fall out on the couch laughing with Pricey. She was so funny.

"I'm thinking about having sex with Tyrese."

"That ain't no big surprise to me, Roni. You should go for it. It's clear you feeling him and he feeling you."

"I know, but I'm still scared. What if I can't do it right?"

"Girl, all you got to do is lay there. If you feel like you want to do more, do more. If not, then don't. Tyrese just gon' be happy that he even with you."

"When should I do it? Where should we do it?"

"You should do it tonight, over his house."

"Over his house? Pricey, I don't know where Tyrese lives."

"I do, Roni, Trip got a extra key to his house and we can call you a cab."

"What am I going to wear, Pricey?"

"Nothing, girl. Ya'll not going on a date, ya'll getting buckin' naked." I let out a laugh and agreed with Pricey. I felt like tonight was the night and I was ready. The cab came a half-hour later and Pricey gave me some money.

"Look, when you get there, take a shower, put on some lotion, let yo hair down and wait for him in his bed. Then, as soon as you can, call me and tell me everything."

"I will. Talk Trip into taking us to have dinner tomorrow night."

"I will. Bye."

I got in the cab and closed my eyes. When I made it over to Tyrese's house, I couldn't believe it. I cut the lights on and was shocked at all Tyrese had. His house was laced and I had to admit the boy had some good taste. Guys had it so much easier than girls; they could always find somebody to work for. Girls—the only option we had was opening our legs or strippin' off our clothes to make some quick money. Yeah, I could have gone down the right path and taken school seriously, but it would be too hard. Who gon' pay for college, food, clothes and any other little thing that comes up? There was no way I could take care of myself and give my all to school. I ran the shower and got in. The water was nice and hot. I could feel the stress leaving my body and I felt better for being there in Tyrese's house. What would he say when he found me in his bed? Would he even want to do anything with me? Did he find me attractive? I stood in front of a mirror in the living room and checked myself out, with my long, wavy, black hair. And I was a nice, thick size, doing it big in a size eight. The only things that I saw that I wasn't too happy about were my breasts, only a size 34C. Now that might have been fine for some white girl, but I wanted me some D's or something.

I went back in Tyrese's room and got under the sheet he had on his bed. He didn't have the air conditioning on and it was a little warm. The scent of him was all around me and I smiled because, from his smell alone, I was ready to have sex. One a clock in the morning and still no Tyrese. Maybe he decided to spend the night with someone else. I noticed some paper on his desk, which sat in the opposite corner of his bed, so I decided to write him something. It was getting late and I was ready to leave, not wanting to put my dirty clothes back on. I found some clean gym shorts and a wife beater to slip on and I called a cab while waiting in the living room. It came an hour later. I put my clothes in a bag and headed for the door. Once I touched the knob, it opened, I was face to face with Tyrese.

"Veronica, what are you doing here? How did you get in?"

"I got an extra key from Pricey and I had come over here to talk to you, but since my cab is here I guess it can wait until later."

Tyrese walked outside and told the cab driver to take off. I was starting to get nervous as the question, "Could I really do this?" kept popping into my head. Tyrese came back into the house and closed the door behind him.

"What you do that for? That was my ride home."

"Don't worry, Veronica. I'll take you home."

"Thank you, Tyrese." I walked to the door and Tyrese grabbed my arm pulling me over to the couch.

"Wait a minute, we not in a rush. Sit down and tell me what you wanted to talk about."

"I'm really sleepy, Tyrese. We can put this on hold for later."

"Naw, I don't think we can, it seems to me that whatever you have to say must be important."

"Why would you think that?" I was starting to sweat as Tyrese put the clues together.

"Well, because you went to Pricey to get my extra key and come over here instead of just calling me on my cell phone so I could come to your place. You got in a cab, knowing that I might not be home. That's why I think what you had to say is important."

"Well it's nothing that I had to say, really, B came home talking shit and I just needed some place to chill."

"B came home? Really? I wonder how he beat me back from Detroit."

"Detroit?"

"Yeah, B over in Detroit handling some things for Dorian. Told me he wouldn't be back for a month."

"I guess he changed his mind, Tyrese. Look, it's really getting late and I need to get home."

"Wait a minute, Veronica. Something's not adding up. Why, exactly, are you wearing my clothes?"

"It was a long day for me and I just took a quick shower, that's all."

"Are you sure there is nothing you have to say to me?" Tyrese smiled and grabbed my hand.

"I'm sure. Now can we leave?" I pulled my hand away and faced the door.

"Yeah, just let me go in here and change my shoes real quick. My feet are killing me."

I watched as Tyrese left the couch and went into his room. I let out a breath of relieve until I realized my little note for Tyrese was still in there. Maybe he wouldn't notice it; maybe he wouldn't understand what it was about. I couldn't take that chance, though, so I got up and ran into his room. It was too late. He had already read it. I could tell 'cause he had a big smile on his face. I had to think fast.

"Can you come on, Tyrese?"

"Veronica, what is this? And what, exactly, is a 'gift?'"

"I don't know what you're talking about. I didn't write that."

"You didn't? Well damn, it wasn't here when I left this morning, and you're the only person that's been in my house."

"Do I have to call the damn cab driver back? I'm ready to go home!"

Tyrese put the note back on his desk and walked over to me. We stood there, almost face to face. I tried not to make eye contact, but couldn't help it. Tyrese had the prettiest brown eyes I had ever seen. He took his hands and put them behind my neck, pulling me into a kiss. I could feel his warm tongue trying to push its way into my mouth and, as my eyes rolled into the back of my head, I invited it in. This was the first time I had been tongue-kissed and I could tell that I was doing it wrong. I could feel the smile spread across Tyrese's lips as he slowed down and I was able to kiss him better. Tyrese pulled the wife beater over my head, exposing my breasts. Before I could cover them up with my hand, he dropped to his knees and placed one of them in his mouth. I almost fell out right then and there. When he finally did move to the other one, I couldn't take it no more. My knees got weak and I fell into his arms. Tyrese just stood up with me still in his arms and gently placed me in his bed, continuing what he had started. I couldn't help but to rub the back of his head and grab the sheets as tightly as I could. He was making me feel things I had never felt and all I wanted was more. What had I been thinking by trying to deny myself this pleasure? Tyrese kissed my stomach and I helped him take off his shirt. Boy did he have a body. That damn six-pack screamed to be touched and I did slowly wanting to cover every inch of his body with my hands. I could feel Tyrese pulling at my shorts and my body stiffened. He looked up at me, whispering, "Relax." He took off my shorts and my legs were closed so tight that I knew nothing was getting in between them. I began to shake. That's how nervous I was. Tyrese sat up and looked down at me, shaking his head and smiling.

"Come here," he said. I lay on his chest and took in a deep breath before slowly letting it out. He rubbed his fingertips up and down my back. I looked up at Tyrese and all he did was smile at me, kissing me on the forehead. I lay beside him, now ready, and slowly opened my legs. It was now or never, with Tyrese, or with nobody else for me. He was who I wanted and he was who I was going to have. Tyrese made his way in between my legs and kissed the inside of my thigh, moving his way up to my center. When he opened his mouth and his tongue touched my wetness I lost my mind. Never in my life had I made so much noise and felt so good at the same time. Whatever he was doing to my body, he was doing it right 'cause, ten minutes later, I felt this explosion of pleasure throughout my body. I lay there breathing hard as Tyrese finally took off his pants, I wasn't nervous anymore. If he could make me feel like that with his mouth, I welcomed whatever else he had to offer. I spread my legs again for Tyrese and it seemed like forever had passed before I felt the warmth of him right outside of my wetness. I licked my lips and closed my eyes as Tyrese entered me. It hurt, like Pricey said it would, but I didn't care. Tyrese was going as slow as he possibly could, making sure not to hurt me too much, and that meant so much to me.

"Damn, Veronica you so tight," he said. The longer we went, the better it felt, and by the time the sun came up, I had come again. Tyrese doubled that and, as we finished, I had this nigga sayin' he loved me. I knew he didn't mean it, but boy, he said it like he did! We slept all that day and didn't wake up until late afternoon. I woke him up by kissing his chest.

"Good morning, Tyrese."

"Yes, it is a good morning and it was a great last night."

"Who you telling?"

"So how do you feel? Was I any good?"

"Do you really have to ask? You are the only person I've been with, but I know you're the best I will ever have."

"Then my goal is accomplished. Are you hungry?"

"Starving."

"Go get in the shower so we can go get something then."

I rolled out of bed and couldn't stop smiling. Last night had been perfect. I couldn't have asked for more. When I got out of the shower, Pricey was sitting on the toilet smiling at me, I couldn't help but to smile back. She handed me a towel and I dried off.

"I brought you some clothes."

"Thank you."

"So, bitch! Tell me what happened!"

"Girl, everything! We had sex all night. At first, it hurt, but then everything started feeling real good. Guess what? Tyrese ate me out."

"Girl, ain't that shit great? Trip do it all the time and I love it."

"Man, it can't get no better than last night, Pricey."

"Yes, it will. Soon he gon' be trying to move yo ass up in here."

"I don't know about all that, but if he keep doing what he doing, we all good."

"I hear that."

After that night Tyrese and me was always together. Sometimes we had sex, but most times we didn't. I was just happy that nothing had really changed between us. Tyrese was still cool as hell and I was falling in love with him. We got so close that he would let me hold his dime bags and stash some shit at my apartment when he didn't want it on him at the moment. He even had me holding his money when he was playing dice, and when he went out of town I went along with him. For two months we were inseparable until I kept hearing another female's name being said in the same sentence with Tyrese's. I took into consideration that Tyrese was older than me and I didn't want to overreact because of some little kid shit, which I knew would be the first thing that came out his mouth. So I didn't say anything when more people brought to my attention that there was another female involved with my man. I just chalked it up to "he say, she say" bullshit and paid it all no mind. That was until I started seeing Tyrese less and less. It seemed like the dude had no time for me, all of sudden. First, I just pushed that shit to the side 'cause my boo was a very busy person. Then when we were together his phone was ringing off the hook and I could have bet money that he was smelling like some knock-off of "Glow" by Jennifer Lopez. Once again, I played it all off as me just being paranoid over nothing, but that shit wasn't easy since Pricey wanted to be in my face about every little thing. Every day it was the same conversation.

"So what the fuck you gon' do about Tyrese?"

"What you mean what I'm gon' do with Tyrese?"

"Don't play the dumb role, you know he trying to play you. Fucking around with that trashy-ass Mexican chick. You need to put his ass in his place."

"Ain't you a blind person trying to give directions? What about Trip?"

"What about Trip? He not cheating on me, and if he was, so what? I'm not in love with Trip like you in love with Tyrese. You setting yourself up for the downfall and I can't let Tyrese get one over on you."

"The way you talking, Pricey, he already has."

"Roni, wake the fuck up. Tyrese is cheating on you. I seen it with my own eyes, Tyrese was at the mall with his rat and they was buying the place up. He tried to play it off like they was friends, but one look in that bitch eyes and I knew he was dicking her down."

"Really?"

"Veronica, I don't want to see you hurt, and if you don't call Tyrese out he gon' get rid of yo ass. Don't no nigga love or respect somebody they can get over on all the time."

"I hear you, Pricey, and I have everything under control, don't worry."

Had I only listened to Pricey, I wouldn't have been at this house party Trip was throwing, looking salty as fuck. Tyrese was on the dance floor with some Mexican chick, having the time of his life. Even then, I tried to let that shit slide, but when they sat in the corner on the couch and the chick was on his lap with his tongue down her throat, everything came to a head. Pricey grabbed my hand and we both went over there to confront Tyrese.

"Tyrese, what the fuck do you think you doing?" Pricey shouted at the top of her lungs, making everyone pay full attention to us. Out the corner of my eye, I could see Trip trying to make his way through the crowd.

"So Tyrese, this the shit you do behind my back?"

"Come on, Veronica, don't play ya'self like that. I seen you when you came through the door. I'll give it to yo face before I punk out and do it behind yo back. This shit ain't no secret, everybody know what it is. I can't help that you finally chose to see what was going on."

"Straight up, it's like that?"

"That's what you get for fucking with these little girls, Tyrese," the Mexican said.

"What, bitch?" Pricey yelled. "You don't want it with us!" I put my hand against Pricey's chest.

"Hold up. Let ol' girl say what she got to say. I want this hoe to talk herself into a grave." Pricey looked at me and stepped back.

"What, little girl?" asked the Mexican. "You not tough! You just lost yo virginity not too long ago and I'm not even sure yo baby teeth is all out." Tyrese laughed at her little joke and I smiled at him. "I mean, get over it, Veronica! No man wants you, especially not mine."

"I hear that," Tyrese said as he held his girl.

"Hell naw! I'm kickin' somebody ass!" Pricey yelled. Just when she was about to lunge at the Mexican girl, Trip pulled her away.

"You not about to do nothing."

"Trip, let me go!" I watched as Pricey was drug away by Trip.

I took one last look at Tyrese and busted out laughing. What was I thinking? He put on his little grin and I walked away, walked all the way home that night. I had not even cried for my mother, but I would cry that night for Tyrese. I had never felt that much pain in my life and the fact that I knew what was going on all along did not help at all. The more I thought about it, the worse I felt. All Tyrese had wanted from me was ass. I locked myself in the apartment for a week, thinking about him. How could I have fallen for his game, why didn't I see him for what he was? How could he be so heartless, and what reason did he have to play me like he did? I kept wondering how this had all happened and where I went wrong, but with to the questions I had not one answer. To make matters worse, he was always riding through my 'hood with the chick in his car. But, with time, things don't seem that bad and emotions always change. It didn't take long for my pain to become anger and I was happy when it did 'cause I knew then that soon someone would pay the price, and all this hurt I felt could be set free. I went outside the next morning and by the afternoon I had all the information I needed. Justice would be served today.

I went back in the house and waited until nightfall. I caught the bus for two hours and needed five transfers before I reached my destination, but when I got there, none of that even mattered. Thanks to all the big-mouthed people in my 'hood, I now knew where Christina, the big-mouthed Mexican slut, lived and that Tyrese was always at her house late at night so he could get some. Just my luck, as I was walking down the street, I saw him climbing out of Christina's bedroom window. I watched him land on his feet, walk over to his car and pull off. I went over to the same window and climbed in.

"Hey baby, back for more?" she asked.

The lights were off and I couldn't even make out where Christina was. I put walked in the direction of her voice. My leg hit her bed and I could feel her arms reaching out for me. I pulled my knife from my pocket, leaned in toward her and put my hand over her mouth. By the time she realized it wasn't Tyrese I had already stabbed her twice. Yep, she was dead, dead as a doorknob. I couldn't see her, but I felt her lifeless body and I was satisfied with that. I picked up the can of gasoline that I'd brought with me, pouring it first onto the door, then on her dresser, the floor and, finally, dumping the rest all over her body. When I lit that match and the flames sprung up in the air I had light to see. I can't express the joy I felt when I saw Christina covered in blood, eyes rolled into the back of her head and shock all over her face. Freedom! I had not a care in the world as I left the burning room feeling a million times better than I had all week. I walked most of the way home, then I caught a cab when my legs started to get tired. What a wonderful night. I slept so well and wasn't mad when Pricey started banging on my door at nine in the morning. I opened the door with a smile.

"Yes."

"Roni, girl, let me in. I got to tell you something."

“Come in. Excuse the mess. I’ve had a hard week.”

“I’m sorry about what happened to you. Tyrese is a fucking dog and one day he gon’ get what’s coming to him.”

“Yeah, one day. So what is it that you have to tell me?”

“You remember the Mexican chick that was with Tyrese?”

“Of course. How could I forget? Her and Tyrese was hoeing me at the party.”

“Why did her house catch on fire and she was the only one who didn’t make it out?”

“Really? Looks like she talked herself into that grave, after all.” Pricey got real quiet and looked at me hard. Putting her hand over her mouth, she hit my arm, making the connection with my earlier threat.

In a whisper she said, “Roni, you killed that girl!”

“Yep.”

“Why her? Why not Tyrese?”

“Come on now, Pricey, you know the rules. Killing one of Dorian’s workers would cost me my head. So, for now, I’ll let Tyrese live.”

“Veronica, you got to stop this shit. What if the police find out?”

“How can they pin anything on me? I don’t have a record.”

“If the police want yo ass, they will find a way.”

“Pricey, don’t worry. This not gone be something I do every day. I won’t have no dead bodies on my hands for a very long time. I’m chilling from here on out. School about to start and I need to go out so I can make me some money.”

“Good, ’cause I don’t want anything to happen to you, Roni. Sadly, you all I got.”

“What you mean ‘sadly?’ You know you love me.”

"Yeah, Yeah, Yeah."

Pricey chilled with me for the rest of the day and we went out to the mall to pick up some things, but that didn't solve my money problems. Nobody wanted anything at the time, so I wasn't making any money from stolen clothes. I needed a new hustle. I started getting into dice games and stashing shit at the crib, but that only covered rent. Once rent was paid, I was broke all over again. So when this guy named Game started talking to me on my way home from school, I made the mistake of half listening.

"Hey, excuse me, Miss. Can I talk to you for a minute?" I stopped walking so I could get a look at his face. He wasn't bad, but from his half-smile, I could tell he wasn't about shit. He parked his car and ran up on me. "Hold up and let me talk to you for a second." I kept walking and he walked with me. "What's yo name?"

"Veronica."

"Would you like to know mine?"

"Sure." I was not impressed with him and he could tell.

"My name is Kanye, but everybody call me Game." I just looked at him to see if the name fit the face; it did.

"Game? That suits you 'cause you look played."

"Damn, Veronica, it's like that? You don't even know me."

"Yeah and you don't even know me, but you in my face trying to spit game."

"How you figure I'm trying to spit game?"

"You don't know shit about me but that I have a nice body and you wouldn't mind fucking me, so you gon' say and do whatever it takes."

"You pretty smart, but you got me all wrong. I seen this sad girl walking home from school and all I wanted to do was brighten up your day." I stopped walking and finally gave Game my attention.

"You want to brighten up my day?"

"Yes, if you tell me how, I will."

"What's the price?"

"No price, just tell me."

"This weekend I want to go to New York and see a play or something. Maybe do a little shopping, have a bite to eat and go out to a club. That would brighten up my day and every day until Saturday, which is in two days. If you could swing all that Game, I might give you my number." I started walking home when halfway down a block, Game called out to me.

"Veronica, where you want me to pick you up at?"

"I'll be around!" I shouted back.

I went home. I had to admit that he had put a little smile on my face. Game hadn't been the first to try to talk to me since the whole Tyrese incident, but he was the first who was able to get more than two words out of me. Dealing with Tyrese had helped me spot bullshit miles before it walked up on me. Now, thanks to Tyrese, all of Chicago knew I was giving it up, so every nigga who spotted me on the streets wanted to try to get at me. Too bad for them 'cause I had made a promise to myself never to allow another man inside of me. I went home and was so bored that I sat down and did some homework. Pricey hadn't been to school all week and life wasn't as fun with her not being around. I was going to call her, but decided against it. Just because my summer love life had fallen short didn't mean hers had to, so I let her be. I slept through most of school the next day, and with all the boredom that consumed my life, I was out of it by the time the weekend came around. I got up Saturday morning and washed my dirty hair plus my funky ass. What to do? I decided to put on my red velour Baby Phat outfit and sat on the couch. By twelve in the afternoon Pricey was calling me telling me I needed to rush over to Trip's place. I got in a cab as soon as I could and went over there, only to find Tyrese's car outside. I called Pricey on my cell phone and told her to come outside 'cause I wasn't going nowhere near Tyrese. I had no love for that nigga and I didn't want him to think anything different. Pricey came running out the house, leaving the front door wide open and got in the cab with me.

"What is Tyrese doing over here?"

"Playing video games with Trip."

"Why am I over here, Pricey?"

"'Cause somebody wanted to see you." Game caught my eye as he was walking to the cab. I looked at Pricey, who was smiling her head off.

"What is he doing here?" I asked.

"He came over here looking for you, said he knew you was my girl and he needed to know where you was."

"How does Game know you?"

"Game doesn't know me know me, but he do know Trip and if anybody know Trip, they know me 'cause that's my shit."

Game walked over to my side of the cab and opened my door. He held out his hand for me. Pricey pushed me out and I had no choice but to take his hand or my ass would have fell on the ground. Game helped me and paid the driver. Everything was happening so fast. When I saw Tyrese come outside I didn't take another step toward the house. I turned my back to Tyrese and looked up to Game as Pricey stood by my side, still smiling.

"Pricey told me you were looking for me," I said.

"Yeah, it's getting late and I didn't want to miss our flight to New York."

"Really? How did you swing that in so little time?"

"I know people. So we still going out?"

"Hell yeah!" Pricey interrupted. "Veronica ain't doing nothing. Go on, girl, and have fun."

I could feel Tyrese watching my every move, so, without words, I got in with Game and we pulled off. In the distance, I could see Trip and Pricey arguing while Tyrese laughed. I could only imagine what that conversation was about. I put my seat belt on and looked over to Game. I couldn't get a read on him because he was holding such a straight face, but I knew he was the bullshit type. All niggas were. And I wasn't about to believe that Game was the exception. I sat back in my seat and waited for him to start asking me all types of questions, trying to get in my head and figure me out and shit, but he didn't. Game drove to the airport and didn't say a word to me; he got a point for shocking me. When we got on the plane I pushed my seat back and went to sleep. When I woke up we were landing. We got off the plane and got straight into a black Navigator. By now, I was starting to wonder where Game's head was at and what he had planned.

"Where we about to go?"

"To see one of Madea's little plays. I forgot the name of it, but I just figured you would want to come see this."

"Why is that, Game?"

"'Cause it's the only thing that you not gon' fall asleep on in the first thirty minutes."

"How old are you?"

"Twenty-three. Is that a problem?"

"Naw, that's not a problem yet. Do you know how old I am?"

"About eighteen."

"Subtract two from that, Game."

"You sixteen? Damn, you don't look it. If we were talking, I would have a big problem with yo age."

"Is that because you run the risk of going to jail?"

"Yes, and because young girls are not my thing. I'd feel like some type of rapist for going out with you."

"Going out, like we doing right now?"

"This is not a date, Veronica. I told you I wanted to brighten up your day and I am a man of my word. Now if chilling with someone who is seven years older then you is a little too much, I understand completely and we don't have to do this ever again."

I sat there quiet 'cause dude was giving it to me like I had him all wrong, and the fact that I was bring all these questions up felt silly. But I had learned my lesson the first time about not speaking my mind and letting shit slide. No matter what Game did or said from here on out, he would still be bullshit to me and, by no means, was I giving it up.

The play we saw was funny as hell. Tears was running down my face, it was so funny. Game surprised me again when we went to dinner and he didn't say a word the whole time. This time I wasn't gon' press the conversation, I was just going to enjoy my food. Right after that we went to the club and, once I got two hard drinks in me, I was on the dance floor with Game. He wasn't giving me much of a reaction, seeing that I was fucking him with my clothes on. We stayed until the club closed and, once again, when we hit that plane, I was out. I woke up over Trip's house and for some hours I lay in bed awake, just looking at the ceiling. I tried to close my eyes when Pricey popped her head into my room, but she had caught me. She jumped in the bed and shook me.

"Get up, bitch. I seen you open your eyes."

"Come on, Pricey, not so loud."

"Alright, just tell me what happened."

"We went to a play, out to eat and to this club. That's all. No sex, no kiss, no nothing, so don't ask."

"What ya'll talk about?"

"Nothing really, Pricey. Did you know he seven years older than me?"

"Yeah, the two losers were talking about it yesterday when you left. I didn't know Game was that old. He look good."

"Yeah, he kinda hot," I admitted. "So what did Tyrese have to say about the situation?"

"Nothing, girl. Talking shit. Talking about all Game want is some ass and you gon' give it up 'cause you so easy."

"That's what everybody think, but they all in for a rude awakening. Feel me?"

"Oh, nigga, I feel you. Tyrese just make his self look like a damn fool 'cause everybody know he was the easy one in ya'll relationship."

"Tell the truth on it, Pricey."

"So are you going to go out with Game again?"

"Maybe. It's not like I have shit else to do. I be at school all by myself."

"Girl, don't try to cut it to me like that. I've been in school."

"School started three months ago and yo ass been about six times."

"It don't matter how many times you go. I bet you my grades tight, though."

"That's cool. I hear you. Just as long as we pass high school, I don't care. 'Cause I can already tell you that college not for me."

"Damn right, Veronica. I don't think they have 'Murder 101' in college."

"Shut up, trick."

Pricey and I shared a laugh. I missed having her around so we could joke and have fun. She was always at Trip's house, being his little wifey. I couldn't hate on her 'cause this was exactly what she wanted. Game and me went out somewhere every weekend after that. It seemed as if he wasn't that bad a guy. I liked the fact that when we went out we talked about everything but us; it made hanging out with him a lot easier. Truth be told, at that point of our chilling with each other, if anybody asked, I said he was "my nigga." I would ride for him and fight any bitch that gave him problems.

I waited outside my apartment for Game one early December day. The leaves were starting to fall off the trees and the sun would set a little earlier every day. I liked this time of year 'cause it wasn't too cold and it wasn't hot anymore. Tyrese fathead self popped up in my face, interrupting the nice thoughts I had running around in my head.

"Hey, Veronica. Stop daydreaming for a second and let me talk to you." I looked up at him and my smile disappeared.

"What do you want, Negro?"

"I just want to talk to you for a minute. I seen yo man had you waiting out here in the cold and figured I'd take the time out to keep you company."

"First of all, I don't have a man and if I was waiting on death I wouldn't want your company. Let's not play games. What do you want?"

"I just wanted to tell you that yo boy Game is a foul-ass nigga. Tells me all the time that he got big plans for you, that I'm not gon' be yo one and only for long."

"That's nice, Tyrese."

"So you saying Game is right?"

"I'm not saying anything. Why are you so damn concerned with who I'm with and what I do anyway? What I do is what I do and that ain't none of yo business."

"Everything you do is my business. You mine, whether I'm with you or not, and I say ain't no other nigga hitting that besides me."

I couldn't help but to bust out laughing 'cause this nothing-ass nigga was so serious. I held on to him 'cause I didn't want to fall from laughing so hard. Game honked his horn to let me know he was there; I looked up at Tyrese and laughed in his face again. He moved my hands off him and I made my way over to Game's car. I wiped my face and cleared my throat as I opened the door.

"Tyrese, you right: No other nigga hitting this," I said. "Not even *yo* ass."

I got in the car and closed the door. I couldn't help but to laugh again when Game looked at me, puzzled. How could Tyrese put his self in the position to be hoed like that? He was such a fool! Later on when I got home that night and went to sleep, I replayed the whole thing in my head. Tyrese was jealous, but why he thought he still had a chance with me was crazy. I was about to milk this for all I could. Maybe I didn't have to kill Tyrese; if I could make him feel the same pain he made me feel, I would be happy. And I think I found me a way to be happy that day. Things, from that point on, got out of hand. My mind was so focused on hurting Tyrese that I didn't realize that I was putting myself in the position to get hurt by someone else. I had started dropping hints to Game, letting him know that I was ready to take this friendship to the next level. Did I mean it? Hell no. Just like he was using me to piss off Tyrese, I would do what he was doing, only better. There was no doubt in my mind that Game was popping off at the mouth to Tyrese now 'cause Tyrese wouldn't be mad like he was if he only knew that me and Game was spending time together. Tyrese didn't care who I dated, but I could tell he cared who I had sex with. What I didn't understand was why Game wanted to piss Tyrese off so bad. But I didn't care. I was too busy laughing at Tyrese whenever he saw me and Game hugged up.

5

I got off on seeing Tyrese get mad. It made me want Game even more. That was the only time I ever really touched Game—when Tyrese was around. And it was like Game knew or something; we would always be around Tyrese. It got so bad that every time they were around each other, any little thing could happen and they were ready to fight. I wanted that shit to happen, too, 'cause I knew Game would fuck Tyrese up. By now, it was February, and me and Game had been together for three months. He had given me one of his cars so I could get back and forth to school when he was out working. He also gave me a key to his place and wanted me to move in with him, but I told him it was too much, too soon for me. He agreed and left it alone. Trip was having another house party and I was excited 'cause I hadn't seen Pricey in a minute. As soon as we got there, I went looking for her. She was in the kitchen getting a drink. I greeted her.

"Hey, boo."

"Roni, long time, no see. What's up?"

"Shit, nothing. How you been?"

"I'm good/ I'm so tired of these damn parties, though. Trip ass love to be around too many people for my taste, but he pay the bills so what can I say?"

"Shit, whatever the hell you want, Pricey. You queen in this house."

"Tell his ass that."

"Come on. I will." I pulled Pricey into the living room where everybody was and we found Trip talking to Tyrese by the window.

"Trip, you need to cut the bullshit."

"What you talking about, Roni?"

"My nigga Pricey just got done telling me that she not feeling this party shit. Your focus should be on her when you not working, not all these ghetto-ass people up in here smiling in yo face 'cause the food and liquor is free."

"Is that so? Come here, Pricey." Pricey walked over to Trip and he gave her a kiss. She smiled and started to blush a little. "That's all I have to do to get you to smile more?"

"Naw, you got to do a little bit more than that." They both cracked a smile and went to the back of the house to their room. I was about to go find Game when Tyrese grabbed my arm and started talking.

"So now you just act like you don't even see me?"

"I wish I had it that good, but I don't. You always seem to be around."

"Come on now, Veronica, enough is enough. You got my attention. What you still hanging with that nigga Game for?" He tried to hug me, but I moved away.

"Don't touch me, Tyrese, and don't play yo'self again."

"Veronica, we both know the only reason you kickin' it with Game is to make me mad."

"Naw, Tyrese, that's where you got shit fucked up. The reason I'm kicking it with Game and not you is simply because Game is better than you. Besides, I've already had you and let's just say I don't even want my own leftovers." I tried to walk away, but he pulled me to him and held me tightly.

"Don't front, Veronica. I was the best you ever had and you was the best I ever had."

"Save the bullshit cause I'm not even hearing you."

I pushed him away and went over to Game; he took me into his arms and kept on talking to his friends. Tyrese ended up leaving early, I guess he got sick of seeing me suck face with Game. I didn't see Pricey for the rest of the night; her and Trip left their own party for sex. Who could blame them? The way Tyrese held on to me brought back memories. Game dropped me off at home and when I made it upstairs Tyrese was waiting.

"About fucking time," he announced.

"What are you doing here?"

"We need to talk, Veronica."

"I don't have nothing to say to you and you don't have shit I want to hear. Just take yo ass home."

"Naw, fuck that. I'm tired of playin' this game with you. I'll be the bigger person and admit that I hate seeing you with Game; or anybody, for that matter. What I did to you was wrong and I'm sorry, but you have to admit that you fucking with Game to get to me."

"No, I'm not. From the beginning, Game approached me."

"Maybe. But since we last talked, you've been all over him and, from what I can see, you only on him when I'm around. Don't deny that shit 'cause I know what you doing and that shit is working."

"Good. Finally, you get what you deserve. But, on the real, what you see between me and Game is all he gon' get, him or any nigga, for that matter."

"Don't tell me I turned you gay or some shit."

"Naw, it ain't nothing like that."

"So you gone stop fucking with Game?"

"Naw! Game still cool people and I like being around him."

"But I know he ain't the nigga you would rather be kissing and spending yo time with. I know I'm sounding like a real ass right now, Veronica, but let's not bullshit each other. I know you love me and I'm gon' be a man and let you know I love yo ass, too."

"What? Now yo ass really going off the deep end! Who said anything about love?"

"I did, Veronica, and I meant what I said."

"We only kicked it for two months and, yeah, the sex was good, but it wasn't no fall in love type of shit," I said, putting up the biggest front of my life.

"Maybe then it wasn't, but now it is. Seeing you with Game and knowing that he holding you down has made my feelings change for you."

"Tyrese, why you trying to kick game to me like you on some marriage type shit? You too fucking slutty to commit yo'self to one person and I'm too young to even be dealing with all this. It's been a long night and I'm tired of playing head games with you. So if you don't mind . . ."

I turned my back to Tyrese and opened my door, but I could feel him on my back: He kissed my neck and pushed me inside. We headed over to the couch. His kisses felt so good. I didn't realize how much I had missed him. I could smell his Axes cologne and that, by itself, made me melt. I was so far gone that I didn't notice, within a few seconds, I was half-naked and Tyrese's mouth was on my breast. Why was he doing this to me? I let myself enjoy his warm tongue on my body, but as soon as he went for my panties, I had to shut him down.

"Tyrese, you have to leave."

"Come on, Veronica don't start this. I want you."

"I'm sure you do, but I'm not a cheater like you. I'm with Game now and, until that end, I can't be with you."

"So drop that nigga!" he shot back at me. I got off of Tyrese and put my shirt back on.

"That's not going to happen. You made your bed, now lie in it. You had me, then you decided to toss me to the side. Your fault, not mine. Truth be told, I love to see you pissed off about me and Game. Why would I leave somebody who wants to be with me for somebody who only wants me when I don't want him?"

"You know what, Veronica? Yo shit gon' catch up with you."

"I'm not worried about it. Good night. Drive safely."

Tyrese got up and left. I could feel his anger, but I didn't care. My feelings for him didn't matter because I knew, at any given moment, he could change his mind and push me to the side again. I wasn't having that shit and, even though all I wanted was his love, my pride had been fucked with. Now, I wanted the chance to laugh at him while he was down. The next month, I couldn't help but notice that things were changing. Out of nowhere, Tyrese gets him a girl and Game started throwing the "L" word around. Game was really starting to get on my nerves. He was like a little kid, always doing crazy shit to get my attention. At first, we were always in the 'hood around his friends, but now, all he did was sit in the house. March 14, 2002 was the day that I finally had direction in my life. This day, everything would become clear to me. I would realize who I was and what I wanted out of life, just like my mother told me to on the day she died.

I watched as Game sat in the kitchen on the phone. He had been on the damn thing all day. I had watched movies for hours and was starting to become restless. It was the same routine damn near every day. Game would pick me up from school, now that he had taken his car back from me, and he would drop me off at his house so we could spend time together. The only thing I went home for was to sleep and change clothes. Other than that, I was always with Game. And with Tyrese out of the picture, I stayed around out of force of habit. He was on this love tip and I wasn't. I could that tell this so-called relationship was coming to an end. Game didn't want me around nobody but him, and when I noticed that I was seeing Pricey less and less, he had to go. There was nothing on TV, so I cut it off and went into the kitchen.

"We need to talk," I said, interrupting his phone call.

"About what?"

"About all this time we have been spending together. I do have a friend that I would like to tend to."

"Who? Pricey? She not nobody." I took the phone from him and hung it up.

"What the fuck do you mean, 'She not nobody?'"

"She not nobody you should be seeing on a day to day basis."

"You tripping, Game. Why is it we don't go out any more? What are you trying to keep me from?"

"Not 'what'—who."

"Who? What do you mean, who? Who are you trying to keep me from?"

"You know who, Veronica. Look, I'm not about to get into this with you. You want to go somewhere, let's go to California for a month. Get the fuck out of Chicago for a while."

"It's starting to dawn on me that Chicago is not the problem, you are." Game looked at me with his eyebrow raised.

"I'm the problem now? Fine. Have it your way. I'll pay for her to come, too."

"Are you hearing yourself right now, Game? You can't just pull people from their lives."

"I pulled yo ass, and what life do you or Pricey have? Two little girls with no guardian, living life. How you think you supposed to live?"

"You right, Game. Look, I'm gon' give it to you straight: We done."

"We done? Give me a reason why, exactly, that is, Veronica."

"I feel like you taking this thing between us a little too serious."

"Maybe I am, so what's the problem? I give you what you want."

"I'm leaving, Game." I sat on the couch and began to put on my shoes.

"You not going nowhere, I made the mistake of falling in love with you and I'm not ready to let you go."

"Sounds like a personal problem to me." Game sat down next to me and wrapped his arms around me.

"Come on, Veronica. Don't be like this. You want to go out, we can go out. Where you want to go?"

"I want to go home, Game. I never want to see you again and I don't want you to turn this into a big, ugly thing. Now take me home." Game jumped up.

"How the fuck can you treat me like this, Veronica? I love you."

"Look at yo'self. You're getting tossed to the side by a sixteen-year-old. You don't have anything that I want. You never did. Now are you going to take me home or what?"

"What about when you said you love me? Did you mean that shit?"

"No, I didn't mean it, loser and don't play that victim role. Your love for me not real, you just figured if you said it enough, I might let you fuck. But too bad for you. After five months, you still not getting shit. Look, Game. I don't want to hoe you or nothing, but this conversation, if it continues, is not going to get better."

"How can you tell me that my love for you is not real?"

I took a moment to look at Game. He was such a loser and I couldn't believe I had allowed myself to hang with him this long. It was time to shut his ass down 'cause he really was getting out of hand. I stood up and put on my jacket.

"Game, your feelings can't be real. Do you remember what you said to me about my age and how you wouldn't take our relationship to that level? I'm wondering were you lying then, or are you lying now?"

"I was lying then, Veronica. When I first saw you, I wanted to be with you. I liked everything about you and I would have told you anything at that point in order to spend a little time with you."

"Do you realize that you're seven years older than me? You have a problem! I don't want to be with no R. Kelly type of nigga! What can I give you that you can't get from a older woman? Why you not dating somebody your age, Game? Is it because all the older girls think you a loser, too?"

"So now I'm a loser? What separate me from every nigga around here?"

"Not a damn thing, Game. That's why I'm not giving it up to none of ya'll nothing-ass niggas. So are you going to take me home or what?"

"Hell naw! You gone sit yo ass here until you change your mind."

I tried to brush past him, but he pushed me back down on the couch. I looked up at him and decided I didn't need all the extra drama. I got up and went toward the back of the house.

"Where you going?"

"To the bathroom! Damn!"

I went to the bathroom and locked the door behind me. I pulled out my cell phone and called Pricey, but she didn't answer her cell, so I left a message. I looked out the window and contemplated jumping, but things hadn't gotten that serious yet. I went back into the living room and sat on the couch. Game sat down next to me and tried to kiss me.

"Nigga, what the fuck do you think you doing?"

"The only thing stopping you from walking out that door is a kiss."

"A kiss? You holding me against my will and you want a kiss!"

"Yes." I went ahead and kissed this fool to see if he would keep his word, and he put his hand down my shirt.

"What is you doing?"

"Come on now, Veronica. You think you gon' just walk away from me like that? I know what you need and if you gon' leave me for good, you gon' have to give me what I been putting all this time in for."

"You better get your hands off me!"

"Come on, Roni. Don't act like you ain't never did this before. Tyrese used to brag about it all the time. Now just open them legs for me." He tried to put his hand in between my legs and I slapped him in the face.

"Damn, Veronica! Look, I'm fucking you today! We can do this the hard way or the easy way. Just relax."

I punched Game in the eye and then I hit him in his throat. While he was trying to breathe, I ran to the bathroom and locked the door. I struggled to get the window open, but as soon as I did, Game kicked in the door and grabbed my leg. As he was pulling me back in, I screamed out, "Let me go!" I lost my balance and hit my head on the edge of the sink. My body fell limp for a moment and I was trying so hard to fight passing out. But I could feel Game pick me up and pull me out of the bathroom. I heard his bedroom door open and I just started screaming. I tried to pull away from him, but he held me so tight, I could hardly breathe. I heard him slam the door and I stood there trying to get my head together. Game walked over to me and I just started swinging. This was not going to happen to me. Game was now a completely different person than I thought I knew. He wasted no time slapping me across the face. I stumbled, but I wasn't about to go down. He came over to me and pushed me onto the bed. As soon as I hit the mattress, it was like something in my head went off and I started screaming louder. I never thought that I would be screaming for help. I could feel Game tugging at my pants and I started to punch him in the head. But it had no effect on him. He kept on doing what he was doing. I guess he was tired of me hitting him, because Game bit me on my chest, damn near drawing blood. I screamed out in pain and when I felt him enter me, I cried. I yelled for help and cried some more. I felt so helpless. I couldn't believe this was happening to me. I could hear his sounds of pleasure. Even after I vomited on him, he still kept going at it.

What seemed like days of horror came to an end when Pricey came through the door, jumping on his back, giving it her all to get him off me, but he tossed her on the floor like it was nothing.

"Dog, what the fuck are you doing?" said Trip as he pulled Game off me and helped Pricey up off the floor. Game stood there with his pants down to his knees, mad that he couldn't finish violating my body.

"How did you get in my house?" he asked them.

"Oh my God, Veronica," Tyrese said, appearing out of nowhere. I couldn't look at him, but I just imagined the expression on his face when he saw me there on Game's bed, covered in vomit. He came over to me and tried to touch me.

"No, no don't touch me!" I said as I jumped off the bed and quickly fell on the floor. "Just don't fucking touch me!"

Pricey came over to me, taking her jacket off to cover me up. She got on the floor with me, taking me into her arms and I just cried. The next thing I heard was fighting, and Trip saying, "No, you know the rules." For the rest of that day I clung to Pricey and she stayed by my side. When we made it to the apartment she ran me a bath and washed my back.

"Roni, I'm so sorry. I should have answered my phone when you called."

"Don't trip off it. I should have never started talking to Game."

"You know it's alright to be upset. I was when it happened to me."

"I'm not upset, I'm just disgusted. Don't worry about me, Pricey. This whole thing has humbled me a lot. I'm not Miss Bad Ass, like I thought, but Game's day will come."

"Veronica, you not thinking about killing Game, are you?"

"Why shouldn't I? Fuck Dorian's little rule. If he don't handle Game, I will. What happened to me today is the worst thing possible. Anything after this is nothing."

"You got to stop thinking like you don't have a fucking care in the world. That's how you got in this mess." I looked up at Pricey, shocked that she would say that shit to me.

"Sorry, I didn't mean that shit," she explained. "All I'm saying is, even though you might take death lightly, I don't. The worst thing that could ever happen to me is losing you."

"I hear you. Like I said, don't worry."

6

Pricey left the bathroom and I thought about what she said. I wasn't living life just for myself, and just in the same way, I would lose my mind if anything ever happened to her. Fine. I wouldn't do anything now. I would let this slide. I washed up and put on some clothes. When I came out of my room, Tyrese was sitting on the couch. I went into the kitchen with Pricey and made a sandwich. Tyrese came over to me and when he tried to touch me, I quickly moved away.

"Look, Veronica. I just came over to see if you were alright."

"I'm fine. Shit happens. I'm still alive."

"I just want you to know that, if it wasn't for Dorian, Game would be dead right now."

"Thank you, I guess."

"Maybe you should go, Tyrese," Pricey said.

"Yeah, I have to be somewhere anyway. Veronica, I'll see you later."

"Sure."

Tyrese left and I sat in the living room watching TV. Pricey stayed the night with me and, even though I told her not to worry, I knew that she still worried. She was the only person who knew what I was capable of and she didn't want to see me put myself in another dangerous position. I was going to be cool, I knew that I couldn't kill all my problems away. All I needed was to learn a little self-control. That was easier said than done 'cause, once news got out about me and Game, it seemed like every nigga wanted to try me. It got to the point where I was fighting every damn day; sometimes it was people I didn't even know. Guys or girls, my age or older than me. I didn't give a fuck. If Game was still living, everybody was going to suffer. I spent all my time in the house thinking of ways to kill him if I could. He spent all of his time telling people how he had me and I wasn't as hot as I pretend to be. Just day in and day out of shit-talking. The boy couldn't keep my name out his mouth. Tyrese and Game stayed fighting and, to my shock, Game was always the one getting his ass whipped. Pricey spent her time with me, making sure I didn't freak out and do something stupid. Every day, I woke up pissed off, ready to fight, and caring about life less and less. I was on the edge and I finally went over it when I fought this girl on my seventeenth birthday. She had been placed in intensive care—and she just happened to be Dorian's so-called "goddaughter." That's when everything came to a head; I was summoned to Dorian's house one day after school. When I say "summoned" I mean two big niggas threw me in a van and drove me there. I was pushed all the way upstairs into a room with Tyrese, Game and Dorian. Dorian was the first to notice me in the room, and he motioned for me to come over to him.

"Here is the star of this ongoing bullshit. Roni, right?"

"My name is Veronica."

"Dorian, this is B's girl," said Tyrese.

"What? Didn't your mother kill herself not too long ago?"

"I think a year is a long time," I said, not happy that he brought up my mother.

"Where is Bernard, Veronica?" Dorian said, annoyed.

"I don't know. I haven't seen him in damn near a year."

"What the fuck is wrong with people nowadays? No wonder you out here running around crazy. Veronica, do you know why you're here?"

"Supposedly, the chick I put in the hospital is your goddaughter, but I can tell you right now I didn't know who she was to you. Had I, I wouldn't have kicked her ass so bad."

Dorian took a moment to laugh. Naw, I didn't care about what he could do to me and I wanted him to be aware of that.

"You're a very funny little girl, Veronica." His smile disappeared and he grabbed me by my neck, pulling me over to Tyrese and Game. "You're the reason why people not getting along like they should. Now I have to clean up your mess and take time out of my day to address things I shouldn't." I pulled away from Dorian and fear popped into Tyrese's eyes.

"Hold up, Dorian, I don't need you to clean up my mess," I said. "Had I had it my way, Game would be six feet under right fucking now. But no, you and your stupid-ass rule stopping me from handling my business."

"Granted, you're a fighter, but you're not a killer," Dorian replied. "I know what a killer looks like and you're not it at all."

"So why don't you let me prove it to you?" I said with a smile.

"First, tell me what the problem between you and Game is."

"Oh, you haven't heard? Game, you've been telling everybody how you had your way with me and you didn't care to mention that you raped me."

"Man, you better get out my face," Game replied.

"Fuck you, you weak piece of shit!"

"That's why you mad, Veronica? 'Cause Game took that shit? Do you know that type of shit happens every day?" Dorian asked.

"Has it ever fucking happened to you Dorian?" Tyrese came over to me and put his hand on my back.

"Calm down, Veronica."

"Get the fuck off me!" I walked over to Dorian and stared him in the eyes. "How would you feel if somebody forced they self on you? Paid no attention to your screams and cries?"

"How did that make *you* feel, Veronica?" Dorian asked, like we were the only two people in the room. I answered him like the person who had done all of this to me wasn't standing there.

"It made me feel weak."

"If it's really so terrible, then why don't you cry now?"

"Crying is for weak people. I said I *felt* weak, I'm not weak."

"So let's see if all this talking has been in vain, Veronica. Kill him," Dorian ordered.

"What?" Game said with fear in his eyes.

Dorian didn't have to tell me twice. I had been waiting for my chance for a month now. I pulled my knife from my bra and slit his throat with ease. When I saw blood squirt all over his shirt, it was like I could breathe for the first time. I felt so at peace, even happy. I laughed when he gasped for air. Game fell to the floor as Tyrese's mouth was wide open. I sat on top of Game, smiled at him and stabbed him in the side, repeatedly, laughing my ass off. I was about to poke his eyes out when Dorian said something that caught my attention.

"Veronica, you're going to have a very bright future."

"What makes you say that?"

"Tyrese, I'm going to need you to leave," he said. "I would like to talk to Veronica alone."

"Alright." Tyrese couldn't even look at me as he left; in a way, it made me feel proud.

"Veronica, this is not your first time, is it?" Dorian asked. I got off of Game and wiped my hands as best I could with his shirt. I cleaned my knife off and put it back in my bra.

"What makes you think that, Dorian? Game really hurt me, and that just sent me over the edge. I had to do something," I said in a vulnerable tone of voice.

"Don't be cute with me. Just answer my question."

"No, this isn't my first time, it's my third. I don't know why, but it just solves all my problems."

"You remind me of myself when I was younger." Dorian sat on his desk.

"Thank you for the compliment, Dorian. So what are you cooking up in that head of yours?" I sat next to him, hitting his shoulder with mine.

"What makes you think that I'm planning something?" he asked, giving me a sideways look. He was surprised that I was so comfortable with him.

"My father has the same look in his eyes right before he leaves. You can't do anything right if you don't have a plan. So what you planning?"

"Does it bother you that Bernard is not around?"

"Not at all. Whether he here or not, my life not gone change."

"So how are you living and paying bills—or was Game your money man?"

"Dorian, I take care of myself. I feed myself and I clothe myself. I don't need any nigga for that. Are we done?" I stood up, angry that he would think I was some kind of gold digger.

"Are you sick of me asking you questions, Veronica?"

"No, but if you're trying to figure me out, you're not going to be able to, so stop wasting your time. You're a very busy man."

"You're right, so let me sum up this little conversation." Dorian came over to me. He was like six-feet-two and thirty years old. He made me feel so small. I didn't like that shit, but as I was about to back up, Dorian slapped me, causing me to fall on the floor. He crouched down and got in my face. I tried to back away, but Dorian grabbed me and pulled me even closer to him. His eyes were so cold. "When I make a rule it is not to be taken lightly, okay? Now I know you've had a hard time with B leaving, your mother dying and the whole Game bullshit, but I don't care. Whatever goes on in yo life, know that what I say is to be followed. This is your warning." Dorian pulled me up off the floor and I pulled away from him, only to be even closer to his face when he pulled me to him again.

"If you ever put your hands on me again, Dorian, I will kill you."

"Are you threatening me, little girl?"

"I said what I said and I meant that shit."

Dorian looked at me really hard and left the room. I went over to Game and looked at his dead body. His eyes were still open and that fear was still on his face. I bent over him, shaking my head.

"What a sad, little man you are, Game. I can't believe you thought you would get away with what you did to me. Bet when you first approached me when I was walking home from school, you didn't expect me to be the death of you. All that glitter ain't gold, and just because I look good don't mean I'm good for you."

I laughed and walked over to the door. It was time to get up out of there. I tried to open the door, but it was locked from the outside. Well, wasn't that something? I went over to the window and saw Tyrese pull off in his car. I felt like I should be jumping out the window 'cause I didn't know what Dorian had planned for me. Then I looked over at Game and realized that I had nothing to worry about. Whether Dorian was going to kill me or not, I didn't care. Even if I did, I wouldn't show any fear. I couldn't be killing people and be afraid of someone killing me, 'cause, most likely, that's the way I was going out. I sat on top of Dorian's desk waiting on him to come back into the room. I ended up falling asleep and waking up in the morning with a gun pointed to my head. Paying no attention, I got off the desk to stretch and I walked over to B, who was standing in the room. He had an upset look on his face.

"Hey, B. Back so soon?" I placed my hand on his shoulder.

"What type of shit have you been in? I saw that dude all cut up. Did you kill him?"

"I think you already know the answer to that B." B looked at me real hard.

"Oh, my God. You crazy just like Martha. I should put you away."

"You would have to be around long enough to commit my ass."

"Who the fuck are you talking to, you little bit- . . ." My father looked at me in shock.

"Oh Bernard, your little Veronica has grown up quite a bit. She is no longer a virgin and that young man who you seen all cut up is the guy who raped your daughter."

"*Raped*?"

"Don't act shocked, Bernard," Dorian said. "You know how shit is around here. What the fuck did you think would happen when you leave a fucking child alone to raise herself? I don't need this little murderer running around fucking shit up, killing my workers."

"Veronica, that guy worked for Dorian, you can't go around breaking the rules," B told me. I rolled my eyes. He could be so clueless sometimes.

"So I have been told, B, but I guess it's a little too late for that speech, seeing that Game is already dead!"

"Yes, he is, Veronica, and you know what happens to people who break my rules," Dorian threatened.

"Let me guess, Dorian. This gun may have something to do with it." I pointed over my shoulder at the big, thick guy who had been holding the weapon the entire time.

Dorian took the gun from him and pointed it to my head. I looked him dead in his eyes as he pulled the trigger; over and over again, all I heard was "click" after "click." He had gone through the whole barrel. The gun had no bullets in it. To Dorian's surprise, I hadn't even flinched, let alone broken a sweat. He smiled at me and hit me in the mouth with the side of the gun. My mouth filled with blood and I laughed.

"Bernard, it seems like you do have a little crazy bitch on your hands."

I stopped laughing and spit in Dorian's face. He raised his hand up to me and I stepped closer. It was time to set his ass straight.

"What? You gon' hit me again? *Hello*, Dorian. Get a fucking clue! I don't give a fuck what you do! If I'm not afraid of death, what makes you think hitting me means anything? You're fucking weak! Yeah, *you*, king of Chicago! But you don't run me. Do what the fuck you want, but you're not going to disrespect me!"

Dorian smiled and started to go to town on me. I was out when he punched me in the face the first time. That beating must've lasted for a while, but the only thing I remember is Dorian saying, "You're a weak little girl and you're not going to last long without me. I could have every nigga in Chicago do what Game did to you. Get yo shit together and realize who's boss!" Then I was picked up and carried away.

"Bernard, have a seat, please." Dorian sat behind his desk and Bernard took a seat in front of him, not sure what to say, what to do or how to act.

"Relax," Dorian said. "I want you here to talk about business. I'm willing to offer you fifty thousand dollars for Veronica."

"What? You want to buy my daughter?"

"Yes."

"I just saw you beat the shit out of her and you want me to just hand Veronica over to you?"

"You saw me hit your daughter and you did nothing. You stood there and didn't say a fucking thing. So what you're telling me is I can beat on your daughter all I want, but she can't belong to me?"

"Dorian, Veronica is only seventeen. What do you want with her?"

"With my guidance, she could be so much more than this crazy-ass, emotional little girl. I could make her into something great. All she needs is to be broken in."

"Veronica is not a horse, Dorian. I can't give you Veronica. Her mother would turn over in her grave."

"Let me get this straight: Out of nowhere, you want to be a father? Keep Veronica from the big bad wolf? How do you think Veronica has been living? Tell me how many people she has killed. How did she feel when she was raped?"

"I don't know."

"Are you willing to die for Veronica?"

"I'm not willing to die for anyone."

"So do I have to get someone to kill *you*, to get what I want?"

"No, all I ask is to let Veronica make her own decision. Wait until she is of legal age, at least."

"You have a point. What am I going to do with a little girl anyway? I do have plans for Veronica, big plans. So this is what's going to happen. Bernard, you're going to be a father. Make sure she goes to school, has clothes on her back, food to eat and, most important, you're going to discipline Veronica. By the time she is of legal age I want her to be very well-behaved. Cut all that talking back shit out and help her find her place. If I don't see improvement in six months, you're dead."

"A year to get Veronica right? No problem."

I woke up in the hospital in a private room with Pricey, Trip and Tyrese all looking at me, sad and shit. Pricey was right by my side, Trip stood over her rubbing her back and Tyrese paced the floor. My eyes were swollen and I could hardly see a thing. My whole body was in pain, but I smiled on the inside 'cause I knew I was the only one who had ever stood up to Dorian. He could do what he would, but I would not be broken. I had lost so much already, and that included any human emotions. Pricey started to rub my hand.

"Damn. All eyes on me."

"Roni, you 'woke! Are you in pain? I can call the nurse so she can give you more pain relievers. How do you feel?"

"I look like shit, Pricey, but I feel fine. Don't worry. How long have I been in here?"

"About three days. I could kill Dorian for doing this to you."

"Trust me I had it coming." I tried to smile, but couldn't. Tyrese came over to me and, even though I couldn't see him well, I could feel his anger.

"Yeah, all that shit you was talking! You lucky he didn't kill you!"

"Excuse me for having more balls than every nigga in Chicago!"

"It's not about having balls, Veronica, it's about knowing how to play the game."

"And all ya'll niggas that work for Dorian play the game like bitches. Nobody is going to run me, and I don't fear no nigga. I'll talk as much shit as I want until Dorian shut me up, and, even in death, I'm still going to be talking shit." I heard Pricey trying to hold back her tears and not let me know she was crying.

"Can ya'll give me a moment to talk to Pricey alone?" When I heard my door open and close again, I spoke. "They gone, Pricey?"

"Yeah, they gone."

"I need you not to worry about me. I'm living to die, and I'm alright with that."

"Veronica, how can you say shit like that? Don't worry about you? Dorian is a dangerous man and you can't just kill him if he pisses you off. Shit don't work like that with him, Dorian will kill you and you won't come back."

"Pricey, I don't care."

"How can yo ass not care? You all I fucking got and you putting your fucking life on the line like I don't need you. If you die, I die and, unlike you, I'm not ready to go."

"What do I keep saying? 'Don't worry.' I'm not wishing for death. I just accept the fact that it is going to come for me one day."

"Veronica, I love you and I will do my best not to worry."

"Girl, you ain't know? I'm not going nowhere for a long time. But if I do, I'm not letting nobody punk me before I go."

"Anyway, I'm tired of talking about that shit. I know you ain't going nowhere for a long time. I just hate seeing you like this."

"Shit, every bruise heal in time."

"Dawg, you should have seen Tyrese earlier when we found out you were alive. Then we came here and his face dropped when he saw you. I think he went in the bathroom to cry. The boy is in love with you."

"I could give a fuck less. Tyrese ain't shit to me; he a weak nigga and I no longer want to have anything to do with his ass. I can honestly tell you that I don't believe in love and I don't have time for niggas no more."

"I hear what you saying and . . ."

"Great," another voice said. "That's what a father loves to hear his daughter say." Pricey stood up and I could feel her anger.

"What are you doing here?"

"I am the girl's father, Pricey; I came to see if big mouth was alright."

"You should have done that when Veronica was admitted to the hospital, not wait until guilt convinced you."

"Boy, you got a mouth on you, Pricey. There is so much of Gina in you."

"You got me fucked up. Why you here? We don't need you."

"From the looks of it, ya'll do. Veronica laid up in the hospital. You off playing house with some nigga. It's only a matter of time before you pregnant and that nigga tossing you out on the street."

"Don't worry about me, B, 'cause it's none of yo business who I'm with and what I do."

"Pricey, I'm yo father and . . ."

"So now you want to be my father and shit! You ain't never did shit for me and now . . ."

Pricey was screaming at the top of her lungs and tears were about to fall, but I knew she wouldn't give B the satisfaction of seeing her cry. Pricey picked up her purse and kissed my forehead.

"I don't feel like dealing with this bullshit. Veronica, I'll see you tomorrow."

"Bye," I said. B sat in the chair that Pricey left empty, and he looked at me.

"Veronica I'm going to be straight up with you. I was wrong for leaving you here so I could go off and do my own thing. You shouldn't be living the way you have been. I'm sorry that you ever met that guy Game. I know if I would have been around that shit wouldn't have happened. Things are going to change from here on out and I'm going to try my best to get this family back on track."

I was rolling my eyes to the back of my head so far that I wound up going to sleep on him. The next morning, Pricey was back, just like she had said she would be. She came every day until I was released four days later. B had come to pick me up and Pricey said she would call me later. I could tell she didn't want to have anything to do with B and I knew the shit would hit the fan when B tried to get this so-called "family" together. Pricey and me was family, but I didn't know what B was. I sat in the house most of the time and went to sleep right after school. The day that the hospital had released me, B dropped me off for class. The only reason I decided to go was so I didn't have to be around his ass. Every time I was at home he would just be the biggest bitch toward me. He would push me down, when I was barely walking as it was. When I talked back he would grab me where my bruises were and, as badly as I wanted to scream out in pain on so many occasions, I didn't. It took me longer to completely heal because B was always making thing worse. Once I did heal completely, I was pushed into this boxing class. My trainer was a bastard, though, and he didn't teach me in the way that he should have. All he did was beat the fuck out of me every day and tell me over and over again, "You're a pretty girl, but if you don't pick up what the hell I'm teaching you, you won't look so good for long."

So, one day, we were in the ring—I didn't want to be there, 'cause the day before, he had kicked my ass something terrible, and he hit me in my already-swollen eye that I had stitches under—he punched me and, as he pulled his hand back, he took my stitches with him. I was so mad that I didn't say a word. I beat that man something crazy and when he was coughing up blood, I laughed. I was assigned a new trainer two days later and kicked his ass, too. Four trainers later, I realized that I had learned all I needed to learn. On the day that I had made the decision to quit being bothered with trainers, I caught the bus to Trip's house to see Pricey. I hadn't seen her, really, since the hospital and I missed her. When I got there, the door was wide open and I could hear screaming inside. Trip's car wasn't parked outside, and once I noticed that, I ran into the house. I found B and Pricey in the living room arguing.

"Get the fuck out my house!" she screamed.

"I'm not going to tell you again to pack yo shit."

"What the hell is going on?" I asked. "B, what you doing here?"

"Veronica, you knew where Pricey was this whole time and you didn't tell me? How many fucking times did I ask you where she was?"

"What would be the point of telling you? Pricey not going nowhere."

"Who the fuck do you think you are, B?" Pricey demanded. "You think you can just come out of nowhere and start running shit? What make you think that I'm gon' do anything you say? I ain't got no love for you, nigga, so you might as well get out of my house 'cause you wasting your time!"

"All that mouth is going to get your ass kicked, Pricey. You got ten minutes to pack." Pricey started to laugh in B's face.

"Fuck you, B." Before I could tell Pricey to move out the way, B had slapped her and she was on the floor. I ran over to her and wrapped my arms around her.

"What the fuck is wrong with you? Don't you ever put your hands on her!" I yelled. The last person who had laid hands on Pricey was dead because of me, and B would get it, too.

"I'm tired of this shit! Get your ass up and let's go!" he shouted.

B grabbed Pricey by the hair and was pulling her towards the door. I was holding on to her, but stopped once I saw that it was making the situation worse. When I stood up and looked down at Pricey crying, I saw red. I ran up on B, him punching him in the head and laying that nigga out. I helped Pricey off the floor and walked her over to the couch. Nothing would've stopped me from killing B that day, but something inside me said it wasn't his time. So I dragged his big ass out the house and locked the door behind me. I made Pricey some tea and fixed her hair. Before she could open her mouth and tell me how all this came about, B was up and banging on the door. Pricey got up and went to the back room; I guess she didn't want to deal with him no more. I sat on the couch trying to ignore the banging sound, so I closed my eyes. But they popped right back open when my air supply was cut off. B's hand's were around my neck and everything was going black, I was about to pass out. Just as my eyes rolled back, I could breathe again, all of a sudden. I opened my eyes and Tyrese was sitting next to me, gently touching my neck. I saw B on the floor and jumped on his ass. We went at it blow for blow, and a bitch was winning! I was kicking his ass and it felt so good. I felt so powerful and I tried to hit him harder every time I threw a punch. Tyrese pulled me away from B and Trip kicked B out his house.

"What the fuck is going on? My fucking door broke!" Trip hollered. "Pricey, what happened?"

"That nigga came in here trying to make me leave and he was dragging me on the floor."

"What? This nigga put his hands on you?" Trip pulled out his gun and went out after B.

"Don't you ever come over to my house again!" I heard him say. "Fuck Dorian's rule! I'll have your ass missing long enough to move the fuck out of Chicago with Pricey, and never be found!"

"And he slapped me, too, Trip! Blow his fucking head off!" I yelled, smiling.

"Veronica, this shit ain't over," B answered.

"Fuck you, B!" I said, still tired and out of breath. Tyrese sat next to me and pulled me into his arms. I pushed him away and went to Pricey.

"What the fuck is that about?" Tyrese asked.

"Nigga, I don't like you. Don't be touching me."

"Pricey, go get the phone book and find somebody to fix my damn door. I been working all fucking day and I want to go to sleep," Trip said. "I'm not dealing with this shit." Pricey went in the back with Trip, leaving me with Tyrese.

"What the fuck is yo problem? B was about to kill yo ass and I pulled that nigga off you," he said.

"What you want, a cookie? Nowadays, somebody always tries to kill me. So what? As you can see, I can handle this shit." I walked over to the hallway.

"Pricey, I'm about to go," I called. "I'll see you tomorrow." Before I could, leave Tyrese grabbed me again.

"Let me go, Tyrese."

"No, Veronica. I want to know why you haven't been answering my phone calls, and why haven't you been wanting me to see you?"

"Why do it matter? We ain't got anything going and we never will. Let me make things real clear: *I don't like you*. I don't want to be around you and I don't want you to touch me—*ever*."

"Veronica, please don't walk away from me. It's hard for me to say what I have to say, but I want you to know, I love you."

"Tyrese, I want you to know I don't give a damn. I don't want you or your love; you're a joke to me. You're a slut and a loser. I don't want to have anything to do with you. Please leave me alone."

I walked away from Tyrese and, as hard as it was, I didn't cry. God knows I loved that boy ever since the day I met him, and I wanted to be with him. But I was never going to put myself in the position to love again. I took the bus home and, before I walked in the door, I did a few exercises to get ready for what was about to go down again. I opened the door and B came out of his room to charge me. We were at it again. If I was going to the hospital tonight, B's ass was going, too. After it was all said and done, for the first time since B had started laying his hands on me, not one of my bones had been broken. B was as fucked up as I was and the feeling of satisfaction washed over me. He laid off me for a while after that. Then I guess he got it in his head that all he needed was to rest up and he could take me again. B had tried everything from sneaking me, to trying to beat me in my sleep. He even tried to jump me while I was leaving school, thinking that I would feel so embarrassed that I wouldn't know what to do with myself. But his best just wasn't good enough. Every time B put his hands on me, his ass ended up on the floor in more pain than he anticipated. Once it finally hit me that I could kick a nigga's ass, I was always in the streets starting shit. Fighting niggas until they gave me my respect. Once I had what I wanted, I cooled down. I was always with a gang of niggas, gambling, fighting bitches for money, smoking weed, running from cops, hopping fences and just having fun. It felt great to be one of the guys. I felt untouchable and, once again, I was the talk of Chicago, so you know what that meant—B and Dorian had to try and figure something out. I heard them talking one day:

"Bernard, what is all this shit I've been hearing about your daughter terrorizing Chicago again?" Dorian asked. "I thought we had an understanding. It's been three months and Veronica is not broken. Why is that?"

"Veronica *can't* be broken. I have tried everything. Those boxing classes you got her into fucked everything up. She fights like a fucking man and she won't listen to anything I say. Veronica sees me as her enemy and she's going to fight me on every little thing. There is nothing I can do, Dorian."

"There is always something. I will admit that the boxing wasn't a great idea, but there is always another way to get what I want. You say that Veronica sees you as her enemy—well then, I want you to get someone else for her to focus her hatred on."

"Who? Nobody makes her that mad but me."

"Except for me. So I want you to tell little Veronica a story and, by all means, get on her good side. I'll take care of the rest."

7

It was like one day I woke up and a curse had been put on me. All of the niggas I used to kick it with were nowhere to be found and, even if I did catch up with them, they would give me the brush off. I had no one to chill with, nowhere to get weed and no one to commit a crime with. I felt so empty and banished from the world. With nothing to do and no one to chill with, all my activity slowed down. What about Pricey? Let her tell it, Trip was always whisking her away to another country, going out of town and leaving my sad ass in Chicago to rot. I sat in the living room looking out the window at the dark clouds and bet myself that, any minute now, rain would fall. Two minutes later, I won the bet and treated myself to some chips. It got to the point where I just wanted to do anything. My dreams were filled with me fighting or killing someone. Those were good times; B had disappeared once again, so I didn't even have him to bother. With all the extra time I had on my hands, I got into material things. The mall was my new best friend and I was always there picking out things that were out of my normal price range. But I felt like I deserved it, anything to eat the time. I was at the hair salon and the nail shop every week, I felt myself changing, but I didn't care. Finally, B came home and, for some strange reason, I didn't feel the urge to fight him. When he popped his head into my room and asked me to come in the living room, I went. It was like I was having an out-of-body experience, because I didn't know this person I was becoming. I sat on the couch and just stared at him.

"I want to apologize for everything I took you through, Veronica. I had no reason to put my hands on you and nor did I want to in the first place." Flashes of us fighting popped in my head.

"So why did you, B?"

"Dorian wanted me to."

"What?"

"I don't know what you did, but somehow you have the biggest drug lord infatuated with you." I sat up and really started to listen to B.

"Infatuated? Dorian hates me."

"You think he hates you, Veronica? How many people do you know who Dorian has let off with a warning? He even let you kill one of his best men."

"Oh, I was going to kill Game sooner or later. Dorian ain't do me no damn favors." I felt myself coming back to reality and anger was coming right behind me.

"You should be dead right now and you know it. Dorian offered me fifty thousand for you and when I turned him down, he threatened my life. So I struck a deal with him. I told him to, at least, wait until you were eighteen so you could make up your own mind about being with him. He agreed with this deal, but only if I broke you out of your smart mouth and got you to follow rules that he wanted you to follow."

"And you agreed with this shit, B?"

"What would you have done? Don't even fucking entertain the thought of risking your life for me, huh?"

"I'm not the fucking parent, B! Why won't you realize that there are some things you're going to have to do for me that don't benefit your ass?"

"Veronica, I passed up fifty thousand because of your ass. Every fucked-up thing I have ever did? Wipe that shit clean. I should be parent of the year for that shit. I just figured it would be better if your father kicked yo ass then just some random nigga—a nigga who gon' kill you once he bored."

"B, let me clue you in: Yo ass figured wrong. Just because you passed up fifty thousand dollars, you haven't proven anything to me. I already know that the only reason you passed on the money was because you felt bad about Game rapping me. Had that not happened, yo ass would have ran off with that money and I would have never seen yo ass again. All this shit might not even be true, but might be another one of B's head games to make me forget all that shit you put me through."

"You don't think I'm telling the truth? Open your eyes, stupid! Why you think you're sitting in the house? Where your friends at? Why do you think you're isolated from everything and everybody? Because Dorian wanted it that way.

He doesn't want anybody around you. Sorry to inform you, Veronica, but you're Dorian's property now."

I left the living room and went back into my room. Was B really telling the truth? Why would Dorian want to have anything to do with me? I go against everything he says and give him the most trouble. It didn't make sense, unless he was one of those freaks that got off on that shit and just wanted to have the satisfaction of ruling over me. I thought hard, but couldn't believe it. Dorian was a sick man but he couldn't possibly be thinking of me like that. B had to be lying; he was so great at this head game shit. He was up to something. I just didn't know what. I had started going back to school on a regular basis because sitting in my room was really making me crazy. I sat at lunch wishing the rest of the year would go by so I didn't have to see the school for three months. I put my head down and was ready to go to sleep, but then I heard someone call my name. When I lifted my head, Pricey was damn near an inch from my face.

"Bitch, wake yo ass up! I came as soon as I heard. How you holding up?"

"Heard what?"

"How Dorian got yo ass on lockdown. I heard Trip talking to Tyrese on the phone. We had just got done having sex and the nigga thought I was sleep. I also found out that the only reason Trip and me been going on these so-called vacations is because Dorian didn't want me to be around you. Tyrese told Trip that they couldn't break the beast the way they wanted, so they found another way. Being alone is a bitch."

"I can't believe this. B was telling the truth the whole time. Tyrese called me a beast?"

"Girl, nowadays Tyrese call you every name in the book. You broke the boy heart."

"Obviously, I didn't break it good enough 'cause he still ain't learned to keep my name out his mouth."

"Tyrese is the last person you should be worrying about. What you gon' do about Dorian? I know you don't want to live yo life like this forever, being known as Dorian's shit—don't touch, look or talk to."

"Don't worry. I'll come up with something."

It was called killing two birds with one stone: I had a plan to fix Dorian and Tyrese. What about B? I had to come up with some head tricks of my own for this man. I was getting older and, like everyone had been telling me, I needed to learn how to play the game if my life was going to change. I needed for the spotlight to stop shining on me until I was ready to handle the shine. First, I needed B out my hair and off my back. I needed him to feel like he had won his little head game. I passed on getting a ride home from school, telling Trip and Pricey to go about their business. Pricey wanted to do lunch the next day and I agreed. Right now I needed to think, put shit together and build up the straightest face I could. I didn't know how I was going to get my life where I wanted it to be. But when I saw Tyrese across the street holding up his cross chain at me, I knew I had to get my plan in motion now. I went in the house and was glad that B was home sitting on the couch, smoking a blunt. This ensured that he wouldn't be trying as hard to read me as he usually did. I stood in front of him.

"I talked to Pricey today and she told me all about Dorian little plan."

"I told yo ass. I don't have to lie."

"Did you know that he sent Pricey away?"

"No, I didn't."

"This isn't fair! I'm too young for Dorian to even be interested in. Why is he ruining my life?"

"I don't know. Maybe I should have given you the life that Pricey has. That girl doesn't have a care in the world and she landed a nigga with money. I don't have to worry about her from here on out."

"B, do you regret being with my mom?"

"Come here, Veronica." B put out his blunt and opened a window to let some of the smoke out. I sat on the couch next to him.

"Veronica, your mom was a wonderful woman, very sick in the head, but she was so in love with me. She loved me so much that I didn't need to be in love with her to have a loving relationship. There were a lot of things that I did wrong that your mother didn't deserve. I just feel like, had I been a better man, we would have been perfect for each other."

"Was mom happy when she had me?"

“I had never known her to be more happy than when you two were together.”

“I miss her so much. I know that if she was here I would never be alone.” I let fake tears roll down my cheek as I looked at B. He had the saddest look on his face, but I could see a smile in his eyes.

“I know it will take time for you to love and trust me, but I’m here for you, Veronica. You all I got and I’m all you got. It’s true that I didn’t want to have kids, but my life wouldn’t be what it is without you. I love you, Veronica, and you’re going to see the change in me.”

“I want to be the family that mom always wanted us to be. I’m going to meet Pricey for lunch and try to talk her into moving in with us. All I have is the two of you now.”

I got up and went to my room. Even with my back turned to him I could feel him smiling. This would all work out in my favor and I was only hoping to make this plan work so I could fix everyone who fucked me over. I had a list, a hit list, some might call it. And once you were on this list, there was no way you were getting off. No matter what, all who were on the list would die by my hand. It would take some time, but all I *had* was time, and just the thought of being able to stick it to these sons of bitches would hold me over. Once I fixed Dorian and Tyrese, I needed to find a life outside of all this. Right now, time was on my side and, as long as it stayed that way, things would always be in my favor.

THE LIST:

TYRESE MCKINNEY

BERNARD PATTERSON

DORIAN JAMES

The next morning, I meet Pricey at school and we stayed for the first half, then we left for lunch. We took a cab downtown and eat in this soul food restaurant. Pricey wanted to sit by a window. That was cool with me ’cause today I wanted to be seen. The whole world was watching me. That’s what it felt like. And I only wanted them to see what I wanted them to see. After ordering our food, Pricey wanted to pick up the conversation from yesterday.

“Trip got cursed out for coming back to Chicago and letting me see you.”

"Tell him I'm sorry. I'm going to see Dorian today and try to tweak this little hold he have on me. What I really need is for Dorian to find some other chick to hold his attention."

"Yeah, that would be perfect, but I heard that Dorian is a very picky man. He found what he was looking for in you and he not about to let you go."

"I don't need him to let me go right now, I need him to focus his attention on somebody else. I just need some privacy to make some moves."

"Well I don't know how you gon' get that, but if you want me to help you in any way, you know I got your back."

"I do need you to get into Tyrese head, make him miss me. Tell him what he don't want to hear and make him want me again."

"Why? Why do you want to have anything to do with him?"

"We have unfinished business. I'm going to make him wish he never fell in love with me."

"I got you, Veronica. I'll have him asking for you in no time. Matter of fact, I'll get Trip to throw a party this weekend."

"Good. Remember, Pricey, that what might take place for the next couple of months was all planned. I'm going to free myself from all this."

"Roni, I don't worry about you. I never have. You control your life and can't nobody take that from you."

"It feels so good to have you on my side, Pricey. If I don't have nobody else, I have you."

"You got that right, bitch, and you bet' not ever forget it."

The rest of the week went by quickly and I was actually looking forward to the party. I had gone to school every day and to every class. I even did my homework. I was ready to have fun and let loose. I wore a skirt, halter top and some pumps. I waited outside for my ride to pick me up and I wasn't shocked to see Tyrese pull up. He wanted me so bad, I could see right through his fake ass. Tyrese wanted everybody to believe that he didn't care about me now, that he even hated me. I knew the truth and this truth was going to hurt him more than he ever tried to hurt me. I got in the car with him and he pulled off.

"Thank you for coming to pick me up, Tyrese. I didn't have money for a cab."

"Don't worry, Veronica; Trip gave me gas money to pick you up. I'm just doing a favor for my boy."

"How can it be a favor if he paid you?"

"Don't start, Veronica."

"Look, I'm sorry for all the shit I said to you. I really didn't mean it. I mean, you wanted me to welcome your love right after I had been raped and beaten. I'll be honest with you. I don't trust men. You cheated on me, my father made a deal on my behalf to a drug lord and Dorian is ruling my life. No man wants love, all ya'll want is sex. So excuse me for calling you out on that bullshit you was trying to feed me about love, Tyrese."

"How was it bullshit? Veronica, how can you know my true feelings for you?"

"Where was yo love when Dorian locked me in his office? You didn't know if he was going to kill me or anything. You just drove off and left me there! Where was yo love then, nigga? The only reason you wanted to be with me was because you couldn't stand for me to be happy with someone else."

Tyrese was pulling up to the house when I jumped out the car and took off running towards the door. If Tyrese were truly in love with me, getting him right where I wanted would be simple. I was taking the guilt route; make him feel bad to get back on his good side. As soon as I found Pricey we went back into her bedroom. I closed the door behind me and broke into laughter. I sat on the bed next to Pricey.

"What? What is it?"

"Thank you for getting Tyrese to come pick me up. This shit gon' to be easier than I thought, Pricey."

"What are you talking about? I didn't tell Tyrese to pick you up."

"He said Trip asked him to."

"No, Trip didn't."

"Really? So he lied. Tyrese trying to act like he don't want to have nothing to do with me, but it's cool 'cause I know he loves me."

"So what did ya'll talk about in the car?"

"I was the one doing all the talking. I made him feel so bad."

"How?" The door flew open and Tyrese stepped in the room.

"Excuse me, Pricey. I would like to talk to Veronica alone."

"Well wait your turn. I'm talking to Veronica right now."

Tyrese picked Pricey up and put her outside in the hallway, locking the door behind him. I could hear Pricey banging on the door, cursing and yelling. I laughed for a while, then stopped when Tyrese sat next to me. I looked away from him and he pulled me close.

"Veronica, I did you dirty and I am sorry about that shit at Dorian's house. What was I supposed to do? I saw you kill Game like you do that shit every day, and then there were rumors that you killed Pricey's mom and Christina."

"So what you sayin', you scared of me?"

"Hold that shit up, I'm not scared of no one. I just didn't think I was ready to deal with that shit. I mean I've killed a couple of people before and, to tell you the truth, it didn't faze me, but the look you had on your face . . . I mean it's one thing to not care about taking someone's life cause that's just how the game is, but to enjoy it like you do? That shit worry me. You could really be the death of me."

"Is that a risk you willing to take or are you just running off at the mouth for nothing?"

"I told you I'm not scared of nothing or nobody."

"Yeah, Tyrese, you talk a good game, but there ain't much you can do. You know Dorian don't want nobody around me, talking to me or anything else." I rubbed his thigh and smiled at him so he could understand what I was talking about.

"If memory serves me right, I had you first. I'll do whatever I want with you."

Tyrese grabbed my face and we kissed. Boy had I missed this! I hopped in his lap and he wrapped his arms around me. I felt him getting hard and he slid his hand up my skirt.

"Tyrese, not in Pricey's room."

"Come on, they not gon' know."

"Yes, they will. Later. Tonight at your house." Tyrese placed his head on my shoulder.

"Why should I wait that long?"

"'Cause it's going to be better if you wait for it."

Tyrese kissed me again and we left the room, going our separate ways. I went to find Pricey in the kitchen. I sat down at the table with her and she pulled out a deck of cards. We found two other people and got a spade game going, and wound up playing cards for most of the night. By one o'clock, the party was still going strong, but I was ready to go. I went to Tyrese and told him to put his car keys in Pricey's room. Then I told him to meet me outside in five minutes. I got his keys and went to his car so I could wait for him to drive us away from there. It had been a while since we had had sex and, to be honest, I was in need. Tyrese got in his car and kissed my cheek, "I like how you think, Veronica."

I smiled at him and he pulled off, I lay back in my seat, closing my eyes. I had dozed off for a minute and woke up in Tyrese's house on his couch. I got up and found him in his bed on the phone, so I sat next to him waiting. He smiled at me and hung up the phone; before he could speak, I kissed him. Tyrese took off my shirt and kissed my chest, I let my head fall back onto his bed. He lay on top of me as we kissed for a while; I grew tired of that and started to undo his pants. Tyrese took off my shirt and, with his tongue, stroked each of my nipples to the point where I had slipped out of my skirt for him. The only thing stopping our connection was my Victoria's Secret panties, but with Tyrese rock hard, they were gone in a matter of seconds. There we lay in his bed naked as the day we were born and I had never wanted anything more than I wanted Tyrese at this very moment. I kissed his neck and waited in anticipation as I felt him inching near my wetness. As he put it in, things changed. My legs locked and, all of a sudden, I was hotter than I should have been.

"Wait Tyrese," I said.

"Come on, Veronica, I need to feel you right now," he said, breathlessly, like he had already been hard at work. I rolled my eyes and tried to get back into the mood. But as he got closer, I started to have flashes of Game, what he had done to me that day and how I'd felt. It was like I was there in that moment. I could see Game so clearly in my mind and I could even smell him.

"Tyrese, stop." Like he had heard nothing I said, he continued and, as the seconds passed, I started to freak out. "Tyrese get the fuck off me, now!" Instantly, Tyrese stopped in mid-stroke and looked down at me with a crazed expression on his face. Just being able to feel him inside me had me going crazy and I began to cry. I could not handle this and I just wanted to leave. Tyrese jumped off of me and, as he reached out to hold me, I jumped off that bed with a quickness. I did not want to be touched.

"Don't fucking touch me!"

"What's wrong? Calm down." Tyrese reached for me again and I stepped back.

"Don't come near me."

"Veronica, tell me what's going on. Why are you crying?" I started to pick up my clothes and head for the door.

"Where are you going? You don't even have on any clothes." Seeing him walking towards me naked was not helping me at all. I made it to the door, but as I tried to open it, Tyrese grabbed me by my arm, tightly.

"Why are you trying to leave?"

"Let me go!" At that point I was acting crazy as hell. I ran to the kitchen and found a knife. Wasn't no nigga gon' hurt me again. Tyrese took a few steps back, realizing I wasn't playing with him.

"Veronica, I'm going to need you to calm down and tell me what's going on."

I didn't respond to Tyrese, I just stood there shaking and crying, uncontrollably. I started to put my clothes on the best I could with my free hand. Tyrese tried to walk beside me and I tried to stab him, but he moved back.

"Don't come near me!"

"Just tell me what this shit is about. Why you freaking out on me?"

I walked towards Tyrese, causing him to back up and I was able to get back to the door. As I opened it, he came at me trying to get the knife out of my hand, but he was too slow and I ended up cutting him about three times before he backed up. When he stepped back I was out. I dropped the knife in the driveway and took off running. I hadn't thought to pick up my shoes, but even with bleeding feet, tear-drenched face and my lungs about to collapse, I was glad to be home, once I made it. I had run all the way back and, as bad as I wanted to stop, I didn't. By the time I made it to my room, my chest felt like it was on fire and my whole body shut down. I crawled to the bathroom to get some water to help ease the pain and, when my breathing went back to normal, I passed out right there on the floor. I heard a banging noise in the distance and then my name as I woke up much later. I felt like shit. I heard the door open and I opened my eyes to see Pricey standing over me.

"Girl, what the hell you done did now?"

"What you talking about? Help me off the floor."

"What the hell is going on here? Veronica, what happened to your feet?" I gave B a strange look after his strange comment, then I looked down. My feet were swollen, purple and black from the bruises and cuts that I had.

"Me and Veronica took up a ballet class and we been working our asses off," I said.

"My feet look just like that, but I'm taking a lot of painkillers," Pricey added. "Veronica, I'm going to get you some clothes together so we can get ready to go to practice. Wash up so we can go. Come on, B, let's give the girl some privacy."

Pricey pushed B out the door and I could hear her reassuring him that I was fine and telling him to go back to sleep. I was still on the damn floor and in some real pain because of my feet. The last thing I could do was stand up. Pricey came back into the bathroom and closed the door behind her.

"Damn, Roni, you not even off the floor."

"I can't stand on these bloody-ass feet. I'll pass out from the pain."

"Come on, I'm gon' get you out of here."

Pricey helped me up and told me to put all my weight on her so it wouldn't hurt as bad when I walked. I did what she told me to, but after we got my clothes on, we barely made it to the pissy-ass elevator before I fell flat on my ass. This shit hurt like hell and I was sweating hard as fuck because I was so mad at the fact that I was injured again. Pricey pulled me onto the elevator and we took it all the way downstairs. That's where she had to help me again when I finally had the strength to get up. But I fell back again when Trip reached out his hand to help me into the car.

"Don't touch me!"

"Come on, I'm just trying to help you." Trip reached out for me again.

"Don't fucking touch me!" I held onto the Pricey and began to tear up.

"What the fuck is your problem?"

"Trip, baby, just open the door for me and drive."

Pricey helped me into the car and sat in the back with me. Having her there with me helped, tremendously, but I still couldn't calm down. I couldn't figure out what was wrong and why I was trippin' like I was. When we made it to Trip's house, Pricey helped me out and took me to the bathroom. I had a seat on the toilet while she ran me a bath, and I started to take off my clothes Pricey handed me some pills and, without asking any questions, I downed them bitches. In a matter of minutes, I wasn't feeling any pain and I was so sleepy. I got in the tub and rolled my eyes to the back of my head as I relaxed. Pricey didn't say a word, she just tended to my feet as I started to wash my hair. That bath did wonders for me and when Pricey gave me some pajamas to put on I was asleep as soon as I hit the couch. By the time Tyrese showed up, I couldn't hear a thing, I was so far gone.

"Bang! Bang! Bang!" was the noise on the other side of the door.

"Stop pounding like you crazy, Tyrese!" Pricey told him.

"I know she in here!" Tyrese said.

"First off, you need to cool the fuck down," she said, opening the door.

"Pricey, let me in this muthafucka and stop playing. I need to talk to Veronica." Tyrese pushed past Pricey and stepped inside.

"Be quiet, Tyrese. Don't you see she sleep?"

"Well you better wake her crazy ass up 'cause we got some shit we need to discuss."

"Hold up, you not gon' be calling my nigga all kinds of names like you done lost yo mind."

"Do you see my damn arms, Pricey? That bitch cut me up like I was some damn sushi!"

"Come here." Pricey grabbed Tyrese by his arm and pulled him into the kitchen. He pulled away from her grasp in pain and they stood face to face.

"Don't be calling my nigga no bitch 'cause I'll fuck you up right here for disrespecting her. You said that you loved Veronica and that you wanted to be with her, right?"

"Yeah, but . . ."

"'But' nothing! How you gon' say all that shit, then when shit not going your way, you flip out? Why would you try to have sex with her anyway?"

"Why wouldn't I? I missed her crazy ass and she was acting like she was down for whatever. Veronica pulled *my* pants down last night."

"That don't mean shit. Veronica don't realize how fucked up she is right now."

"Fucked up over what, Pricey?"

"Hello? The last time Veronica had sex, it was forced. I was raped when I was a little girl and only considered having sex with Trip. Trip was, technically, my first. Even though what happened to me happened many years ago, that shit still in the back in my head. The worst feeling in the world is having somebody take the most precious thing that we have. Just picture what it would feel like if a nigga raped you."

"Hold up, that shit ain't happening."

"Shut up and just listen, Tyrese! If a nigga held you down and forced his self on you, you couldn't stop anything that was going on—think about all the pain you would feel. Somebody ripping your self-respect from you."

"I know what you sayin' and I was ready to kill Game for what he did to Veronica, but I thought me and her was better than that. I would never hurt her like that. Never. I love her stupid ass."

"Then you have to take your time and show her that she can trust you. Veronica just had a panic attack and, from here on out, you gon' have to take things slow."

"I hear you, Pricey." Pricey left Tyrese in the kitchen and went back to her bedroom to sleep. Tyrese went into the living room and waited for me to "wake up," not knowing that I had heard the whole conversation.

Later that day, I was feeling a lot better. That was until I saw Tyrese sitting on the couch across from me. He was asleep and I was getting the fuck out of here so I didn't have to face him. I stood up to get my cell phone, but fell right back down. I felt my feet instantly start to throb and I was ready to pop another pill. Tyrese woke up and tried to help me up, but I pulled away from him again.

"Don't touch me!"

"Veronica, I'm not gon' hurt you. I just want to help yo dumb ass off the floor." Tyrese reached for me again.

"I said don't touch me! I'll cut yo ass up again!"

"Come here." Tyrese picked me up and I started kicking and screaming.

"Let me go!"

"Shut up! Listen to me!"

"Pricey!" I hollered. "Pricey!"

"What's going on? Tyrese let her go!" Pricey ran over to me and grabbed me out of Tyrese's arms. We sat together on the floor and I held on to her for dear life, crying my eyes out again.

"Fuck this shit! I can't handle this mess! I can't be dealing with this crazy-ass bitch!" he yelled.

Tyrese left the house and Trip stood there looking down at the both of us, realizing he didn't want to deal with us, either. So he left with Tyrese. Pricey held on to me and rocked me in her arms.

"Veronica you need to talk about this, get out how you feeling."

"I don't know how I'm feeling! I'm just scared. The thought of having someone do what Game did to me again makes me freak out, 'cause, on my life, that shit is never happening again."

"I know how you feel. Remember when it happened to me and you helped me through it. I was so mad and I felt so bad."

"You ain't got shit to worry about 'cause I'll ride on that nigga in a minute."

"And I will do the same for you, Roni. I was just mad that I didn't make it there sooner. I shouldn't have ever talked you into going out with his ass." Pricey started to cry right along with me, hurt that I was so hurt.

"This shit is nowhere near your fault," I sobbed. "Game was just a sick fucking pig and I didn't see it coming, just like you didn't."

"So why are you holding this shit against Tyrese?"

"I'm holding this shit against every nigga I come across. Why is Tyrese even important?"

"'Cause, Roni, he love you and he want to be with you."

"Love? He just want some ass, just like all these other niggas, and I'm not offering."

"Veronica, you can't make every nigga pay for what Game did."

"Oh, but I am, and if you can't support me, then we ain't got shit to talk about. I made up my mind and I'm sticking with how I feel."

"Roni, you have to let this go. You have to forgive in order for you to be able to move on. If you don't, then you're always going to be unhappy."

"Then so be it." I moved away from Pricey and she gave me a funny look.

"Fine, Veronica. Be like that. But the more you push people away, the worse your life gon' be. I'll call you a cab."

Pricey left the living room and I stayed there on the floor thinking. Yeah I did have a problem that I needed to address, but if solving my problem meant forgiving Game for what he did, then that shit just wasn't going to happen. How could I forgive someone like him? That would be like saying that what happened to me was all right. When I killed Game I thought that everything would be fine after that, but, even now, he still has a hold on me. I just hated the thought of some guy touching me, being near me, and sex? I was totally turned off by the thought. I went home later that day and sat in my room, just thinking. What if I never got over this shit? I didn't want Game to have that type of power over me, but all I had in me was fear, and with fear came anger. I was so hurt to the point where I did shut everybody out. Things after that went downhill. I stopped talking to Pricey and every time a dude came close to me, I would fight him to no end. I was getting kicked out of school every other week. B knew what I was going through and didn't bitch about it, but he told me I needed to figure out how to deal with life in a better way. I respected him for that and just figured my best bet was to take a break from the world for a moment. So I locked myself in my room for a while until I felt like I was stable enough to deal with the world. Even when my mother died, I had never been this unhappy. I sat on the couch one afternoon watching TV when I heard the door open, and in walked Tyrese. I stood up ready to defend myself.

"You need to get the fuck out!" I said.

"I'm not going nowhere. See, I made the mistake of falling in love with yo ass and, try as I might, I can't shake that shit. I've given you enough time to get yo shit together, but it seems like you getting worse and worse. So I'm here to help you get over what is bothering you, and I'm not leaving until we fix this shit."

"I'm not gon' tell yo ass again, Tyrese."

"Veronica, I got all day. I'm not leaving. If you want me out, you gon' have to put me out yo damn self."

"Not a problem."

I went over to Tyrese and punched him in his mouth as hard as I could. When he stumbled back, I tried to push him out the door, but he wouldn't move. I pulled my fist back ready to strike him again, but he held on to my wrist.

"Just because I love you don't mean I'm gon' let you beat on me."

"Fuck you, nigga! You can keep yo love to yo'self."

When Tyrese pulled me to him for a kiss I lost my mind and flipped out right there. I was biting and kicking all over the place. I stomped on his foot and tried to break free of him. I smacked him in the face and spit on him. I did whatever I could to hurt him for damn near a half hour, but he still stood there with me, holding me while I had my tantrum. I started to cry from being so angry. Then I was all out of breath and too hurt to move anymore. I let Tyrese hold me in his arms as I cried as hard as I could. He just wrapped his big arms around me and told me that everything would be okay. I just cried until I couldn't cry no more and was too weak to fight. He carried me over to the couch and let me have my space while we talked. I sat there with my knees in my chest and my own arms wrapped around myself. I felt so small and so helpless. Even though I knew that I could give any guy a run for his money if we went head-up, something inside of me said I would lose. I watched as Tyrese touched his lip and smiled.

"Veronica, I don't want to hurt you. What happened that night you were over my house just got out of hand. I don't want to rape you; I want to give you the utmost pleasure. I want you to feel safe with me and be able to trust me. I'm sorry for what Game did, but I'm not him. I would never hurt you like that and I need you to believe that."

"I can't. I can't trust that it won't happen again, 'cause what if it does? Just the possibility has me freaking out."

"I know, but I'm telling you right now that you don't have to worry about that shit with me. I won't do you like that and I won't let any nigga touch you in a way you don't want to be touched. Had it not been for Trip, I would have killed Game that day. I would kill anybody for you, Veronica; I'll do whatever it takes to make you happy."

"Tyrese, please don't do this. I just can't have sex with you."

"I'm not asking you to have sex with me. I'm asking you to let me hold you, to let me take care of you and to let me help you to feel better." I felt fresh tears run down my face and when Tyrese tried to wipe them away, I just let him.

"I'm not asking you to let your guard down all at once 'cause I know you can't, but you got to talk to me, tell me how you feeling. Let me know what's going on so you don't feel like you have to fight me off."

I thought about the plan that I had come up with to pay Tyrese back for all his wrongdoing towards me. Boy how the tables had turned. He was giving me all the opportunity in the world to get close enough to him to shatter his ass. Even though I was going through so much shit right now, I had plans to carry out the shit that I needed to. My undoing was the reason I couldn't trust. If I was able to stab Tyrese in the back now when he was only trying to help me, why should I allow myself to believe that he wouldn't do the same to me? What made me any different from anybody else? I soon realized that all I had at the end of the day was me, and I needed to be true to myself. I couldn't go back on what I said I'd do just because the sun was shining right now when, any day now, my storm could come back and I would have missed an opportunity to make things right, once and for all.

"Do you want to know what I was thinking when we were having sex? Do you want to know why I was freaking out?" I asked him.

"Yes, I do want to know."

"As soon as you were inside of me, I went right back to that day Game raped me. I saw his face, I could smell him, I could feel the bruises on my face and I could even feel his sweaty body on top of mine. That was the worst day of my life and, as much as I try, I can't sweep that shit under the rug."

"I'm not asking you to, Veronica, I want you to be able to tell me how you're feeling at all times, so I don't push you to the point where that day plays out in your mind."

"It's not just you, Tyrese; I've been getting into fights with every guy in my school for just looking like they wanted to do something. I can't stand for no nigga to be close to me—to even be in the same room as me."

"I know and I'm not trying to rush you; just talking is good enough for me."

"We'll see."

We sat on that couch for hours talking; everything that I had felt since that day Game took advantage of me, I told Tyrese about. It felt so good to talk and to cry, to have him there with me. I won't front. I needed that shit. I needed to be able to get all the things I had been feeling on the inside, out. He just sat there, never complained, never said he had to go and never tried to move closer to me. Tyrese just let me talk; let me say everything I needed to say. That night when I went to sleep was the greatest sleep that I ever had. Tyrese left at around three and I went to sleep that night feeling a million times better. I went back to school happier and talked to Tyrese every day after that. It took me a couple of weeks to fully be comfortable around him, comfortable enough to let him hold me and comfort me when I cried. Everything was really pretty innocent, nothing sexual at all. We didn't even kiss and Tyrese seemed okay with that. We fell back into our old routine of hanging out on the weekends and him picking me up from school. Things were going great until Tyrese had a little meeting with Dorian late one night. I was at his house and we were watching movies when the doorbell rang.

Once he opened that door, I knew it was going to be a long night. Three big niggas came in with guns and told us to get in this black van. What could we do? We were outnumbered and had no guns on us. I hadn't killed anybody in what seemed like forever, so I was ready for war, I wanted to fight. And I thought about all this as I sat in front of Dorian, a man that I couldn't stand, and a man who had played such a big role in fucking up my life. I was not holding back tonight.

"Tyrese, I see that you have been getting awfully close with this young lady."

"Dorian, trust me. It's not what you thinking, we just friends. Veronica having a hard time right now and I'm helping her out. Yeah, we chill together, but it's nothing more than that."

"Word around here is you said that you are in love with this young lady and you didn't give a fuck who was pissed about it."

"Yeah, I said that and I meant that shit, too. But it don't matter what I say or how I feel. Veronica not where I'm at, so, like I said, we chilling."

I was so proud of Tyrese for how he was standing up to Dorian. This was the same nigga that had left me in a room with a killer, and now wasn't afraid to be killed by this same man. But, like I said, I had plans for Tyrese and my plan would be no good if he was dead. Naw, I had a far worse fate for Tyrese, one that would make him suffer. Death for him right now would be more than he deserved. I looked at Dorian and saw that he could care less about Tyrese's life and was about to prove it in a minute. I stood up out of my seat and Dorian looked at me with a smile, 'cause he knew he was going to have to beat me down again and couldn't believe that I was so hard-headed.

"It don't matter what Tyrese said 'cause I ain't tied down to nobody! I can talk to or fuck any nigga that come my way if I wanted to Dorian, and who would care?"

"That's not the point right now, Miss Veronica. Have a seat."

"I don't feel like sitting down, Dorian. Tell me what the point is."

"Tyrese know the rules and he knows what happens if you don't follow my rules."

"What rule could you be talking about? The rule that says you own me?"

"Exactly, Veronica."

"Who the fuck do you think you are, Dorian? I will do what the fuck I want, with who I want, and there ain't shit you can do about it!" Tyrese grabbed my hand and told me to cool down. I was getting mad and it was just a matter of time before I did some stupid shit.

"Naw, fuck that, Tyrese! What right does he have to rule over my life?"

"I have every right, Veronica. If you haven't noticed, I'm running shit around here and what I say goes."

"Don't you realize how pathetic that makes you look, Dorian? You desire a girl, you fucking pervert! The thought of me ever being with you makes me sick."

"Shut your fucking mouth before I beat the shit out of you!" Dorian said as he stood up from his seat and walked over to me. Tyrese stood in front of me, fearing that Dorian would hit me.

"Naw, move out my way," I said as I stepped into Dorian's face. "Do you think I fear you, nigga? Did you think that it would be easier to control me because I was young? What? Yo ass can't handle being with a grown woman 'cause you know she ain't gon' take yo shit? You thought that staking your claim on me to all of Chicago would break me? That somehow I might be tamed? Well take a look, Dorian! That shit ain't working! I'm still me and I still don't give a fuck about *shit*! How yo plan working out for you now?"

"If you ain't the dumbest little girl walking the face of the earth, I don't know who is," he replied.

"Dorian, you want me and you don't want anybody else to have me! A child! You want to be with a child! What does that say about the man that you claim to be?" Dorian didn't say anything for a while. Then his eyes went dead and I wasn't shocked when I fell to the floor from being slapped. Tyrese helped me up.

"I will not be disrespected, Veronica! The fact is, what I say goes and if I find out that ya'll are together, Tyrese, you're dead! Veronica, just know that I know plenty of niggas who are far worse off than Game, and who would love to meet you." My face lit up with anger and I went over to Dorian looking dead in his eyes.

"If you mean what you say and something does happen to me, when it's all said and done, you better kill me before I kill you."

I could see the shocked look in Dorian's eyes. Just the thought of anyone standing up to him was unthinkable and, to have me, a little-ass girl, threatening his life left Dorian speechless. Tyrese pulled me out of there before Dorian could think of what he was going to do about my disobedience. My face was stinging like crazy, but I smiled anyway. I know I got to Dorian and that shit made me feel great. Tyrese dropped me off at home and, since that night, I hadn't seen him in damn near a month. Pricey came to see me one day, a while later. I guess word got around about the whole Dorian thing 'cause she came to me asking a million questions.

"Where you get off threatening Dorian James?"

"Girl, that shit happened so long ago. Who told you?"

"Roni, it's all over the streets! People sayin' that you a dead woman and shit! What was you thinking?"

"I was thinking that I'm not gon' allow anybody to run my life. Have you heard from Tyrese lately?"

"Him and his girlfriend Deborah been seen all over. She just moved in with him a week ago. She real pretty and she go to college. They were over our house not too long ago and she didn't seem like the type Tyrese would go for, but he was smiling the whole time."

"Really? All that shit that nigga was trying to feed me, and as soon as shit get tight with Dorian, he move on! And to think I was going to take him off my list . . ."

"Yeah, I knew you was gon' be mad. Just don't kill this one, okay?"

"If she know how to act and she don't get in my way, I won't, but I'm way behind on my plan."

"What plan?"

"You'll see."

I talked to Pricey for a little while longer and I tried my best not to show her how heated I was. Boy was I mad! Tyrese was such a punk, but, most importantly, he needed to be paid back for all this shit he tried to pull. I spent the night at Trip's house, so I wouldn't have to do a lot of traveling that night, 'cause please believe I was going to confront Tyrese's weak ass. I waited until Pricey was asleep and Trip went out to make his rounds, and then I left. I could see the living room light on as I walked up to Tyrese's house. I pulled out my cell phone and called him.

"Hello?" he mumbled.

"Bring yo ass outside right now."

"Hey Trip, you outside?" he said, faking so his girl could hear. "Yeah, I'll be right there." No less than five seconds later and Tyrese was standing right in my face.

"What are you doing here?" I could see the fear in his eyes, he was such a punk.

"What are you doing with a girlfriend? For weeks, all you was spitting in my ear was that you loved me."

"Don't come at me like that, Veronica. I meant what I said."

"Like hell you did!"

"Veronica, lower your voice."

"I'm not doing a damn thing! You better get rid of her before the bitch come up missing! You wanted me, now you got me!"

"Can we talk about this tomorrow, Veronica? Shit's not how you think it is and I don't want to draw any unneeded attention to us."

"Either we talk about this now or you gon' have a lot more to deal with than Dorian."

"Are you threatening me, Veronica?"

"Handle yo shit. I'll be waiting in the backyard."

I left the front porch and went to the back where I told him I'd be. I don't know what lie he told her, but she was out of there in a matter of minutes. Tyrese came to the back door and let me in. I stood in the kitchen ready to finish our heated conversation. Tyrese tried to hug me and I pushed him away. He had a pissed off look on his face.

"Don't be trying to suck up to me now! Tyrese, you been with this girl for a month and you didn't even care to tell me! After all that bullshit you tried to feed me about loving me, I knew you was full of shit!"

"Hold up, don't be jumping to fucking conclusions. Veronica, the only reason I'm with Deborah is for us."

"For us? Where you get that shit from?"

"If you don't remember, we were facing death a month ago. Deborah just someone to take the attention off of us. We can't be together if I'm with Deborah, and that's what I want everybody to think."

"So when were you going to tell me? Why this bitch in yo house if ya'll relationship is just for show? You full of shit!" I turned my back to Tyrese and he eased up behind me, holding me. I lend my head back on his chest.

"Veronica, I know you don't see it now, but the only reason I'm with Deborah is because I don't want you to be in harm's way because of me. I'd rather love you from a distance then to love you only for a moment because some murderer don't want me to be with you."

"I kinda understand where you coming from, but you should have told me. Just think about how it was told to me—like you was trying to play me or something."

"Veronica I'm just thinking of you. I love you and I don't want nothing to happen to you."

I turned to face Tyrese and we kissed. I could feel how reluctant he was, but enough time had passed. My plan needed to be put into action now. I pulled him over to the couch and we continued to make out, but I was ready for bigger things. I took his shirt off and started to kiss his chest. I could hear him moaning softly. Tyrese grabbed my hands and started sucking on my fingers, and then he said to me: "You're not going to flip out on me this time, are you?" I stopped kissing him and looked him dead in the eye. Normally, this would be the time where I went off, but I was on a mission today. I gave him a weak smile, taking off my shirt and bra, and then I popped a boob in his mouth. Maybe that would keep his ass quiet long enough for me to get the job done. As he did his thing, I started to take my panties off and I whispered in his ear, "Take me to your room." Once again, Tyrese stopped what he was doing and started to run off at the mouth. Standing up, he placed me to the side, taking my hands into his.

"Veronica, you know we don't have to do this. I'm not rushing you. I love you and if you thinking that you have to do this 'cause of me, I'm fine."

I gave Tyrese that "whatever" look, 'cause I knew that every nigga that was sexually active needed a daily nut or they would go crazy. I stood in front of Tyrese naked and it did get me a little excited to see the desire in his eyes. I pulled down his pants and his big ol' dick flopped out at me. I smiled 'cause this is what Tyrese wanted. He was hard as a brick. I pushed him back down onto the couch and slowly started to ride him. When he started to kiss my neck and rub my back, I just tuned the whole thing out. This was not about Tyrese, this was about me being happy and making sure that every wrong was righted. Out of nowhere, he stood up with me still in his arms and, I don't know, what he was hitting, but the shit was driving me wild. I felt so light in his arms and the way he was stroking me was making me get closer and closer to orgasm. Just when I was about to reach a climax, Tyrese bent me over the couch and started going at it from the back. Then, ten minutes later, I came harder than I ever thought I could. Right after that, I felt a warm build-up inside me. Tyrese came. He came right inside me. I didn't think that this was going to happen so soon. With what little strength Tyrese had in him, he carried me to his room and we got under the cover. Tyrese went right to sleep and I lay there thinking more about my plan. When would I tell Tyrese I was pregnant? I knew it right away. And how would we deal with Dorian when he found out? Now things could go one or two ways: Dorian could find out, kill Tyrese and try to kill me, but that's when I'd kill him. Or I could let Tyrese stress himself out to the point that he drove himself crazy, and then tell him I got an abortion. I didn't want Tyrese to die yet, and not by Dorian's hands. I wanted to do it myself, but I couldn't. My whole plan basically consisted of just stressing everybody else out—pissing Tyrese off and getting Dorian out of my hair. I didn't know, really, what was going to happen. For all I knew, this little stunt could leave me with a bullet in my head. But deep down, I knew I wasn't going to die soon. I had a lot more damage to do. I took a short nap and woke up at three in the morning to go home. I called and told a cab driver to meet me around the corner, so all the attention wouldn't be on Tyrese's house. He wasn't shit, but a scary-ass bitch and I couldn't wait to stick it to his ass.

8

The next couple of months were very strange for me; Tyrese had his own life with Deborah. They had their little relationship, but he would always come to me, at least twice a week, so we could fuck. Now I knew that no other girl would put up with some nigga having his cake and eating it, too, but I started looking at it from a different point of view: Deborah kept Tyrese out of my face when it came to serious shit. He wasn't always trying to have deep conversations with me, either. He wasn't always talking about love anymore and I really didn't have to deal with him outside of sex. Tyrese's being with Deborah kept me focused on what I wanted out of all this. I didn't have to worry about my feelings getting in the way of my plan anymore. It was easy to play somebody when you already knew he or she playing you. Tyrese told me that he wasn't sleeping with Deborah, but Pricey told me that they always got a hotel room downtown on Saturdays. Everybody thought I was so stupid. Then, to top everything off, Dorian started seeing some white chick named Dawn, and word was that I was bumped off the wifey list. She was number one. Don't get me wrong: It was great to have Dorian out my hair, but how could Tyrese be punished when the person who was supposed to do the punishing didn't care what I did anymore? Dorian was throwing an engagement party at his house and the shit was making me sick. I rode with Trip and Pricey to the party that I really didn't want to go to, but I knew Pricey would be bored out of her mind if I wasn't there. It was a nicely mixed party; I assumed that all the white people there were related to Dawn, but some of them looked like they could be in the drug game. When we entered Dorian's house, Trip went his separate way and left us to entertain ourselves. Pricey pulled me over to the open bar and, once I downed two drinks, I was feeling better. That was until Tyrese showed up with Deborah. This was so unacceptable! Before I could go and confront him Pricey pulled me outside by the pool.

"What is you doing, Pricey?"

"Before you go over there and make a fool of yo'self I want you to admit something to me, first."

"What?"

"Admit that you mad that none of your admirers are admiring you anymore. Tyrese with Deborah and Dorian about to marry Dawn."

"You know what, Pricey? All this shit ain't nothing but a show. Dorian still want me and Tyrese, well Tyrese give me what I need, so I'm not trippin' off him being with Deborah. I could care less what these niggas doing 'cause I know, at any given moment, I could have them full-time if I wanted them."

"Hold up, Veronica. You fucking Tyrese?"

"I sure am. Twice a week at that. So when I see him with his so-called girlfriend I know I'm the only one on his mind."

"You ain't nothing but a rat, Veronica. Why would you want to be the bitch on the side?"

"It's all about pulling my plan off. I want you to get the word out that I'm pregnant with Tyrese child before I'm completely out of the limelight."

"*What*? Pregnant! You haven't even got your period yet?"

"The only person who know that is you, Pricey, and you not gon' let my little secret out, are you?" I asked, knowing that I was lying.

"Whatever you cooking up, it's gon' be bad and I would love to be a part of it. I have sat back and watched Tyrese try to play you, and it's about time that he got what was coming to him. At least, you not killing nobody." I put one arm around her shoulder and smiled.

"That's why I love you so much. You always got my back. Let's go back inside and break some hearts."

"I feel that, Veronica."

We went back inside and there was a big crowd around Dawn. I listened on as Dorian talked about her, how happy he was to have her and how pretty she was. If you asked me, the bitch was too skinny and too pale to be attractive. Dorian's eyes met mine and he pulled Dawn over to my direction, breaking through the crowd to get to me. I could always count on him; I was looking great that night. Hair done, toes and nails done, rocking the fuck out of this black Gucci dress.

"Dawn, this is Veronica, the girl I was telling you about."

"This is her? This is the girl? You talked about her like she was special or something," the bitch said.

"Dorian, I'm very happy to see that you've found someone who knows her place," I replied. "I know how you like them." Dorian laughed and left us standing there.

"Veronica, I want to thank you for passing up on Dorian."

"Yeah, he not my type. Makeup irritates my skin, so I can't cover up Dorian's love taps like you can." I quickly rubbed under Dawns' eye and, sure enough, there was a black ring.

"You're going to pay for this!" Dawn said as she ran up the stairs

"You don't know me very well," I said.

I got myself another drink and found a seat. I saw Pricey waving for me to come over there. When I stood up I felt someone touch my hand. I turned to see this very great-looking Italian guy who, on first sight, I wanted to bone. He looked so good that he gave Brad Pitt a run for his money. I wasn't even upset that he touched me. I slowly pulled my hand from his, but he pulled it up to his lips and kissed it.

"Hello? Don't you want to know my name before we jump into foreplay?" I asked him.

"Nope, I just want to enjoy." I laughed as he kissed the back of my wrist and licked my fingertips.

"Alright now, you starting to get a little out of hand. I'm not that easy."

"Oh, I know. Trust me. You haven't done a thing to make me think that, but I have a problem with being a little over affectionate with outstanding-looking women."

"Well you need to get your problem under control, 'cause people might start thinking you're the easy one."

"Only if I cared. I'll behave for now 'cause I don't want to scare you off. So what's your name?"

"First, you sexually harass me, then you ask my name."

"You can never say that the first time we met was boring."

"You're right. My name is April, and yours?"

"My name is Frankie Ridley."

"So are you related to Dawn?"

"Yeah, she's my cousin through marriage. Are you related to Dorian?"

"No, my father is friends with him and we were just invited. I would much rather be doing something better with my time."

"I wouldn't, April. Meeting you makes all this worth my time."

I smiled again. I was really feeling this Frankie character, and I was even about to ask him for his number, but someone is always raining on my parade—B came out of nowhere and tried to pull me away, but Frankie wasn't having that shit.

"Hold on, my man, I'm talking to this lovely lady."

"I don't give a fuck. This is my daughter and I can drag her away from any conversation I want to."

"You think so?" Frankie asked. I liked him more and more. He was being so disrespectful right now that I could tell he had a bad side to him. I stepped in between them when B let my hand go.

"B, let me finish up here and I'll meet you by the stairs in one second."

"Naw, you need to bring yo ass now."

"Don't show out tonight. How mad would Dorian be if you get into it with Dawn's cousin?"

"You have a second," B said, walking away. Frankie took my hand in his again.

“Will I see you again tonight, April?”

“Probably not.”

“Well then I should give you my number now so you can call me later.”

I took a moment to get his number and he walked me to the stairs. On the way, I saw Pricey smiling at me, and Tyrese with the most pissed off look I had ever seen. I laughed to myself and enjoyed the fact that this sexy guy wanted my attention. When we made it over to the steps he kissed my neck and walked out the door. Boy, he was smooth and I was not hating him for that. Once Frankie left, B grabbed my arm and we walked upstairs.

“That’s the kind of nigga that will fuck you over and throw yo ass away when he done.”

“Well, B, he won’t be any different than any other nigga in my life.”

“Whatever. I care about you, so I’ll warn you about the shit you got yourself into again. Dawn is not happy with you, so you know what that means?”

“Another bullshit excuse for a nigga to put his hands on me. Yeah, yeah, yeah, I get it.”

I went to Dorian’s office and closed the door in B’s face. He wasn’t gon’ do shit and he couldn’t talk Dorian out of being mad, so what good was he? I looked over at Dawn and she was smiling at me. Why did people always think they had the upper hand when it came to me?

“Veronica, have a seat,” Dorian said.

“Okay.” I sat down.

“Did you touch Dawn?”

“I brushed her just a little bit,” I said with a smile.

“See Dorian, this is the shit I’m talking about! This bitch thinks she untouchable! Put her in her place for me.”

“Why don’t you do it yourself, you whiny-ass bitch?” I asked. Dawn slapped me without thinking and, as I stood up, Dorian raised his hand for me to stop.

"If you hit her, you're going to have to deal with me." As if he had said nothing, I punched Dawn. He slapped me. Then kicked me when I was down and I could feel Dawn smiling.

"Fuck her ass up, Dorian! Kick her again!"

"Dawn, get out!" he ordered.

"What? No, Dorian, I want to watch."

"Are you telling me no? Get out, go get your face together and go down there with your company."

I stayed on the floor not saying anything 'cause I knew Dorian would hit me again and I didn't want to be sitting up in the house healing this week. He helped me off the floor and I was shocked. I looked up at him and wondered why he was being so nice.

"Dawn's something else, ain't she, Veronica?"

"She doesn't really seem to be your type."

"Well I couldn't have the one I wanted," he said with a smile. And I had to jump on it. To be honest, Dorian was what I wanted my husband to be like, just not so damn disrespectful and abusive, of course.

"You just went about it all wrong," I explained to him. "Respect is a big thing with me and you don't seem to have that for me. You're attracted to me, but you want to beat me. All bruises don't heal and, the way we go at it, I wouldn't be so attractive for much longer. You treat me like your own personal property and I'm not going for that shit."

"I see. And you not gon' change."

"I might change one day, but not into the woman you want me to be. I want you to know that I'm happy that you have Dawn. She's what you need right now."

"Don't bullshit me, you happy that I'm not on yo ass no more."

"You right, Dorian, but I never said I wouldn't want you to be on my ass one day."

"What?"

I leaned in toward Dorian and kissed him. Any other nigga would be confused, but Dorian just went with it. He cleared off his desk and sat me on top of it. Straight to the point, that's how I liked it. Dorian ripped my panties off and pulled my waist to him. I was on the edge of the desk on my back and Dorian stood in front of me. I looked up at him and the look in his eyes got me hot. He was about to fuck my shit up! Dorian pulled down his pants, slowly, and I couldn't believe what this nigga was packing. He had to be about eight or nine inches and, for a moment, I got scared 'cause I didn't think I could take that shit. But when he put that cocky-ass smile on his face, I knew I had to try. To my surprise, Dorian was a very sensual lover. He didn't go fast and he didn't do me, roughly. He was stroking me just right, kissing on my legs and pinching my nipples. Dude was driving me wild and I couldn't contain my loud moans. Actually, I wanted somebody to hear. By the time Dorian had pulled me up and bent me over the desk, I had come, like twice. As he slapped my ass from behind, I came again. I felt his hot cum splash all over my ass and some slid down my crack. I had never been so satisfied in my life. Dorian slapped my ass one more time and I fell on the floor. He laughed as he put on his pants and headed for the door.

"You're going to be something else, with time, Veronica."

"I'm a fine wine, Dorian," I said. "Just wait for me."

"I will. Believe me, I will."

I tried my best to get up, but I couldn't. My legs were like Jell-O, and I soon realized that I wasn't going anywhere. I took my hair down and let it fall all over my face. I was burning the hell up. I called Pricey on my cell phone and told her to come get me from upstairs. In a matter of seconds, she was there and I was holding my face like I had gotten the beating of my life. Trip picked me up and we were out, so I spent the night with Pricey. When I got there, they put me right in the guest room and left me alone. I was sleepy, but I wanted to tell Pricey what happened so bad I couldn't sleep. Then when Trip left at around two in the morning I started screaming out Pricey's name. She ran to my room and cut on the light.

"What? What's wrong? Is your face hurting again?"

"Girl, I've never felt better."

"That's it. Dorian finally beat yo ass senseless. I'm going back to sleep. It's too late for this shit and I'm tired."

"Too tired to hear about the sex me and Dorian had?"

"What the hell . . . ?" Pricey jumped into bed with me. "What are you talking about? You had sex with Dorian?"

"Yes, girl. That's what we was upstairs doing. You didn't hear us?"

"Yeah, I heard you screaming, but everybody just figured you was getting your ass kicked. Dawn was downstairs smiling her head off, enjoying that shit, and Trip had to hold me back so I wouldn't beat her ass. When I realized there was nothing I could do, I started to cry, I was so mad."

"I'm sorry that I made you cry. You know if I ever get my ass whipped, I wouldn't give nobody the satisfaction of hearing me scream."

"I know, but when I seen Dawn smiling and Dorian come downstairs with this hard, emotionless look on his face, I freaked out."

"I told yo ass to stop worrying about me. I got this, ain't shit gon' happen to me."

"So do Dorian got a big dick?"

"Pricey, that nigga got the biggest dick in life! I don't even remember how many times I came. Dorian got that work and now I'm starting to second-guess not being with his ass."

"What? You don't want to be with that crazy-ass nigga! As hard-headed as you is, a month into ya'll relationship, Dorian would kill yo ass."

"You right, that's why I'm gon' call Frankie and try to get to know him a little better."

"Are you talking about that fine-ass Italian nigga you was talking to tonight?"

"Yeah, that was him."

"Oh bitch, that nigga was a piece of art! You better get with his ass."

"I am as soon as I get Tyrese off my back. Did you see how mad he was when I was talking to Frankie?"

"Don't even mention that nigga's name around me, he such a bitch. When everybody thought you was getting yo ass whipped, that nigga left with Deborah."

"Yeah, I know he a bitch and that's why I'm about to cut his ass off next time we cross paths. I'm done with him."

"Good."

Pricey and I went to sleep in the guest room, but had to wake up a few short hours later when Trip came in the house with Tyrese, drunk as fuck. When I heard these niggas come in the house I jumped out of bed so quick that Pricey bounced up, too. We ran into the living room and found them lying on the couch, still laughing and being loud. Trip took one look at Pricey and pulled her into their room; I saw liquor make Trip horny. I looked at Tyrese, rolling my eyes, and I went back to the guest room. I was not wasting my time with him anymore; I was moving on to bigger and better things. I wasn't surprised when he followed me to my room, but if he thought we were cool, he was in for some shit. Tyrese grabbed my arm and tried to kiss me, but I pushed that nigga back.

"Don't even try that shit with me. Be up on Deborah."

"Come on, ma. Don't start that shit. I told you that the bitch is just for show."

"You must take me for some type of fool, don't you?"

"Do you really expect me to answer that shit? Why you trippin', Veronica? I didn't act crazy when I saw you all up in dude face tonight. I don't want to argue with you tonight. Just let's go to bed right now, try to work things out." Tyrese tried to kiss me, but remembering what Pricey said about him being at the room with Deborah had me heated and ready to have it out.

"If you think yo weak dick gon' get you out the mess you made, think again."

"When did my dick become 'weak,' and why you trippin'? You know the situation between us; I'm trying to get the attention off us."

"Naw nigga, what you trying to do is make me out to be some kind of a fool, and I'm not having that shit. You can keep all that smooth shit to yo damn self 'cause I'm done with you. We don't have shit else to talk about."

"Come on, Roni. Tell me what this is about. You know I love you." The fact that this bitch just said that shit to me like he had never done no wrong made me hit the roof.

"You so full of shit! You don't love me, Tyrese! You love yourself and I don't have time for the bullshit no more. I know that you been taking Deborah to the room, fucking her. Even being bold enough to bring her over to Dorian house."

"Veronica, whoever been planting those lies in yo head, you need to tell them to step off."

"Save all that, Tyrese. You just let Deborah know that you a family man now, and you don't have time for her no more. No more trips to the hotel and spending money on her ass 'cause you got a baby on the way." I couldn't believe I said what I said. I had said it so good that I even believed myself for a moment. I was going to take it back, but the look on Tyrese's face told me to let this play out.

"What? If you don't want me to see Deborah no more, that's fine, but don't play like that, Veronica." I could see the fear in his eyes and I had to twist the knife in a little deeper.

"Tyrese, when have you ever used a condom with me? When have I ever told you I was on some type of birth control? When did you even ask me?"

"I didn't think I had to. What type of bitch want to have a baby this young? I can't believe you could be so stupid!"

"I don't know, Tyrese. How could I? But don't worry, because even though Dorian probably gon' kill us once he find out about our bundle of joy, it makes me feel so good knowing that we love each other." I bit my tongue as hard as I could so I wouldn't laugh.

"We got to get rid of it."

"I'm not getting rid of nothing. I'm having this baby and, hopefully, you'll live long enough to see your child be born. If not, I'll be sure to give the baby your last name or whatever."

"This shit not no game! Dorian will kill us!" That's when I got real mad 'cause, finally, I could see past all of Tyrese's game, and saw that he really didn't give a shit about me.

"You think I give a damn? I'm willing to die, as long as yo selfish ass come with me! I'm not doing no favors for you! It's time for you to face the music."

Tyrese's eyes went dead and he stood there for a moment, thinking. He looked at me with worry on his face and I smiled at him. I wanted him to know that I wasn't joking. Tyrese lowered his head and left Trip's house. I fell to the ground laughing 'cause the fact that Tyrese believed everything I had just said made me so happy. When a week passed and the streets were saying Tyrese had disappeared, it was the icing on the cake. This nigga was actually running scared over what he thought was going to happen to him. Every day that passed while Tyrese was on the run from his imagination, I felt better. While he was gone I got a little closer to Frankie. I had been bored one weekend and decided that I would go to the mall to kill some time. I went from store to store picking up a couple of things and laughing at the people working there. As much as I stole, they never caught on.

"Excuse me, Miss. I'm going to need you to empty your bags," I heard this male voice say from behind me. I was too shocked to move, but I was about to make a run for it until I was hugged from behind.

"I'm just playing with you, April. Chill," I looked up at Frankie's sexy ass smiling down at me. I finally stopped holding my breath and relaxed.

"You almost got me for a second. You was about to get knocked out."

"Yeah, whatever." Frankie let me go and we stood face to face.

"I should report yo ass. You know taxpayers like myself have to pay for all that shit you take."

"Well you better start doing what I'm doing then. That way, you won't just be giving your money away."

"Naw, I got too much bread for that shit. I'm wiping my ass with fifties, but do you, ma." For the first time ever, I felt a little bit embarrassed for having to steal. I didn't want Frankie thinking I was poor.

"Naw, I was just doing this 'cause I'm so bored, that's all." Frankie gave me a "bullshit" look, but didn't say anything more about it. We left the store.

"So April, what did I do so wrong that night we met for you not to call me?"

"Nothing, it just slipped my mind for a second, but I was going to call you."

"So what you doing today?"

"Nothing much."

"Why don't you let me take you out to dinner?"

"Sure, why not."

Frankie was the good that finally poured into my life. For almost three months, we became inseparable. Well . . . almost. See, I'm a girl who needs her space. When Frankie asked me to move in with him, I told him that I wasn't ready for that. I really wasn't, but whenever he wanted more of me, red flags would pop into my head and I would pull away. So we were serious, but not too serious. Frankie was giving me money like the shit was going out of style and I never spent not one cent. I saved everything. The only time I wore new clothes was when he bought me something, which was all the time because he said he didn't want me stealing anymore: "My girl shouldn't have to steal a thing; I'm gon' take care of you." As nice as it was to hear that type of shit I wasn't going to play the fool no more. If a nigga was doing something for you, trust that one day you was gon' have to do something in return. But when he said that shit, the only thing that was running through my mind was I didn't want to be tied down again. I didn't want to be nobody's "girl" and I realized that love shit was played out. For some reason I didn't rush things with Frankie. Please believe I wanted to jump his bones, but every time I found myself faced with the choice to have sex, I didn't. But I did please him in other ways: Frankie was addicted to oral, giving and receiving, which was great with me.

I wanted to have dinner with Pricey and Trip, but Trip wasn't having that shit. Pricey told me he said that shit would be disrespectful to Tyrese. As bad as Pricey went off when he said that shit, I told her not to fuck up a good thing and to let Trip have this one. I wasn't cool with what Trip had said, but he was good to my sister and he loved the shit out of her so I wasn't gon' come in between them over no bullshit like having dinner. Tyrese had been gone for almost three and a half months. Everybody said he was down South somewhere and I could give a fuck less. As I allowed myself to get happier and happier with Frankie I knew a storm would come any day now. With perfect timing on Frankie's and my three-month anniversary, which was held at this wonderful Italian restaurant that his grandparents owned, it came. Pricey was there because most of Frankie's family came, and she was the only family that I had. Frankie had gone all out with balloons, streamers, cake, gifts, and he had rented us a limo. This was better than any birthday that I ever had and it wasn't even my birthday. We sat there full, ready to die from over-eating, but when Frankie's grandmother came out with our cake, everybody perked up and was ready to eat all over again. Frankie lit the candles on it and I smiled at him. He was so sweet for doing all of this. Before I could blow them out, Tyrese caught my eye. He was standing in front of me with the most evil look on his face. I sat back and looked him dead in his eyes. He bet' not try no stupid shit.

"This what you been doing all the time I been gone? Playing house with this bitch?" he said. "We about to have a baby together and you with him? You ain't shit but a fucking slut!" Everybody's mouth was wide open and, of course, all eyes were on me. I blew out the candles and stood up in Tyrese's face.

"Do you hear me, bitch?" he repeated. "You not shit!" I slapped Tyrese in his face and in the time it took for him to raise his hand to me Frankie was up and ready to scrap. I placed my hand on his chest.

"Don't. I can handle this, Frankie," I said. "Tyrese, we can talk outside if you feel this passionate about the situation."

"Come on." He tried to grab my arm, but I pulled away from him, he could see that I wasn't in the mood for his shit so he just walked out of the restaurant. I kissed Frankie on the lips.

"I'll be right back and I'll tell you whatever you want to know. Don't worry."

"Take your time. I'll save you a piece of cake."

"Thank you."

Frankie just kept giving me reason's to fall for him. He didn't know who Tyrese was to me and he didn't know what Tyrese was about, but I could see that he didn't care. Frankie didn't give a damn about what Tyrese and I used to have 'cause he knew I was with him. I loved how sure he was of things and how much he knew about me without knowing specifics. I went outside and found Tyrese on the side of the building pacing around, trying to get hyped. I walked up on him and stood at the side of the building. This dude was not about to have my energy. He didn't even deserve that much from me. Tyrese stopped pacing and we stood face to face.

"Man, what you doing with that clown? Are you sleeping with him?"

"Not yet."

"Good, 'cause I don't see how we gon' try to work out things with that chump all in yo face. You need to go back in there and let him know he out the picture."

"I'm not doing nothing, I'm with Frankie and that shit ain't gon' change."

"Look, you need to cut the bullshit out! We about to have a baby together and I be damn if my baby mamma was with some other dude." I burst out laughing. He could not be serious. I took in a deep breath, trying to calm down.

"Where is all this shit coming from? Your punk ass left town and didn't want to have anything to do with me. Now you talking all this 'baby' shit. I told yo ass that night that you left that I was done with you, so stop embarrassing yourself."

"I'll be straight up with you. I've been doing a lot of thinking and I want to be with you. Since yo ass ain't changing your mind about getting rid of this kid, I figured, let's just make the best out of this." I could feel myself getting heated and, at that moment, I wanted to fight Tyrese, but I didn't want to give him the satisfaction of making me mad.

"The only reason you trying to be with me is because of this kid?"

"Naw, ma, you know I got feelings for you and, out of all the chicks I have ever kicked it with, I'm glad you the one who gon' birth my child."

I fought back the feeling of wanting to vomit 'cause the thought of birthing this nigga's child made me sick to my stomach. The cool approach wasn't going quickly enough for me, so it was time to get gutter. I wanted Tyrese out of my life once and for all, and I was going to say anything to make sure that happened.

"Not only do I not care about how you feel about me, I don't care to be the mother of yo child. When you left, I made sure we had no more reasons to talk. I found me someone who is way better than you and I got a abortion." His face dropped from shock.

"Don't act surprised. I didn't want to be with you, let alone have a *mini*-you growing inside of me. Be for real!"

"You killed my baby?"

"I sure did."

"Why? Why would you do some stupid shit like that, Veronica? I know I wasn't happy with the idea of being nobody father, but all I needed was time and yo ass couldn't even give me that!"

"You want to know why?" I stepped up toward his face and the fact that he didn't want me nowhere near him made this that much sweeter. "Why would I want to have a baby with someone so weak? What would you be able to offer with yo scary ass? Don't nobody have respect for you. Your ass ran! Why would I sit up here and have a baby with you, knowing that yo ass ain't shit? You can't stand up for yo damn self or me, so why do you think you would be able to do it for a child? I don't want to have nothing to do with you, period, so I tied up all loose ends."

"You heartless bitch!" Tyrese started choking me and I laughed weakly as I felt my last breath coming to an end. Out of nowhere came Trip pulling Tyrese off me, and Pricey helped me up.

"I'm gon' kill you, bitch!" he yelled. I caught my breath and laughed stronger this time.

"Don't you get it? Don't you see, Tyrese? I want to see you hurt, I want you to hate me and I, for damn sure, want you to feel as much pain as you can. You let your emotions get the best of you and, to me, you're nothing! You're nothing!"

Tyrese charged at me and I pushed Pricey aside so she wouldn't get hurt. From there on, it was blow for blow and, for a minute, I gave it to Tyrese, but my boxing skills were a little rusty. One small slip up and Tyrese was beating the shit out of me. Before he blacked both of my eyes, what I saw in him would last me a lifetime. I had killed a part of him and the shit felt good. Even when I slipped unconscious, I went out with a smile. The last things I heard were Pricey and Trip screaming at Tyrese to let me go. Then Frankie was speaking Italian so I knew, from that, he was mad and he wouldn't let nothing happen to me. I woke up back in the hospital, not hurt as bad as the last time, but my body was sore, nonetheless. I smiled when I saw Pricey by my side; she was the only one who could make me genuinely smile. I sat up slowly as she handed me something to drink. I took a sip and spoke.

"How long have I been out?"

"Only for two days. Veronica, the doctor said all you really need is rest. Time to heal."

"Same ol', same ol', Pricey. I know the deal. They should just let me have my own room and hold it for me until the next time I come back, 'cause you know someone's always trying to whip my ass."

"They all seem to be doing a great job, too, crazy!"

"Come on, Pricey. Don't start. I told you not to worry. The sooner you stop, the less stress you'll have. Just remember, no matter what happens to me, I always come out on top."

"Yeah, bitch, I know yo ass not going nowhere for a long time—whatever that shit you be talking. That still don't mean I want to see yo ass all in the hospital, looking like shit."

"Thanks for your love and support."

"I'm not joking. This shit got to stop."

"I know and I promise it will. I'll try to be a good girl. So tell me what everybody's talking about, give me the dirt."

"Once again, yo mess became everybody's mess. There was about to be a war between Dorian and this guy named Hector. Now, Hector is Frankie's cousin, who is deep into the drug game and just became partners with Dorian because of Dawn. You know Dorian about to marry into the family or whatever, so they decided to mix business with pleasure. But when Frankie seen Tyrese beating on you, they got into it. No lie, Frankie kinda gave it to Tyrese, but Tyrese held his own. Anyway, everybody had to break them up, but Frankie wasn't letting that shit go. He wanted Tyrese dead and you know Dorian's little rule."

"Yeah, I know—lucky Tyrese slides again. So where do you think Frankie's head's at? You think he still want to be bothered with me?"

"Fo' sho. He love you, but the way everybody been talking about you having Tyrese's baby is probably wearing Frankie down."

"I'm not pregnant, Pricey."

"I know that, but yo little lie just caught up with you is all. Everything should be cleared up in a couple of days. Dorian's and Dawn's wedding is next week."

"What about Tyrese. How he doing?" I asked with a smile, hoping Pricey would tell me what I want to hear.

"You *real*, sick, Veronica. You know you fucked him up. He not working, not going out, all he do is sit in his house."

"Good."

I lay back and was proud of myself for being able to get a plan together and see it through. Frankie was there the day that I was released from the hospital and he took me back to his place. I knew he had a lot of questions because the truth was that Frankie knew nothing about me, and the shit he did know was all lies: from my name to my age, to where I lived and what I was doing with my life. Frankie thought I was twenty, that I had my own place and that I was a full-time college student. I wondered how much of that he already knew was a lie by now. We sat down on his couch and I put together something to tell him. I wasn't in love with Frankie, but I liked him a hell of a lot, he treated me right and I didn't want to hurt him. But at the same time, if he wanted to end it, I wouldn't lose shit over the situation. I told myself I wasn't getting into the relationship bullshit again, and I meant it. Frankie was twenty-one and, as he explained, was at crossroads in his life. His cousin Hector had offered him a job, but Frankie wanted to go to culinary school. He wanted to become a chef and open his own restaurant. Frankie wanted somebody to love and take care of, which was cool with me 'cause I needed to be taken care of. What I didn't need was his love, or all the heavy shit he was trying to put on me about wanting to get married young. That shit went in one ear and out the other. The only reason I kicked it with him was to have my sanity. For every piece of good, there is bad, and to every right, there's a wrong. Well Frankie was the other part of my life, the good part. He was what I had when Veronica's life became just a little overwhelming and "April" needed some enjoyment.

"April, how long were you involved with Tyrese?" he asked.

"About two years, off and on." Good. He was still calling me April.

"So why did ya'll break up?"

"Tyrese didn't want to be tied down to one girl."

"So are you going to have his baby or not?"

"No, Frankie, I'm not. I . . ." I didn't know what would sound better, abortion or miscarriage. Frankie would probably think I was heartless if I said abortion, since he couldn't wait to have his big family. I put a sad face on and said, "I miscarried about a couple of days before I seen you in the mall that day. Tyrese left the state when I told him I was pregnant, that's why he didn't know."

"If he didn't even want to be a father why did he attack you about it?"

"Attack me? That was not the first time me and him got into it like that." I saw the anger in Frankie's eyes and knew I was winning him over. "Anyway, Tyrese said he had been doing a lot of thinking and he was ready to be a family man. I told him what happened and he was fine with that, but he still wanted to be with me. He wanted me to leave you. When I said no, we just got into it."

"I hate him, April, and I want you to know he's a dead man."

"Frankie, please don't. I don't want you in this any deeper than you are. I know you selling for Hector so you can go to school, but selling and killing somebody are two totally different things. Fuck Tyrese. He is no threat to us. We're together and that's all that matters. Besides, I don't want there to be problems in your family because of me. I know Hector and Dorian aren't seeing eye to eye about what's going on. I don't want all of this to come in between Dorian and Dawn, or Dawn and her family. Just let this go so we can move on with our lives."

"You right, April. I don't want to be in any more shit, but I want you to know I love you and I'll do anything for you."

"I know and you know I feel the same, Frankie."

"Good 'cause I wanted to ask you to do something for me, but I don't want you to think the wrong thing."

"Anything, Frankie. What is it?"

"Come with me."

We got up off the couch and headed to the back of the house to the bathroom. I wasn't shocked when I saw the pregnancy test on the sink, but I made a mental note not to underestimate Frankie as much as I have before. I started to undo my pants and Frankie grabbed my hands.

"April, I don't want you to think I don't trust you. If you don't want to do this you don't have to."

"Frankie, stop it. This is the least I can do for you." I smiled at him and opened the box.

"Call me when you're done," he said. I grabbed his hand this time.

"Oh no, Frankie. I don't want you to have a doubt in your mind. You sit here and watch me take this test. I don't want your mind clouded with the thoughts of babies while we're doing a little baby-making ourselves."

Frankie smiled at me or at the thought of finally being able to have sex with me. I took the test in front of him with a smile; I knew I had nothing to worry about. I laughed to myself at what Frankie said about trust. If he had me doing all this, he didn't trust me, and he shouldn't, but, at least, let's be real. When the test showed that I was not pregnant Frankie kissed me and made me dinner. I stayed the night with him and went home in the morning. It's funny 'cause after all that mess, the next week I came on my period for the first time, and that shit was no fun.

B was home and I had to say that, during those last couple of months, we had found a nice little way to co-exist. Now that Dorian wasn't all up on me, B wasn't on my back anymore, either. Realizing that I was never going to change, he just schooled me on all the things I needed to know about the life I was going to live. He stopped trying to lie about every little thing and, from that point on, he trained me. When I look back at it, my mother's death date is the day I started to live. It was the day I opened my eyes and found which path I was going to take. From that point on, I knew who I was and what I wanted out of life, and when I realized that my real eighteenth birthday was right around the corner, I was ready to stand on my own two feet. But, as time changes, so do people, and boy do they change in very big ways. As I got older and the street life became some really dangerous shit to fuck with, B didn't want me to be involved. I mean it was complicated with B, because he had outright told me that I was on my own once I turned eighteen, but had said that the streets should be my last option for money. I had some respect for my father because he helped me see a lot of things. He taught me so much and he gave me a way of life, a way of thinking, if I chose to fuck with the streets. When B found out about Dorian getting married and not having his name on me no more, he shocked me for the first time in my life. He stayed in Chicago, he stopped going out, he stopped trying to jump on me and he sat his ass down to be a father. B pulled me to the side one day and just explained that shit. "I always pride myself on being a man, not the best man, not the most loving or dependable and, for damn sure, not the man you turn to for help, 'cause I only care about myself. With all that said, I thought I was a man, but I'm not 'cause I don't take care of my shit. Like it or not, and I don't, for the record, but you are my responsibility. So from here on out, I'm gon' handle my shit." Don't think that, from that point on, things were great between me and B 'cause that was far from how it was.

"My job is to prepare you for life on your own." B said that every time he beat my ass or signed me up for some self-defense class. He let me know every day that I was a girl and shit would be twice as hard for me in the game.

I wished somebody would whisper that shit into Pricey's ear. She was still with Trip after all of this time and the girl was spoiled. Trip had been in the game for a minute—had a house and three cars to show for it. He loved my sister and proposed to her a couple of months after I got out of the hospital, but it seemed like neither one of them wanted to get married anytime soon, 'cause they wouldn't set a date. I knew Pricey wouldn't marry Trip because, even though he treated her right, I could tell that she still wouldn't let herself really love him. When she used to speak all that shit on men and how all they were good for was money she meant it. Since her and Trip got together, Pricey's little "friend" came to pay her a visit for the first time after she had three abortions. She kept fucking around with those pills, missing dates and shit. I told her ass that she needed to get "fixed" or something. They put her on that little birth control shot, but, anyway, she was a grown woman in her own right, a loud ghetto-fabulous, gorgeous woman who would only have the finer things in life. Her and Trip had basically been all around the world. Pricey loved to get out of Chicago and shop. If shopping was her job, the girl would be a millionaire, putting in overtime every day. She was in high demand like me. Even though Trip had branded her as his woman, that didn't stop niggas from trying to holla. This, in turn, had Trip always getting into it with some stupid nigga. Pricey loved attention, couldn't get enough of it, and welcomed it all, but if Trip did what Pricey did, she was going off. Any chick she saw within ten feet of Trip, she was fighting, and I was always right there her. Point blank: Pricey and Trip loved drama. They were a match made in heaven, but Pricey didn't want to see it. In fact, the more she fell for him, the more she made Trip into her enemy. Pricey had a separate banking account and when she felt like proving something to herself, she would leave Trip for whatever little reason and stay in the little apartment that she rented. Yeah, she told me one day that she realized that she was too dependent on Trip and had to have her own. I could feel that 'cause there was only really one person in life you should ever depend on: yourself. For my eighteenth birthday, we got each other's name tattooed on the back of our necks. I put no one above her and it was the same for her. That was the only thing that wouldn't change, the fact that we loved each other.

When Frankie proposed to me a week after I told him about Pricey's engagement, he might have taken it the wrong way. I think he thought that I was trying to give him a hint, but that was not the case. When I saw him pull a small box out of his pocket, I was not fazed and didn't waste time telling him no. Frankie asked why and I fed him some bullshit about being too young, which I was, and about not being "ready for that type of commitment," which I meant. The real reason I didn't say yes, though, was because I didn't love him. I would never love him and I could never see myself as someone's wife. Frankie wanted things that I didn't and it wasn't fair for me to play as if we had a future when we didn't. We really didn't even have a relationship, 'cause while I was with him, I had two other men. So when he said he was leaving Chicago and moving to New York to go to school, I told him to go. Frankie was so wonderful and, if I wasn't for me being the person that I was, we would've been great together. Frankie was the type of guy who was perfect for any woman.

9

I was walking home from high school at two o'clock in the afternoon when I saw Tyrese McKinney and wanted to punch myself. He was a block away with some other guys playing dice and he was looking so good. Out of all of the people that I knew, he had changed the most. Not only was he the sexiest man in the world at six-two, one-hundred-eighty pounds of muscle, long hair that he kept braided, dark, smooth skin that was covered in tattoos—and if my memory served me right, he had a big dick, too. But his looks are not what attracted me to him all over again after five months of not speaking. It was the person he had become; his attitude is what made me want to jump his bones. Tyrese had become the coldest person in Illinois, the top nigga on Dorian's team. It was said that Tyrese was Dorian's actual right-hand man and he took that job seriously. He had killed numerous people who didn't do what he wanted. Tyrese had a "fuck everything" type of attitude and would shut anybody down in a second. One time this dude stepped on his shoe and didn't say sorry, so Tyrese pistol-whipped him. I was there when it happened because everybody had come to see a high school basketball game. I watched as blood squirted out of the boy's face and Tyrese hit him with his gun over and over again. I was so hot and I wanted so badly to throw myself at him, but I knew better. Everybody, including me, knew that I was the most hated by Tyrese. I don't know why he felt the way he did when it was clear that I was the one who changed his life and made him head nigga in charge. Tyrese had taken in everything that I said about him being weak and changed all that around. He didn't have feelings and neither did I, but I wanted to change that, if only for one night. Since Frankie had left, I hadn't been fucked right. I dipped inside of the corner store across the street from where Tyrese was; his back was to me so I knew he hadn't seen me. I grabbed me a pack of gum and walked out. The man behind the counter didn't say anything. Even though I hadn't killed anybody in a while, I still had a nice little rep, so people knew not to fuck with me.

But I didn't have what Dorian and Tyrese had. I wanted to be feared and respected. There was always some nigga I had to put in his place for calling me out my name or thinking he could touch me because I walked past him. I didn't want niggas to have to second-guess me, I wanted them to know that I wasn't the one-period. So every day, I fought for that respect, no matter who it was I had to fight. For now, I was basically your all-around 'hood bitch. Chicks hated me and niggas respected me. I would fight anybody, be it girl or guy, and ten times out of ten, I won. I was a beast with weapons, and always carried two blades if I couldn't bring my guns along, which was hardly ever. I jumped fences like all the other niggas, bagged weed and cut up coke for B. That's why niggas was always pressing Pricey and me. We looked better than any bitch you could find and we could roll with the hardest niggas around. That's what every guy really wants, a chick that's beautiful who can hold shit down. I checked myself before I left the store. Besides Pricey, I really had no competition. But her and me were like night and day in the looks department. Where I had long hair, Pricey had hers short in a pixy cut. I was very light-skinned because of my mother and Pricey was dark because of our father. I had gray eyes, Pricey had hazel eyes. I was five-ten, but Pricey was five-five. She was loud and I never really talked that much. Pricey really didn't have big boobies. She was like a B cup and I was a D. The only thing we did have in common were our fat asses. I felt damn sexy in my Baby Phat outfit, jeans and a t-shirt with my hair pulled back in a long ponytail. I was about to squeeze into the tight circle of men playing dice until Trip caught the corner of my eye. He was across the street sitting on the hood of his car on his cell phone, smiling and shit. I rushed over there and took the phone out his hand.

"Who is this?" I barked into the phone.

"Bitch, who is you and why you on my man phone?"

"Hold up, hoe! Trip is my sister's man and if you don't want yo ass beat, you'll realize that shit real quick!" Trip was laughing and shaking his head.

"Veronica?" I heard the voice say.

"Pricey, is this you?"

"Girl, yeah, it's me."

"Oh my bad, Pricey." I hit Trip on his thigh.

"You could have told me you were talking to Pricey."

"Naw, I love to watch you and Pricey make a fool of ya'll selves."

"Tell Trip I said shut up," Pricey said.

"Pricey said shut up." Trip got off the car and walked over to his boys playing dice.

"'Ey, Veronica, good looking," my sister told me.

"You know I got you, Pricey. So why you ain't come to school today?"

"Girl, fuck school. We almost out. My ass missing a few days won't hurt."

"You know we got finals coming up."

"Yeah I know and I'm gon' be there. What you doing?"

"I was walking home until I spotted Tyrese fine ass."

"What is wrong with you, girl? Tyrese and you don't mix. Ya'll never have, so you need to let that little fantasy of yours die."

"Whatever! You know I'm not even trying to hear that."

"I know, but you keep on playing with fire, Veronica, and you gon' get burned."

"Well start lighting my ass up, 'cause I want him."

"I'm done with you. Tell Trip to bring some KFC home 'cause ain't shit here."

"Alright."

I got off the phone with Pricey and went back across the street to give Trip the phone and the message. Some guys stopped playing so I jumped in on his spot. I took a hundred bucks out of my bra and put it down on the big stack of bills. Money talks 'cause the whole time I had been around them, this was the first time they realized that a female was around. Tyrese looked up, saw it was me and handed back my money. I took it and put it back on the stack. About two-thousand dollars was up for grabs and I was going to be in on this.

"If you don't pick yo money up, you not getting it back."

"You think so, Tyrese? Hand me those dice and I bet you I could prove you wrong."

"I'm not handing yo ass shit, now get the fuck out of here."

"I'm not going no damn where. I put my fucking money down, so let me roll."

"Come on, Tyrese, let her roll once, so she can go about her business," Trip said, seeing that things were getting a little heated.

"I'm not gon' repeat myself," Tyrese said.

"What? You scared?"

"Bitch, please! No rat will ever put fear in my heart," he answered with a smile. He gave the dude standing next to him a five. All the guys laughed and so did I.

"As much as you changed, Tyrese, you still a bitter little bitch yo'self." The whole group fell quiet; nobody had talked to Tyrese like that and lived. I wasn't fazed because I was just living to die anyway, and no nigga was going to disrespect me.

"Veronica I'm not in the mood for this shit, take yo money and get the fuck out of here."

"Why you making this hard, Tyrese? Let me roll and, if I fuck up, I'm gone." He looked around at the other guys and tried to figure out what he should do. Out of nowhere, he ran up on me and slapped the shit out of me.

"I told yo dumb ass to go on somewhere! What's wrong with these young bitches nowadays? Tell them one thing and they do another!" I pulled my shit together as I heard everybody agree with Tyrese, and pulled out my blade. I was about to cut his ass up, but Trip held me back. Tyrese turned around and his smile had faded.

"Bitch, you trying to stab me? You think you can take me?"

"You might have all these niggas fooled, but I see the bitch in you!" I yelled. Tyrese pulled his gun out and pointed it to my head.

"Come on now, Tyrese, you know me better than that. I could give a fuck less about dying. So what you really trying to prove?"

"Come on, Tyrese, let this little shit slide," Trip said. "You know Veronica ain't right in the head." Before I could object Trip put his hand over my mouth. "Let me handle this shit."

"You better handle it before I do," Tyrese warned.

I was talking so much shit as Trip picked me up. I was so pissed off that I was kicking, damn near fighting Trip so he would let me go. Tyrese just laughed and went back to his game; he wasn't getting away with this. I put my life on that shit. Trip threw me against his car. A feeling of shock came over me.

"Veronica, let this shit slide—Tyrese will kill you! Don't put me in this position. You my nigga and everything, but I'm not taking no bullet for you."

"I can take care of myself."

"I know you can, but just don't do this shit while I'm here. If you want to try to sneak Tyrese on yo own time, go for it, but not now."

"Trip, just don't get in the middle of this. Whatever happens, happens."

I pushed Trip to the side, causing him to stumble backwards and I ran back across the street. Just as Tyrese turned around I kicked his gun out his hand and punched him in the mouth, causing him to fall. His lip was busted and I put my knife to his neck. He tried to sit up, but I pressed down on his neck even harder. Tyrese sat still with a smile on his face.

"So what you gon' do now, Veronica? Either way, I'm gon' fuck you up, so make it good."

"I'm going to get my money back, since you don't want to play with me. Then, since I don't have my piece on me, I'm going to run."

Just like that, I was gone. I knew that Tyrese would run after me, but I had a pretty good chance of being faster than him. But getting home never seemed to take so long! I looked back and Tyrese was a block away. If he caught me, it was a wrap; not only would he kick my ass, but, most likely, I would be in a body bag at the end of the day. Dorian didn't have his name on me no more, so I was unprotected. I finally made it to the door, but had six flights of stairs to run, since the elevator was out. I didn't even take in a breath when I started hitting those steps and I knew, when I finally did get a chance to rest, that my chest was going to burn. I made it to the second floor when I heard the door open. I knew without even looking back that it was Tyrese, but I kept on moving. My chest was on fire, my mouth was dry and I felt like I would pass out at any moment. I didn't know how I was still going, but I was not about to face Tyrese while he was mad. With only two more floors to go, I tried to pull out my keys, but they fell on the floor. I didn't stop. If I had to kick down the door, I would. As soon as I got to my guns I could face Tyrese and his. I was going two steps at a time, but I soon figured out that he had to be doing about four, 'cause what little breath I had was knocked out of me on the fifth floor when I was slammed against a concrete wall in the hallway. Without getting a chance to recuperate, Tyrese damn near took me off my feet and threw me through the window. The only reason I didn't fall to my death was because of the bars that kept us locked inside of this place. I felt the glass cut through my back and I let out a moan of pain, but when I saw Tyrese smile at the sound that I made, I knew not to make it again.

"Do it hurt, Veronica?" he said with a smile.

"You know all this abuse is like foreplay to me," I said with a sick smile.

"You were always a sick bitch."

I put my hands down to my waist and found my blade. I pulled it out and cut him an inch below his left eye. I went for the stairs again, but, once my foot hit the first step, I fell, face-first, on the floor.

Damn it! I figured I wasn't gon' make it to my guns before there was a bullet in my head, so I decided to talk my way out of this.

"I appreciate all of these love taps, but I think I'm suffering from some internal bleeding," I said.

Tyrese picked me up off the floor and I was back up against the wall. I scrunched up my face because I felt chunks of glass go even deeper into my back. I felt him reaching for his gun and I started to talk again. "You know what? Fuck it, kill me! Shoot me!"

"Oh, I'm about to." I heard him cock his gun and knew I had to say something better.

"Just answer me this one question."

"What?"

"Why do you act like we don't have no fucking history? We haven't talked in months and now all this disrespect. You know how I am, Tyrese. I won't be dismissed and I won't be disrespected. I'll die first."

"I see."

Tyrese stepped back and, for a moment, it looked like he didn't want to kill me. But who's to say what was going on in his head. Before I could speak, Tyrese punched me in the face, then the stomach, and once I fell to the floor, he started to kick the shit out of me. As good as he looked in Timbs, I wished he didn't have them on right now 'cause I thought that, at any moment, he would break one of my ribs. I damn sure didn't want to go through that shit again. I heard Trip telling Tyrese to stop and thanking him for not shooting me.

"Come on, nigga. That's enough. Veronica got the picture. Let's just take her to B and let him handle this."

"He ain't gon' do shit, so if yo boy want to beat on me some more, let him. 'Cause I'm not trying to deal with his bullshit no more."

I stood up off the floor and looked him in his eyes. I didn't have to wonder for long what he would do because, in a blink's worth of time, he punched me in the eye. When Tyrese pulled me closer to him by the hair I began to laugh and smile. I would only allow myself so long to feel pain. Most people cried when they were hurt. I laughed. I have my mother to thank for that.

"In my eyes, Veronica, we have no history and I was never with a rat like you."

"If that was true, you wouldn't hate me so much." I tried to wrap my arms around his neck and kiss him, but he pushed me, causing me to fall onto the steps.

"Don't fucking touch me!" he yelled. I got up with a smile still on my face.

"Fine. Be mean," I said.

He and Trip followed me upstairs and I opened the door. I left it open 'cause I knew they would follow. B was sitting on the couch. He took one look at me and went back to watching TV, but when he saw Tyrese, he was livid.

"What happened to you, Tyrese? Who the fuck do I have to ride on?" Tyrese and Trip looked over at me and B caught on quickly.

"What? Every time I send you out, you do something stupid!"

"You mad at me, B? Tyrese got one little scratch and I'm standing here with a black eye, busted lip, glass in my back and bruises all over me!"

"That shit ain't new, Veronica. Tyrese, have a seat and let me get ya'll something to drink. Veronica, go in there and get something for the boy's face."

"Get the fuck out of here! Do I have to run down the list of my injuries again!"

"Don't you be getting loud with me! I'll beat yo ass until you pass out." Before B could get his next word out, I walked over to him.

"I know ya'll work for Dorian and ya'll have this loyalty for one another, but don't threaten me. Don't ever fucking threaten me." B and me locked eyes.

"Just do what the fuck I asked," he said.

I went to the back, knowing that I was in no shape to fight B today, not after fucking with Tyrese earlier. I watched from the bathroom as Trip admired our dining room, B had the place pretty laced.

"Please have a seat, gentlemen. So Tyrese, what happened?"

"You know your daughter like to run off at the mouth," he said.

"She wanted in on a dice game, but Tyrese wasn't having it," Trip added. "He was about to shoot her in the head before I got there."

"Hell, Tyrese, you should have shot her dumb ass! Maybe a bullet is just what that crazy-ass girl need, 'cause God knows beating her is pointless." I came out with some Neosporin to clean up his cut and a Band-aid.

"Nice to know how you really feel, B."

"You already know I don't give a damn, so you better learn your place. You not gon' always come up against somebody as nice as Tyrese who will let your big-mouth ass slide."

"As much as I could say, B, I won't even waste my time." I put the Band-aid on Tyrese's cut and let my hand caress his face for a moment before I went to my room. He moved away.

"Look, Tyrese, I'm sorry for the trouble."

"Don't worry about it, B. Can't nobody control that crazy bitch."

"Damn right. You know her mother was the same way. Both of them hoes crazy." B laughed and Tyrese got up to leave.

"Alright B, we got rounds to make. We'll holla," Trip added.

"Cool. Veronica, come walk them downstairs."

I got my jacket off before B started calling for me again. Blood was basically pouring from my back, but did anyone give a damn? Hell naw! I just went to the dining room so I could be done with Tyrese. I had had enough of his sexy ass for today. I stood in between him and B.

"What do you want?" I asked.

"Go walk them downstairs and apologize to Tyrese." I looked up at Tyrese and could see the smile on his face again.

"Whatever," I said, walking downstairs as they followed me. I laughed when I saw Trip's car parked outside, windows down and keys still in the ignition. Nobody had touched it.

"Tell Pricey I'll call her later and not to worry."

"Alright." Trip got in the car, but Tyrese's bitch-ass sat on the hood, waiting.

"Don't you have something to say to me?"

"Not really. Have a safe trip."

"Naw, that's not it, Veronica. Try again."

"What's the point of me saying it if you know I don't mean it, Tyrese?"

"Because you were ordered to and I wonder what B would say if I called him and told him his daughter didn't do what he asked."

"He wouldn't say shit. We would just be bucking and, even though I don't feel like fighting nobody else today, I will. What's two or three more bruises?"

"You a real sick person."

"Tyrese, you don't know the half of it and I won't say sorry for defending my name. If I got to fight every day for the rest of my life, I will not be disrespected by anyone. That goes for even your fine ass."

"Girl, you don't have a chance in hell. Let it go."

I walked back upstairs and Tyrese got in with Trip. It was going to be hard breaking him, but I would, eventually, and then I would toss his ass to the side again. I went to my room and took the chunks of glass out of my back so I could run me a bath. As I sat in the hot tub I recalled so many times when the clear water would turn red, from one nigga's beating or another's. I couldn't believe that my beauty was still intact, but I was thankful. I closed my eyes and relaxed for a moment before I had to get out to put bandages all over my body. Now was the hard part, healing a hundred percent. I wasn't tired until I took those pain pills and, once they went into full effect, I was out. I didn't sleep long 'cause around two in the morning my cell phone started going off. It was Paul, this white police officer I had been talking to for almost a year. It was funny how we met and how I always ended up getting out of shit.

I had started that long walk from Trip's and Pricey's house to mine and it was past one in the morning. I had turned down Trip's offer to give me a ride and I didn't have money for a cab. Something just told me to walk that night, and I was glad I did. I had spotted the police car following me when I was halfway home and my first instinct was to run. But then I realized I had done nothing wrong. I kept walking, thinking about how much I hated the police, and, the more I thought on it, the closer they got. When I was about fifteen minutes away from my place, they pulled up on me. Two white cops got out. The one shining his fucking light in my face was a fat, sloppy piece of shit and I knew he was about to give me a hard time. The other, Paul, stood by the car while his pig partner approached me.

"Is someone picking you up tonight, or have you stopped working?"

"Sorry, I'm not a hooker and I would appreciate if you'd stop blinding me with yo light."

"I would appreciate if pieces of shit didn't walk the streets, but here we are."

"Whatever. Can I finish walking home or would you like to continue with this pointless conversation?"

"You're a smart nigger, aren't you?" I took a moment to look at him so I could remember his face if I ever caught his fat ass in my 'hood when I had my piece on me. He was dead.

"I don't have time for this." I started to walk and this fat bitch walked up on me, placing handcuffs on me.

"What the fuck is this! I haven't done anything!"

"Come on, Billy. Don't do this," the other cop said.

"Paul, never miss an opportunity to put these sluts in their place."

I felt Billy's little meat get hard behind me and I just knew this motherfucker wasn't trying to do what I thought. Billy pulled me to the back of the cop car and bent me over. Once he started to try to undo my pants, I lost it.

"Get the fuck off me!" Billy pulled out his nightstick and slapped me across my back.

"Shut up, bitch!"

I started to kick and scream as I felt Billy's pants fall to the floor. He didn't try to take mine off any more. He just pulled out a knife and cut them off. Once again my pride would be stripped from me, and I could do nothing with my hands behind my back. I felt his little-dick ass push up against my behind and my eyes filled up with tears. This shit couldn't be happening to me again. I tried to scream, but every time I did, Billy would choke me. When I felt him pushing himself inside me, I got angry and I looked over at his sorry-ass partner, who had his head down trying to act like this wasn't going on.

"Fucking pig-ass police! Ya'll ain't shit! How can you just stand here and let this shit happen! You hear me fucking talking to you!" Paul looked up at me and looked away with shame.

"Shut up, bitch!" Billy said You're just mad because I'm not paying you!"

"I'm not a fucking hoe, you dumb piece of shit and, even if I was, it wouldn't give you the right to do this!"

I started to scream and cry even harder when I realized no one would save me. I would be a victim again and there was nothing I could do about it. "Somebody please help me! Please!" I slid to the side and let myself to fall on the floor; I was going to make this as hard as possible for Billy.

"Get up, you stupid bitch!"

"Fuck you, pig!" I kicked Billy in the back of his knee and he fell to the ground. I got up off the ground and tried to run, but was tripped by the fat slob. Billy got up and started to beat the shit out of me with his nightstick.

"Billy, that's enough!"

"Fuck this black bitch!" Before I knew it, Billy was laid out next to me and I watched as his eyes rolled to the back of his head. Paul helped me up and I tried to pull away from him.

"Calm down. I don't want to hurt you. Just let me call you a cab." Paul helped me back over to the car and took the cuffs off me. I intently rubbed my wrists to try to make them feel better. Paul got a blanket out of the trunk and put it around me.

"Thank you. Thank you so much," I said. But there was a part of me that wanted to take Paul's gun and shoot both of these bitches. I was so happy that he saved me, though, so I just thanked him.

"Don't thank me. I shouldn't have let it go on as long as I did. I'm sorry." Paul went over to Billy and slapped some handcuffs on him.

"Billy won't be too happy when he wakes up."

"How can you work with somebody like him?"

"I don't know. The force is just not what it used to be, I'm thinking about leaving all together. So what exactly are you doing out here so late anyway?"

"I just left my sister's house and I didn't feel like staying the night. I walk home all the time; I guess I won't be doing that anymore."

"I don't want you to live in fear. You shouldn't have to."

"Thanks, but if the police are the ones out here that I should be worried about, then why should I risk it with just any ol' body?"

"I'm sorry. Not all of us are like that. What's your name, by the way?"

"April."

I sat there talking to him until my cab came and Paul gave me fifty dollars for the ride. I don't know why I gave him my number, but I was happy about it later on. It seems that Paul was something of a pushover and, for some reason, he decided to stand up for me. But Paul was full of shit that night, because, out of all the time we'd been talking since the incident, didn't mention leaving the force anymore. After a week of talking I was ready to cut him out my life, until he invited me to dinner at this upscale hotel. I met him there and when I arrived he was already seated.

"April, thank you for coming. Have a seat, please."

"No problem. What's wrong?"

"Let's order first."

"Okay." We ordered our food and I was really wondering what all this was about. I noticed that Paul didn't have his wedding ring on and he seemed nervous.

"Alright, we ordered. So what's this about?"

"Can we just wait until after dinner? I have a room upstairs and I want to tell you something."

"Excuse me? I don't think we ready to be going to no room."

"April, it's not like that. I just really need to tell you something, but I can't say anything right now. If it will make you feel better, I don't have any kind of weapon on me."

"Oh, I'm not worried; I just don't want you to expect anything."

"I don't. Please, let's enjoy our meal."

We finished dinner and went upstairs. I didn't really think that Paul would try to hurt me. I just didn't trust anybody. So, even though I knew he wouldn't do anything, I still didn't know what was going on and I didn't like that shit. After dinner, Paul walked into the room first and sat on the bed. I sat in a chair across from him, waiting. When he didn't say anything, I spoke up.

"What is this about?"

"About a year ago, me and a couple of my fellow police officers raided this black guy's house because we were sure that he had drugs in there. He was one of the workers of a drug lord we have been trying to get for years now."

"Who is this drug lord?"

"Dorian Fletcher. He's the reason my life has been turned upside down."

"So what happened with this bust?"

"We knew this guy was involved with drugs, and this was his house, but we couldn't find anything. We already didn't have a warrant to show, and things got out of hand. One bullshit comment led to another and the next thing I knew, half of my partners were beating the crap out of him. I told them to stop. I said that he had enough, and his girlfriend stood next to me, pulling me, begging me to make them stop. But I just stood there with her and we watched my fellow police officers beat this man to death. Blood was everywhere and when that woman wouldn't stop screaming they took her in the back and shot her. They covered it up, made it look like a drug deal gone bad. Two basically innocent people were murdered and I didn't do anything, I didn't tell anybody. Every night I have nightmares about what happened. My wife left me and I've isolated myself from everybody at my job. I have nothing and, April, I just don't know what to do." I sat there, speechless.

"I feel so bad, I feel like I need to be punished." For the first time since Paul started talking, he looked at me. "April, I want you to beat me." My mouth dropped open and I couldn't believe what this crazy white boy wanted me to do.

"What?"

"April, I need you to do this for me. I know you're mad about what Billy did to you, so just take your frustration out on me."

"You can't be serious. There are other ways of dealing with your demons."

"I've tried everything already. I told my wife and she left me. I went to the victim's funeral and begged for forgiveness. I've even prayed. I'm at the point where I can't keep living like this."

"Damn. You dealing with a lot of shit."

"April, just try for me. If you're not comfortable, just stop."

I couldn't pass up this opportunity to kick a cop's ass. I had to take it. I got up out of my seat and started to beat the fuck out of that white boy. When I thought about all them niggas in my 'hood that took a swing on me and kicked my ass, I gave it to him harder. I couldn't even recognize Paul once I tired myself out and stopped. His face was bloody and bruised. I gave him the once over to make sure nothing was seriously wrong with him. There wasn't, but I noticed a wet spot on the front of his pants.

"Did you piss on yourself?"

"That's not piss."

It took me a moment, but once I realized what he was saying, I made it up in my mind that I would never be talking to this freak again. What type of person gets off on being beaten? I gathered my things and was about to run out the door until Paul pulled out hundreds and I froze. "Here is a thousand dollars; I want you to have it. Thank you for helping me." I didn't question it. I just took the money and left. That's really how this crazy relationship started. Now Paul calls me every once in a while to get his fix and pay me for it. He sometimes takes me to the gun range and helps me improve on my skills. He was calling for our usual appointment tonight.

"Hello?"

"April, it's Paul can I see you tonight?"

"I'll be over your house in a hour."

"Alright. I'll be waiting."

What can I say? I'm addicted to easy money. I got up and called a cab. When I arrived, Paul was waiting in his car. He got out to pay my fare and we sat back in his car. He drove to the gun range and we let off a couple of rounds, then went right back to his place. Within two minutes of walking in the door we were fucking on Paul's couch, and five minutes after that he was asleep. I got up and walked around his house to see if I could find anything of use. Every chance I got, I went through Paul's things to see if he was collecting any evidence on any of my niggas in the 'hood. If I ever did come across anything I would take them make copies so I could let these niggas know where they were fucking up and, if I was cool with the person, I would just do some editing. After I took a shower I picked up Paul's wallet, taking my share, and then I called me a cab again. I needed to find a dude who could do for me and have the dick to keep my attention. Good thing I didn't have to deal with dudes on a regular basis. I made it back home and was shocked that B wasn't there. I went to sleep 'cause I did have plans on going to school. I knew Pricey would show up asking me questions about my day and how I escaped death once again. Getting dressed the next morning was not an easy task, my body hurt so bad. So I just decided to make it easy on myself and wore some cute sweats with some gym shoes.

I went to school and was shocked when the day ended that Pricey was nowhere to be found. The walk home was boring so I took my time. No point in rushing home if there was nothing there for me. I wished I had my own place. I'd hook it up the way I wanted it to look and just walk around naked if I pleased. B was bringing me down, holding me back; he wouldn't talk to Dorian for me so I could get a job. I went home after school, not feeling up for much and thought about calling Josh so I could go shopping, but I didn't feel like dealing with his fat ass. After being with Paul and his small penis, I didn't want to deal with another one. So I sat in my room thinking, thinking about when my day would come, when I would make my own money and have my own shit. Graduation was right around the corner and I only had so much to live off of once B decided to kick me out. I went to sleep for what seemed like only minutes, but as my cell phone woke me up, I noticed that it was now dark outside.

"Hello?" I answered.

"Girl, get yo ass up! I'm coming to get you in like five minutes. Dress cute."

"Pricey, where we going?"

Click! The trick had hung up on me.

I got out of bed and slipped on some tight black pants and a red tank top. I put on my black Forces and my holster that held two forty-fives. Wherever Pricey was taking me I would be ready for anything. Finally, I put on the matching black jacket and went downstairs. As soon as I opened the door to go outside, Pricey pulled up and I jumped in her G-Wagon. I noticed that she was dressed to impress, so I knew we were headed to a party. I sat back and listened to music with my nigga, not surprised when we pulled up to her house. I got out the truck and we went in. The music was so loud, and everybody in Chicago was there. I was glad that I thought to bring my pieces 'cause, as soon as some shit jumped off, it would be nothing for me to pop a nigga. The first person I saw once I was in the house was Tyrese and he smiled at me, but I rolled my eyes. I knew he was full of shit and I just wasn't for it tonight. Pricey handed me a drink and we made our way to the dance floor. Now I'm not the type of girl that goes out of her way to look good, or to attract a lot of attention to myself—that was Pricey's thing—but when I hit the dance floor it's over. Dancing was like breathing for me. It came so natural and I never missed out on an opportunity to move. Had the desire and passion been there, I would have gone to college so I could dance, become a choreographer or something. But the truth was that the only thing I would ever go out of my way to do was kill people. Nothing compared to the joy I felt when I took a life. Sick, huh? Yeah, but that's just me. My father would always say that I was born to take lives. Every time I got into a fight I damn near killed the person.

I stayed on the floor for most of the night, and the times that I wasn't dancing I was getting drinks, telling niggas to get out of my face. I figured if I ever was to hook up with a guy, I would be the one to approach him, not the other way around. Besides, most of the guys who tried to spit at me worked for Dorian, and I had learned my lesson from that. Tyrese grabbed my hand before I could go back on the dance floor. He was drunk and I could see sex in his eyes. I had almost learned my lesson. I smiled at him and stood my ground.

"What do you want, nigga?"

"Let's go in the back so we can talk."

"I can hear you just fine right here."

"You not still mad about the other day, are you?"

"I wasn't mad then. What you want?"

"Let's dance."

I walked to the dance floor and Tyrese was right behind me. I loved a guy who could keep up with me, and since I already had a thing for Tyrese, when he suggested we leave, I thought nothing of it. After dancing to a couple of songs I was ready to fuck anyway. I could feel his hardness pressed up against me and I was ready to go. I would get what I wanted tonight and I was happy for that. Tyrese had sold his house a year ago when the attention from the police was on him after a shooting. Now, he stayed in this apartment right outside Chicago. I noticed over the years that Tyrese pulled away from everybody by moving and only really associating with Trip. I had never been to his apartment and I felt a little proud that I was one of the few girls that did get to see his place. As soon as Tyrese got the door open I jumped into his arms and we went at it. It had been too long since I kissed him and the shit was great. He had gotten bigger and being in his arms made me feel so small and sexy. I pushed him down on the couch 'cause it was taking too long to get to his bedroom. My shirt and his shirt were off in a matter of seconds. Damn, his body was tight! I kissed his chest and then went right for his spot on his neck. When he opened his mouth and let out the sexiest moan, I knew I was on it. I took my bra off myself just so I could feel the heat from his body pressed up against me. I loved Tyrese so much and he was the only person that I had ever wanted to be with. He finally wrapped his arms around me and held me tightly; even though I didn't trust him, I felt safe whenever he was around.

"Damn, I want to fuck you so bad, Veronica," he said, breathlessly, with words full of passion. I looked him in the eyes.

"Well let's go then. Take off them pants." I went for his neck again and undid his belt before he grabbed my hands.

"Stop," he said. I looked at him like he was crazy.

"Why?"

"I can't do this."

"What you mean you can't do this? Yo 'boy' is up."

"I know, and that shocks me, but I'm not fucking you." Tyrese pushed me to the side and started to put his shirt back on. I sat there, still half-naked. Confused.

"Run that shit by me again, Tyrese." I was so horny and I was trying my best not to just *take* the shit from him.

"Veronica, do you still love me?" I scrunched up my face at his question and sat there not sure of what to say.

"Man, you know I'm always gon' love yo stank ass. What is this really about?"

"I saw you tonight looking pretty cute and just knew I wanted to fuck, but when I get you to my house and the liquor finally leaves my system, I wonder how I even let a rat like yourself grace my doorsteps." My face dropped to the floor when Tyrese said that. I didn't try to hide the shocked look on my face.

"What?" I was barely able to get the word out.

"I mean you're just a kid. When I touch you, I feel sick. The thought of me sliding up in you is disgusting." I slowly put on my clothes and let the anger build as he spoke. "I mean everybody know about the white men you be tricking for and I was about to break you off. I'm fucking up. Veronica, you not even on my level and I just remembered that I could do much better."

"I see." I started to put on my shoes and could feel Tyrese smiling.

"Can you hurry up so I can take you home and go find someone who can give me a proper nut tonight?" I laughed to myself and jumped off that couch so quick into his arms again. I started punching that nigga in the face and, once I felt liquid on my hands, just the thought that it might be blood made me give it to him harder.

"Get the fuck off me!" he screamed as he pushed me, while I scratched the shit out of him. I hit the ground hard, but jumped back up like it was nothing and tried to punch him again. But he was ready. Tyrese slammed me against the wall so hard that I fell back onto the ground. This time I couldn't get up so easily. Still mad as all hell, I hit that nigga in the nuts and Tyrese wasted no time grabbing me by the neck and lifting me back to my feet. I swung wildly at him and tried to kick the shit out of him before that darkness could take over. Just as my eyes were about to roll to the back of my head, he slammed me back up against the wall, repeatedly, until I stopped trying to hit him. He finally let me go and there I sat on the floor, doing my best to not fall out. I let my breathing go back to normal as I watched Tyrese grab my guns and jacket. He came back over to me, grabbing a fist full of my hair, and pulled me to my feet. Tyrese dragged me like that all the way out of his apartment to his driver's seat and pushed me into his car.

"Sit yo ass down and don't say shit! If I have to pull over, I'm beating the fuck out of you! Don't be mad at me 'cause I don't want to be with you, bitch! You a fool for thinking that I would stick my dick inside of you, hoe! What a joke! About as funny as you saying that you love me!" I tried to open the door and Tyrese smacked me in my head. "Don't be stupid, Veronica! It's a long way to your house from here. Just sit the fuck back and let me take you home."

I was too hurt to even speak. My heart was really hurting and I couldn't look at him. The fact that he meant what he said is what cut me deep. We hadn't talked or spent any time together for so long, but I still loved him the same way I did that night that I gave him my "gift." Now, he hated me with a passion. I wondered what it was that kept my love so strong for Tyrese and what it was that made him hate me with the same degree of love I felt. I sat there; my ego and pride more hurt than anything. The ride back to Chicago was so long. I just wanted to jump out of his car and put this whole night behind me. For a moment, I wanted to say "fuck it" by turning his wheel so the car could flip over, hoping that I would live through the crash and he wouldn't. *Vanilla Sky* his ass! But, with my luck, I would fuck around and kill my fool self. When we finally made it to my building, Tyrese unlocked the door so I could get out. As he pulled off, I could hear him laughing over his music, and right then, I wanted to cry. But I didn't. About a block down, he threw the rest of my things out the window and I went to go pick them up. I had never wanted somebody dead so bad, and, eventually, I got everything that I wanted.

10

I went in the house and fell out on my bed, but could only enjoy sleep for a moment when my cell started ringing off the hook. I answered it with sleep still in my voice and half-listened to the person on the other end.

"Hello, my sweet Veronica. Sorry to wake you."

"Dorian?" I forced myself to sit up.

"Yes, it's me. I want to see you today."

"Okay."

"Get dressed and someone will be there to pick you up in twenty minutes."

"I'll see you soon."

I jumped out of bed and got in the shower, I didn't have much time to get dressed. Dorian waited for no one. My relationship with him had gotten better. Dorian let me know that he respected me and, from that point on, we had no more problems. I tried my best to follow his rules and he didn't freak out when I made mistakes. I hadn't seen much of him, either, since he'd gotten married. I put on a red Baby Phat pants suit and some black heels. I didn't have time to flat-iron my hair so I just put it up in a bun. Dorian's favorite color was red and, if I wanted to start working for him, I needed to impress him. It was all about being on Dorian's good side after he got rid of Dawn. Word was that the dirty bitch was fucking one of Dorian's bodyguards. When he found out Dawn was five months pregnant, on the night he confronted her she swore it was his. I heard that all Dorian did was laugh, and the next day there was no sign that Dawn ever existed. Dorian was truly cold-blooded and I wasn't trying to fuck with the nigga, not just yet. He was single all over again and he kept his house full of very attractive ladies. He was like the drug lord version of Hugh Heffner. But even with all the hoes he had, the few times I went over there for a party, or whatever, I could tell that he still wanted a piece. I waited outside for my ride and debated on whether I should call Pricey to tell her about my fucked up night with Tyrese. I decided against it 'cause I knew all she would say is, "I told you so." I knew better than to think that anything good could come from a bastard like Tyrese in the first place. What can I say? I like everything I'm not supposed to have.

When Tyrese pulled up in front of me I wasn't even mad. That's just how my life was. I opened the door, got in, put on my seatbelt and looked out the window. I had no intentions on saying a word to him, but Tyrese enjoyed rubbing things in my face so he had everything to talk about that morning.

"How did you sleep?"

"Fine."

"Did you hook up with somebody after I left?"

"Nope."

"I did. This *bad* bitch, too! I just came from over her house not too long ago. Just as my ass getting out the shower, Dorian call me." I could feel him looking at me, waiting on a reaction.

"What?" I asked without looking from the window.

"You're just so not yourself. You really shouldn't let me effect you so much."

"Okay." He wanted a response from me.

"So the bitch I was fucking last night had the best mouth a nigga could ever ask for. She had a fat ass, too, and let me hit it from the back."

"Sounds like wifey material to me," I said, sarcastically.

"Naw, if that was the case, I would have went ahead, settled and married you."

"What is that supposed to mean?"

"It mean that if I wanted to marry a hoe like the one I was fucking not too long ago, I wouldn't have wasted all this time and just married you."

"Lucky me. I missed a bullet. Can you not speak to me for the rest of the ride?"

"I could, but I'm not. I'm in the mood to talk. So do you feel stupid for throwing yourself at me the other night? I was telling Trip about it and he was kinda embarrassed for you."

"Naw, I don't feel anything. Not yet, but there is a time and a place for everything. When yo time come, I hope you can back up all this shit-talking."

"What you trying to say?"

"I'm not *trying* to say anything. I'm saying that one wonderful day, when you don't have Dorian to hide behind, I will kill you."

"I look forward to this day."

Tyrese didn't talk the rest of the time; he just turned up his radio and drove. I wondered what Dorian wanted to see me for. With me staying out of trouble, we hadn't seen each other in a while. When we arrived at Dorian's place two bodyguards told us to follow them, which we did, and found Dorian in his gym working out. For a thirty-four-year-old man, Dorian was fine as hell, and if he got his shit together long enough, I would be with him. I watched him run on his treadmill, all sweaty and sexy; damn I needed to be fucked! I took a deep breath and caught a look at myself in the mirror; it was time for me to be professional today. If I wanted a job and respect, I had to play it cool. Dorian finally noticed that I was in the room and got off his treadmill. He walked over to me and gave me a kiss on the cheek. I tried my best not to blush, but I knew he could see what I was thinking in my eyes. That's why he looked at me for so long.

"Thanks for showing up at such short notice."

"No problem. So may I ask what this is about?"

"Well something popped up and I have to deal with it today. I've let things get out hand for too long."

"So what can I do?"

"Always willing to help out," Dorian said with a smile.

"You know me; I might end up having fun."

"I'm glad you said that. I was talking to your father not too long ago and he told me that you wanted a job. Is this true?"

"Yes it is."

"What kind of job are you looking for?"

"You know what I'm into, Dorian. I want to make your problems go away."

"Really? Now why would you want to do all that for me?"

"It's a job, right? Besides, what other teams compare to yours?" Dorian laughed as I grabbed his hand. We heard Tyrese smack his lips from where he was standing behind me. Dorian let go of my hand and stepped a little closer to Tyrese.

"Problem?" he asked.

"Naw, I'm cool," Tyrese said with a straight face.

"Good. Now Veronica, do you really think you want to be down with my team? It's almost easy to get in and impossible to get out." I took a look at everybody in the room and back at Dorian, with a smile.

"I think I can handle myself."

"And if you can't . . . ?"

"Then I won't accept anything less than a long, painful death. I want to be beaten. Pull my teeth out, break my bones and rip my tongue out for wasting your time. You don't have to worry about me, Dorian. I know what I'm getting into and I look forward to my future working for you. Give me a chance and I promise I won't back down." I could feel everybody in that room's dick get hard and I was pleased at what I said.

"Boy, did you grow up! Well let's see if you're full of bullshit or not. It all sounds good. Tyrese, I want you to come with us outside. Follow me."

Tyrese and me walked behind Dorian to the back of his house. In the distance, I could see someone sitting in a chair and someone else standing over him. It wasn't until I saw the guy standing up punch the guy who was sitting down that I realized how serious this was. Then I saw the man in the chair—who was tied up—was B! Dorian told us to stop about fifteen feet from B and we did.

"Veronica, it seems that one of my trusted workers was doing everything but his job. Smoked my weed, had crack parties and spent my money that he owes me on a house that he bought in California, somewhere to run to, once I found out. But it seems I'm not as stupid as he thought. This man has worked for me for years. A man I trusted, and even liked, broke all of my rules. What do you think I should do about that, Veronica?"

"Kill that nigga."

"Really? You do realize that that man over there is your father and if you want a job with me, here is your first assignment."

"I don't have my guns with me, Dorian." The look of shock lay deep in his face; I knew they didn't think much of me. I could damn near hear Tyrese saying how full of shit I was. Dorian suppressed his smile and looked over at Tyrese.

"Tyrese, let Veronica see your gun." Tyrese pulled it out and looked over to me.

"Does anybody have a glove I can put on?" I asked. "I don't know how many bodies are attached to Tyrese gun."

"Veronica, don't waste my time," Dorian said. I took off my jacket, exposing my black lacey bra and took the gun from Tyrese. I started to walk over to B, but stopped once I saw his face. He was all cut up, bruised and there was, like, maggots in his skin, he was really in bad shape. By this time, Dorian and Tyrese were standing next to me.

"Veronica!" B said. "Veronica, are you there, for real?" I looked at Dorian.

"Yeah, I'm here B."

"Baby, I fucked up. I fucked up."

"I see."

"I need you to get me out of this. I know you have some money saved and I promise I will pay you back. Just talk to Dorian for me, do something."

"B, you know there ain't nothing I can do. You put me in a real fucked up position. You know I'm trying to get on, get a job and shit."

"Veronica, we already talked about that. This ain't the type of business you want to get in. Look at me."

"As touching as this is, I have other shit to do," Dorian interrupted. "So Veronica, are you handling this or not?"

"What is he talking about?" B asked. I walked over to him, placing my hand on his shoulder.

"Come on B, you know what this is. You fucked up and you got to go. Dorian putting me on if I can cut you out, so you know what that mean." I cocked the gun and pointed it to his head.

"Wait! Wait a fucking minute! You gon' do this to me? I'm your fucking father!" B couldn't even open his eyes and I was trying to hold back my laugh.

"B, remember what you told me: Don't go out with fear. Suck that shit up!" I said with a smile.

"You are really a sick bitch and I'm gon' see you in hell!"

"I love you, too, Daddy."

Bang! Bang! Bang!

"It's always one to the head and two to the chest," I said. I kissed my father on his cheek and handed Tyrese his gun. He was completely shocked. I put on my jacket then looked over at Dorian.

"Would you like for me to wait for you in your office?"

"Yeah, I'll be right up there." I went into the house and left the men there to talk. Little did they know that they would have the same fate as B. As God was my witness, I would kill them, too.

"So what do you think, Tyrese? Should I put her on?" I heard them talking as I walked away.

"You couldn't have asked for a more worthless person. She loves to kill and I don't think she will betray you."

"I know all that but, will she be a problem? How do you feel about her?" Dorian asked.

"Me, personally, I hate the bitch but, as long as she stay out of my way, everything is everything."

"Great. So I'm going to have you watch her until I feel she's ready to be on her own."

"What? Come on, Dorian! Man, don't play me like that. I don't have time to babysit."

"You have all the time in the world."

I sat in Dorian's office waiting for him to come in. I couldn't help but think about B and what I had just done. But it's what I really *had* to do, once I thought about it. Where would I live with him gone? How would I make money? I had to have this job because I couldn't pimp white guys for the rest of my life. I mean I could, but I'd rather not. Had it not been me who killed B, it would have been somebody else so why shouldn't I benefit from all this? Hell, if anybody should kill him, it *should* have been me after all the shit I had to deal with because of him. Did I feel bad for killing my father? Naw, not at all. I mean he was about to move on with his life in California and not tell me anything about it. I mean, it wasn't like I was going to ask him if I could go, but all B cared about was his self, and it was time for me to start being a little selfish my damn self. Dorian came inside and told Tyrese to wait until he called him. He had a seat at his desk.

"So how much do you want, Veronica?"

"Fifty thousand dollars a person for the first year and eighty thousand after that."

"Done." He called Tyrese in.

"Veronica, you're going to be staying with Tyrese for a while, until I feel like you're ready to handle shit on your own."

"*What?* I can't stay with this nigga! If you leave me alone with him . . ."

"You're not going to do a damn thing!" Dorian said. "Both of you will not turn this into a fucking headache for me. Get out, Veronica. I'll call you in a couple of days."

"What if I stay with Trip?"

"Veronica, good day." I went over to Dorian and kissed him on the cheek.

"See you soon."

What could I do? His mind was made up and even if I did have a little trick up my sleeve to make him change it, it would be twice as hard to get him to do what I wanted with Tyrese standing there. Live with this nigga! Dorian wanted me to *live* with this nigga! How could I sleep in the same building with him and not slit his throat? This was about to be a challenge, but I wouldn't let Tyrese fuck up what I had finally gotten. I left and we drove over to his apartment. I was not feeling this shit and I knew this nigga would give me nothing but hell. I called Pricey and she said she would be on the way in a minute. I followed Tyrese upstairs and sat on the couch waiting for her. Tyrese went in his room and came right back, standing in my face.

"Look, the room on the left is yours. Ain't no bed, so I guess you'll sleep on the couch. I don't buy no groceries, so you eat what you pay for. There's a laundry room down stairs and that's about it."

"Fine."

I got up and went to my room, Tyrese was not playing. There was nothing in there, but I was happy to see that all my clothes were in the closet and my guns were on the floor. I looked out the window and saw Trip and Pricey pull up. I went back to the living room, but then to the kitchen when I saw that Tyrese had made himself comfortable. I had a seat at the table while Tyrese started to play video games. When I heard Pricey banging on the door I got up to answer, but Tyrese beat me to it.

"Don't touch nothing that's not yours."

"Whatever, nigga." I stepped back and let him open the door. Pricey came in and gave me a much-needed hug. I pulled her into my room and closed the door behind me.

"What's up, girl? What you doing over Tyrese house?"

"I'm living with this nigga now."

"What? Fuck you mean you living with Tyrese, Veronica?"

"I mean this is where I rest my head at night now, Pricey."

"How the fuck did this happen?"

"Dorian put me on today, and I had to kill somebody for him. That person just so happened to be the dude I was living with at the time."

"B! You talking about B? You own father, Roni?"

"I can't help that the nigga fucked up and had to be taken care of! This nigga was fucking with Dorian's drugs and his money. Bought a fucking house in Cali!"

"Get the fuck out of here! I knew he was always a dumb ass. So how much you making?"

"Fifty thousand a person."

"I feel that. I would have smoked B ass for five dollars my damn self. So how long you got to be shacked up with Tyrese hoe ass?"

"Not long, I hope. Tyrese probably set this whole thing up so he could give me as much hell as he can." Tyrese pushed my door open and stepped inside.

"Bitch, I didn't want yo ass to be nowhere around me. This was all Dorian's idea."

"Bitch, was I talking to you? I'm in here talking to Pricey. Mind yo damn business!"

"If you speaking my name, it is my business. Don't think you gon' live in my house and disrespect me."

"Nigga, fuck you! You ain't shit no way!"

"I was something when you was trying to fuck me the other night. How can you love somebody who ain't shit, Veronica?"

"You ain't shit but a fucking female, always running at the fucking mouth, just like a bitch!" Tyrese walked up on me and grabbed my arm, tightly.

"What did I just tell yo stupid ass!" I pulled away from Tyrese.

"Get the fuck off me!"

"Hold up. Ya'll was about to hook up last night?" Pricey asked, shocked that I didn't bring this to her attention.

"Veronica ain't tell you, Pricey? She was grabbing at my dick, tough! But I pushed the bitch to the side 'cause I decided I didn't want her slut ass," Tyrese smiled. And I decided that I was not going to be no more "bitches" that day. I punched that nigga in the face and we were fighting, once again. Trip and Pricey jumped in, quickly, to break us up, Trip pulled Tyrese back into the living room while Pricey closed my door.

"Fuck this! I don't need this bullshit! I hate that bitch-ass nigga!"

"I hate yo ass, too!" I heard him yell.

"Cool down, Roni." She walked over to the door and locked it this time.

"Naw, fuck this shit. I don't know who he think he is, but I'm not dealing with this shit on a day to day basis." I walked over to the window and thanked God that we were, at least, only on the second floor. I opened the window and put one leg out before Pricey came over so she could try to stop me.

"What the hell you doing? You gon' brake yo fucking legs!"

"I have my cell phone. I'll call you later."

I jumped out the window and looked back up at when I heard the door kicked in. Tyrese stuck his head out the window and I gave him the finger, then took off running. I saw a bus go by and went for it. It was half a block away, but once it stopped to let somebody off, I caught up with it. Something told me to look behind me and I was happy to see that Tyrese was running, and not driving in his truck. I jumped on the bus, paid the fare and sat in the back. There was no way that Tyrese was going to catch up with me this time. I smiled to myself as everyone looked at me crazy, 'cause, by now, Tyrese was cussing me out, saying how he was going to fuck me up when he got his hands on me. I gathered my breath and pulled out my cell phone.

"Joshua Smith," a voice answered.

"Hello, Mr. Smith. I work for Steve McKnight and he is looking for a home in Illinois."

"Really? Well I'm about to head home, but you can call me tomorrow, or I can call you later on tonight." "What's the number?" I asked.

"Just call the Ritz downtown and ask for me."

"No problem."

Joshua hung up the phone and I figured out the best way to get downtown. I missed those days when things didn't have to be so hush-hush between Joshua and me. Everything was cool until his wife found out that we were together; now I had to call, giving all these fake-ass names. Our conversations were always brief and straight to the point. We had codes for everything and, to tell you the truth, if he wasn't the main person cashing me out, I would have cut him off long ago. Joshua was a fifty-five-year-old, horny-ass white man that needed ass, at least, twice a week. I met him at an Italian restaurant that Frankie took me to one time. When Frankie went to the bathroom, Joshua slipped me his card and I called him a week later. Ever since then, I'd been kicking it with the old dude. The only reason I didn't leave him alone when his wife found out about me was because Joshua always needed somebody to go on trips with. While his wife was gone out of state shopping, visiting family in Texas and having her little tea parties, Joshua always wanted to go out of the United States, so I was there. We took trips to Africa, France, Japan and India. I went all around the world with Joshua, and he bought me clothes, shoes and gave me over a half-million dollars during the time we were together. Why should I let him go just because his wife was in the picture? I felt that, if she loved him like she said she did, she would pay Joshua more attention. That's all my boo really needed, and he wanted to feel young, so what better way to feel young than with a young, black girl to help him out? I got off the bus and got on the subway heading to the hotel. I made it there within the hour. I went to the front desk and gave Joshua's name. A room had already been reserved and champagne was waiting for me. I opened the bottle and killed three glasses real quick before he got there. I was happy that sex didn't last that long between Joshua and me. He had stopped taking his Viagra a month before, so it was nothing but quickies ever sense. I guess he just realized he didn't have to work hard with me. It didn't matter if he did it for hours or for minutes, I would still moan the same and tell him he was the king. The problem was never how long Joshua could last; the fact of the matter was that he had a tiny penis and it wasn't doing anything for me. But he'd never know that.

After he came in and did his thing, Joshua rushed out of the room as quickly as he rushed in, talking about his wife was throwing a dinner party and he had to hurry back. He left me a thousand on the table and went about his business, promising that we would take a trip soon. No sweat off my back. The room was paid for and I had a place to sleep for the night. I got in the shower and called down to the front desk so they could change my sheets and send my clothes to be dry-cleaned. I put on a robe and got into my fresh bed under the covers, so I could look at my phone. Pricey had called me twice and this other number was there about six times, so I knew it had to be Tyrese's. I called the number and he picked up on the first ring.

"Yeah."

"Hey, sugar. What you doing?"

"Thinking of ways I'm gon' kill yo stupid ass, Veronica."

"Aww, ain't that sweet. I was thinking the same thing. So do you miss me?"

"Yeah, I wish you were here right now so I could beat yo ass. Why play these games, Veronica? Just tell me where you are so I can kick yo ass and be done with the bullshit."

"As tempting as that sounds, Tyrese, I think I'm going to stay where I am. I'll see you tomorrow if you learn how to be nice."

"Either way, today or tomorrow, you getting yo ass whipped."

"Love you, too, Tyrese. Bye."

How did I go so long without having him in my life? Tyrese kept me with a smile on my face, laughing at his dumb ass. He really believed that he put fear in my heart; that, as strong as he was, I couldn't give it to him on a right day. The sooner he came to the realization that he wasn't going to run me, the better off we would be. I sat back and debated whether I should order room service. I thought about calling Pricey, but I knew, for sure, that Tyrese was watching her every move. I didn't have no plans on seeing his face again tonight and I didn't need the drama. Before I could drift off to sleep, Pricey called again.

"Which hotel is it this time?" she asked me.

"Is Tyrese with you?"

"Roni, do I have stupid written all over my face, that nigga want to kill you right now. I wouldn't play you like that."

"Is Trip around?"

"Girl, Trip is in the back sleep and I'm on my cell phone."

"The Ritz, downtown."

I hung up with Pricey and cut on the TV. I wasn't getting no sleep no time soon, now that she was on the way. In record time, Pricey was outside of my room within five minutes of hanging up the phone. I got out of the bed and let her in. She picked up the phone so she could order us dinner. I sat on the bed next to her and counted the seconds—which were only three—before she started asking questions.

"Why you ain't tell me that you and Tyrese hooked up?"

"Because we didn't. He got me back at his house half-naked just so he could tell me I was a hoe and take me home."

"Damn, that's fucked up. I told yo ass you were going to get burned. Leave that nigga alone. Tyrese is heartless."

"I'm not losing sleep over the situation. I'm still gon' do me."

"Alright, Roni. Me and Trip not always gone be there to pull Tyrese off of you."

"I can take care of myself. I'm not giving Tyrese a second thought. If he wants to buck every day, then we can do that. The longer it takes him to realize I'm not to be fucked with, the more problems we will have."

"Well I'm just gon' say this, Roni. A hard head makes a soft ass and you keep on fucking with Tyrese, it ain't gone be nothing pretty."

"I hope you give him this same speech."

"Girl, please! You know I can't stand that nigga."

Pricey ordered a movie while we waited for our food. Once we got done eating, we went downstairs to the spa and got massages. I couldn't wait until the day came when I didn't have to be on some white guy's tab. One day I would have my own chips. Pricey decided she would stay the night with me, so we stayed up drinking and eating dessert. When check-out time rolled around the next morning, I didn't want to leave. Pricey could barely keep her eyes open, so I drove her home and told her to pick up her car from me later on. I parked outside of Tyrese's apartment and took a deep breath. "Here we go," I thought as I got out and went upstairs.

I stood outside the door wondering if I should even deal with him now or if I should go spend some time with Paul. Before I could turn around, Tyrese opened the door and pulled me in by my collar. He slammed the door behind him and pushed me up against the wall.

"Don't you ever go to sleep?" I asked.

"No."

"Look, I'm not in the mood to play-fight with you. The fact of the matter is, Tyrese, you're not going to stop me from living my life and you're not going to disrespect me. You stay out of my way and I'll stay out of yours." Out of nowhere Tyrese tried to punch me in my face, but I moved my head to the side. He let me go and looked at his hand, in pain from hitting the wall.

"Look, you know I can box. I would hate to beat yo ass in your own house." Tyrese tried to punch me again, but I moved and smacked him in the face.

"Tyrese, you not fucking with me. I know you mad, but you really need to let the shit go."

"I'm gon' fuck you up!"

Tyrese tried to charge me and I kicked him in his chest. He hit the floor and started to cough up blood. I went to his linen closet to get a rag and wet it with cold water. He was still on the floor when I handed him the rag, but he wouldn't take it, so I knelt down and put it to his mouth—a stupid move 'cause now he had his hands around my neck. I didn't lose my cool, I just slammed my head into his. Missing his nose, I hit him in his mouth, which made him release me. By now, I was pissed. I leaned in and punched him in the face.

"Here I am trying to be nice to yo punk ass and you try to choke me!" I kicked him in his side, making him moan out in pain. "I told yo stupid ass to leave me alone!" Tyrese jumped up and slapped the fuck out of me, and, in return, I kicked him in the nuts.

"I'm not dealing with this shit!" I said, grabbing Pricey's keys and heading back downstairs. It didn't take long for him to run down after me. As soon as he ran up on me, his head went through Pricey's passenger window. Glass was everywhere and blood was all on the inside of Pricey's car, on her seat. Afraid that Tyrese's fool self would cut his neck trying to get out, I pulled his head out the window for him. I thought he was just going to fall on the ground, but he punched me in my head and I was out from a one-hitter quitter. I woke up in the hospital again. Tyrese had stitches in his head and so did I. Pricey looked down on me, shaking her head. I could see her mouth moving, but heard nothing and I was out for a second time. I woke up again a short time later and was pulled to my feet by Trip. Pricey was still in my face, but now I could hear her loud and clear.

"Come on, Roni, snap out of it. Walk this shit off!"

"Not so loud, Pricey. Give me a minute." I tried to push Trip away, but he held onto me tight.

"Get yo shit together, then I'll let you go."

"Look at you, Tyrese," Roni said, looking at the other bed in the room. "I should fuck you up for this. I'm not gon' tell you no more not to put your hands on my sister."

"Don't talk to me. That bitch got what was coming to her." I couldn't walk right then, but that didn't stop me from smacking Tyrese in his stitches. Trip put me down on the ground real quick to hold back Tyrese.

"Naw nigga, cool down. Enough is enough. All this fighting between ya'll has got out of hand! I got to pay to get Pricey damn truck cleaned and get the fucking window fixed."

"Dawg, you know I'll give you money on that shit. Cool out."

"Fuck that, Tyrese. We all work together now. You need to let that abortion shit go. What happened, happened."

"Abortion? That's what you been upset about this whole time, Tyrese?" asked Pricey. "Veronica, tell him! Tell this fool you was never pregnant. Veronica!" I lay there on the cold floor, not wanting to speak. Who cared if Tyrese's feelings were hurt over a baby that never existed? If it was a knife in his back, I would twist that shit.

"Of course, there was a baby!"

"Bitch, stop lying! Veronica was never pregnant. When she told you that, the girl hadn't even gotten her period yet."

"What?" Tyrese sat back down on his bed.

"Veronica, tell him."

"I ain't got shit to say to that trick." Pricey walked over to Tyrese.

"Veronica was just mad when she found out about you and Deborah. So she came up with that little lie, hoping that Dorian would take you out, but when you ran off, she just stuck with the lie to keep you out of her face." Tyrese got up and left. Pricey helped me off the floor and I did the best I could to walk to the car with them. I needed to lean on Pricey most of the time and when the time came for me to go inside of Tyrese's apartment, Pricey didn't want to let me go.

"Pricey, stay yo ass in the car," Trip said. "I'll be right back." He helped me up the steps and let me inside. Tyrese wasn't home.

"Look, Veronica. Tyrese shouldn't be back for the rest of the night. I'm gon' leave you the number to a Pizza Hut. If you don't have no money, put it on Tyrese tab."

"Thanks, Trip. Tell Pricey not to worry, I'm feeling better already." I gave Trip a weak smile and he shook his head.

"Girl, you a mess."

I lay back on the couch and turned on the TV, but the light gave me a headache, so I just lay there in the dark. I tried to sleep, but every half-hour I would wake up, wondering if Tyrese had made it home yet. I couldn't believe, out of all the things that I had done to him, he hated me because he thought I had an abortion. The same nigga that skipped town because he didn't want to face his responsibility as a man—if I had been pregnant, for real. I mean, this was the same dude that didn't have love for me or anybody else, and I'm to believe that he wanted to be a father! I laughed a little to myself and fell back into my short sleep. Every time I woke up, I would think: What if I really had been pregnant? Would Tyrese really be the father he was talking about outside of the restaurant that day? Hell, even if things had played out the way I said they were, and I was pregnant, I would have gotten an abortion anyway. I did agree with B on one thing. The worst thing I could ever do is have kids. I wasn't the type of person who liked to be tied down and I was not willing to take care of nobody but me. Like father, like daughter. When the front door finally opened at five in the morning, I jumped off the couch ready to fight again. Tyrese looked at me with a strange expression.

"Oh, it's just you." I went to the bathroom and pulled the hotel toothbrush from out of my pocket so I could brush my teeth. I needed to go shopping today. I left the bathroom and Tyrese was sitting on the couch, so I made my way to the kitchen.

"Can you come here for a minute? I want to talk to you."

"Look, I haven't even woke up yet. Give me a minute before we start bucking again."

"Naw, it ain't shit like that this time. Have a seat."

"Okay." I sat on the other end of the couch from him.

"Why did you lie to me about being pregnant?"

"Why did you lie about fucking Deborah?"

"Is that it, Veronica? You was jealous?"

"Don't even try to play me like that. You know it didn't have nothing to do with being jealous!" I had to stop talking 'cause my own yelling was hurting my head. "You fed me all that bullshit so I figured I should pay you back."

"What bullshit was that, Veronica?"

"Please, don't start with me. You already know what I'm talking about, so let's not do this."

"Alright, maybe I did lie about fucking with Deborah, but I did love you."

"Don't start this shit, Tyrese. If you trying to get back at me for hurting your feelings, save that shit. I don't want to hear it."

"Can I fucking finish my damn sentence? Shit! You can't never just listen!"

"Whatever. If it's that important, go right ahead." I looked Tyrese in his eyes.

"I did love yo stupid ass. It was just that I loved you more when you weren't mine, and when we were together, it was just different."

"Different how?"

"Different like I couldn't see you right next to me, but I saw you so clearly when you was on Game arm."

"Just wanted something that wasn't yours," I said.

"I know I was wrong, but I felt like, whether we were together or not, you was always mine. When you were fucking with Game and that other nigga, what's his face?"

"Frankie."

"Yeah, whatever. When you was kicking it with them, it really wasn't shit to me, 'cause you was mine and I could have you whenever I wanted. It was just when you pushed me away that I felt like I wanted you more and that I needed to be with you."

"A nigga into games," I said. "Well I can't blame you. I am fine as hell."

"That you are, but I did some thinking tonight and I'm gon' get off yo back. We cool?"

"It's whatever. I'm following your lead." Tyrese got up and went to his room, closing the door behind him.

This was going to be interesting.

I went back to sleep and didn't wake up until eleven in the morning. I got off the couch to see if Tyrese was still home. I knocked on his door and called out his name; he opened the door quickly, and didn't look like he just woke up at all.

"Did you go to sleep last night?"

"Yeah, why?"

"Nothing. Whenever you dressed, could you take me up to CVS to pick up some things?"

"That time of the month?"

"No, I just need a toothbrush and some deodorant."

"Give me a minute." I sat on the couch and cut on the TV. I was feeling much better, but not very attractive with these stitches on my eyebrow. Tyrese got in the shower and put on his clothes, then we left. With him mentioning "time of the month," I knew it was only a matter of time, so I picked up some pads, too.

"I knew it," he said. "Don't be embarrassed, Veronica. All girls go through this. It's nothing to be ashamed of."

"I know that, fool. I don't know how long I'm gon' be staying with you, so it's better to be safe than sorry, alright?"

"So are you going to get the one with wings or the ultra-thin?"

"You are so immature, Tyrese."

I finished getting what I needed and he took me to get something to eat from the Coney Island right up the block. When we got home I went right for the shower with my bag of goodies. I needed to shave everywhere, badly, and to wash my hair. Damn! I'd forgotten to get some flat irons so I could straighten my hair. I got in the shower and stayed there for two hours. Something about hot water running down my body just did it for me. I got out, but forgot to bring a towel, so I got back in the shower.

"Tyrese, can you come here, please." When I heard the door open I stuck my head outside the shower curtain. "Can you please hand me a towel? I forgot it."

"Nope," he said, closing the door.

"Tyrese, stop playing! I'm gon' get water on the floor." He left and came back in the bathroom with a towel in his hand.

"I'm not your damn maid." He put the towel on the sink and left.

"Thank you."

I dried off, lotioned up my body, put on some deodorant, slipped on my underwear and started to blow-dry my hair. As soon as Tyrese heard the dryer he came running in the bathroom to snatch it out of my hand.

"What did we go to CVS for, Veronica?"

"To get me what I needed, but I forgot . . ."

"Sounds like a personal problem to me," he said as he closed the door.

"You are such a ass!" I wrapped the towel around my head and brushed my teeth again. I opened the door and saw that Tyrese was sitting on the couch with some guy. Tyrese jumped off the couch and covered me up with my towel.

"Get off me! What are you doing?"

"I have company. I don't need no half-naked chick walking around. Show some self-respect, Veronica."

"Excuse me! I didn't know you had company and I'm not hardly naked. All my private areas are covered. Besides, my room is two feet away." The guy stood up and walked over to us with a smile.

"Hi, my name is Richard Martin. I just started working for Dorian."

"Same here. My name is Veronica." I was trying to play it cool.

He extended his hand and I shook it. Right off the bat, I was feeling Richard, one of the flyest white boys I ever had the pleasure of meeting. There was something about him. He had a little "nigga" in him. He didn't *sound* white. He reminded me of a sexy-ass Eminem or something.

"Nice to meet you," he said, slowly letting go of my hand.

"You, too." I looked at Tyrese and tried not to smile at Richard. "Negro, can you move so I can get to my room? Hurry up!" I pushed past Tyrese and went to my room, closing my door. I listened to them from the other side.

"So this who Dorian got you shacked up with? Dawg, you were talking like the chick was ugly or something. I would love to have her walking around my crib half-naked."

"Don't be fooled. All that look good ain't good for you."

"I'll take my chances with her fine ass."

I stood in front of the closet wondering what I should wear today; it was still early, but I decided against putting on some pajamas. Most of my closet was filled with Baby Phat, my favorite name brand. I put on this black skirt and a black shirt with the black string going across the back. I decided to slip on some red heels that had a black toe; I had nowhere to go, so I just left my hair up in the towel. I went back into the living room and all eyes were on me. Since Richard was in the room, I was feeling that shit. Now, Trip was there, too, and they were all playing video games. Trip saw the way Richard was looking at me and called him on it.

"'Ey,' dawg, don't be looking at my damn sister like that. Veronica, go put on something else."

"No. There is nothing wrong with what I have on. I'm just showing off my legs, not my ass and not my boobs, so get off my back."

"Still, as you can see, niggas don't know how to control themselves."

"Trip, man you better stop putting me on blast. I don't mean no disrespect, Veronica. I just think you're attractive," Richard said.

I wanted to say I felt the same way about him, but I didn't, so I said, "Thank you, Richard. Trip, you really need to chill. Where my sister at?"

"Sitting her ass in the car, waiting for the tow truck." I went downstairs and told Pricey to come up.

"What the fuck are you doing down here? Bring yo ass. There is a fine piece of ass upstairs!"

"Straight up? You gon' get on?"

"I want to, but he work for Dorian so you know how that goes. I will not be burned twice. But can you ask him how old he is, get some info for me?"

"I thought you said you wasn't gon' get on."

"I'm not, but I need something to fantasize about. I need facts!"

"You so crazy."

When Trip saw Pricey come in, he wanted to talk shit.

"What yo ass doing up here when I told you to wait for the damn tow truck?"

"Who he talking to, Veronica?" she asked.

"I'm about to go put the chairs in my room," I said.

"Put who chairs in what room?" Tyrese asked. Here we go again.

"Tyrese, don't start. Me and Pricey gon' sit in my room and watch for the truck."

"Ya'll better stand 'cause ain't gon' be no re-arranging in my place."

"You so fucking childish! Fine! I won't touch yo shit!"

"I know you won't." I started toward my room, but stopped when Pricey grabbed my arm.

"Hold the fuck up, Tyrese. You not gon' be treating Veronica like that. If my nigga want to move a chair, she will, and if I want to get out of the damn car, I will. Stupid-ass niggas think they run shit. Bitch, pick up a chair!" I did what Pricey said, 'cause when she got annoyed like that, it wasn't a pretty sight.

"You better put my shit down!" Tyrese said to Pricey.

"Why don't you get off yo ass and make me?" She put her chair down and stepped into his face. Pricey was the prissy type, but she would still kick anybody's ass if she felt pushed to it. Before Pricey could prove herself, she noticed Richard.

"Hello. Who are you?"

"Hi, I'm Richard."

"Have you met my sister, Veronica?"

"Yes, I have."

"Pricey, don't start," Trip said, knowing where this was about to go.

"I'm not talking to you, I'm talking to Richard," she said with a smile. "So Richard, how old are you?" Pricey sat on Trip's lap as I went over to the window, looking out for the tow truck.

"I'm twenty-one."

"What happened to your little rule, Veronica?" Tyrese said out of nowhere. "You know the one: Never date guys that work for Dorian. No offense, Richard, just that I been there and done that."

"You are such a asshole, Tyrese. Why don't you explain to Richard how yo ass wasn't man enough for me, either? We all make dumb decisions. I don't know why I have to keep re-living mine." I went to my room and Richard met me at my door.

"I am a little offended, Veronica. I would rather you not talk to me because of my character, not because of who employs me."

"See, I told you the young, white man got a good head on his shoulders," said Pricey. "Would you like to go out with my sister, Richard?"

"'Ey, look this ain't no motherfucking love connection! Pricey, mind yo business, and Richard, get back to the game!" Pricey looked at Trip to see if he was going to correct Tyrese for his comments, but he didn't. She jumped out of his arms and walked back over to me.

"It always be the nigga that's not getting no pussy that fuck it up for everybody. Veronica, grab your chair and come on. I'm stuck with a no-balls-having-ass nigga. Maybe you're right about guys that work for Dorian." She slammed the door to my room behind her and we sat by the window. They kept talking shit.

"You better watch your fucking mouth!" Trip yelled.

"Trip, I don't see how you deal with that girl. She got too much mouth for me."

"And that's why you ain't with nobody, Tyrese! Shut the fuck up and let's play."

"What do Veronica have against men who fuck with Dorian?" asked Richard.

"Nigga, you still on that shit?" Tyrese asked.

"Look Richard, I'm gon' be real with you," Trip said. "Veronica not somebody you want to fuck with. She my sister and I love her, but her ass is crazy. She a fucking murderer and she will cut yo ass in a second."

"I think I can handle myself, Trip, so why don't you put me on?"

"Richard, don't waste yo time," said Tyrese. "Veronica is a big-time hoe, can't stay faithful to save her life."

"I could change her mind."

"Here *you* go." Tyrese said, becoming annoyed.

"If ya'll haven't noticed, she a bad-ass chick. I need a broad like her on my arm to add to the other one. Don't worry, Tyrese. When I'm done with her you can have her all to yourself, once again. Look, it was nice, but I have shit to take care of. See ya around."

"Nigga, you don't have a chance. You ain't got what it takes to deal with a psycho like Veronica, so hang the shit up."

"Thanks for looking out, Tyrese. I'll keep that in mind."

"Richard kinda cute, Roni," Pricey told me. "You said you ain't had no dick in a while."

"I also said I would cut off my arm before I got with another one of Dorian's fools."

"He look like he a cool dude, but you know it might be a act. You just have to take that chance and see."

"Yeah, maybe."

"So how are you and Tyrese doing? Even though the bitch was talking shit, I see you ain't got no new bruises on your face."

"Besides him being a asshole, I ain't had to kick his ass since yesterday, but who's to say what will happen tomorrow."

"You know what we should do, Veronica?"

"What?"

"Go out to eat and go out to the club. I feel like dancing tonight."

"I feel you, but what we gone drive?" Pricey waved Trip's keys at me.

"Pick-pocket queen," I smiled.

"You better know it, Veronica. Besides, Trip dick not good unless he mad about something."

"You sick. Let me do something with my hair."

"Let that shit air dry so we can go right now."

"Red Lobster?"

"Of course."

I took the towel off my head and followed Pricey. We ended up meeting Richard downstairs and he started running off at the mouth about something.

"Veronica, it seems like somebody not over you."

"If only I gave a damn, Richard. So what's your angle? What do you do for Dorian?"

"I make people talk. And sometimes I do pickups."

"I see. So you got a girl?"

"Well that depends."

"Depends on what?"

"Depends on what I have to say to get a taste of you," Richard said, running his fingers through my hair. He was in my personal space and I was loving it.

"Just answer the question, honestly, please."

"Yes, I'm seeing someone. But that's a small factor that can be taken care of, if there is a possibility of you and me."

"You are a very cocky man, Richard."

"I know, I'm hung like a bull. Don't let my race fool you."

"Maybe a little too cocky." I left Richard standing there.

We didn't waste time getting into Trip's ride and pulling off. Pricey was a beast behind the wheel, so I knew we would get to Red Lobster in no time. Later on, Trip told us about the conversation he had with Tyrese before they ever knew we were gone:

"Dawg, don't get bent out of shape about Richard. He didn't know about you and Roni."

"He know now," Tyrese said.

"Yeah, too bad he don't give a damn."

"That nigga got a lot to learn, Trip. I'm not worried. Veronica know better." Tyrese got up and looked out the window.

"You the one who has a lot to learn. The bigger the ass, the harder Roni fall. And Richard seem like the king."

"It seem like I'm not the only one who have a lot of learning to do, Trip. Pricey and Veronica gone." Trip jumped up.

"What! I know her ass didn't . . ." Trip patted his self down and realized his keys were gone.

"I'm gon' kick her ass!"

"You know you a sucker for her. Don't try to act for me."

"What about you?"

"What you mean?"

"I mean now that you know there was never a kid, you don't have shit to be mad about. So when you gon' get at Veronica? That's in-house pussy."

"You can get up off that dream. I learned my lesson. Veronica don't let shit go; she just waiting for me to slip up so she can stab me in my back."

"I know you still feeling her, so it's only a matter of time. Just like I'm weak for Pricey, you weak for Veronica and that's just how shit is."

"Yeah, whatever."

We fucked up some crab pasta at Red Lobster, and them biscuits? They couldn't bring them quick enough for us! We sat in the booth, stuffed, breathing hard, and happy. I didn't feel like going to the club no more. I just wanted to go home and go to sleep. I could see that Pricey felt the same, but we didn't want to go back to Tyrese's house to face the music no time soon. So I said, "Let's go to the movies," and she was down for that. After the movies we went back to Tyrese's, but he and trip weren't so we drove around the spots they collected money from and still couldn't find them.

"I know he just doing this to piss me off, Roni," Pricey told me. "He bet' not be in no hoe face!"

"Chill. That's how he wants you to think. Besides I don't think he doing nothing wrong. He never do."

"Naw, I got this feeling in my stomach right now. Think, Roni. Where could they be?"

"If they not picking up money, they have to be making money. So where would they be selling right now?"

"Trip told me about this white boy he was supposed to be meeting in the court this week."

"Don't nobody do real business on the court. Let's roll over there." Sure enough, when we made it to the court, the dude Trip was in the process of selling some heavy coke to was the po-po.

"Shit, Pricey! That's the hoes in blue! Look over by the bleachers, all the way down there on the other side of the court. They by the tree and they like three cars away. Wait right here," I said, getting out.

"Oh my God, Veronica! Don't let anything happen to my baby, please."

"I got this. Chill and don't bring no attention to yo'self." I started to walk over to them. I could see people moving in, so some shit just fell out of my mouth.

"Trip, something wrong with Pricey! She in the car, her eyes rolling in the back of her head!"

"What? Hold up, my man," he told the undercover. "I'll be back. Talk to my boy, Tyrese." Trip stopped what he was doing and ran over to his car, passing me by. I slowly walked over to Tyrese, wondering if I should save his ass or not. When I was a couple of feet away I recognized the white boy Tyrese was talking to.

It was Paul.

"Paul! How are you?" I walked up on him and slipped into his arms as Tyrese gave me a look. I could still feel people moving in.

"Paul, this is my brother Tyrese. Tyrese, this is the guy I was telling you about. You know the one who kick it with the people Dorian don't like."

"Yeah, I remember. Look my man. It's a little too late for my little sis to be out—and don't you think you a little to be old to be talking to her?"

"It's not what you think," Paul said.

"You don't have to explain anything, Paul. I'll call you tomorrow."

"No you won't," Tyrese told me. "Come on. Let's go. Now."

Tyrese and me jumped in his car and pulled off like nothing was wrong. Trip and Pricey had already left, so we met them outside Tyrese's place. Tyrese and I got in the back seat of Trip's car so we could talk and figure shit out. Pricey was holding Trip's hand, shaking a little. All eyes were on me.

"Veronica, that white boy was five-o?" asked Trip.

"Yeah, and it was more than him out there. Police was setting ya'll up, about to rush ya'll niggas. Don't fuck with them white boys 'cause they all five-o."

"Shit, that mean they watching me. Fuck!"

"Chill, Trip," Tyrese said. "You ain't sell to that dude. Just having a few meetings won't hold up in court. They can't prove shit, and Uncle Mike still got us on his books at the auto shop, so it look like we working that nine to five shit. You just got to lay low for a minute."

"Thank you, Veronica. If you didn't come when you did, I would be looking at some serious time right now," Trip said. Pricey started to cry as Trip kissed her hand.

"Trip, I'll holla at you tomorrow," Tyrese said.

"Alright, Tyrese."

"Hold up, Trip. You need to park yo car somewhere else for a while. The cops don't know about your apartment in New York, I'm sure, so take Tyrese's car and go there," I said. "If they know yo car, they know yo spot and they gon' be watching you, having people come up to your uncle's shop, looking into his books if they ain't did that already."

"She right, Trip," said Tyrese. "You got to get the fuck out of here for a while until we can figure out how much shit they got on you."

We all got out of the car and Tyrese gave Trip his keys. I gave Pricey a hug and told her I had everything under control. In a couple of days she could come home. If I had to kill every cop that saw Trip's file, I would. Then I would find the file and make it non-existent. Trip and Pricey pulled off headed to New York, making no stops, and I reminded them to throw away their cell phones just in case. For so many police to be covering Trip, they must've had something serious on him. Tyrese got rid of Trip's car and I got rid of Pricey's. I would call Dorian the next day to let him know what was going on. I told Tyrese to pick me up from my old apartment after we got rid of the cars. He pulled up in his other ride, a Maybach. I got in and we started talking about the situation we were all in.

"How long has Trip been fucking with Paul?"

"About a week, feeling him out," Tyrese said.

"That means they been on Trip for, at least, a month or two. They can't have too much; ya'll don't discuss ya'll work over the phone, but I'll see what I can find out."

"So that was one of yo white boys? What was his name—Paul?"

"Don't start, Tyrese. Paul or anybody else I kick it with is not important."

"So what are you getting out of kicking it with them then?"

"If you must know, Paul lets me know who the spotlight is on in the 'hood. I go through his files and see if my niggas are in the limelight. If they are, I take them out and, from time to time, I go to the gun range. Just somebody to play with when I'm bored or need to get away."

"I see."

"Despite what you think, I'm not a hoe. I just like to have a life outside of all this. Keeps me sane, living two lives, I guess."

"Only you could find peace in craziness, Veronica. Don't you ever miss being with a real nigga?"

"Sometimes. But with these white boys, it's all the benefits without the drama."

Tyrese didn't say anything else to me for the rest of the ride home and I didn't press it. Part of me wanted to know what he thought of me and the other part of me knew he didn't lose sleep over what I did or did not do. I couldn't sleep that night myself, so I was debating whether I should call Paul and try to see him. I didn't want to rush this 'cause I didn't want him to become suspicious about me. I sat up on the couch and turned on the video game. Tyrese had gone straight to his room with the phone to his ear. I wanted to call Pricey, but I knew she hadn't made it to New York yet. Tyrese finally came out of his room and grabbed a controller so he could play the game with me.

"We going to talk to Dorian tomorrow," he said.

"Alright."

We didn't stay up to late playing, 'cause Dorian expected us early the next morning the next day. I went to sleep for a couple of hours and got back up to take a shower. I went to my room and decided to just wear some jeans with a simple Baby Phat shirt. Dorian was in his office waiting for us when we got there, but when we sat down, I could see the anger develop in his face and he jumped out of his seat to get a better look at me.

"What the fuck happened to you?" I looked puzzled for a moment, then I touched my stitches like they were new. With Dorian looking so angry, I just pointed to Tyrese.

"Tyrese, what happened?"

"We weren't seeing eye to eye, so we found a common ground."

"What the fuck did I say? I don't want to deal with this bullshit! There will be no fighting! I had a job for you, Veronica, but you can't do it looking like shit!"

"Don't worry. I can take care of my face. I can still do the job."

"Naw, you can't do shit until I say you can. Tyrese, you better get this shit under control, right now."

"Everything is cool. Me and Veronica are cool. No more bullshit, no more fighting." Dorian smiled and patted Tyrese on the back.

"Good. So, other than this bullshit, what do you have to present to me?"

"The police were on me and Trip last night. We were about to sell to a cop, but Veronica I.D.'d him before we could. Trip and Pricey are in New York laying low."

"How much do they have on him?"

"I really don't know, but it couldn't be much 'cause, for about a week, Trip had been playing dude to the side."

"I see. They have something on him."

"I can find out what it is, Dorian," I said. "I know someone."

"What precinct does this cop work at?"

"Twenty," I said.

"I have people there. Give me a few days and everything will be taken care of. Veronica, I want you to get Trip's file and bring it to me tomorrow."

"No problem."

"Tyrese, I want you to take Veronica with you on your night rounds, since Trip is gone."

"Okay."

"Alright, I have some calls to make. See you soon." Tyrese and I got up to leave.

"Oh, Veronica. Here . . ." Dorian handed me a big Louis Vuitton purse and told me I did a good job.

I didn't look inside the purse until I was back in Tyrese's car. Inside it was the money that I had earned for killing my father.

11

"So, was it worth it?" Tyrese asked me as we rode.

"I would have taken B out for less than fifty-grand, if that's what you're asking. I'm about to be grown in no time. I had to get in where I could."

"So this was just business? Killing your father, I mean."

"Not just business. It was personal as well, Tyrese. No one will hurt me and walk away from it. Judgment Day will come for all."

"When will mine come?" he said with a smile.

"No time soon. Don't worry your pretty, little head."

"I won't. From what I've seen, you only attack when people can't do anything about it."

"You can always do something about it. It all depends on how strong your will is. Besides, even if someone was at their best and wanted to go up against me, their best isn't good enough to fuck with me at my best."

"We shall see, Veronica."

When we made it back to his place, I saw that I had missed a phone call from Paul. Instead of calling him back, I figured it would be best to wait until later to deal with him. He never wanted to see me in the daytime, so I knew that finding Trip's file at his house was going to take some work. I put my money away and went to sleep after Tyrese left. When I woke up, I walked to the Coney Island up the street and got me a chicken salad. I ate there and walked back home so I could get dressed to see Paul. Since Tyrese was nowhere to be found and he wasn't answering his cell phone, I called a cab. I didn't want to call Paul ahead of time to let him know I was on the way over there. I needed to see his face and take in how he reacted to my popping up unannounced. I stood outside of Paul's door with my hair in two ponytails and my cute little school girl uniform on. I had a job to do tonight. I knocked and, as soon as he saw that it was me, he pulled me into his house, slamming the door behind him.

"April, what are you doing here?"

"I saw that you called me earlier and thought we were on for tonight."

"You fucked up last night! I was doing a bust before you blew my cover."

"My brother and his friend? You were about to bust them?"

"Yes."

"Why? They don't do anything illegal except for gambling on the corner."

"We don't want them. We want someone else that they might know. Look, I'm telling you too much. Maybe we should cool down for a while, take a break."

"If you want me to get my brother to talk to you, I can."

"Really?" I moved over to Paul and ran my finger through his hair.

"Look, baby, you know I don't want to come between you and your work. If I can help, I will. But don't push me away."

"You know I don't want to, April."

"Then don't."

I kissed Paul and he carried me to his room. After a minute of him sucking on my neck, about to make me vomit, I put a sleeper hold on him. I couldn't play tonight. Out like a light, Paul would stay that way as long as I needed him to. I got off him and went looking for Trip's file. I found it in Paul's office lying on his desk. Could this guy be any dumber? I took the file and looked around a little bit more, but found nothing. I made it to the front door before my phone started ringing, I stood there so still that I forgot Paul couldn't hear anything. Then I relaxed and answered it.

"Hello?"

"You called me. What you want?" Tyrese asked.

"I have the file."

"Where you at?"

"Pick me up at the grocery store up the street."

I walked up the couple of blocks to the grocery store and stood there waiting. Nobody was around. When Tyrese pulled up I got in his car, but it took him a minute to pull off.

"What the hell do you have on?" he said, looking me over.

"Just drive so we can get this file to Dorian, please." Tyrese drove like a madman on the way to Dorian's house. I didn't care. I wanted to give this file to Dorian and return it to Paul so I could be done with his weak ass. Dorian met us in the living room.

"Veronica, what the hell do you have on?" I looked down at my uniform and baby doll shoes.

"Look, I got your file." I handed it to him.

"Good, but I don't need it. I found out that I seem to have a leak in one of my police departments, and the day after tomorrow, I want you to take care of it. Tyrese, drop her off, and Veronica, take care of your face. I don't need nobody tipped off."

"No problem."

I took the file from Dorian, leaving so I could get it back to Paul's. I didn't want Tyrese to know where Paul stayed, just in case I needed to run away from him in the near future, but I knew he wasn't going to let me catch a cab. When I got back to Paul's, he was still laid out in his bed unconscious. I took off his clothes and took off my shoes. I sat on the edge of his bed and put smelling salts up to his nose, so he could wake up. Paul opened his eyes and I began to put my shoes back on.

"Where are you going?" he asked, sitting up, placing a pillow over his private area.

"Baby, look at the time. I have to go. You've been passed out for hours."

"Really? I don't even remember falling asleep. I'm sorry, baby."

"Don't worry about it. Any time that I get to spend with you is better than nothing."

"You're great, April. You know that?"

"Yeah I know, Paul. So are you."

"If you're not doing anything tomorrow I want to take you shopping."

"Alright. Call me when you get up and I'll come over after class."

"Okay, see you tomorrow."

I kissed his forehead and left. I was glad he didn't try to walk me to the door 'cause Tyrese was waiting parked outside. I closed the door behind me and got back into the car with him. He looked at my outfit again, shook his head and pulled off. Tyrese let me into his place and then left right away; with all the running around I had just done, I decided to go to bed early. Realizing that I hadn't been to school in a while, I figured it was best for me to go the next morning. Besides, it was the best place to kill some time before I went to see Paul, and the cab fare to his house would be cheaper. When I got done getting dressed for school, it dawned on me that I had no way to get there. Living with Tyrese, I was a ways from my school. I looked out of the living room window and his car was outside. Shit, I really didn't feel like asking him to take me, but I wasn't trying to waste money on two cab rides, either. I knocked on his door before I opened it and, before I could peak inside, his face and my face were an inch apart.

"What are you doing up so early, Veronica?"

"I need a ride to school, if you don't mind."

"Why you trying to go to school today? Your ass ain't been going."

"That's beside the point. All I need you to do is drop me off."

"I can't help you. Catch the bus." Tyrese slammed the door in my face and locked it after that.

"Come on, stop bullshitting!" I was yelling and coming closer and closer to being pissed off.

"Stop banging on my damn door!"

"Well open this muthafucka up then!" I could hear Tyrese coming back to the door now and, when he opened it, I stood there with my arms folded.

"Bitch, I said stop banging on my damn door! I'm not taking your dumb ass nowhere!" When I took a step, the door was slammed in my face again. Fuck this shit! I kicked the door in and stepped inside Tyrese's bedroom.

"I try to be nice to yo ass and you pull this shit on me . . ." Just as I finished my sentence, he jumped up and I could finally see why he was acting all shitty. The nigga had some broad lying up with him.

"Get yo ass out my room!"

"Fuck you, bitch! I told you I need a fucking ride to school and you blow me off because you got a hoe up under you! Get yo black ass up and take me to school!" Tyrese got in my face.

"Didn't we already have a talk about this shit, Veronica? This is my fucking house and your ass is the guest. You not running shit! So sit on that couch and wait until I have time for you."

"You got me bent! Yeah we had that little weak-ass conversation and it seems like I'm not the only one who can't stick to what we said. You want to disrespect me, Tyrese, so I'm gon' act a fool. Put this bitch out. Say yo goodbyes and let's roll out."

"Look, little girl, I'm not gon' be too many more of yo bitches, alright?" she said.

"Hoe, if I don't address you, don't speak. Alright?"

"You got me fucked up! I don't play around with nobody's kids and I won't be disrespected!" she answered. I almost laughed when the chick pulled a blade out on me. Within the blink of an eye, my gun was pointed at her head.

"Now what the fuck you gon' do with that?" I asked her.

"Nothing. I'm not gon' do nothing. I got a kid at home, I don't want to get into it with you."

"I know you don't. You just need to keep that in mind for yourself."

"Veronica, put that shit away," Tyrese said. "You not gon' do nothing."

"Just like I didn't do nothing with Christina, Tyrese?"

"What? So you really were the one who killed Christina?"

"Sure did. I'm tired of playing games with you. This can be easy or this can be hard," I said, cocking my gun back, ready to pull the trigger.

"Tyrese, please just take her to school," the broad said. Even though both of us were not on the same page at the moment, I'm sure Tyrese felt just as sick as I did when he saw her crying her eyes out.

"Bitches fold up so easy nowadays," I said, just a minute from ending this girl's life. I was about to leave a mess for him to clean up when we heard a knock at the door. Tyrese left the room, letting me know he didn't care about her life. When I saw Richard walk in, I put my gun away and left the chick in the room.

"Hi, Richard," I said with the biggest smile on my face.

"Hi, aren't you supposed to be in school?"

"I can't get a ride," I said in Tyrese's direction.

"Richard, get this crazy girl out my house before I kill her."

"Come on, Veronica. Let's go. I don't want you to be late." Before me and Richard could leave, Tyrese grabbed my arm, tightly.

"This is not over. We still have plenty to talk about." I pulled away from him.

"You don't have anything to say to me that I would want to hear."

I made my way downstairs, not worrying about what Tyrese had in store for me. If the nigga was smart, he would realize that I'm not to be fucked with. I have to admit that when I saw Richard's motorcycle I looked at him for a moment. I mean the first time I saw him, it was like dude was smooth as hell, had on his custom-made suit, looking all clean and shit. But from what I made up in my mind about him, he didn't seem like the type to have a motorcycle. I stood in front of him for a moment and really looked at him. Richard had a very tan complexion, like he had just come from vacation somewhere hot. But he wasn't too tan, like some white people who overdo the shit, looking damn near black. Not Richard. He still looked good enough to suck dry. He stood six feet with light blue eyes and a solid body, not as impressive as Tyrese's, but I could tell he could put a hurting on my pussy. I thought about the comment he made about being "hung like a bull" when me and Pricey were leaving the house that day. His hair was jet-black, cut short, and he was dressed nicely. The one thing that made him stand out the most, though, was how classy he looked. I don't really know how to explain it; he had on jeans and a t-shirt, but it just looked so expensive. Like the hundred-dollar blue jeans the celebrities buy and the vintage shirts that cost an arm and a leg. Richard was not a flashy guy, but I just knew he was working with a lot of paper because he carried his self that way. Richard reminded me of Dorian; Dorian never had to do much, everybody just knew he was the shit, and that's the vibe Richard was giving off. Like he didn't try—like he put no effort into his style, and I was feeling the shit out of that.

"Yeah, I just can't put my finger on it." I stopped touching him once I reached his belt buckle.

"Maybe you should try to figure it out a little longer." I leaned my head against his back and smiled.

"Just take me to school, please."

Richard started up his motorcycle and sped off. He had to be doing, at least, eighty the whole way to my school and it was the most fun I had had in a while. I thought we were going to crash so many times, but I didn't say anything, I just held onto Richard tighter. If I was going to fall off this bike, he was too! When Richard popped a wheelie in front of my school I was hooked. I got off the bike and took off my helmet with a smile.

"What?" he asked. "Why are you smiling?"

"I got to get me one of these bitches right here."

"Oh, you enjoyed yourself? Most females be screaming for me to slow down."

"Shit, I wanted you to go faster! Damn, you got me all hyped up. I don't even want to go to school."

"So don't go, Veronica. Fucks with me today. Word is you don't do shit now that you living with Tyrese ass."

"I really want to, Richard, but I have shit to take care of today, besides school, so I really can't fuck with you."

"What type of shit?" Richard moved a little closer to me and I took in his smell. All I could think was, "Boy, don't tempt me."

Instead, I said: "Not that it's any of your business, but I'm meeting up with one of my male whores today so I can pick up some things and get some shit done." Richard came closer until we were an inch apart.

"So what you saying is this whore taking you shopping and getting your hair done, so you don't want to miss out on that?" Richard looked down at me and I was so close to his lips that it took all I had not to go in for the kill.

"It's free and I don't break my plans for no one."

"I'm not just anyone, Veronica." Then he grabbed the back of my neck and kissed me. Normally, this would not be acceptable, but shit, I wanted it so bad. I pulled myself together, but didn't push him away.

"All guys are one and the same to me, Richard, and you're no exception," I said, turning my back and walking into the school.

"I guess I just have to show you different! I promise I'm gon' make you eat them words."

"The day I eat those words is the day you eat me out."

"What you doing this weekend?" I turned around to Richard when I reached the door and smiled at him. Then I gave him the finger and went inside.

I heard him pull off and I smiled. I liked him. He was blunt about the fact that he wanted to fuck me and that shit was a turn on. As usual, I had not been in school for about two weeks and it only took me a day to catch up with all the work I had missed. For fun, I got Pricey's work for her and decided I would do it so I could turn it in the next day. That goes to show just how easy school was for me. I was happy when Paul called at two, saying he had already made my hair appointment and to call him when I was done so he could pick me up. I left school and saw that the bus was pulling up so I caught it downtown to the hair shop. I decided on getting really long bangs to cover up the stitches, and got the rest of my hair curled. I called Paul just as I was getting done, and he showed up to pay. I was happy to see that he drove his truck; that meant I was going to be doing some serious shopping. We went to the mall and I got some summer clothes. March was coming so it would be warm in a minute. Besides, I had plenty of winter clothes. Hell, I had plenty of clothes, period. What I didn't have enough of was shoes. I thought of Pricey as I shopped. I knew at that very moment she was doing the same thing I was, shopping her ass off. Paul took me out to dinner and by eight that night, Tyrese was blowing up my cell phone. I excused myself from the table and went to take my call in the ladies room.

"Hello?"

"Where the hell are you, Veronica? You said you were going to school and school is over."

"Is something wrong? Do you need me for something?"

"Hell naw. I have my shit on lock."

"Well then what the fuck do you want?"

"I have to leave town for a while and I'm not gon' be here to let you in."

"I think I can manage, Tyrese. Besides, I have the key you gave to Trip. Just make sure you're back in time to take me to see Dorian tomorrow morning."

I hung up the phone and went back to my table where Paul was waiting. I finished up the last little bit of my food and we went back to his place. We watched some movies and when Paul fell asleep on the couch I called a cab. The ride home was peaceful and I tried my best not to fall asleep. The cab driver helped me with my bags for an extra twenty. I didn't care that the pig wanted extra money as long as I didn't have to do it by myself. I peeled off my clothes, sleeping only in my underwear, but before I drifted off on the couch, I replayed my day. I always did this so I could see what I could have done better. Being a crazy, murdering bitch doesn't come easily. It takes work. I didn't like the fact that I was getting too comfortable at Tyrese's place. Even if I didn't see him as a threat, rule number one was never let your guard down.

I needed to do some research on Richard. Since he took a liking to me it would be nice if I knew who he really was and if I should shut him down ahead of time. I hoped he checked out 'cause when the time was right I was going to fuck the shit out of him on that motorcycle. I had to put Paul on hold for a while; we were spending too much time together. Most importantly, I had to move the fuck away from Tyrese. The nigga didn't respect me and we just weren't going to work out as roommates. I closed my eyes and slept lightly, but I woke two hours later when he walked through the door. I opened one eye and watched him; he went to the kitchen and got a bottled water, then headed for his bedroom. Normally, it took him eleven steps to get from the kitchen to his door, but on the eleventh step I didn't hear his door open. I pulled my twenty-two from between the couch cushions. When I could feel him over me I sat up and pointed the gun at his head; just as quickly, his gun was pointed at my chest.

"You're good. Nobody has ever been able to pull out they heat in time, Veronica. I might be falling off just a little bit. Dorian said he didn't need to see us until close to noon, so sleep as long as you want." Tyrese smiled as he turned to go to his room.

"You don't worry me, Tyrese. I just made up my mind that I won't tolerate being hit any more. I know you mad about Christina and you're going to pay me back for killing your ugly girlfriend, but I don't care. The bitch shouldn't have been running off at the mouth."

"Veronica, I could give a fuck less about some damn Christina. Whatever you have to do to make you feel better is your business. Just know that the day you take me out is the day that we go to hell together."

"Yeah, we will see, Tyrese."

I went back to sleep and woke up around ten in the morning with Tyrese nowhere to be found. I cut on the TV and watched the news for the weather. Then I made some cereal before I got in the shower. I needed to get ready for my meeting with Dorian. I was actually excited about the work he had for me. I wanted to take somebody out so bad that I could just cum from seeing someone take their last breath today. I decided to wear white; something about the color made me feel untouchable, made me feel sexy and, since today I was going to be able to do my job, I really wanted to be feeling like myself. So I got out the shower and oiled up my beautiful, black body, then put on some lacey panties with the matching bustier. I stood in the bathroom mirror, putting on a touch of makeup. Hanging with Dorian I needed to look older. I loved to be in sexy things, I loved my body and, if I could, I would live my life in nothing but Victoria's Secret clothing. I went to my room so I could slip on my clothes. It was almost eleven and I knew Tyrese would be up any moment talking shit about me not being ready. I put on a white turtleneck with no sleeves and some long white pants. I decided to wear silver shoes, with silver sunglasses, then I put on my gun holster and my knee-length, white pea coat. Just as I was getting my purse together, Tyrese came in.

"Come on, I'm ready to go."

"You are so damn predictable, Tyrese." I noticed him checking me out when I left my room.

"You look different. You cut your hair and you have on makeup."

"You still look like shit."

"Just come on." We went downstairs and got in his car so we could go to Dorian's.

"Why are you all dressed up?"

"This is not me dressed up, this is me being professional, Tyrese. I have more than just Baby Phat in my closet, even though I do have this bad-ass Baby Phat suit. I should have worn that."

"So what did you do yesterday?"

"Nothing. Went to school, got my hair done and went shopping."

"With who?"

"With Paul. Why do you want to know?"

"Because I met up with Richard in the late afternoon and he was talking like ya'll about to get together or something."

"He's fuckable, but all he did was give me a ride to school, nothing more."

"I don't know, Veronica. It seems like Richard might be your type—a complete asshole who wants nothing more from you than pussy."

"Then ya'll have more in common than I thought. First of all, I don't have a type. And I don't even know dude well enough to be thinking about hooking up with him right now. Get over it."

I couldn't stand Tyrese for nothing, he was always doing that, trying to get me to tell all my business so he could use it against me later. But, little did he know, I wasn't ashamed of anything. I wonder what Richard told him. It had to be something out of the way because when Tyrese told Richard to take me to school, he thought nothing of it. I needed my own place bad; living with Tyrese was starting to get old. I couldn't stand to sleep on his lumpy-ass furniture, and not having my own whip was killing me. I was going to talk to Dorian about all this today and see what he had to say. I hoped he was in a good mood and, at least, willing to listen to me. We made it to Dorian's house and, just my luck, he was not happy at all. We found him in his office and he was cursing someone out on the phone.

"Don't fuck with me, okay? Have my shit by next week or we will have nothing to talk about! I told you what I needed from you and if you can't do your job, you're out." Dorian slammed the phone down and looked over at me.

"Have a seat, Veronica. Tyrese, wait for me downstairs. I want to talk to her alone."

Tyrese left.

"I see that you're not very happy, Dorian. What can I do?"

"Always willing to please. I like that, Veronica. You look nice."

"Thank you."

"How have things been between you and Tyrese?"

"As good as they're going to be, seeing that I see him every day, we stay in the same place and it really doesn't help that we don't like each other. But I won't let that bother me. Dealing with him is just business."

"So, honestly, what do you want, Veronica?"

"How do you know I want something?" I smiled at him.

"I can read you very well, so what is it?"

"I want my own place, own ride and I really want to start working more. I feel like I'm just sitting around doing nothing."

"I see. I have a black truck for you downstairs; you are to take that truck about twenty minutes down the road to this restaurant called Sugar and Spice. Go in there and I want you to find this man," Dorian said, handing me a picture of this huge, white guy. Without him telling me, I recognized the man.

"Do you know who this is, Veronica?"

"Steven Willis, captain of the main police station in Chicago. Very popular."

"He used to work for me, but Willis decided that he wanted out—so you're here to make sure he gets what he wants."

"No problem, Dorian."

"Good, that's what I like to hear."

I left Dorian in his office, went downstairs and hopped in a black Envoy truck. The keys were already in the ignition. I put my purse in the passenger seat and put on my white gloves. I started the truck up and headed to where I needed to be. Once I got there, it was easy to spot Steven. One would think he had not a care in the world. Nobody should ever think that they were safe, especially not fucking with a guy like Dorian. I sat at my table and ordered a salad while I watched Steven's fat ass eat three dishes. It didn't look like he was even chewing. He was just a fat, fucking pig. He looked like a dirty cop; I know he thought he was above everybody, untouchable. After a salad, two glasses of water and a piece of pie, I realized I could eat myself to death waiting on Steven to finish. I paid for my food and went back to my truck. All I really needed to know was if he was alone or not, so I waited for him to come out. When he did I started up my truck and put it in drive. When Steven pulled off I was right behind him. He was pushing a little sports car and I was wondering how his sloppy ass got into it. I didn't feel like following him around all day and I knew if I let him make it back to the city, killing him would be harder than I was up to doing that day.

I was five minutes away from Sugar and Spice when I decided to make my move. We were the only two people on the road right now, so why not? I lowered my window with my gun in hand and fired at the two back wheels of Steven's sports car. That instantly made his car go flipping into the air. I watched that fat man and I could hear his screams. Then I counted down from five to one before his car flipped for the final time. Just my luck, the damn car was upside down and Steven didn't have sense enough to wear his seatbelt, so he was half in the car, half out. I parked my truck fifteen feet away and walked up to him. I couldn't believe he was still alive, but it wouldn't be for long.

"Oh my God, please help me. Call for help."

"Chill, Mr. Willis. Relax and don't worry about a thing." I took one of my guns from the holster and cocked it.

"Oh my God, please don't kill me. Whatever you want, I'll give it to you. I'm the captain of the police."

"I wouldn't be throwing that around, Steven. That's what got you into this mess."

"You tell Dorian to kiss my ass. I'll see him in hell!"

I aimed. *Bang! Bang! Bang!*

"Yeah, yeah, yeah, Steven. I'll let him know."

I got back into the truck and drove back to Dorian's house. Why does everybody try to talk their way out of death? I'm not pointing a gun at you for no reason. Your cries are not going to make me change my mind. If today is your day, go out with strength and some pride. Besides, Steven Willis was asking for death by eating the way he was. I parked the truck and went inside, I ran up to Dorian's office, finding him, Tyrese and Richard there. What was going on?

"Veronica, you're back quick."

"Well he was easy to take care of, Dorian."

"I'm glad you feel that way. Have a seat." I sat down next to Tyrese after Richard gave up his seat for me. What a gentleman.

"I have something big coming up that I need you and Richard to take care of. It's a month from now, but I want ya'll to start preparing. Richard will walk you through all the things you need to know."

"Okay."

"Hopefully, you didn't fuck up your job today, so we can move on to the next target without any problems. Tomorrow, Tyrese is going to take you to get a car and I'm setting up a place for you stay as we speak."

"Thank you. I really appreciate this. Oh, and Steven said he will see you in hell and to kiss his ass." Dorian smiled at me.

"Those were his last, dying words?" he asked. "What a bitch." We both enjoyed a small laugh at Steven's expense.

"Richard is going to take you where you want to go. I need to talk to Tyrese for a while."

Richard and I left. I had heard what I needed to hear: I was getting my own place. Richard opened the door for me as we left.

When we made it downstairs, one of Dorian's guards handed me a duffle bag. Tomorrow I would have my own ride. Richard opened his car door for me and we left, but before we did, I took notice that Tyrese was looking at me the whole time.

"So where would you like me for me to take you Veronica?"

"Somewhere we can talk. I want to hear all about you."

"What exactly do you want to know?"

"Everything, Richard. How old were you when you first killed someone?"

"My first time? When I was about six years old I pushed my little sister down the stairs 'cause she had a toy I wanted. After that, my mother was so disgusted with me that she dropped me at my grandfather's house and I never saw her again. There is nothing underlying what I do. I don't bring my emotions into it. It's just all business, everybody has a reason for the things they do, and mine is . . . Well I just have to have more. More money, bigger house, the best of everything. What easier way for me to get what I need?"

"You a ruthless fucker. I can see it in your eyes, you're cold."

"So how old were you when you first killed somebody, Veronica?"

"Sixteen."

"Explain."

"My sister's mother," I said, looking at Richard with a straight face.

"Pricey is your sister, isn't she?"

"Yes."

"So why did you kill Pricey's mom?"

"Because she wasn't treating Pricey right and I wasn't having that shit. So the bitch had to go."

"So let me get this straight: Your mom killed herself, you killed Pricey's mom and you killed both of ya'll's dad?"

"How do you know all my business, Richard?"

"I know more than you want me to know. When I first saw you at Tyrese's, half-naked, I thought, 'Damn, I want to get to know her,' and then, when you opened your mouth, I knew I had to have you. So I did some research."

"I see. I appreciate your dedication, but as fair warning, the more you know, the worse you're going to have it, Richard."

"I look forward to it. You'll come to find that we are a lot alike."

"I'll be the judge of that. So where you from? 'Cause I know everybody in Chicago and I know you have never lived here."

"You right. I'm from a little bit of everywhere. It didn't take me long to figure out that living with my grandfather wasn't going to work, so I found places here and there. I just got out of jail not too long ago."

"Jail for what?"

"Beating up some guys in Texas. They only gave me a couple months, and when Dorian heard that I had been locked up again, he invited me to Chicago to stay out of trouble for a while. So right now, I'm staying with my boy Kelly. But this weekend I'm moving into my own apartment."

"Kelly? That's yo friend? Man, him and me used to clean up when we gambled together. He's cool people. I'll beat a bitch ass for him."

"Yeah, he was the one who told me all yo business."

"Well if you didn't hear it from Kelly, you would have heard it from somebody else. So have you even tried to find your mother?"

"Why would I do that? Veronica, if I did find her, I don't think things would go to well between us."

"I hear that. That's why it wasn't so hard for me to kill B. He treated me and my mom like shit for so long that when the time came, I didn't have to think twice about it."

"Look, we're almost back in Chicago. You hungry?"

"It's still early and I'm not that hungry, but if you want, we can go by your place so we can finish talking."

"That's cool."

We sat there in silence for the rest of the ten-minute drive to Richard's. I played with the thought of sleeping with him in my head. Should I or shouldn't I? From the conversation we just had, I was feeling him a little more. It wasn't just about his look. I took a peek at his lap and tried to figure out if he had a big dick or not. Richard looked at me while I was checking him out and laughed.

"Veronica, I'm not expecting you to have sex with me, nor will I push it to happen. Chill."

"Yeah, tell me anything. I know you want me and you'll play any little game you can to get me."

"I don't play games. It's a waste of my time. If I get you I'm gon' keep you. I don't want somebody I don't fully know and vice versa. It's no game. If you just so happen to fall for me, that's your own doing. Besides, it's forbidden."

"Forbidden? Is that what Dorian told you? Why is everybody so worried about who I fuck? Richard, never accept the first thing handed to you."

Richard pulled up to this apartment complex. It wasn't like the projects where you have this big, tall building with a lot of apartments. This complex had all the apartments lined up next to each other. Once Richard parked, I got out and he opened the door for me. The first thing I saw was his bike in the hallway. I walked over to it as Richard locked the door behind him and I sat on it.

"I love this bike. When I get some more money, after I buy my truck, I'm getting me one. And you want to know something else?"

"What is that?" Richard said, leaning against the wall.

"You're going to teach me how to ride it."

"If you know how to ride a bike, you can ride a motorcycle."

"I hope so."

I got off the bike and looked around his place. The kitchen had everything: stove, microwave, a refrigerator, but no table, and, like, a couple of dishes. Not how I expected Richard to be living, but I guess you have to make do with what you have. I looked at him standing against the wall. It was "forbidden" that we kick it, huh? Fuck that. I needed to, at least, know if Richard was even worth the trouble. I moved closer to him and repaid him for the kiss he gave me the other day—with tongue as interest for his ass. Just as I was starting to cup Richard and feel to see if his package was big enough for me to unwrap it, Kelly came out of nowhere.

"Veronica?"

"I can't believe this," I said in a pissed tone.

"Believe what, Veronica?" Richard said with a smile, looking at Kelly.

"My damn luck. Hi, Kelly."

"Hey! I haven't seen you in a while." Why did this fool come over there and give me a hug and pull me completely away from Richard?

"Okay," I said, pushing Kelly about five feet away. He was my dog, but the only people that were that close to me where my sister and the niggas I just happened to be fucking at the time.

"So Veronica, where you been staying? Somebody else already moved into yo old apartment and nobody seen you or yo dad around here. Rumor has it that you killed him and now you hiding out."

"You know what, Kelly? You talk too much. I'm working on getting my own place, staying with a friend."

"Cool. Come upstairs with me. I want to show you my new TV."

"Kelly, I don't care about no damn TV! Don't you have some where to be?" Kelly looked at me. Then at Richard.

"Yeah, I was just leaving. Walk me out."

"Nigga, you know where yo car at! What do I look like?"

"I ain't going nowhere if you don't come with me. Have ya'll forgotten this is my place? And if ya'll need to be together that bad, then get the fuck out and find somewhere else to go." I rolled my eyes at Kelly; this nigga really thought he was running shit. Granted, this was his place, but nobody took him seriously.

"Go ahead, Veronica. Anything to get this cock-blocker out the house," Richard said. I smiled at Richard, then grabbed Kelly by the arm and pulled him outside. We stood by his car and he unlocked the doors.

"Get in."

"What? Why?"

"Veronica, just do it. I have something to tell you."

"What did I tell yo ass already? You talk too much. One day somebody gon' kill yo ass for saying the wrong thing."

"Maybe I shouldn't tell yo stupid ass, since you act like you know everything now." I looked at Kelly. What could it hurt if I listened to him for a minute.

"Fine, you have my attention." I got in his car and he did the same. Kelly then locked the door and I looked at him like he was crazy.

"Cool out. I just want to talk."

"Alright then, talk."

"How long you been fucking with Richard?"

"Not long. I've only known him for a couple of days."

"Damn, you work fast."

"Shut up! Can you get to the point?"

"First off, you don't need to be fucking with him 'cause he got a girl named Karen who he stay with, 'cause you know the nigga don't stay with me, for real. That's what he just tells people as a cover."

"Kelly, I don't care. I'm not looking to take his girl, Karen, place. I just want some dick."

"Still, don't fuck with Richard. Dude is crazy. I mean, no bullshit. Everything he done told you is a lie. I did some research on him and the boy is nuts; like as crazy as you, 'cause I heard what you did to Game. I don't blame you, but damn."

"Kelly! Can you get to the fucking point?"

"Richard killed his sister!"

"Is that it? He already told me that."

"Veronica, the boy killed his mother, too."

"No, he didn't. He doesn't even know where she is, he doesn't even want to know."

"Let me break it down for yo slow ass. I see Richard told you only a little bit of the truth, so I'm gon' give it to you whole: When he killed his little sister, his mother called the cops on him and they questioned him for hours, trying to get him to confess. Somehow, Richard smart ass convinced the police that it was all his mother's idea—that she had killed her daughter and he was just taking the fall for her, like she had wanted him to. Police start looking at him like, 'He just a kid, so it had to be the mom.' They locked her up and put him with his grandparents. Which was a big mistake 'cause his grandfather was touching on him and doing all types of crazy shit to him. This had been going on for years, since he was a baby or something like that. This went on for years until Richard was thirteen and, finally, went to his grandmother and told her what was going on. She then tried to kick him out the house and, when that happened, he flipped out and choked her to death."

"What did he do to his grandfather?" Here I was eating up everything Kelly was saying. One thing about Kelly was he talked about everybody's business, but it was always fact. He was always right, and I had a feeling that he was right on the money about Richard.

"He waited until that fool got off work and stabbed him to death. He made the whole thing look like a break-in, and when the police caught up with him, Richard said he hadn't been home in days. He said he had run away 'cause his grandfather was abusing him and, when he told his grandma, she kicked him out. When the police did a physical on Richard it was clear he was being abused, so they bought it."

"What about him going to jail? Is that true?"

"Yeah, he got locked up in Texas for beating his girl's best male friend to death 'cause she went to the movies with him."

"Damn, he told me he only got a couple of months. I know he had to be there for some years."

"Yeah, he would have been, but Dorian got him out early."

"How do Richard know Dorian?"

"He didn't. When Richard was in jail, his cell mate was Mike, a old worker for Dorian, and Richard was telling Mike everything he had done and how he was going to get his mother after this. So when Mike got out, he was telling Dorian about this crazy guy he met in jail. You know Dorian always looking for somebody new to be on his team. He made some calls and Richard was out the next week. Dorian made it possible for Richard to find his mother and, once he had killed her like he wanted, he promised Dorian his loyalty for the rest of his life. The rest is history. Once Richard got Dawn off Dorian hands, he was in, a part of Dorian's team."

"So that's what happened to Dawn? How long Richard been out of jail?"

"About three years. He only did a year in jail. He been in and out of Chicago. Dorian always have him overseas, setting shit up in London. Dorian got people in every major state overseas."

As soon as Kelly said that, all I heard was a loud blast, and my bad-ass white outfit was covered with red. Kelly's blood was everywhere and as his lifeless body slid over to his side of the broken window where glass used to be. I saw Richard with his gun still pointed at the car. We made eye contact and then he smiled at me. I opened my door and walked over to him. We stood face to face.

"Thank you for fucking up one of my favorite outfits," I said.

"My bad. I'll buy you a new one."

"I told Kelly that he talked too much." I went back into Kelly's place and grabbed Richard's keys out of his jacket pocket, then went back outside. I walked over to him while he was talking on the phone. When he got done, Richard pulled me to him and we kissed.

"I'll see you later on tonight for dinner?" I asked.

"You know it, Veronica."

"Bye, bye."

I got in Richard's car and pulled off. This was the start of an interesting relationship. Kelly? Yeah, that was fucked up, I know, but the fact was, when he started talking about how Dorian ran his business, he had to go. Kelly wasn't part of the team and he knew too much. I was surprised he was still alive long enough to tell me the little bit that he did, and I was going to kill him myself when he got done, but Richard beat me to the punch. Kelly was my nigga, but I worked for a higher power and he was called Dorian. That's just how the game was. Nobody but Dorian's workers were exempt from death, and even workers had to go when Dorian felt it was time. I drove to Tyrese's so I could change clothes and get ready for dinner. I found Tyrese on the couch with Trip playing the video game and eating pizza. Trip took one look at me, jumped to his feet and damn near ran over to me.

"What happened to you?"

"Nothing happened to me. I'm still alive." Tyrese finally looked my way, and when he saw blood on me, he got all in my personal space.

"Whose blood is that, Veronica?"

"Kelly's."

"Who killed him?"

"Richard."

"Why?"

"Why not?" I asked with a smile.

"Don't bullshit with me!"

"Cool down, fella. There is no need to yell."

"Don't play with me," Tyrese said in an angry voice.

"Kelly was talking about Dorian. He knew too much. About people overseas working for Dorian and shit like that. Now if you would excuse me, I need to get in the shower."

I walked past Tyrese and went into my room. What to wear? It all depended on if I was giving it up to Richard after dinner that night. By the time I took off all my clothes to get in the shower, I decided against giving Richard any of this pussy until he was straight with me. I took a long, hot shower and washed my hair. I didn't want to, 'cause I had just gotten it done, but I figured that Kelly's blood had splashed there, too. Before I could get out of the shower good, Tyrese was walking in on me. I was naked. He had no respect for my space. I didn't let the shit get to me. It was nothing he hadn't seen before.

I got out, grabbed the towel to wrap around my body and pulled out my toothbrush and toothpaste. Before I could handle mine, he was asking me questions.

"What was you doing with Kelly, anyway?"

"I went over his house with Richard."

"Why?"

"Nothing better to do."

"So what was ya'll doing in the car together?" It seemed that Tyrese had done some research while I was in the shower.

"We were talking."

"About Richard and what a psycho he is?"

"Basically, he was trying to warn me about Richard 'cause he thought we were talking, and the conversation slipped to Dorian. You know the rest."

"Did Kelly think something was going on between you and Richard 'cause he caught ya'll doing something?"

"Nobody has fucked me today if that's what you're asking, Tyrese. I'm not stupid. I know Dorian said Richard is off limits and I get that."

"So where you about to go?"

"Out to eat."

"With who, Veronica?"

"None of yo business! I've been nice enough to answer all of your questions, so far, but don't push it. Who I go out with is not important."

"I know you going out with Richard. I seen his car parked out front, so I know he'll be over here to pick it up. Richard is not worth getting fucked up over, Veronica. Leave that white boy alone. You know he have a girlfriend, so why even take it there?"

"Thank you for being all up in mine, Tyrese, but I'm just going out with a friend. Nothing more, so get off my back."

I pushed Tyrese out the bathroom and, luckily, he walked out with no problem. Thank God. I brushed my teeth and did the usual: oiled up, dried my hair the best I could, and put it in a bun. I went to my room and decided on a white Versace dress that I had picked up in Las Vegas the year before. They had wonderful shops there and I need to go back. I was picking out shoes when I heard a knock at the door. I slipped on some silver shoes and walked out into the living room. Tyrese looked at me, then cracked the door open just an inch or two. He told Richard that I would be down in a minute. I grabbed a coat and tried to leave, but I knew he had something on his mind. Before he could grab at my arm and try to stop me I stood in his face.

"What? What do you have to say?"

"You know you shouldn't be going out with him. What do you see in him? What part of 'bad news' don't yo dumb ass understand?"

"Like I told you, I'm just going out with a friend."

"Not wearing something like that."

"Whatever you say. Anything else? I do have somebody waiting on me."

"Let that bitch wait!"

"Don't be mad, Tyrese. You will always be my number one. Don't feel like I'm trying to replace you. You my baby."

"Don't fuck with me, Veronica. I'm just trying to look out for you."

"I'm a big girl. I can take care of myself, but why don't you go do what you do best? Get mad at me for living my life and go pick up a hoe for the night."

"Damn, you know how to piss me off! Fine, leave!" I started to open the door, but Tyrese closed it and put his head against the door.

"Alright. I don't want you to go out with Richard. I don't care if he's just your friend. Stay with me tonight. We can watch some movies, chill, have a good time."

"The only reason you want me tonight is because somebody else does. Please let me by." Tyrese walked over to the couch and cut the game back on. I opened the door.

"Remember I tried to look out for you, Veronica."

"Don't worry. I'll pay you back."

Richard took me to one of the best restaurants in Chicago, a place that you needed two months reservation to get into. Richard had a couple of words with the man at the door and we were seated in no time. Right over to the VIP area we went. Nobody was in this room and there was candle light everywhere. I hadn't really looked at Richard when we were in the car riding, but now that I had a good look. Dude was rocking the shit out of a Sean John suit. Keep it together, Veronica! I sat down and Richard ordered us a bottle of Cristal. I was about to get fucked up tonight.

"So how much of my life did Kelly tell you about before I . . . Well, you know."

"Enough to know you can't be trusted. Enough for me to lose a little respect for you 'cause you lied to me. Enough for me not to be pressed about you. Enough for me to know you ain't even a real criminal. You sloppy and you just so happened to luck up when it came to Dorian."

"What the fuck you mean I'm not a real criminal?"

"What the fuck did I just say? I don't even know why I came out with yo ass tonight. I'm sure yo dick not even worth me pretending that I'm interested in you, or even ignoring the fact that you have a girlfriend."

"Who the fuck do you think you talking to?"

"We're the only two people in this room and I'm, for damn sure, not talking to myself. Why did you lie to me?"

"I didn't lie to you, necessarily. Most of the things I said were true."

"Bullshit! I wanted dick, but now I don't even want that." I stood up to leave and Richard met me at the side of the table, grabbing me by the back of my neck.

"You better not fucking walk out on me!"

"And if I do? What are you going to do?" I started to laugh and pulled away from him. "You have a lot to learn, Richard, a hell of a lot."

"This ain't over, Veronica."

"The shit hasn't even started yet. You have to work at it now. Impress me."

I walked to the front of the restaurant and out the door. It was cold as fuck. I looked up the street and was shocked to see that Tyrese was parked a couple feet away. I smiled and stared while walking to his car. Just as I made it, Richard was walking out and spotted me. He gave me the finger and we went on our way. What was that about? Richard was getting too comfortable too soon. I like a guy to stay on his toes. I like to keep drama going. It's more interesting that way. Besides, Richard wasn't going nowhere. Tyrese didn't say nothing as we drove home, but, as soon as we walked through the door, he took me in his arms and kissed me. I allowed it to continue to the point when he started to put his hands in between my legs. I pulled away from him and sat on the couch.

"Chill out, Tyrese. We not fucking."

"Why not? You left Richard tonight for me. Don't play games."

"Don't *you* play games. You know I didn't know you were going to be outside, and what goes on between me and Richard has nothing to do with you. It started with me trying to get the truth out of him, but once I added the whole thing up, I just got turned off. Richard is going to have to do a lot more to get in between my legs."

"Give my dude some advice. Tell him to give you about a hundred to hit that."

"The going price for guys who I have no desire to have sex with is, at least, ten grand. Why you think you not getting it for free no more?" Tyrese pulled me by my hair and into his lap. I looked up and smiled.

"Yo crazy ass just want somebody to be a asshole to you. Richard too fucking nice." Tyrese pulled my hair tighter and kissed my neck.

"You might be on to something, Tyrese: The last time I fell hard for somebody, they were a complete asshole."

Tyrese kissed me again and we stayed like that for most of the night. I hate to admit it, but, besides Pricey, Tyrese was the one person who knew me the best. He got my madness and respected it, to a point. He never questioned why the hell I was so crazy. He just went with the flow, like we were one in the same. Tyrese ordered pizza and we played the game for the rest of the night. Before I went to sleep he told me Dorian had given me the okay to get a car, and tomorrow when things were taken care of, I was to go met him at his house. Tyrese slapped me in my head, waking me up the next morning.

"What?"

"Richard on the way over here so he can take you to get your car."

"What? Why you not taking me? I'm not trying to fuck with Richard today."

"Not my deciding, ma. This was Dorian's call." Tyrese went back in his room and left it at that. I went in his room and stood by his bedside.

"Why does it matter if you take me over Richard? I'm just going to get a ride. If Dorian don't want us to hook up, then why put us together?"

"I don't know. Why don't you ask him?"

"I will! You are so fucking weak! All you do is take Dorian's damn orders! Shit!"

Tyrese rolled over and put his back to me. I walked out and slammed the door. It pissed me off so much that he didn't care enough about me to show any kind of emotion. He wasn't mad or nothing. I was, for sure, about to get to the bottom of this. Fucking Richard was just trying to fuck with me. I took a long, hot shower so I could try to relax a little bit, but it was hard. I was not in a good mood. I got out of the shower with the towel wrapped around me and went into my room. Richard, who was waiting inside, said hi to me and I just grunted at him. I put on some blue jeans, black high-heel boots and a black shirt with the string that tied in the back. I wore my hair down and put on some big, black sunglasses. I opened my bedroom door and headed out when Tyrese called me over to him. I stood there for a moment with my back to him and looked at Richard. Time for him to learn a thing or two. I held in my smile and slowly walked over to Tyrese.

"Veronica, who do you belong to?" I thought about the question for a moment, then looked over my shoulder at Richard and smiled. I remained quiet as I turned to face Tyrese.

"Veronica!" he shouted.

"What?" I said with a smile

"I asked you a question." Tyrese was such a fool.

"I belong to myself. You are just the guy who dicks me down right." Tyrese wrapped his hands around my neck and pulled my face to his. We were so close, our noses were touching.

"Don't fucking play games with me! I won't tolerate your disrespect!" Tyrese kept choking me until I pushed him away and made him fall. My stupid little man fell hard and I wasted no time jumping on that. I kissed him until I felt him grow from under me.

"You already know the answer to yo question. Don't show out for company." Tyrese stood up with me in his arms and put me down so I could stand on my own feet.

"You bet' not forget that shit, either!" Tyrese slapped me on my ass and I was on the way.

I walked downstairs with Richard and stood outside his car as he unlocked his door.

"Aren't you going to open the door for me? Be a gentleman."

"Open the damn door your damn self, bitch!"

"Oh, you're mad. How cute." I got in.

"So you back with Tyrese?"

"No, he just knows how to show a girl a good time."

"Oh, so you one of those bitches who likes for a guy to keep they foot in yo ass. Now I get it."

"For your sake, I wouldn't call me a bitch too many more times."

"So let me get this straight: I either have to pay you or slap you to get what I want?"

"Think what you want, Richard. Fact is, you're not bad enough for me. You don't do shit, you don't even have a rep. Hell, my rep is harder than yours. I'm a known murderer and you're known for being a clingy punk."

"Fuck you, bitch!" I balled up my fist and hit Richard square in the nose. Blood was gushing out of it and I watched as he tried to gain control of his car, 'cause we were on the freeway by now.

"Are you crazy?"

"Yes, but you don't comprehend too well. I told you to watch yo mouth. Be a good boy."

"Fuck you, bitch!" Richard paid me back with a blow to the chest. Once I caught my breath, I was in Richard's lap, choking the shit out of him.

"Get the fuck off me! We're going to crash!"

"I've survived worse. I hope you can." I felt the car abruptly move from lane to lane. I was laughing the whole time. All the cars that were behind us were losing control and, had we stayed on the road any longer, there would have been a pile-up that everyone would have remembered.

"Veronica, move!" I saw all of the cars slowing down and everything went back to normal. My smile faded as I turned around, seeing that we were going up a ramp, not hurting people.

"You're no fun." I got off of Richard and got back in my seat.

He pulled into a gas station, barely putting the damn car in park and ran over to my side. The look he had on his face turned me on and, as I was about to smile, Richard pulled me out of his car and slapped the shit out of me. I fell to the floor and he was on me, giving slap after slap, after slap. I was in pure shock. I couldn't believe he was doing this. After the shock of taking six to the face left my body and I kneed him in the nuts. I rolled over on top of him and repaid his slaps with punches, blow after blow. Richard yelled out in pain and we spent a good half-hour fighting. Richard didn't give it to me like Tyrese or Dorian would, but he did kick my ass. He wasn't trying to break me, but he wanted to get his point across. Dorian hit me like he wanted to kill me and Tyrese hit me like I was a stranger who had crossed him. After fighting, me and Richard were exhausted. What a workout that was. Richard didn't say nothing. He just picked me up and placed me gently back into his car. He turned on the radio and drove farther out of Chicago so we could go to one of Dorian's car lots. As I sat there going over what just happened in my mind, I thought that we might just have something between us. I didn't want to over-analyze, but I figured the best thing to do was to just let things unfold as time went on.

I thought of my car and I really didn't know what I wanted. Nothing too flashy and nothing that made it seem like I didn't have money. I went inside with Richard and let him do all the talking 'cause I really didn't feel like dealing with people today. I went to the back of the lot and found my baby, this black 2004 Range Rover. It was love at first sight and I had to have her. I handed the salesman a duffle bag full of cash and he handed me the keys. Richard opened the door for me and I got in.

"What a gentleman you are."

"Can this gentleman have a kiss?"

"No." Richard pulled me to him and took the kisses; he was learning.

"Look, I have bad news and I have worse news, Veronica."

"Give me the worse news."

"Your apartment is right across the hall from Tyrese."

"Why is that bad news?"

"That's not the bad news. That's the worse news."

"Okay, what's the bad news?"

"You can move in today." Richard threw my new apartment keys at me and I smiled.

"You don't seem too happy for me."

"You know I'm not. I don't want you nowhere around him."

"Why is that?" I asked, getting in Richard's face—I loved fucking with people.

"'Cause I'm trying to build with yo crazy ass and I can't do that if you keep running back to his ass."

Richard closed my door and I started up my truck. I drove back to my apartment and I was shocked when Richard kept driving instead of trying to come in. I thought, for sure, he would want to come upstairs and spend some time with me. I opened the door to my new place and saw I had a lot of work to do to get this place how I wanted it to look. The bathroom had to be completely done over, the kitchen needed to be bigger and some hardwood floors put in. Some paint wouldn't hurt, either. I called around, setting shit up so I could get this shit going. I wanted my apartment to be done in a week so I called my boy Chris and told him I needed to see him in a couple of days to get my shit. Chris was this guy who I went to school with, and the neighborhood booster. He could get you any and everything. Boy was so good he made enough money to take care of his girl and their four kids. He knew some people who worked at this storage lot and got discounts on storage space if he hooked a couple of people up with some free stuff. So I gave him money here and there to hook me up with the best and make sure my shit didn't get stolen out of my space. Soon I had flat-screen TVs, radios, couches, a bed frame, desk, all the shit I needed to lace my new apartment. Most important was all the money I'd gotten from pimpin' these niggas. I had two million to my name, but I wanted more, much more. The lights would be put in the next day and the bathroom would be started on, along with my bedroom floor being put down. I was excited about this I felt so ready. Ready for what? Any damn thing.

12

I wanted to take my truck to get fixed up. No, not no hoe-ass rims and TVs and shit. I needed some gun compartments to be put in, and some bullet-proof windows on my shit. I was thinking about some sounds, too, but I thought I might wait on that. I went over to this young cat named Damien's car shop. Damien also worked for Dorian. He tracked drugs through his shop to make things run a little smoother, just something the cops didn't expect. I went up there and Damien put me ahead of the line and started working on my car immediately. Everybody who worked for Dorian knew who I was and what I did. In fact, I was getting mad respect for taking one of the top policemen out. While I waited for them to finish I walked down a couple of blocks to go pick me up a corned beef sandwich. I sat there taking my time to eat and enjoying myself when my phone started going off. It was Tyrese. I debated on whether I should answer. I knew the shit earlier had only been a show for Richard and I was wondering if Tyrese had gone back to his old asshole self. Since things were moving kinda slow at the shop, I went for it.

"What?"

"I need you to make this run with me, Veronica."

"Come pick me up."

"Where yo car?"

"My truck is being worked on right now, so if you want me to make this run with you, you need to come pick me up from Damien shop."

Click.

I finished the rest of my food before I headed back out to meet Tyrese at the shop. He needed somebody to make this run with him bad. If he didn't, he damn sure wouldn't have called me. I was the last person he wanted to work with and I knew that. I went back to my truck, put my gun holster on and then my jacket. As I put a blade in my bra, under my titties, Tyrese pulled up.

"Boy, what I wouldn't give to be that blade."

"Shut up." I got in his car and we pulled off.

"You look nice. Is that your Range Rover?

"Yeah."

"Great choice."

"Cut the bullshit, Tyrese. Don't worry. I got your back. If shit pop off, no bullet will touch you. This is business. I'm not going to fuck up."

"Good. 'Cause we fucking with yo boy Franky's people. Dorian and Hector's relationship hasn't been the best since Dorian took Dawn out."

"Well shit happens. Too many people bring their personal feelings into business. That's where all the shit gets fucked up."

"You one to talk."

"I took B out without a problem."

"You don't care about B. What if something happened to Pricey?" My heart stopped for a moment and I started to feel sick, then I started to get mad.

"Nothing will ever happen to Pricey. Nobody is that stupid."

"I see. You know it's only going to be a matter of time before Dorian wants you to take care of Hector."

"Yeah I know. Business is business."

"What if Dorian wanted you to take out Pricey for some reason?"

"That won't happen."

"Just what if, Veronica?"

"Then that will be the end of the game here in Chicago. Mind your fucking business! I didn't want to spend my fucking day with you anyway. You have a lot of nerve trying to sit up here and talk to me like we friends."

"Don't show people your weakness, Veronica. You won't last long."

"Fuck you. You haven't even seen the worst I can do. If anything was to ever happen to Pricey, everybody will suffer. So whoever does try to think about harming my sister should plan to meet their Maker."

"Sounds good."

I wasn't surprised when we pulled up to Hector's house, but I was surprised to see Franky sitting with Hector in the living room, counting money and chopping up rocks. When me and Tyrese walked into the room, Franky jumped up and gave me a hug.

"Hey, baby."

"Hi, Franky. When did you get back from New York?"

"A couple of days ago. Hector called me and filled me in on things."

"Filled you in on what?" Franky took my hand and we sat down on the couch. Hector and Tyrese kept their eyes locked on one another. "Told me that you're working for Dorian now, that you're a murderer, and just a couple of days ago you got rid of Steven Willis and your own father for Dorian."

"Aww, baby, had I known that you were interested in what I did for a living, I would have told you."

"Would you have told me about the white dudes you were fucking while we were together?"

"Sure, had you asked." I put a smile on my face and Franky slapped me.

"You nothing but a fucking liar! Everything you told me was bullshit, Veronica!"

"As entertaining as this is, Franky," Tyrese said, out of nowhere, "I came here to do business with Hector."

"What business is that?" Hector asked.

"You know Dorian has been asking you for his shipment from Cuba, so where is it?"

"It hasn't come in yet. You tell Dorian he'll get his when it's time."

"That's not good enough, Hector. Dorian said we need to leave here with some product or some money."

"I don't have, neither, so what will we do about that, Tyrese?"

I could feel the tension in the air and it didn't take a genius to figure out that a gun war was about to take place in this very room. Shit! All I had on me was two forty-fives. I hoped Tyrese had some serious shit on him. It was a shame. I was actually liking Franky like this. His balls had grown back since I last fucked with him. Everybody was silent until my cell phone went off. I had a gut feeling that it was Dorian and when I flipped it open my feeling was confirmed. I walked a few feet away from Franky and answered my phone.

"Hello?"

"I want you to handle Hector and anybody else that gets in your way."

"Okay, I'll call you later."

"Who was that, Veronica?" Franky asked with a grin on his face.

"One of the white dudes I'm fucking." His smile faded and he left the room. I sat back on the couch across from Hector and I could tell he was sitting on a gun. He hadn't moved since me and Tyrese came into the house.

"Hector, why would you tell Franky all those fucked up things about me?"

"'Cause they're the truth and I felt like my family had a right to know he was being made a fool of."

"I see. But why now? Why after all this time?"

"'Cause I can sense when things are about to come to a head."

Hector looked past me and I couldn't help but turn around to see what he was looking at. My heart dropped when I saw a gun pointed to Pricey's head. She was being held against her will by Franky. When I saw that her lip was busted and that she had been crying, I lost it. Trip was standing beside Pricey and Franky with a gun pointed to his head as well, by someone I had never seen before. I stood to my feet and focused on Hector.

"You have just made the biggest mistake of your life."

"Tell 'em, Roni!" Pricey said with a smile on her face. She knew I would never let anything happen to her.

In the blink of an eye, both my guns were drawn and I had already taken out the guy who was holding Trip at gunpoint with a shot to the head only a few inches from Trip's face. Trip walked over to Tyrese and he handed Trip a gun. Tyrese got on the phone and told someone to come in. A moment later, Richard was behind Franky with his gun pointed to his head.

"Let Pricey go or you're dead!" he said. Franky pulled his gun from Pricey's head and she went to Trip.

"Tyrese, watch Hector," I said. I let my left hand fall to my side, putting one of my guns back into the holster. I turned my back to Hector and walked over to Franky.

"I underestimated you, Veronica. They told me you were a beast, but I didn't believe them." Franky gave me a smile and my gun smacked it off his face. He instantly hit the floor and I was on top of him.

"You crazy bi- . . ." I pointed my gun at Franky's temple.

"I wouldn't finish that statement if I were you," I warned him. "I hate to kill you 'cause you were one of the few good fucks I actually had." Pricey laughed for a short moment.

"Yeah I know. Too bad I didn't know I was fucking a hoe."

"You have so much mouth. Let me help you out." I pulled the blade from my bra.

"How are you going to help me?" he asked with a nervous laugh.

"You want to talk so much shit, but your mouth isn't big enough." I swung down on Franky's face and cut both his checks to his jaw bone. He screamed out in pain and tried to jump.

"Still with the noise, Franky?" I held my gun over his head and was about to shut him up for good.

"If you lay one more hand on him, bitch, I'm going to kill your sister myself!" I jumped up off Franky and pointed my gun at Hector. Before I walked over to him I looked down at Franky. Maybe I was being too hard on him. He just had a broken heart. Hector, on the other hand, was being stupid.

"What did you say to me?"

"You heard me, bitch!"

I shot Hector in the same wrist of the hand that was holding his gun and it flew out of his hand. I was on top of him and, now, Franky's fate was Hector's 'cause I pounded my gun in his face until my hands was covered in blood and there was no more of his face left. The whole time this was happening I was screaming at the top of my lungs.

"You stupid muthafucka! You were so sure of yo'self! You don't even have back-up here! You thought you and Franky's weak ass could take me out! You don't have the balls to take Dorian's business from him! Don't ever speak my sister name, bitch!"

I must have really been doing some shit, 'cause all eyes were on me. Everybody was so focused on me that they didn't notice when Franky got off the floor and pulled a gun from his back. He had already pulled the trigger before I could turn around and I saw Trip go down. Then, as Franky let off another shot, Tyrese shot Franky. I didn't see Pricey or Richard. Who did Franky's second bullet hit? I jumped up and ran to Pricey. Richard was on top of her. He had taken a bullet for my sister. Everything had happened so quickly. Tyrese helped Trip up. He wasn't dead. I helped Richard off floor and leaned him against the wall.

I went to Franky first. Two to the chest and one to the head, the same went for Hector, even though he didn't have much of a head left. I got the third guy for good measure, too. Once again, we were taking another trip to the hospital. As long as Pricey was okay, it didn't matter. While Trip and Richard were getting taken care of I sat with Pricey.

"What happened?" I asked. "How did you and Trip get caught up?"

"We were on the freeway coming home a little early 'cause Dorian called Trip the night before and said everything was cool. Anyway, we get pulled over by the police, so we stop and they tell us to get out the car. Next thing I know, we in handcuffs in the back of a police car and headed to Hector house. Franky was talking shit about you being on the way and how he was gon' fuck you up. I knew you would take care of everything."

"You need to get into some kind of self-defense classes, or I gotta start taking you to the gun range or something. I don't like the fact that you out here, helpless. I can't have anything happen to you, Pricey. I will lose my mind."

"I see. The way you beat Hector face in says it all."

"I got my own apartment, finally."

"Say what?"

"For real."

"Oh, that's cool. Now you don't have to stay with Tyrese. You can come over my house until you get your spot together."

"Yeah. I can't believe Richard took a bullet for you."

"Girl, I know! He don't even know me like that."

"I know. Tyrese ass ain't do shit."

"You know what it is, Roni? I think Richard in love with you. You didn't give it up while I was gone did you?"

"No! You know I'm not fucking with nobody that work for Dorian."

"Girl, you bet' not sleep on Richard. He saved my life. The way I see it, you owe him the cat for saving me. I command you to give up the pussy." We both busted out in laughter for a while at that comment.

"I'm not trying to go down that road with him. Been there and done that."

"Yeah, Roni, but you haven't been there with Richard or done *that.*"

"Shut up. My mind made up."

"Yeah, we'll see."

"Come on, ya'll. We can go," Tyrese said, walking up.

"Ya'll go ahead. I'm going to stay with Richard for a while."

"Don't bother. His girl on the way."

"Pricey, I'll call you later on tonight. Stay safe." I hugged my sister and found it hard to let her go, but I did.

I went to Richard's room and found him sitting on his bed. I walked over to him and gave him a kiss. I stopped, then looked at his wound. He had been shot in the shoulder. I was happy for that. He could be dead, had Franky been a good shot. I thought about my next move as I took off my coat.

"Thank you so much for saving my sister's life. You don't know how much that meant to me. If you ever need anything, I have your back. I owe you my life for what you did today."

"Don't think twice about it, Veronica."

"No, really. No bullshit. You have my respect from this point on."

"Thank you, Veronica." I kissed Richard, this time deeper. He deserved the pussy, like Pricey said, and I had no problem giving it to him now. I had given my body to men for much less, so I could do this. If this is what Richard wanted, he could have it. I pushed him back on his bed and got on top of him. As soon as I went for Richard's belt, he stopped kissing me. I looked at him with a funny expression.

"Veronica, my girl on the way. I can't fuck with you."

"Why not? I thought you was running shit in yo relationship."

"Don't start with me. I said what I said. Please get off me."

"You cannot seriously be turning me down."

"But I am, so can you move." It took all I had not to show the shocked look on my face, but I held the shit back. I got up and put on my coat.

"You'll be kicking yourself for this later," I said. As I was about to leave, an Asian woman came in running over to Richard.

"Are you okay? What happened?"

"I'm fine. Just ready to go home."

"Okay, let's go. Let me help you. I made your dinner already and I straightened up."

"You're so good to me. Let's go home." They got up to leave before she spoke.

"Hello."

"Hi," I said, dryly.

"Who are you? My name is Karen. I'm Richard's girl."

"I'm ready to go, Karen," he said. "She is no one."

Karen closed her mouth and continued to help her man out of the door. As I waited on my cab back to Damien's shop, I thought about what Richard had said: I was nobody. The shit was crazy to me. All this time he had been trying to start some shit with me and now that his ugly, little whore came into the picture, I wasn't shit. That's a nigga for you. Since I had a choice in the matter, I vowed from that point on to never be second place in any guy's life. Not even the rich white men who were giving me money like it was falling out the sky.

I was happy to see my truck when I made it to Damien's shop and even happier that it was finished. As soon as I picked up something to eat for dinner, my phone was going off.

"Hello?"

"If you not spending the night with Richard, the door's open. I'm about to go get something to eat," Tyrese said. I rolled my eyes at the thought of wasting any more time with Richard.

"Alright." I made a u-turn and started for Tyrese's place.

"You okay?" he asked.

"Yeah, why wouldn't I be? Is Trip cool?"

"Yeah, that nigga can take a little bullet."

"Yeah, that nigga pretty tough."

"Is Richard alright?"

"He'll live." I parked my car and met Tyrese on the steps as we hung up our phones.

"Here go your key, in case you plan on leaving again tonight."

"Thank you."

Just like that, Tyrese was gone and I was back on the couch. It had been a long day. I was so tired, I hoped Dorian didn't want to see me early the next morning, 'cause I was sleeping in. I made myself get up and get in the shower. That hot water felt so good on my skin that I didn't want to get out, but I did. I slipped on a big t-shirt and, in a matter of seconds, I was asleep. When my cell phone started ringing a couple hours later I was beyond pissed off.

"Hello?"

"Hi, Veronica. We're outside of your apartment and you don't seem to be in. My name is Carry and I was supposed to put in your lights this morning at nine."

"Give me a moment." I put on the jeans I wore the day before, and grabbed my keys. I had totally forgotten that they were starting to work on my place today. I opened the door and let Carry in.

"When you're done, I'll be right across the hall. Is cash fine?"

"Yes, cash is okay."

I went back to Tyrese's to sleep, and three hours later, Carry was done. The people who were going to do my hardwood floors were there. I found time to talk this contractor to look at my kitchen and bathroom so I could make the changes I needed. I knew he would be there any minute so I just got out of bed. Tyrese was still sleeping when I got out of the shower. I should've paid his ass back for waking me up the other day, but I went against it. I put my hair up in a ponytail and put on a wrap-around dress that stopped at the middle of my calves. Damn, I was one sexy woman. I went over to my apartment and caught everybody together, paid Carry real quick and told him it was nice doing business with him. I didn't feel like waiting until the end of the week.

"I've been doing some thinking, guys, and I want my apartment done by Wednesday. Now money is not a problem and I tip very well. The kitchen has to be done, the bathroom, and I want the walls to be painted. Bring in as many men as you need. Be creative."

My cell phone started ringing and I wasn't surprised that it was Dorian.

"Hello, Dorian. What can I do for you?"

"I want you to keep an eye on Richard. Take care of him for a little while and then, when he has healed up, training will start. I have something big coming up and I'm going to need the both of you."

"Not a problem," I said. But I was pissed. That bitch, Richard, had a chick to cater to him, so I wasn't needed. I would only go over there and show my face to make Dorian happy.

"Alright, call me when you're almost done so the rest of my things can be moved in," I told the crew. "Do you need money to buy supplies or do you already have some?"

"I'll need supplies" the contractor said. I went to Tyrese's place and grabbed a couple-thousand to get him started. I paid the contractor and went to go check on Richard. When I arrived at his house I found him and his chick in the middle of the stairs. I couldn't tell if they were going up or coming down.

"Hey, Veronica. What you doing here?"

"I'm here to keep a eye on you, make sure you heal up right."

"I'm fine, don't worry about me. Karen is taking great care of me." I sat my purse and keys on the kitchen table and walked up the steps to Richard.

"Now what are ya'll trying to do?"

"Go to the kitchen and make me something to eat."

"Let me take you back upstairs and she can make you something to eat. I talked to Dorian and he said he wants you in top shape so we can work on something big he's planning." Karen looked at Richard for approval and he nodded at her.

"Veronica, I know you just following orders, but trust me. I'm okay. I've been in worse shape."

"Be that as it may, Dorian gave me orders. I won't be here long." I put Richard's arm around my neck and I helped him back up to his room. I sat beside him after he got into bed.

"Alright. Do you want your TV on?"

"Naw, just hand me the remote control, please."

I was about to stick my finger in the hole that resided in his damn shoulder, but Richard was acting like he wanted me to leave and shit. Like I was bothering his ass! I didn't want to be there in the first place! If he wanted me to leave, I would. I could find better shit to do. When my phone started going off and I saw that it was Pricey, I moved over to the other side of the room.

"Yes'em."

"Girl, what you doing? Where you at?"

"Over Richard house, babysitting him, like Dorian told me to."

"What's wrong with that? I thought you liked Richard."

"I did until he started acting all stank and shit, like he want me to leave. I'm here trying to help him and he trying to act like he don't want me around."

"I'm not acting," Richard said.

"Shut the fuck up while I'm on the phone."

"Well shit, I see how you treating that man. When did you get over there?"

"Just a minute ago, and I'm treating him fine."

"A minute ago? You should have been by that man bedside when he woke up. Why didn't you stay the night?"

"Why would I?"

"You are so simple, Roni. This man took a bullet for me! You need to be treating him like a god. The boy has real feelings for you and you treating him like another fucking assignment that Dorian gave you. Would you even have come to see him today, had it not been for Dorian?"

"Maybe." I wanted so badly to tell her what happened before the shooting, how Richard had tossed me aside like Tyrese and every other nigga had done, but I couldn't.

"You need to go to Richard and tell him thank you. I could be dead right now, Roni. Dead. Think about that. I got to go. Trip calling me. Bye."

"Bye."

Pricey was really upset with me. Was I wrong? I had told Richard thank you. He was watching TV now and he didn't even look my way when I walked over to him. He was mad, and Pricey was right. If Dorian wouldn't have called me, I wouldn't have come to see him that day.

"Richard, can I talk to you?" He turned the TV off and looked me dead in the eye.

"Go ahead."

"I want to say thank you again for taking a bullet for my sister. That shit really means a lot to me and I will forever be in debt to you." Richard smiled at me.

"You know I would do anything for you, Veronica. I just can't lose Karen, and I know you not willing to keep us quiet, so it is what it is." That put a half-smile on my face. I guess I had to take the good with the bad.

"Thank you." I leaned down and kissed him on the cheek. I was ready to go, so I got up.

"You're welcome."

I left and drove to Pricey's; time to face the music. Shit, how much could she say? Pricey knew Richard had a chick. She better get off my back. I would stay with her for a while, until my place was together. She wouldn't be on my case that bad 'cause she would be too busy taking care of Trip. I pulled up to their house and Pricey let me in without a word. I sat on the couch waiting on her to finish up with Trip. I closed my eyes. I was still a little tired and needed a nap or something. I felt Pricey sit down and I opened my eyes.

"Go head, explain."

"Explain what?"

"Why don't you like Richard?"

"He not my type."

"What? He too nice for the big, bad Veronica?"

"Sometimes he can be. Why you making a big deal out of this? Richard ain't shit, just like all these niggas. The white boy got a chick he love and he just want me for a side piece. I don't play that shit no more, so fuck his weak ass."

"You tried to fuck him and he turned you down, didn't he?"

"You know it. Pricey, what's wrong with me?" I placed my head in her lap. She was all I had and I was starting to realize that shit.

"Nothing is wrong with you. Other than the fact that you crazy and you really have fucked up taste in men. The nice ones bore you and the mean ones hurt you."

"I know. Fuck'im. I don't need no man. All they do is bring drama. I'm trying to stack my bread up. I really don't have time for no dude."

"So what's been going on between you and Tyrese? Did you fuck him while I was gone?"

"Naw, a kiss here and there, but that's about it."

"That's good. Don't worry. I have a feeling about Richard. He gon' come around."

"I don't want him to come around, I want to take a trip and relax somewhere in the sun."

"I hear that. I was freezing my ass off in New York."

"Pricey! Come here!" I sat up off Pricey.

"Go tend to yo boo. I'm cool."

"Get some sleep. I want to go shopping early in the morning tomorrow."

I went to sleep and woke up before the sun rose. I needed to go back to Tyrese's to grab me some clothes. I took Pricey's keys so I could lock the door and not disturb them when I came back. When I made it home I was happy to see that they were still working on my place. It was coming along, nicely. I opened Tyrese's door and, to my surprise, he was home playing the game.

"Hey, Veronica. Stayed with Richard last night?"

"No." I smiled, happy that Tyrese could still be jealous about where I was and who I spent my time with.

"Good. I had company last night and I didn't want to have a episode like we did last time, so that was cool."

"Sounds like everything worked out for you." I went into my room and got a suitcase together.

"Dorian called me, said we need to make a run tonight," Tyrese said.

"Cool. Just call me."

"How long you going to be gone?" he asked, seeing the suitcase.

"A couple of days." I went over to the bathroom and grabbed some more things.

"A couple of days doing what?" I smiled at him. He was standing in the bathroom doorway now.

"Taking care of some things, like Dorian wants me to do."

"Yeah, whatever." I pushed past Tyrese, but he grabbed me by my neck and kissed me.

"Remember what happened to you the last time you tried to make me jealous."

I pulled away from Tyrese and flipped him the bird. He was such an ass. Back at Pricey's, I went into the bathroom, got in the shower and decided to wash my hair. Then when I got out, I had the feeling to do my feet and lotion every inch of my body. I looked at myself in the mirror, hair pulled back into a ponytail; all curly, shorts, wife beater and some house shoes on. Sometimes I got so tired of being me. Franky was such a fool. He just had to fuck up a good thing. Not a good thing for him, but a great thing for me. I needed two lives. I couldn't live Veronica's life twenty-four hours a day. The shit was stressful. I put on a pot of coffee and started watching TV in the guest room. I kept looking at the clock. How was Pricey gon' want to go shopping "early in the morning" and not even be up? It was going on ten o'clock, so I knocked on Pricey's door and she popped her head out.

"Give me a minute. You took yo shower already?"

"Yep." I went and laid out my outfit. I heard the doorbell ring soon after; Pricey was already in the shower, so I shouted to her that I had it. Just as I was walking in the living room, Trip had opened the door for Tyrese. I wanted to jump back real quick, so he wouldn't see me, but it was too late. I got another cup of coffee.

"I thought you said that you was staying with Richard?" Tyrese asked.

"I never said that."

"Why you over here bothering Trip when you could be at my place."

"Trip, I didn't know I was bothering . . ." Trip threw his hand up and went back to his room. "Anyway, I thought it would be nice for me to sleep in a bed while I waited for my place to come together. Besides, I think we've been spending too much time together."

"I agree, but we have shit to do, so don't forget about tonight."

"Yeah, whatever you say." I went back to my room and Tyrese followed. I was so over me and him. "What kind of run do we have to make tonight?"

"A long one, so get yo mental together."

"I'll be ready, don't worry." I sat in my bed and looked up at Tyrese.

"What, Veronica?"

"Just wondering when you leaving so I can get dressed."

"Oh, I need to leave now?"

"I would think giving me my personal space wouldn't be a problem. I don't harass you when you trying to get dressed."

"Whatever, dawg." He left and I got dressed. I walked out of the room and was happy to see Tyrese gone.

Pricey and I were on a mission, so we went to every store there was in Chicago and spent grand after grand all day. After a lot of crazy shit went down, we just shopped to get back some of the shit we lost. Clothes removed stress and the reality of how serious our lives were. We didn't talk much, though. I had nothing to say and Pricey wasn't about to force a conversation out of me. I was a little upset when it started raining later on. It was too cold for rain, but that didn't stop it from fucking up my day. I wished my place was together so I could be in bed watching movies all day. I just felt so in a funk that nothing was making me happy. I felt like something was missing. I took Pricey home, put her bags in the house for her, then kept on rolling. But where to go? What to do? I rode back to Tyrese's apartment and he wasn't home, so I decided to go in and put my clothes up. They were still working on my place. Richard called me before I could figure out my next move, asking me to come over. Karen had to leave for some reason and he felt that it would be best that I look after him, all of a sudden. I didn't have nothing else better to do. I found him in his room and I sat on the bed with him. It didn't take us long to start doing something stupid.

My first mind said, "Push him off and curse him out." I didn't want him thinking I was some type of hoe, but it felt good. He felt good. Being with him felt good. Maybe he was what I needed: somebody my age, who I could relate to. Our kisses became deeper and I thought: "What the fuck. Why shouldn't I fuck Richard? I'm grown. I don't have no man, so what's stopping me?" When Richard went to unsnap my bra from behind, it hit me—fear. I was afraid, afraid that love would sneak up on me again, afraid that I might end up with the short end of the stick again. I pulled away from Richard and looked him dead in his eyes.

"I can't fuck with you like this. We work together. I have rules and I need you to respect that."

"Veronica, are you okay?"

"Yeah, I'm cool."

"Look, I don't want this to be a thing between us. I like you, but I can control myself."

"Who said that you controlling yourself was the problem?"

"Your mother was white, wasn't she?"

"Yes, she was."

"What was she like?"

"Crazy as hell."

"Okay. Well what do you miss about her?"

"Why do you want to know, Richard? You're so random."

"I want to see if this parent shit is something I missed out on." He was trying to move on from the fact that we weren't going to be fucking that day.

"Then you asking the wrong person. My father was shit and my mother was crazy."

"You seem to have turned out alright."

"Yeah. If killing people for a living is alright."

"You know what I mean, Veronica. So what do you miss about your mother?"

"The truth? The more you know, the more reason I have to kill you."

"Death is promised. Continue." I smiled at Richard and gave him some eye contact for the first time since we started talking.

"Every year of my birthday, my mother would wake me up at 3:42 in the morning and pull me into her arms. Most of the time, I would be dead to the world sleep and couldn't remember a word she said to me. Then there were other times when I would listen to her tell me how much she loved me, how I was her world and how I would always be her baby, perfect and all."

"Sounds like I have missed out." I smiled to myself. My mom was crazy as the days were long, but she still loved me like any other mother could, with all her heart.

"Maybe you did miss out. Give me some popcorn."

13

Richard passed the popcorn and cut on the TV. We spent most of the time watching movies, then I cooked and got some rest so I could make the run with Tyrese that night. God knows how long that fool was going to keep me up. I fell asleep on the couch and Richard woke me up in the middle of the night, handing me my phone. I sat up and looked at the Caller ID. It was Tyrese. What a surprise.

"Forgot about our run, Veronica?"

"No, I was just waiting on your call. You on the way?"

"Yeah, I'm outside."

"Alright."

I got off the couch, ran upstairs to slip on some blue jeans, some gym shoes, and grabbed a jacket. Couldn't leave the house without my two best friends: When I got in the truck with Tyrese I put my holster on. Tyrese had a smile on his face as he pulled off. He thought he knew me so well. I wasn't about to correct him, once again, about what was going on between me and another guy. Not knowing for sure would hurt him more than my just telling him what was happening. I put on my safety belt and faced the window, just to give it a minute.

"You and Richard fucking?"

"Would you believe me if I said no?"

"No."

"Then you already have your answer."

"Veronica, just answer the damn question."

"No, I haven't fucked him yet, Tyrese."

"Yet?"

"You know me, it don't take much to get my panties off. Just some smooth words and some cash, and I'm theirs."

"Tell me about it."

"I just did."

We both fell silent for the rest of the ride. Tyrese didn't care to mention that the run we had to make was more like a full-day trip. We had to go all the way to Ohio to visit some people. Cleveland was a ways to be going. But Tyrese drove and didn't say a word. I wanted to call Richard and tell him not to wait up for me, but I thought that was a bit much and I didn't feel like hearing Tyrese's mouth about it. What the fuck was in Cleveland anyway? I hoped it was somebody I could kill, 'cause after paying for my apartment to be remodeled, my cash would be a little low. By the time we made it to Cleveland the sun was shining and I was pissed that Tyrese didn't tell me I would need a change of clothes. Bitch made me sick. Another hour of driving and I was starting to get antsy, so I pulled out my phone and called Pricey.

"Hey girl, heard you was spending a lot of time with Richard," she said.

"Can that not be the first thing you say to me when you get on the phone? I do have a life that don't involve men."

"For example?"

"What do you mean, 'For example?'"

"I mean tell me something about your life that don't involve a guy you fucks with."

"My job."

"Bitch, please! You fucked your boss, one of his workers and about to fuck another one. The people that you kill are men. Face it: Men are in every aspect of your life. Ain't shit wrong with that. I'm just saying don't deny the shit."

"I see. You have a point and I will review that at a later time."

"Tyrese around?"

"You know it. We making this run to Cleveland."

"Cleveland! That ain't no damn run, that's a fucking trip!"

"I know. But you know how he is."

"Yeah, I know, Veronica."

"Can ya'll hoes not talk about me like I'm not sitting right next to you?" Tyrese asked

"Fuck you. Focus on the road and get where we need to go."

"Tell his ass, Roni. So you fuck Richard yet?"

"No. And I don't think I will. If I just think the shit through and not act on impulse, then I'll be fine. You think I would have learned my lesson."

"That's what I be saying, Roni, but you hard-headed. Plus, don't be holding that shit over Richard head, 'cause he seem cool. Just take yo time and feel him out, first."

"I hear you. What you doing today?"

"Nothing. Maybe go to the show, do a little shopping. I was thinking, Roni . . ." Long pause.

"Thinking what?"

"Oh, nothing."

"Slut, don't lie to me. What was you thinking?"

"Don't hoe me, okay?"

"Girl, just tell me."

"Alright, I was thinking about having a baby. I mean I'm not really doing nothing with my life, and I be so lonely in the house all by myself."

"I see," I said. "You want me to give it to you real or fake?"

"Real, man."

"Pricey, you know you can't deal with no baby crying in the middle of the night, wiping ass, never being able to go out partying and shit. Then you have to share Trip's attention with somebody else. Shit won't be all about you no more."

"You do have a point. The spotlight must be on me at all times. Maybe I'll just get a puppy or something."

"That sounds more your speed. Besides, it's hard enough keeping you safe. I don't want to have to worry about nobody else. But whatever you decide is cool with me. I'm gon' hold you down."

"I know. Look, the show start in a hour and I still have to get dressed, so call me when business taken care of."

"Alright."

I hung up the phone and took off my safety belt. I was feeling confined. I let my seat back and was about to go to sleep until I felt Tyrese's hand on my stomach, moving north.

Tyrese was a joke. Who the fuck did he think he was? I was so over him, I didn't care how good he looked or how many orgasms he made me have. All that wasn't worth the drama he brought into my life

"Are you out of your damn mind?"

"You tell me," he said. I pushed his hand off me and turned away from him.

"I don't know why you keep hoeing yo'self. I'm not just here for you to poke at when you want. Be professional, for a damn change!" A moment passed before I felt a slap against my ass.

"Get the fuck out of here, Veronica. I know you better than anybody. You want me and you want me to want you. If Richard wasn't pressing you so hard, letting yo ass know you could have his dick whenever you wanted, then you would still be throwing yo pussy at me." I turned to face Tyrese and let my chair back up.

"What world are you living in, nigga? Ain't nobody thinking about you. I'm done with you. Trust me. I've had my fill."

"Lie to yo'self if you want, Veronica. We both know the truth. Just remember: Richard a little boy. He just don't compare to a grown-ass man like myself."

"You are such a turn-off."

"Whatever. So Pricey thinking about having a baby?"

"Naw, she know better than that. She ain't ready to have no baby and neither is Trip."

"That I can agree on. Them niggas can't stay together for more than two months at a time."

"And they can't stay apart for more than two weeks."

"Yeah, they both out of they fucking minds."

"So when you gon' settle down and have some kids, Tyrese?"

"I don't know. When is best for you, Veronica?"

"Shiiiiiiiiiiiiiit. Nigga, please! I'm never having any kids. Don't want to fuck nobody up like that, and I'm, for damn sure, not mother material."

"I don't know. If you love yo kids as much as you love Pricey, they might be alright."

"Well since it's my choice, I'm not having any."

"In that case, since I can't count on you to birth my child, when I have time, I'll find some respectable chick and let her carry my seed."

"You think you might marry this chick?"

"Naw, I'm not the marrying type."

"That's for damn sure."

"Look who's talking. You could never be any man's wife. You would never be faithful."

"What? I can be faithful."

"Not if I'm not your husband."

"I'm done talking to you. You so full of yo'self."

"With good reason."

I turned away from Tyrese with a smile on my face. He was so cocky and full of his self. When I woke up we were at an airport. My guess was we were still in Illinois. I didn't wake up fully to see, but I was looking out the plane's window. As soon as I sat down, thoughts of Game entered my mind. We were on Dorian's jet. The last time I had flown was with Game. I didn't let my anger take over me, completely. I just took a deep breath and went back to sleep. By the time we landed, I was in need of some damn answers. I wished Dorian had told me what the hell was going on, up front. That way I didn't have to be in Tyrese's face. When we got off the plane, a black truck was waiting for us. I sat there waiting on Tyrese to fill me in on what was going on, but, of course, he didn't.

"What we here for? Who do I have to take out?"

"Don't worry about it right now, just chill."

"I'm not in the mood for this shit. Fill me in so I can get my mind right, do what the fuck I got to do and be done with this shit. Grown-ass man like to play games. Get a fucking hobby or something."

"That little temper of yours is going to get you in a lot of trouble one day."

"Yeah, Tyrese. I look forward to that damn day, too. So, like I asked, what am I here for? Is this about money or babysitting your ass?"

"It's always about money, Veronica. We found out that yo little boyfriend Richard is sleeping with the enemy."

"Who? His little Asian bitch the po-po? Get the fuck outta here!" I let out an evil laugh and Tyrese gave me a crazy look.

"Cool down! I haven't even told you who you have to kill yet. For all you know, yo white boy might be out the game by yo hand."

"Do you think I give a fuck? Either way, I'm getting paid. Richard ass not above nobody."

"What happened? You was feeling dude a couple of days ago. He turn you down, too?"

"You know what, Tyrese? Fuck you. Don't kid yo'self. I could have you and any other nigga that I wanted. Just tell me who I have to take out."

"You right. It's the Asian bitch. I don't know what Dorian want us to do with Richard, but he might be out, too."

"Damn," I said, surprised. "Can I ask you a serious question?" Tyrese looked at me and sized me up for a moment, then nodded at me. "If you knew my time in the game was up, would you tell me?"

"I wouldn't have to tell you, Veronica. You would know. Nobody gets cut for no reason."

"I mean if somebody was building a case against me or some shit like that."

"Yeah, Veronica. I would tell you what was going on."

"You fucking liar. You wouldn't tell me shit, you would get off from the shock on my face when Dorian sent whoever to take me out. Just promise me this: I want you to be the one who takes me out, not nobody who do that shit on the sneak." Tyrese sat silent for a minute, then looked at me.

"Alright."

I left it at that, I didn't say anything else. I wanted Tyrese to take what I said to heart. When people talked about me in the future I wanted them to say that I was taken out by the best, not just some random nigga trying to come up. I didn't want to be caught on some set-up shit. When my story is told by other criminals who admire me, I want them to say, "Veronica Avery was the realest bitch in the game. She feared nothing." When I go out, I want to know my time is up and I want to stare my killer in the eyes and just take that shit. Hell yeah. That's what I want. We pulled up to a hotel and got out. I kept my mouth shut and let Tyrese handle things. I was in need of a shower and some new clothes. Maybe if I stayed off Tyrese's back, he would look out for me or something. We made it up to a room and my clothes were already laid out on the bed. I smiled to myself and ran to the bathroom. I used up all the hotel lotion and cursed at the fact that the damn bottles were so fucking small. I put on my black jumpsuit and pulled my hair back into a ponytail. Tyrese was sitting on the bed when I came out, but he quickly got up and headed for the door.

We left the room.

Tyrese had stopped by the hotel to let me do what I needed to do and I was feeling that. I would be cool for the rest of our time in Cleveland. He gave me that, so I would be on my best behavior. We walked down the hallway and got on the elevator so we could take it to the thirtieth floor where I had already figured Richard and Karen were. I just stood behind Tyrese and watched as he pulled a key card out of his pocket. Once the door was open, everything happened so quickly. The last thing I heard was Tyrese yelling at Richard, asking him where Karen was. When I saw Richard point to the bathroom I disconnected myself from their conversation. I opened the door and drew my gun, damn near ripping the shower curtain down. All of a sudden, I was filled with anger and I wanted this bitch dead. She was a fucking cop and, to make matters worse, her fucking man had rejected me once. Without a blink, I shot Karen in the chest and she flew up against the wall. I turned my head to the side and looked out of the bathroom. Richard had jumped up, but was held back by Tyrese. I smiled at Richard, thinking to myself that I had paid him back. It hurt me when he didn't accept my advances and now it was my turn to hurt him. Even though the pain wasn't equal it was all the same to me. I shot Karen in the head the second time and watched as her lifeless body fall down in the tub. The shower water helped her blood run down the drain. I put my gun away and walked casually out of the bathroom. Tyrese let Richard go and he brushed past me with a quickness, falling onto the bathroom floor when he saw Karen. He reached out to her, but pulled back when he realized there was nothing he could do. I looked over at Tyrese and rolled my eyes. Richard was about to feel so stupid when we told him about the woman he thought he loved so much. He got up off the bathroom floor and walked past me and Tyrese to the window that was across the room.

"Look man, I wanted to explain before Veronica made any moves, but you know how she is." Richard didn't say anything, he just lend his head against the window and started rubbing his face into it. Yeah, he was freaking out.

"I don't fucking want to hear this shit! I don't want to hear it!" I didn't notice when Richard reached for the gun, but I felt that sharp, fiery pain in my flesh; my leg, to be more exact. I just reacted. My gun was out and Tyrese was holding my arm. I looked at Richard. He was so crazy—it was love at first shot.

"Hold on, ma, you shot to kill. I got this," Tyrese said. "Richard, put the gun down. I know you don't want to lose yo life over some damn cop."

"What?"

"You stupid son of a bitch!" I yelled. "You shot me! You shot me in my fucking leg!" I couldn't believe that he had been bold enough to shoot me. That shit was so hot! Maybe he could handle me after all.

"Fuck you, Veronica! You lucky it wasn't the head!"

"Everybody just shut the hell up! Veronica have a seat." Tyrese helped me into a chair, but I was still cursing under my breath. "Richard, put the gun down before you do something else dumb. Karen was working for the FBI; she had so much shit on you, it wasn't funny. Karen had you linked to over five murders and had a case building on Dorian."

"See?" I yelled. "The bitch was playing you the whole fucking time! Stupid muthafucka!"

"Fuck you, Veronica! I still don't want you!" Tyrese cracked a smile when he heard that.

"I don't give a damn. I was just offering you pity sex anyway. Get over yourself." Richard walked over to me, so I stood on my feet. It was whatever. All I had to do was get him to love me and then . . .

Before I could even finish the thought, it was slapped out of me. All I could do was smile at Richard. It took all I had not to kiss him in the mouth. Tyrese pulled Richard away from me and in came two big niggas. Just like that, Richard was gone. I hoped they didn't hurt him too bad. I had plans for Richard, big plans. Tyrese helped me and we were off to the hospital, once again. The bullet had gone right through, so I would be fine. When we got back to Dorian's jet, Tyrese sat next to me.

"You know what, Veronica? I'm actually proud of you. You took that shot well. Didn't scream out in pain or show any weakness."

"I've been through worse. The bullet just felt like a bee sting. I'll be cool. So what do you think Dorian is going to do to Richard?"

"I'm not sure. He told me he has invested too much in him to kill him, but he doesn't want this fuck-up to go unpunished. So God knows what that could mean."

"Cool, I'm not feeling up to no road trip. Sorry."

"It's fine, Veronica. You did what you were supposed to do."

I took a moment to look at Tyrese. He was being a little too nice for my taste. Not to say that him being nice to me was wrong or anything, it was just out of his character. I wondered what he was planning in that big ole head of his. I didn't think about it too long. My thoughts went to Richard again. Did he really mean what he said about me? It didn't matter because, even if he hated my guts, at least he was feeling something. I could build off of *something*. He was so fine. The way his eyes went cold when he pulled the trigger and the way he slapped me—not in a "I want to kill you" kind of way, but in a "I want to make my point" kind of way. I respected Richard and now I was ready to have him. I thought of our moment, me and Richard's, the moment when he realized that he loved me. The moment when he understood who I was and everything I was about. Oh, I couldn't wait. My body ached for him and now I cherished the time that we had once kissed. The love of my life had saved my sister, made me respect him and fall in love with him in a matter of a week. Funny how quickly I fell in love! But I could tell it was love 'cause what I was feeling for Richard was totally different than what I had felt for Tyrese. With Tyrese, there was lust, the feeling of wanting him to want me. And being that attracted to someone for so long will make you think you have feelings that you don't. Richard, on the other hand, he just met all my standards. I couldn't wait to tell Pricey. So I made my way to the jet's bathroom and called her on my cell phone.

"Hello?"

"Hey, Pricey. I have news for you."

"I was talking to Trip and he finally told me what Dorian had planned for you and Tyrese. I can't believe Karen was a cop! So how did Richard take things? Was he mad? Did he fuck her up when ya'll told him? Where you at anyway? What did Richard say to you?"

"Damn! If you stop asking me a million and one questions, maybe I could tell you something."

"Excuse me! I just wanted to know. Go ahead, Miss Thing."

"Alright. I'm in love with Richard."

"What! When did this happen?"

"Right after he shot me."

"What! Richard shot you, Veronica? Why?"

"'Cause I killed Karen in the shower."

"Why did you kill her in the shower?"

"'Cause she was a cop! Plus, I was mad that Richard had turned me down when I tried to offer him sex."

"When was this?"

"Today. Crazy! All this happened today."

"No, fool! I'm talking about when you offered Richard sex. When did you do that and why in the hell would he turn you down if he was trying to get at you that whole time?"

"This was after the whole Franky thing, at the hospital when everybody left. He said that he loved his girl too much and I was going to be second place, and shit like that; that he couldn't fuck with me like that because I wouldn't be able to keep my mouth shut."

"Who the fuck do that white boy think he is? You don't do no damn second place for no average dude like Richard! He on the same damn level as you is!"

"That was what I was thinking when he said that stupid shit to me. So when Tyrese filled me in on the Karen situation, I was like, 'Hell yeah! Richard gon' try to play me for that bitch and now I get to take her ass out.' So when it was time to do the damn thing I went in, not saying a word. I just busted in the shower and took her ass out."

"Damn. So where Richard at now?"

"On the way to Dorian house, I'm sure. Karen had a big case on Richard and Dorian, so who knows what Dorian gone do. Just as long as Dorian don't kill my boo, it's all good."

"Explain this to me, Veronica, 'cause I think I'm missing where you coming from. Now why are you, all of a sudden, in love with Richard? I don't get it."

"Girl, I couldn't put it into words, even if I wanted to. Today I just saw a different side of Richard. I love him, Pricey. I really love him."

"I believe you. But I don't know what woman in her right mind would fall in love with the man who shot her."

"Who ever said I was in my right mind?"

"Lord knows, I know *you* not, but whatever make you happy."

"Now, all I have to do is make him stop hating me so we could build our new relationship, and everything can be good."

"Roni, you crazy. I can't wait to see all this happen."

"Me, too, Pricey. Me, too."

When the jet landed back in Chicago, Tyrese carried me to his truck. What was wrong with him? Maybe he was feeling guilty because he let me get shot or something. Whatever it was, I was about to ride the wave, 'cause, knowing Tyrese, the shit wouldn't last. When we made it to the apartment I was happy to see that they were starting to move my things into my place. I decided to sleep at Tyrese's, start off fresh in the morning. I needed to go pick up little things, like dishes, pots, pans, towels, a comforter for my bed and whatever else. I sat on the couch getting ready for bed, having a hard time taking off the damn jumpsuit.

"Here, let me help you." Tyrese sat on the couch with me and started pulling at my clothes.

"It's cool. I'm fine."

"Chill out, Veronica." I relaxed and let Tyrese help me take the suit off. My leg didn't really bother me until I started moving it too much.

"Thank you," I said, trying to get up and get my pajamas, but Tyrese pulled me back down.

"Don't worry about it. I got you. Let's see. What do I want to put you in tonight?"

"Tyrese, you really don't have to do this. I'm fine. It's nothing but a little flesh wound. You making this out to be more than what it is."

"Veronica, just enjoy. This is the one time I try to be nice to you and you can't handle it. Be easy. Your mouth is starting to annoy me."

"There's the Tyrese that I know."

"Shut up." I watched him look through my closet and shook my head when he pulled out one of my long, silk gowns.

"No. Why do men actually think we sleep in those things? They are just for that little moment before sex that we wear to impress ya'll. Nothing more, so hang that back up and hand me a long, white t-shirt, please."

"A guy can dream, can't he? Here you go." Tyrese put the shirt over my head and picked me up.

"What are you doing now? I don't have to go to the bathroom."

"Girl, I'm not taking you to no bathroom. You can sleep in my room tonight."

"How many times do I have to tell yo ass that I'm fine? My leg is not about to fall off or anything. I am not handicapped."

"Look, you stupid broad, I'm trying to take care of you! So get your ass in this bed and go to sleep." Tyrese laid me down in the bed a little rough.

"Where you gon' sleep?"

"On the couch. I know you want me, but I don't think yo legs can handle me spreading them tonight."

"Nigga, you wish."

"Yeah, I do."

Tyrese left the room and closed the door behind him. I hoped he was just playing, 'cause I wasn't even trying to fuck with him like that. The thought of Tyrese, sexually, was making me sick. Time changes a lot. About a month or so earlier, all I wanted was him, but now he was far from my mind. It didn't take long for me to get to sleep. The whole night, I tossed and I turned. It didn't feel right being in his bed, but I tried to make the best out of it until, finally, my eyes popped open at eight in the morning. I washed up and dressed. The weather was getting a little better and it wasn't that cold outside, so I thought I could get away with a long skirt and a fitted t-shirt. To my surprise, Tyrese hadn't woke up yet. He was dead to the world, sleeping good. I was glad 'cause I know all he would try to do was stop me from leaving. I grabbed my keys and I was off to the mall to handle business. Of course, I wasn't carrying bags home, so I asked them to rush-deliver everything to my place at one o'clock that day. I would be home by then. I had a bite to eat at Olga's before I headed home. As I was finishing my meal, my cell started ringing.

"Hi, sweetheart. How are you?" It was Dorian.

"I'm fine, thanks for asking. What can I do for you?"

"Nothing. Just checking to make sure you're okay, I heard what happened. Don't worry, Richard is being punished."

"Don't hurt him too bad, Dorian."

"Why is that?"

"I mean you want him in good shape for the big thing you have planned for us. Just think about the recovery time, that's all I'm saying."

"I see. For a moment there, it was sounding like you have feelings for Richard."

"Why would I have feelings for someone who shot me?"

"The same reason you had feelings for someone who went upside your head every other day."

"Play-fighting with Tyrese is one thing, being shot by Richard is another."

"Whatever you say. So how is that leg doing?"

"Fine, it barely gives me any problems. I'm just waiting for the wound to close up. Don't think this will stop me from doing anything that you need, Dorian. Whatever you need me to handle, I can."

"I know you can, but, for right now, I want you to chill. Maybe tomorrow you can come see me so we can discuss things. I'll let you know."

"Not a problem, I look forward to it."

"Bye, Veronica."

I paid for my food and headed back to my own place for the first time; just as I got settled on the couch, there was a knock at the door. I knew it was Tyrese before I even looked in the peephole. Maybe I could pretend I wasn't home.

From the angry look on his face, I could tell that he knew I had been gone and he knew I was back. I opened the door to face the music.

"What the fuck is this I hear about you telling Dorian that you alright and you ready to work? You been shot, Veronica!" He just walked right in. I closed the door.

"Yes, Tyrese. I was shot, but I'm not dead. I told you I was fine."

"You are fucking limping around here! How in the hell is that fine?"

"First of all, cut all that loud talking out in my place! Second, what I do has nothing to do with you, and third . . ." Before I could finish what I had to say, there was another knock at the door. "Just get the door, Tyrese."

"Why don't you do it your damn self, since you fucking superwoman and shit? A bullet can't stop you from doing a damn thing, let alone answering your own door." Tyrese opened the door and went back to his place slamming his door behind him. I walked over to the waiting delivery man, so I could sign for my things.

"Thank you," I said.

"Do you need help with your things, Miss?"

"Can you just set everything on the kitchen counter?" I grabbed my purse as he did that. so I could give him a tip. As he made his way out the door I gave him a twenty.

"Oh no, Miss, I can't take this."

"Don't worry about it."

I closed my door and went to my room so I could make the bed. Once I did that, my leg started throbbing, so I lied down. I would put everything away later. I looked at the giant chaise at the foot of my bed and was glad that I had them put it there. I grabbed my remote control and watched as my big screen TV rose up out of nowhere. I loved my place. They had done a great job. I couldn't wait to take a bath because my bathroom looked great. Everything was perfect. At least it was for about five minutes, before I heard a loud knocking sound at my door—again. I started to not get up, but it didn't sound like a normal knock. Why was I not surprised to see all my clothes in the hallway on the floor, and my shoes being thrown at me, as many as Tyrese could carry in his arms at one time. I just stood there and rolled my eyes.

"Why are you doing this?"

"Fuck you!"

"What is the point? What are you even mad about?"

"Girl, you know the fool just crazy," I heard someone say. I turned my head to see Pricey walking up the steps with Trip behind her. I hugged her and we just watched as Tyrese carried on like some type of madman.

"Hey, Veronica."

"Hey, Trip. What's wrong with yo boy?"

"I couldn't even begin to tell you." Tyrese finally made his last trip to the door, laying my guns on top of the huge pile of my things. He sat on his couch, turning on his game.

"Alright baby, I'll see you later." Trip gave Pricey a kiss, went inside Tyrese's place and closed the door behind him.

"Girl, what in the hell did you do to Tyrese?" I threw my hands up in the air.

"I don't know. I just told him I didn't need him treating me like all my damn limbs had been cut off. He was going off on me about wanting to work and I just told him I was fine."

"Yeah, I knew some shit was going down when I heard Tyrese yelling on Trip cell phone. I don't know what about, because Trip left the room. He just realized I be listening to his conversations and shit." I grabbed my guns and sat them on the table. Pricey grabbed as many clothes as she could and headed to my room. "I just told Trip to come on and let's see what was going on."

"I am so glad I have my own place and I don't have to deal with his ass no more."

"Trip is almost better, so he can start making runs with Tyrese again."

"Thank God, I can live my life Tyrese-free." We took turns going back in forth to my room hanging up my things. Once we were done, I got back in the bed. My leg was throbbing now. Pricey sat next to me and we watched TV.

"Nice place you got here. I love how you have it set up. Nice and chic, real simple and elegant."

"Thank you. The only fucked up part about getting shot is the damn recovery time, this little hole is slowing me down."

"Trip said the same thing not too long ago. Hell, it comes with the job, I guess."

"I understand that and it would have been cool, had I not been shot by somebody I work with. Feel me?"

"Yeah, I hear that. But look at the bright side. You have time to relax. You know all Dorian gon' do is work you like a dog when you get better."

"Shit, at least I'll be getting paid. I'd rather be working my ass off making bread than just sitting on my ass with no money in my pocket."

"You have money, about fifty thousand coming yo way."

"Yeah I know, but my birthday coming up in a minute and I want to take us to Paris to shop, and then maybe Africa to relax."

"Africa? I've already been there twice. Let's go to China."

"I hear that. I could fuck with China for a while. That's why I need to be making some money right now 'cause this time and every time after this, I'm paying. No more tricking these white guys for money; I'm making my own way."

"There you go, boo, I'm so proud of you, but for real—you should really rest up. You've killed and pimped so many people for all this, so enjoy."

"Shut up." We both laughed for a second.

"Who would have thought, Veronica? Two 'hood girls living the life. Doing it big and shit, traveling around the fucking world, having a ball."

"I know, but I'm not gon' get too comfortable, 'cause I want too much."

"You'll have it all, sis. Don't forget you said you was taking me on this trip, 'cause I know yo ass will try to push me aside for Richard."

"What? You know I wouldn't play you like that."

"Whatever, Roni. You know how you do."

"Girl, please. I think it's gon' take me longer than two months to get Richard even feeling me like that."

"I doubt that shit. No one can resist my sista. Look at Tyrese ass over there, freaking out 'cause you didn't want his ass around."

"Pricey, Tyrese can let that dream die, 'cause ain't no love between me and him."

"You finally over that nigga?"

"Yes. I'm moving on to bigger and better things."

Pricey and I talked for a little while longer before Trip came knocking for her. She left and I ordered ribs from this soul food place that I knew about. After I ate like a pig I went to sleep and didn't wake up until five that evening. Dorian hadn't called me, probably because of something Tyrese said to him. Shit, I was not a homebody. But wasn't much I could do with a bum leg. Maybe he would call tomorrow, I hoped. But tomorrow came and went. I had put away all my things, fixed up my closet the way I wanted to and went grocery shopping. When day three became day four, I was about to rip all of my hair from my head. Pricey hadn't called me, my hoes hadn't called me, Dorian hadn't called me and, to top it off, I had nowhere to go or no one to see. I needed to let some of this energy out of my system. I almost went to knock on Tyrese's door, I was so desperate. Finally, I said fuck it and went to the gym. I was there for hours, trying to get my leg better. I worked on every part of my body, especially my stomach, because it would be summer time in a minute and I was all about showing skin. So that was my routine for the next week: wake up, take a shower, eat a little something, work out all day, come home, cook, take a bath and go to sleep. My leg was doing much better. All I needed was a phone call from Dorian.

Someone had told me that he went out of town and wouldn't be back for another week. It was cool 'cause I had found something to do with myself, but I was starting to worry about Richard. What had Dorian done to him? Another week passed and, when my phone woke me up at noon, I was happy to see it was Dorian finally calling me.

"Veronica, get dressed and come to the house." A big smile came over my face

"I'll be right there."

I was so happy. Not only did Dorian want to see me, but he sounded mad. That meant I would be working in no time. I slipped on some blue jeans and a cute Tupac, button-up shirt with some black gym shoes. When I made it outside, Tyrese was getting in his car as well; we hadn't spoken since his little freak-out earlier, and I was fine with that. I damn near raced to Dorian's house, I was so excited, and I ran up the steps when I got there. When I made it to his office, his door was already open and five other guys were standing by his desk. One by one, each guy looked up and couldn't take their eyes off me. Dorian didn't notice I was there until he realized he was talking to himself.

"Ahhh, Veronica, come here. I want you to meet everyone." I walked over to Dorian and he put his arm on my shoulder.

"Everyone, this is Veronica. She'll be working with you."

"Doing what? Washing our clothes while we handling business?" I looked over at the bitch with balls who said that dumb comment.

"Excuse me? I don't wash clothes, little boy, and if I were you, I would be real careful what comes out of my mouth."

"Why is that?" I looked at Dorian and he gave me the nod. I walked over to him and got in his face.

"Because I don't like to be disrespected." Before he could get out another word, he was laid out on the ground, knocked out. I went back to Dorian and he put his arm around my shoulder again.

"Like I was saying, she will be working with you all. Here comes Tyrese. Now I can explain everything. We seem to be having a problem with our Cuban friends. Once word got back to them about Hector, they decided to cut me out. This was fine with me because I have another connect there, and I'm not losing money, so I spared their lives. But now these Cuban fuckers have waged war and I'm losing out on good product. So what I want you all to do is make this problem go away."

"Cool, Dorian. I don't understand why you have all of them here," I said. "Just send me down there. I'll take care of business and come back." He gave me a playful hug.

"My sweet Veronica, there is more to it than that. There are roughly eighty to a hundred people I need taken care of, people who are natural-born killers. This will not be an easy task. You are a small team of people and I can't say, for sure, you all will be coming back home."

"How do you want us to go about this Dorian, pick them off or a group execution?" He smiled at me. I was the only person really into the job, but, shit, I need some paper, and it wasn't going to come to me looking all scared like these pussy niggas.

"That is up to you and your team. Training will start five days from now. You all have a month until you ship out."

A *month* of training? Where did Dorian get these bitch-ass niggas from? Who in the hell needed to train when it came to outright killing people? Just point and shoot.

"Before you all leave, we do still have one more matter to deal with," he said. "Tyrese, bring him in." Tyrese left the room and came back with Richard. I gasped when I saw his face; the boy was fucked up. I'm sure it looked worse than it actually was because he was white and every bruise showed up on him. But still . . .

"Veronica, it's all up to you."

"What is that, Dorian?"

"Sink or swim?" he said, looking in Richard's direction.

"Swim," I said. "He's a killer and we need all the help we can get. You see yo boy still laid out over there from one hit."

"You have a point. Alright, take him home, fix him up and bring him back in five days."

"No problem." Tyrese handed Richard over to me, but he wasn't moving his legs so I let his ass fall. I didn't mean to, but I felt myself losing my balance.

"Oh shit," I said, holding in a laugh and smiling at Dorian.

"This is what I'm talking about, Dorian. She not ready for no big shit like this," Tyrese argued. "Her leg is still fucked up. Let her sit this one out." I looked at Tyrese like the fool had lost his mind.

"Who the fuck are you to tell me what the hell I'm not ready for? I got this shit! Don't fucking worry about me!" I know Tyrese didn't like the way I was talking to him in front of all of these men, but he was pissing me off.

"Look, bitch! I'm just trying to look out for you!"

"Dorian, if you send me with this emotional pussy right here, and that lame on the floor, I'm *sure* everybody won't be making it back from the job," I said. I was looking out for me and Richard.

I bent over and flung Richard over my shoulders. What Tyrese didn't know about me was that I could bench press about two hundred pounds. I was handling shit. I walked past Tyrese and called him a mark-ass nigga, then kept on going about my business. I put Richard in my truck and headed home. I had to fix him up the best I could in five days; I had a feeling Dorian was not playing about this training shit, and he was going to work the fuck out of us. I got Richard home and laid him out on the couch. The way he was acting, you would think that he was dead. His lip was busted and his jaws were swollen, but he was in good shape because nothing was broken. I started to take off his shirt, but Richard grabbed me by the arms on the third button. He opened his eyes and they were red. He had a crazy look on his face. It didn't take me long to piece things together when he wrapped his hands around my neck and started choking me. He was upset.

"You killed Karen!"

"What did you expect me to do? Dorian wanted her gone," I said, pulling at his hands. But I couldn't move them.

"No! You did it for pleasure!"

"What? I did it because it was my job! Let me go!"

"No, I'm going to watch you die and enjoy this, just like you enjoyed killing Karen."

"If you kill me, you're a dead man yourself. Dorian will kill you, personally." I started to panic. I didn't know how long I would be able to hold on.

"Fuck, Dorian! I could have killed him a long time ago! I could give a fuck less about him!" Richard pulled me to my feet. Was this it? Naw, fuck that. This was not how my story would end. I punched Richard hard in the chest and kicked his legs from under him. He fell on the floor, hard, letting me free from him. I gasped for air and recovered quickly. I jumped on top of him and slapped him in his face.

"You bastard! I saved your fucking life today! I could have let Dorian take you out, but I spoke up for you!" I hit Richard again. "I could have killed you myself that day you shot me, but I didn't! The fact of the matter is Karen was a fucking cop. She was going to put yo ass away, once she had enough shit on Dorian. Yes, I did kill Karen, more for myself than anything."

"Why? Why would you take her from me?"

"Because you hurt me! You turned me down when I tried to give myself to you. You hurt me then and you're hurting me now. You hurt me and I hurt you back!" I jumped up off him and kicked Richard in his side. I went to the kitchen and poured me a drink. "You know what? Fuck it. What's done is done. Karen was a cop and she's gone. You can try to kill me and Dorian, but you will lose and you will die. So get over this shit and get ready for another job 'cause, this time, if Dorian asks, I won't be saving you." Richard got up, walking toward me. I put my glass down and met him halfway.

"How am I hurting you now? Why didn't you let Dorian kill me?"

"Because I like yo white ass and I want you around a little longer." Richard stared at me for a while and then bust out laughing.

"You *are* a crazy bitch, like Tyrese said."

That's what I get for telling the truth and having feelings and shit.

"I would advise you not to call me a bitch again Richard. Bad things will happen."

"Well, let me be clear Veronica. I wouldn't touch you if you were the only pussy in the world to fuck. I don't want you. You're nothing to me."

"Fine. Business it is. Just have your shit together in five days. I don't need you making me look bad." I walked over to my door and opened it.

"You can leave now, Richard."

"With fucking pleasure."

Once I locked my door, I ran to my room and buried myself under the covers. I cried my eyes out for three days, the heartache was so painful. I loved Richard so much and he hated me with a passion. There was nothing I could do about that. Nothing I could say would make him love me, not even if I said sorry for killing Karen. I wasn't sorry, but I would've said it to make Richard happy. The more he pushed me away, the more I needed him. How could this be happening? I finally found someone that I respected and loved, but he didn't want me. I felt helpless, like I had reached a dead end. I finally rolled out of bed and took a bath to wash away all the pain, but when I got out and dried off, the pain was still with me. So I went to the gym, my new home away from home, but I found myself crying the whole time I worked out. I was a mess, and the next day I had to go to Dorian's and see Richard there. I couldn't even control my tears. How was I going to be able to keep it together around him? When I got ready for bed, I thought about the situation, what I had lost and what Richard had lost. He lost a girlfriend, who was a cop, who I don't even think really loved him. I had lost my pride, my heart, my joy and all of my mental armor. That's when I got pissed: Richard had made a fool of me! This was why I didn't do this love bullshit! Shit like that happened and I started acting like a weak female! Fuck Richard if he didn't want me. I wouldn't force the shit. I could have any man that I wanted. Hell, I could buy me a shitload of pretty white boys, if I wanted to. Richard wasn't the only one in the world.

I woke up the next morning, pumped. I was ready to whip some ass. It was straight gym-wear today, no cute shit. I wanted to fuck some shit up. I rode to Dorian's in silence. I wanted to let my anger grow. I was holding on to it and running as far as I could with the shit. I was not to be fucked with. Everybody was in Dorian's gym when I arrived. Richard glanced at me, then turned around. The bitch. Tyrese did the same. The mark. Dorian welcomed me with open arms, and put a smile on my face.

"How are you, Veronica?"

"I'm fine, Dorian, and you?"

"I'm great." I got a little closer to Dorian.

"How do I feel?" Dorian cracked a smile and I licked my lips

"Is this how she got the job? Fucking the boss? 'Cause I still don't get it," said the same stupid, fucking nigga that I knocked out! I pushed past everyone and kicked him in the mouth with everything I had in me.

"Don't worry about how I got my job, bitch! Worry about how you're going to keep your life, once we make it over there where yo ass not safe no more!" I took my size-ten foot and pounded it into his chest over and over again until blood spurted from his mouth.

"Veronica! That is enough!" I stopped and looked up at Dorian.

"Whatever you say, boss."

"You don't like him? You know what to do. If not, stop putting on a show for everyone. He is not your example." I looked at the gun Dorian pulled out and took it. I needed something to bring me down.

BANG! BANG! BANG!

"No example, Dorian. I don't want to prove myself to any of these niggas, or the white boy over there. I just haven't been working for so long that I need a hit every now and then. Somebody to kill, something to do."

"I understand, but save it. We have bigger shit to deal with."

Dorian left the room and everybody just stared at me. Fuck'em. I walked over to a mat and started to stretch so I could work out. These niggas better be some kind of killers or they were not going to make it in no damn Cuba. If I put fear in their hearts, then they were dead. Once I got done stretching, I went over to the treadmill and ran for about an hour, then worked on my upper body for about two hours. I looked at the other guys bullshitting around, half-ass working out and shit. We were in that gym for four hours before Dorian came back and told everyone to follow him to the gun range he had downstairs. As soon as I put that automatic in my hand and loaded it up, I was in heaven. Dorian had every type of gun laid out for us to use; as soon as he left, I went to work. I mean I hit every target there was right on the bull's eye. Yeah, I was the shit. After that, Dorian had us go outside and work on this little obstacle course. I mean it wasn't really little. There were two walls, two mud ponds we had to swing across, and we had to crawl on the ground and do all type of shit. It was a great day. I had so much fun. I could tell that everyone was impressed with me, but I could care less. I was just sizing up the competition. I knew how Dorian worked. There would be benefits for the strong and consequences for the weak. The only one who was on my level was Tyrese, and I couldn't read him today. He was so focused that I couldn't see any emotion in him. Then I looked over at Richard. He wasn't at his best, but he was still better than the other no-names Dorian had hired. I was so disgusted. How could Richard not want me? Crying over his little cop! I felt myself about to do something stupid, but stopped in my tracks when Dorian came back outside. We all stood in a group waiting for him to speak.

"This job pays a cool million. The possibility of death is very high and you will be training like this every day for a month. Hopefully, that will be enough. Tyrese, Veronica, and Richard, I want to see you in my office. Pack your things up." I was the first to reach Dorian's office and he was sitting at his disk. He smiled at me.

"Close the door please, Veronica." I did what Dorian said and went to him. He pulled me into his arms and I laid my head on his chest. Boy, did I need that.

"I've been watching you all day. I'm impressed with how together you are."

"Thank you, Dorian. I'm just ready to go to war, do what I need to do."

"I see. Tell me why, exactly, are you upset today?"

"Best way to train, I believe, is when I'm mad. I just don't think about anything, I just do what I need to do. Sorry about the mess I made downstairs, he was just trying me."

"I know." There was a knock at the door and we both knew who it was.

"You want me to get that?"

"Yes," he said. I debated in my head as I walked to the door: Should I fuck Dorian? I needed a little contact from the opposite sex every now and then. If you can't fuck the one you want, fuck the one who wants you. I opened the door for Tyrese and Richard; realizing how much shit I had to go through for even dealing with them, I went against fucking Dorian.

"Come in, gentlemen." We all walked to the front of Dorian's desk and waited for him to speak.

"As you can tell, this is a serious situation. You three are the best that I have and the others downstairs are just bodies. I'm trying to get them in shape so they can pull their weight when all of you get to Cuba. I expect that you all will be the only ones to make it out, so I need for everyone to be on the same page. Look out for each other, don't worry about any of the other guys, just do your job and come home. So that means this little love triangle you all have going on needs to be postponed until you get back. Even though its great motivation for you, Veronica, I need you to have a clear head. Whether you all like it or not, you're all partners. If one of you don't come back, the other two will wish that you did. I'll see you all tomorrow."

The three of us left Dorian's office and got into our separate cars to head home. I had to get my mind right 'cause there was no fooling Dorian and I didn't want to make him mad. I just wanted to do my job and get my mill. That was the kind of money I needed to take my birthday trip. I beat Tyrese home and entered my apartment, heading straight for the bathroom, I needed to take a long, hot bath. While my water was running I started to make myself dinner.

I felt like steak and lobster. I had worked hard and I needed to reward myself. I got in the tub and turned on the TV that was in the wall right below the shower head. This was the life. I switched on the jets in the tub so they could spread over my body. I was a little stressed. I lay like that for a half-hour, then washed up and got out the tub. Before I could lotion up, there was a knock at my door. I slipped on my silk robe and answered, surprised that it was Tyrese, but I welcomed him in anyway.

"Hey, Veronica. You busy?"

"Naw, come in. Just about to eat dinner. I'm not going to eat all this. What you want, steak or lobster?"

"Damn, it sound like Dorian paying you a little too well."

"Naw, I just know how to manage my money. Sit down and I'll make you a plate."

"Veronica, you sure? I don't want to fuck up what you had going."

"You cool. So what's this about? I haven't seen you at my door in two weeks."

"Yeah, I wanted to apologize for my behavior last time we were talking. I was just trying to look out for you, but I see I was taking that shit overboard."

"I accept your apology, and thank you for being man enough to admit your faults. I do appreciate what you were trying to do."

"Yeah, I just wanted to clear the air so we wouldn't have any problems working together."

"Now that you brought that up, do you know what Dorian was talking about when he said we all had a love triangle going on? 'Cause I know you hate me and I know Richard hate me, and to be honest, I can't stand ya'll either." I sat his plate down in front of him and went to my room so I could put on my pajamas. When I came back out I was surprised that Tyrese hadn't started on his food yet. I sat down across from him. "Thank you, Tyrese. You didn't have to wait on me to eat, go ahead."

"It's fine. I think what Dorian meant about the love triangle is that I'm in love with you, you're in love with Richard, and he loves you as well." I looked at Tyrese getting a little hot-faced. I was about to ask him a question and I didn't know if I could handle the answer.

"That's not true. You don't love me, right?"

"I respect you now and who knows where that could lead, but, as of right now, we just cool." A big smile came across my face.

"That's what I'm talking about. You respect me now? What brought about this new and lovely change?"

"The way you handled yourself on our last job. You're not the same girl that I used to know."

"I hear that! Dig in! Enjoy your food." I was happy with the situation. Tyrese respected me. At least, I had him on my side. We ate dinner and chit-chatted about nothing important, but it was nice to have company.

"Alright, Veronica I'm on my way out. Go to bed for training tomorrow."

"Alright, thanks for coming by. See you tomorrow."

Man, I had Tyrese's respect. That would have been great to have when we were a so-called couple, but this was cool. I went to sleep feeling a lot better. Over the next month, me and Tyrese became so cool. It was just like old times when we would talk for hours and go out, but there was nothing romantic there to fuck it up. We were friends and I let him know when we made it to Cuba that I would take a bullet for him without a thought to stop me. He didn't say anything, but I knew he felt the same way. The night before we were supposed to leave for Cuba, me and Tyrese had dinner with Trip and Pricey. I hugged her and told my sister that I loved her before we headed back home. She had been the second person in my life who I had told "I love you," and knew, without a doubt, that I meant it. I knew I was going to make it back from Cuba, but I didn't want it to be a question that Pricey had to ask herself while I was gone. I loved her. When Tyrese and I made it home, Richard was waiting outside of my door. I looked at Tyrese and he was looking at Richard.

"What are you doing here?" I asked

"I wanted to talk to you."

"I don't think you have anything to say to me that I would want to hear."

"Just give me a moment of your time."

"Go ahead." Richard looked at Tyrese; there was tension between them.

"In your place, please," Richard added. I looked at Tyrese.

"Fine. Only a moment." I opened my door and let Richard in. Before I could walk in behind him, Tyrese grabbed my arm and closed the door in Richard's face.

"What are you doing?" I said with a slight smile. Tyrese didn't say anything. He just opened his door and pulled me inside with him.

"Tyrese, what's up?" He still wouldn't say anything. He just turned his back to me and put his hands over his face.

"Say something. What is this about?" Tyrese turned to me and we kissed. Damn! Just how I remembered: his lips so soft and his spit so sweet. Before I got in too deep, I pulled away from him.

"What is this shit about?" He was up to something. This passion was coming out of left field.

"I think I'm falling in love with you."

"What! Are you serious?"

"No."

"What?"

"I mean I don't want to lose you."

"Lose me, Tyrese? Lose me to what? What are you talking about? You're not making sense."

"I know what Richard over here for. He is going to try to get with you."

"What makes you think that?"

"I just have a feeling."

"Bullshit. Nigga, be real."

"Alright, we hang with some of the same people and he been telling niggas how he feeling you and whatnot. So you know me. I got a little braggy and told that nigga he had no chance 'cause you was mine."

"What? Why would you say that?"

"'Cause, Veronica, you *are* mine. You can't say we don't have something between us."

"Do you love me, Tyrese?"

"Naw, I just . . ."

"Don't want nobody else to have me. We back at this shit, Tyrese! Come the fuck on, man! What the fuck is your problem? I thought we was cool, I thought you was my nigga, but I see how you get down. It's only fun to hang with me when somebody else want me."

"Come on, Veronica, we cool. It was just some shit that got out of hand, don't take it like that."

"Then what was the kiss about? Why couldn't you come at me on some friend-type shit and just let me know what was up. Hell, I would have left Richard alone if you would have said something. 'Cause I respected you, I would have heard you out. I value your opinion. You a dirty nigga, and the bitch across the hall ain't no better." I went for the door and Tyrese stopped me.

"I'm sorry. Don't let this fuck up this good thing we got going."

"I didn't fuck up a damn thing, Tyrese. You did." I opened the door to leave and, this time, he didn't stop me. I went into my place and Richard was sitting on my couch.

"You might as well get the fuck out. Tyrese told me everything and, to tell the truth, I don't want to fuck with either one of you." Richard walked over to me.

"What, exactly, did Tyrese tell you?"

"That you want to talk to me, all of a sudden, and he been kicking it in your face that he spending time with me."

"So where in that am I at fault? I haven't lied about what we had, I haven't smiled in your face to make someone else mad. What have I done wrong since we last spoke? I know I was wrong for trying to kill you, and what I said to you after that was no better, but you took away what I thought was my world."

"What you *thought* was your world?"

"I asked Dorian for all the information Karen had got on me, and the facts were there. She didn't love me, she was just waiting for me to fuck up one more time. Actually, she hated me. You know, because of all the female murders I had committed."

"I see. So what now?"

Richard walked closer to me and I took a step back. He put his hands up in the air, quickly, to show that he was unarmed, and I stood still. Richard walked over to me and took me into his arms. Before I could object and push away, he kissed me. If I could put the feeling of love into words, only then would anyone understand where I was coming from. I had thought I knew what love was—what it felt like when I was with Tyrese. But now my whole body shook and I felt my legs going weak. When Richard pulled away, he took my last breath with him. Oh my God, I think I came on myself!

"What will happen now is we will let things fall into place," he said. "I won't proclaim that I love you to hold your attention, but I will say this, Veronica: I want to explore the possibility of being in love with you."

I couldn't believe this nigga had just spit the best game that I ever had the pleasure of hearing. I didn't know what to say, what to think. All I knew was that I was feeling all these feelings that I never thought I could. I was ready to take off my clothes and fuck the shit out of Richard. I was ready to cut the tough shit and love him like nobody else's business. I was ready to stand behind him and have his back until death. I was ready to give Richard my world and make him my god. I was shook, scared as hell of these feelings. I actually feared what would come. Richard let me go, kissed me one more time and left. I sat on the couch and tried to take everything in. There was no doubt about it: I was a sucker for love. I could kill, steal, and beat someone nearly to death, but when it came to love and being loved, I couldn't get my dome straight. Which made me think as quickly as I could before my feelings overwhelmed me. The last time I was in so-called love, I had given myself way too quickly and put myself in the position to be violated. I had to be careful, though. This could just be another way for Richard to get revenge on me for killing Karen. I tried to shake the kiss, but I spent the rest of the night dreaming about it, and when the morning came we all met up at the airport to board Dorian's private jet. I couldn't stop smiling when I spotted Richard. I sat down and waited for him to get on. He and Tyrese had come on one after the other. Like musical chairs, they damn near raced for the seat next to me and Richard beat Tyrese to it. I was happy about that. Before I could get out a word, Richard grabbed my hand and kissed it. I smiled and looked over at

Tyrese, who shook his head, turning to face the window. I faced Richard. He had a smile on his face as well. I slowly pulled my hand away. Was Richard playing the game Tyrese had been playing with me? The thought of false feelings coming from Richard brought me down off my cloud and back to reality.

"To make sure that our feelings are genuine, maybe we shouldn't be involved like this at work, keep it professional in a professional setting," I said.

"When you say 'we,' you really mean me, and you think I'm putting on a show for Tyrese."

"If the shoe fits," I said.

"Just so you know: I'm nothing like Tyrese," he whispered in my ear. "I wouldn't stab you in the back. If I fuck you over, you gon' see it coming. Fuck that bitch. I wouldn't waste my time trying to put on a show for him. I do agree with what you said, though, so I'll keep it professional. Oh, and last night I couldn't stop thinking about you. I didn't want to leave. When this is all over, I want to spend time with you. So make time for me."

I couldn't hold back a smile. Richard pulled away from me, brushing his cheek against mine. He got up and sat somewhere else. I couldn't believe I was falling for all this game. I just never saw myself falling for the nice guy. I mean Richard was no angel, but he came at me right, made me smile. I liked his sweet talk. We gave each other looks whenever one of us moved around and my smile was met with his. Half-way through the flight, Tyrese got up and sat next to me. I rolled my eyes.

"What, Tyrese?"

"Chill the fuck out, I came over here to apologize to you."

"Don't sound like no apology to me."

"Give me a fucking minute! Shit! I was wrong for doing what I did by fucking with Richard's head, but I did enjoy spending time with you. You my ride-or-die chick."

"Whatever you say."

"I mean, we cool, Veronica?"

"Sure."

"Good."

He got up and walked away. We would see if he was for real or all talk. I felt Richard looking at me, but I didn't look at him this time. For the rest of the ride, I went to sleep, and when we landed it was night time. We all got in a van that took us to one of Dorian's little hideouts. I sat my things down in the living room and sat down on the couch, I hadn't really woke up yet. Everybody left the planning up to Tyrese and he wanted to go in right before morning to do what we had to do. Everybody was feeling that 'cause nobody wanted to be there longer than we had to, but, at the same time, we hadn't checked the place out. We didn't know who we would find in there, but Tyrese didn't care. He was trying to kill everybody who was in the house at the time. What if the leader wasn't there? He could always get more people to back him and come back stronger. There was no perfect plan for what we were trying to pull off. We were new in town and bringing any attention to ourselves would just be bad. I was the first to hit the shower so I could get ready. I needed to get my mind right. I got dressed and went to the living room. Richard was there. He hadn't taken a shower yet. Tyrese was upstairs, along with the other guys. I stood by the steps for a while, watching Richard pace around the room. He stopped in his tracks and looked at me.

"Come here." I didn't move. I was studying him. "Veronica. Come here." I took a step, then stopped before I took another one. "I want to whisper something in your ear."

I laughed and moved closer to him, but there were still five feet between us.

"I know you said that I need to keep my distance, but . . ." Richard rushed me and held me close. "It's hard for me not to touch you." He kissed my neck and I wrapped my arms around his back. This felt good.

"I can't wait until we get back to Chicago. I want to take you out. What do you want for your birthday?"

"I don't want anything. I finally have money of my own and I enjoy doing things for myself. Wait a minute." I pushed Richard away from me. "How do you go from zero to ten just like that? Last I remember, you wouldn't touch me if I was the last woman on earth. What happened to that? I know you're just waiting to fuck me over because of Karen. Look, forget all this! Just fuck it! You no different." Richard grabbed me from behind and placed his arm around my neck.

"Listen to me, Veronica. I'm nothing like them other bitches, okay? I'm not going to lie to you because I'm not about stabbing anybody in the back. I meant what I said. I have always had a thing for you, but I had to stay true to Karen."

"What about the night we went out to dinner?"

"I don't know. I kinda let things get out of hand. I wanted you and the chase was there, so I went for it. When I was shot, the first person I thought about was Karen. Look, that was the past. I'm here telling you I want to have something with you, no bullshit." I turned to face Richard. We were still close, embraced in a hug almost.

"I'm not ready, Richard. You just need to let this go."

"I can't and I won't." We shared a deep kiss, then Richard let me go and went up the stairs without a word.

He was good. I stepped onto the porch outside to cool down. There was never a moment before a job where I felt like something would go wrong. Call it what you want, but I knew I wasn't going to die; well not today at least. I knew that I had many years in this game because I was serving the devil so well. I'm no fool, I knew all this shit would catch up with me one day. Karma is a bitch like that. Sometimes I would lie in bed in the middle of the night wondering how I would go, who would do it and how much time would pass before I'm forgotten. My daydreaming came to an end again when Tyrese stood next to me and tried to put his hand in mine. I turned to face him.

"Don't start, Tyrese. Focus. We have work to do."

"Did you give Richard the same speech?"

"Yes." I rolled my eyes and made my way to the front door.

"Veronica, wait. My bad. I just came out here to say, when all this shit is said and done with, maybe we can play the video game at my place or something." I smiled at Tyrese. He was so full of shit. When it came to Tyrese, I felt that, at least, the nigga was consistent with his. He didn't shock me.

"Yeah, we can do that," I said.

I went back in the house and started to strap up, I had my.45s next to my breast, two baby-guns on my ankle, a big-ass blade on my thigh, a gun tucked in my belt behind me and, finally, two killa machine guns. I was ready. I was so fucking ready that I felt like going by my damn self. We all loaded up in the van, once again. Execution time. Once the house was in plain view, we put on our eyewear and our gas masks. The next hour and a half was full of nonstop explosions. There were six of us: three in the front, three in the back, broken up into teams. You would have thought we were fucking SWAT or something, with our headsets on, dressed in all black. Team A was me, Richard and one of the no-names. Team B was Tyrese and the other two lames Dorian hired. As soon as we heard Team B come in through the front, we busted threw the back door. Richard was the leader of Team A. After ten bodies fell, we finally made it to the front and found that, already, we were down a man. Six turned into five within minutes, and I whispered to myself, "Fuck." Shit, at this rate, we would lose two more men by the time we made it to the third floor, which was okay as long as that two didn't include Tyrese, Richard or me. People were dropping like flies and once the other two no-names saw that one of us was already dead, they stepped their game up. We was hitting everything in sight, but still no head, no boss. I started to get the feeling that our target wasn't here. Finally on the third floor, I was hot as fuck and wishing we hadn't worn black. We made it to the bedroom at the end of the hallway. The doors were closed, so we all stood to the side.

"Who wants to kick the door down?" Tyrese asked us. We all looked at the two lames still standing.

"Don't look at me. The last muthafucka that broke down a door in this bitch is dead now," one of them said. "Ya'll not fooling us. We know what's going on, how we're not supposed to make it out of here and shit like that."

"Fuck that pussy talk, I'll do it!" I said, making my way to the door. I started lighting that bitch up. If there was someone standing behind it, they were laid out now. I kicked the door in and moved to the side so Tyrese could go in. We found some Cuban chick banging on the wall.

"Let me in! You piece of shit, I hope they kill your ass!" she yelled. Tyrese cocked his gun. "Please don't kill me! Pedro is in here, but you're not going to be able to get in. It has a lock and it's bulletproof."

"Enough! Richard, take her. One of you check under the bed and the other, the closet. Veronica, take a look at this and tell me what we can do," Tyrese ordered.

I found the switch that opened the door. Just like the girl had said, this bitch was behind a big-ass safe lock and there was no way we were getting in there. I turned to Tyrese: "The only choice we have is to blow the house up. Hopefully, we'll kill him. He not gon' give us the lock number and I didn't bring my tools to crack the lock."

"This was the whole point of the fucking trip, Veronica!"

"I know that! What do you want me to do? Maybe the safe can't handle dynamite."

"Alright, I want you two to set up the dyno. Veronica, you get ready to set this bitch on fire. I know how much you love a good fire anyway." I smiled at Tyrese and started for the door.

"What about her, Tyrese?" Richard asked about the girl. "What do you want me to do with her?"

"Do what you feel. I don't care."

"Cool."

Richard pushed the girl to the side and let off five rounds on her ass. She didn't even have a chance to scream. I shook my head and left the room. The boy was sick, and I loved him for it. There was a lot of liquor in the kitchen, so I used that to light the fire. There were so many dead bodies littering the floor. I went to every floor and drenched each one. By the time I made it back to the third floor, the two lames were done with the dyno.

"Alright, everybody outside." We followed Tyrese.

"Light it up."

I lit a match and, within seconds, the whole house was up in flames. We waited in the back for the big bang and when the safe dropped, we walked over to it. The door was cracked open as we approached. We all drew our guns. One of the lames opened the door, helping Pedro out. This bitch was still alive. Pedro pulled away from him and smacked him in the face.

"What were you thinking, Martinez?" Pedro asked the lame. "I could have died with that stunt you pulled!"

"I had to do what they said. They would have killed me. Besides, I knew everything would have been fine."

"Who is the leader?" Martinez pointed to Tyrese and Pedro walked over to him.

"Put your guns down, I have a proposition for you." Tyrese still held onto his gun, tightly, and Martinez pointed his gun to my head while the other lame did the same to Richard.

"There has been enough bloodshed for today. I have five-million for each of you back at another location. What do you say to that, my friend?"

"I'm not your damn friend."

"Wrong answer." Pedro pulled out a gun that he had behind his back. The old fuck was quicker than Tyrese had expected. "Drop your guns!" Pedro was ready to kill Tyrese. I looked at him. He wanted me to try to take the shot, but I didn't want to risk it. If I shot Pedro, he could have shot Tyrese. I looked over at Richard and he was willing to let Pedro kill Tyrese. I dropped my gun and looked at Tyrese again. He was disappointed.

"Now you, white boy."

"I'm not dropping shit."

"Richard, drop your fucking gun!" He looked at me and did it.

"There you go, young lady. Help your friend," Pedro said. "You look very familiar."

"This is the bitch that killed Hector and his cousin," said Martinez.

"Really? This is Veronica? This is Dorian's little prized possession? Come here, Veronica. You are a very pretty girl. Dorian told me you were the best fuck he ever had."

"What?" Tyrese and Richard said at the same time.

"Really?" I replied. "Would you like to find out for yourself?"

"As tempting as that sounds, I know your game. You're a snake and a whore. Martinez, call the others to come pick us up." The guy who was holding a gun to Richard's head started looking at me.

"You know, Pedro, if you don't want her, can I have her, real quick?"

"Do what you want, Rule. After you're done—kill her."

"Fuck all that!" I thought to myself. I needed to make a move before this bitch-ass nigga made a call. We couldn't take on any more people, not just the three of us. I started to walk over to Rule and undid my shirt.

"What are you doing? Stop walking."

"Cool down. Shit, why fight it? You're about to kill me anyway. Don't be scared of this pussy, come get it." Rule put his gun down and told Martinez to watch me. Oh, they watched, alright. We started kissing and I went for his belt. We were so close that I could smell his hot breath.

"Yeah Rule, tag that pussy," one of them said. Just as Rule smacked me on my ass, I reached for the blade on my thigh and slit his throat. Then I threw the knife at Martinez and stuck him right in his eye. Richard shot Pedro and Tyrese picked up the gun, finishing off Pedro with another shot. If a gun couldn't get the job done, pussy always worked. Men were always thinking with their dicks.

"Now, you finally want to do something," Tyrese said.

"Shut up! Let's get the fuck out of here."

"Did you really have sex with Dorian? How could you fuck him? He don't give a fuck about you!"

"And you do, Tyrese? Look, I don't need this shit right now. I just want to go home, alright?"

"You did fuck him, didn't you? I mean I knew you were a hoe, but damn, yo boss? A man who beat your ass like you were a dog! You are one sick bitch."

"Just don't say anything else to me." I could tell that Tyrese was hurting over this. He thought I belonged to him, and he looked up to Dorian, so he felt betrayed.

"Now, be real Veronica. What the fuck is wrong with you? Why would you even get involved with Dorian?"

"Tyrese, what is the difference if it was Dorian, or you, or Game or anybody else? Ya'll niggas are no different! What have you done that Dorian hasn't? You beat on me, just like everybody else, you lie, you cheat, you use me and ya'll all treat me like shit! Because Dorian is the boss he supposed to be different? He supposed to be off limits? Fuck you! Don't none of ya'll bitches care about my well-being. I do what the fuck I have to do to run my life. So all this checking me bullshit needs to stop, 'cause I'ma do what the fuck I have to do to survive. Fuck you!"

Tyrese didn't say a word and I was on the verge of tears. Why? I like, call it the mirror effect: You could live your life however you wanted, but with that, came denial. I mean I have been with a lot of guys, more than I care to admit, but I never thought I was a hoe. Then there go that mirror everybody wants to hold up in my face. What have these men done for me? And why was I giving all of myself to men who hurt me? There was no question in my mind that I was a little crazy, but hell, it ran in the family. As time went by, I wondered if maybe I might have some type of emotional problems. All these damn feelings and letting Tyrese get to me like that. I needed some serious time off.

14

We didn't go back to Dorian's hideout. We just drove all the way back to where the jet was. I wasn't sleepy, but I pretended anyway. I didn't want Richard to say anything to me. I didn't want anybody to say anything to me. By the time we made it home, I didn't have a chance to run and hide back at my apartment anymore; Dorian wanted to see us. I was the last to make it to his office. He walked over to me, ending his conversation with Tyrese, and giving me a long hug.

"I have to be honest, Veronica. I didn't think you were going to make it back."

"Why is that?"

"This is not a first-timer's job. It takes years before anyone can take down a kingpin."

"I see." Dorian let me go and looked at me hard.

"What's wrong with you?" Then he looked at Richard and Tyrese. "Give us some privacy."

"No, they don't have to leave. I just want to know why, after everything you have done to me, why must you slander my name? Not only do I work like a dog for you, but I'm loyal to you, I've done everything you've asked and, still, you have to tell everybody how you fucked me? How well you keep your little bitch in control, right? I work so fucking hard for respect and you niggas do everything you can so I can't have it."

"Veronica . . ."

"Dorian, you don't have to even say it. You don't owe me shit, I just work for you, nothing more. You give me a job and I'll do it. You give me an order and I'll follow it. Everything is okay." I felt so numb to the whole situation at that point.

"Well your money is here. Take it and you all can leave."

I grabbed my money and headed home with one of Dorian's other workers. Richard had offered me a ride, but I said no. I had put Dorian in a bad position. If he said sorry, then he would look weak. If he didn't, the relationship we had would be destroyed. Dorian was more than my boss, and he was more than just a guy who I fucked for no reason. I fucking respected him, I had love for him, and he was the only guy who I'd always thought I knew where we stood. I ran me a bath and went to sleep when I got in. A couple of hours later, there was banging on my door. I knew it was Pricey and I knew that if I didn't open my door she would break it down, so I let her in.

"What is your problem? Why didn't you call me when you made it back home? And why in the hell did you tell Tyrese that you had sex with Dorian?"

"I didn't tell him anything. Did Tyrese tell Trip that I had sex with Dorian?"

"Yeah, he called crying about something, talking shit. So what happened?"

"We were over there handling business when our target let out the news. What can I say? I wasn't going to deny it, especially not for Tyrese feelings. I don't even care anymore. Everybody knows I'm a hoe. No sense in pretending, I'm not fooling anybody."

"A hoe? What are you talking about? You're not a hoe; far from it."

"Pricey, I fucked guys that I barely knew for money."

"A *lot* of damn money!"

"Even a high-priced hoe is a hoe. That shit don't even matter. I could give a shit less about the title. I just feel . . . bare. Like everybody can see right through me. How can I walk in a room with my head held high with everybody knowing things about me that only the people I love should know about? I feel naked. Everybody knows my story, everybody has an opinion. I can't put it into words. I feel dirty and used."

"Roni, you are a goddess. Who cares what they say or what they think? They might know your story, but they don't know you. You're my fucking hero, my world, and I love you. I respect you and I need for you to know what your true worth is."

"I don't know what my true worth is. I'm fucking giving my body away to every fucking dick that can get me ahead."

"I don't know what to say. You're playing the fucking game, so you got to make this shit work for you. Having the head nigga in charge is not such a bad thing, and, last I remember, you were in love with Tyrese, once upon a time. Those other guys were a way of life. How would you have eaten? How would you have been able to stand on your feet? Don't trip off what you can't change, just learn from it."

"I know you're right. I just wish he didn't have to find out like that."

"Who, Tyrese?"

"No, fuck Tyrese!"

"Then who are you talking about?"

"Nobody." I wasn't ready to tell Pricey how serious my feelings for Richard had gotten.

"Don't lie to me, Veronica. Are you talking about Richard?" she asked, reading my mind.

"Yes. The night before we left, oh my God, Pricey, he kissed me and my whole world went upside down. I have never wanted somebody so bad and I don't want nothing to fuck this up before we can let it grow, you know?"

"Get the fuck out of here! My sister's *really* ready to be in love! Go for it. I hope Richard is the one for you."

"Who knows . . . I don't even want to face him."

"I'm sure he will understand. So what we doing for your birthday in a couple of weeks?"

"I don't know. I don't even want to do anything anymore. I just really need the time off. Where do you want to go?"

"I was thinking maybe Jamaica or, like, China."

"I like the sound of Jamaica: shop until we drop."

"Hell, yeah. So what do you want for your birthday?"

"For you to make time for your sister."

"You know I am, Veronica. Now, for real, what do you want me to buy you?"

"Nothing. I just got a mill for the job we just did. Nobody has to get me anything."

"Well you know I am, so fuck you. Look, I'm going to holla at you tomorrow. Maybe we can do lunch or something."

"I really just want to lay back until my birthday, chill at home. Just call me."

"Alright, Roni. See you soon."

When Pricey left, she took all my bad feelings with her. What would I do without her? She was my breath of fresh air and I loved her for it so much. I started on dinner and felt that I needed to make a phone call.

"Hello?"

"I see you're still hard at work, still in your office."

"You know my work is never done."

"I know. Dorian I just wanted to call and say sorry. I didn't need to show my ass like that."

"No, Veronica, you had every right. You're one of my best workers and the least I could do is give you that respect. I just want you to know that when I let our little secret out I didn't mean it in a 'you're my whore' kind of way. I was excited because I had just had the best sex of my life, but that is no excuse. I don't want this to fuck up our relationship."

"Dorian, we good. I owe you a lot, I'm on your team and ain't shit changing that."

"Good. I know your birthday is coming up soon and I want to give you a party at my house before you go out of town."

"Sounds great. Thank you, Dorian."

"Not a problem. Look, I need to tie up some loose ends."

"Okay, see you soon."

I hung up the phone with a smile on my face. I was the "best sex" Dorian had ever had. He was just probably blowing smoke up my ass, but I didn't care. I sat in the living room, eating. I wished Richard was there with me. I couldn't believe I was digging dude this hard. Around three in the morning before I went to bed I heard someone at my door trying to get in. I grabbed my gun and flew out to the door. It was Richard.

"What are you doing?" I asked him. He gave me a big smile and a kiss.

"You really need to get me a key." Richard came in and closed the door behind him.

"Excuse me, a key? Now why would you need a key?" Richard sat his overnight bag down in the living room. "And why in the hell do you have that with you?"

"You said that we could do this, but we had to keep it professional. So I figure if we can't spend time on the job, we need to make up for the time we lose. So this week, your place, and next week, mine."

"You cannot be serious. Don't you think you're moving a little too fast?" At this point, I had a big smile on my face, trying not to laugh.

"No. Come here." Richard wrapped his arms around me and kissed my neck. "You don't know how hard it was, waiting all day so I could come over. I knew Pricey would come to see you and ya'll would talk forever. Then I didn't want Tyrese all in our business. He already telling the world what a hoe you are." I pulled away from Richard and went into the kitchen. He was right behind me.

"Don't act like that, Veronica. I don't care about your past, just as long as that shit don't happen from this point on. 'Cause you know I will kill you." I lifted my head and made eye contact with Richard. "I don't give a damn how many men you have been with or for what reason. Just know that, from this point on, you're mine."

"You know you're really sick, right? My past doesn't make me any less attractive to you right now?"

"No."

Richard turned me around with my back to him and he eased up on me. I could feel him getting hard. He took my hair out of its ponytail and let my hair fall, moving it all over to my right shoulder. He then wrapped his arms around my waist: "I know you're the sexiest woman in the world, you have everything that I want and all I want to do is please you." He was killing me with this whisper shit. God, I was so wet. Damn, he could get it if he just made the move. I lay my head back against him and relaxed my body. Richard could do whatever he wanted to me. He unwrapped his arms and I leaned most of my weight onto the counter. He went for my waist and I knew he was about to pull my pants down. He started to lift my shirt up over my head and then he pulled down my panties. I stepped out of them for him and he told me to spread my legs. I mean, by this time I could feel my wetness running down my thigh. I had never felt this way before. Richard finally backed off me and I could feel his eyes burning a hole into my pussy. I wanted to scream at the top of my lungs, "*Come and get this pussy!*" But instead, I just bit down on my bottom lip to compose myself. I could hear some movement behind me and, as I started to turn around, Richard put his hand on my back and said, "No, don't move. I want you just like this, the first time." The first time? What was he talking about? Richard went back to making noise behind me and I just stood there in anticipation. I wanted him inside me so bad. When I felt kisses on my ass, I tried to turn around again, but his hands were firmly on my waist, keeping me in place. "Relax, Veronica." I took a breath and closed my eyes. I was trying to figure out what his next move would be, but I couldn't. I felt the kisses on my ass again and I couldn't tell if he was standing up or what. Just as I was trying to picture what it was he was doing, I felt warm liquid on top of my warm liquid. One stroke, two strokes . . . what was he doing to me? I felt him start to move his right hand around to the front of me and, in one second, he found me. With his tongue deep inside me and his right hand rubbing on my clit, I was on the verge of cumming.

By now, I was bent over the damn counter. My arms were the only thing keeping me up. My body was in flames and pleasure had me screaming at the top of my lungs. Richard took his tongue from me just as I was about to cum. I wanted to cuss him out, but I couldn't catch my breath. Damn, he was already putting the work on me. A minute later, he was back at it. This time, he rammed two figures inside me and started to eat my ass. Oh my God! I pushed into him and started to move my hips around while grabbing my own breast. Two minutes later, I was cumming all over Richard's face. I mean I came so hard that my knees got weak and I thought I would pass the hell out. Richard stood up and wiped his face with his hand. With a big smile, he licked his fingers. "You taste great."

I couldn't speak. Richard took me into his arms and carried me into my room. I couldn't believe how maxed out of energy I was. I wanted to help take off his clothes, but I was taking deep breaths trying to prepare for what was to come. I didn't give a damn if this white boy only had three inches to work with; if he could eat me out like that every time, I would marry his ass. Richard's body felt so hot on top of mine. We were on the covers and it, literally, felt like my skin was on fire. I spread my legs and I waited. His face was an inch from mine, so I couldn't help but kiss him. I got lost in it and wrapped my arms around his back, pulling him closer. I could feel the head of his dick right outside of my lips. I took a deep breath and he entered me. Perfect fit! There wasn't any pain and it wasn't like I was loose or nothing. It was perfect. I let my breath go and enjoyed the rest of the night. When I say the boy wanted to go all night long, he was really trying, but I told him I needed rest. That was the first time I couldn't keep up with anyone in the bedroom. I didn't wake up until late afternoon and Richard wasn't in the bed. I wondered if he had left. I went to the kitchen and smiled when I saw him cooking.

"Yes, that's what I want to see: naked and ready," he said. I looked down at myself to confirm what Richard saw.

"What are you making? It smells good."

"None of your business. I ran you a bath, so go get in and I'll be right there with our food."

"Cool." I went to the bathroom and got in the hot bath Richard had made for me. This was just what I needed. I lay back and closed my eyes. I was so relaxed.

"Don't go to sleep on me again," I heard him say.

"I'm not going to sleep. Are you going to join me?"

"How can I say no to that kind of question?" Richard took off his clothes and I couldn't believe what I saw.

"Oh my God! Did I do that?" He looked at his chest and his back in the mirror.

"Yeah, those are all your love marks."

"I'm so sorry. Do they hurt?"

"Naw, they feel good. Keep it up." Richard got in the tub with me and leaned his head against my breast.

"Last night was good, Richard."

"Then wait 'til you see my great." I smiled and kissed his cheek.

"Are you going to feed me now?"

Richard grabbed the tray he had brought with him and sat it on the edge of the tub. He turned around so we were facing each other. It was filled with fruit and little sandwiches. I was surprised that it tasted so good and actually filled me up. Sex in the tub was good, sex on the couch, good, sex in the kitchen was nice, sex on the table was really good, and sex on the floor was okay, but then we hit the bed and I experienced greatness. That's all me and Richard did for a week—have sex and talk. We didn't go out, not once, and when I ran out of food, we went to his place. I had completely forgotten that my birthday was coming up and was a little depressed when Pricey called me, asking me what I was wearing that night for my party. Time to get back to reality. Richard and I had spent two weeks together and I was in love with this guy. I caught a cab back to my apartment so I could get ready for my party. And guess who was there knocking on my damn door like the loser he was. Yep, Tyrese. But not even he could piss me off this time. I was on cloud nine and I was not coming down.

"What do you want?" Tyrese turned around and looked at the overnight bag hanging from my arm.

"Where have you been? I've been trying to get in touch with you for a whole damn week." I walked over to my door and opened it.

"I have a cell phone. You could've called me if it was important."

"I could have, but I didn't. So where have you been all week?"

"Are you coming to my party?" I asked with a smile on my face.

"Yeah. Dorian want everybody there."

"Oh, that's nice. Well I'm about to get dressed so I can go, I'll see you then." Tyrese walked over to me and grabbed me by the shoulders.

"Veronica, where the fuck have you been!" I looked up at him, hearing him for the first time since we started talking.

"Cool down! Damn! I was out. I'm safe. Now mind your own business. Like I said, I'll see you at the party."

"Whatever."

Tyrese left and I took a shower. What to wear? I was eighteen. Who would have thought my destructive ass would have made it this far? I was feeling good and I wanted everybody to know it. I decided on a gold, silk dress. It was long, with spaghetti straps, and it was hugging every curve. Yeah, I was doing it classy tonight. I felt older. Hell, I felt better. Pricey called and told me she was on her way to the party, asking if I had I left yet. I told her yeah. I didn't want anybody to know where I was going first, so I got in my truck and went for a little drive. When I reached my destination I grabbed a blanket out of my truck and started walking. I stopped in front of her tombstone and placed the blanket on the ground. As I lay down and closed my eyes, I could see my Mom's face.

"Damn, I miss you so much. It's been hard without you, Mom. I'm trying to be strong, but . . . forget it, it doesn't matter. Pricey has given me a reason to live. She is so good to me, and I found somebody. His name is Richard and I'm in love with him, Mom. I know, right? Me, in love with a guy. Who would have thought? So many things have changed. I hope you're looking down on me, still. I can't wait to see you again. Love you, Mom."

I got off the ground and made my way back to the truck. Every year for my birthday, I took the time out to go see my mother. I made it to Dorian's at around midnight. I had left my cell phone in my truck while I was at the grave site, and Pricey had called me, like, nine times. At Dorian's, the party was going on strong. Pricey was waiting for me at the door.

"Where the hell have you been!" Pricey gave me a hug and pulled me into the house, closing the door behind us.

"I had to take care of some things."

"Okay, well you here now, so let's turn this bitch upside down. Oh, and I heard you have some fly-ass gifts coming your way."

"So what you get me?"

"Roni, you said all you wanted was my time, so . . ."

"So yo lame ass ain't get me nothing?"

"You know I got you something." We went into the living room where the majority of the people were. Dorian waved me over.

"Veronica! Come here. I thought you weren't going to make it." Dorian gave me a long hug, once I was in reach of him.

"Where else would I be, Dorian?" He was still holding on to me when I saw Richard come from the pool area.

"I don't know. Where were you?" I placed my hand on his chest and moved in closer to him. I didn't want everybody to be in my mouth.

"I went to go spend some time with my mom." Dorian kissed me on the cheek.

"You are something wonderful, Veronica. Let me go get you a drink." I could tell he was kinda drunk. Pricey came and pulled me over to the dance floor before I could go talk to Richard.

"Come on. Dance with me and have some fun!"

"Alright."

Dorian had someone send me a drink and I danced with Pricey for as long as I could, which was only three songs. Every time I turned around I was being pulled into an embrace of some kind. Everybody wanted to wish me a happy birthday and give me money, which I wasn't mad at, but I missed Richard. My eyes were on him the whole night and his were on me. He would give me a wink now and then, and I would give him a smile. After cutting the cake and having a bit to eat, I met Richard on the dance floor. This was the first slow song the DJ had played all night and I was so happy I was in Richard's arms.

"You smell good," I said.

"You look great, Veronica." I smiled and leaned my head on Richard's chest.

"I missed you today." Richard bent down and kissed my neck.

"You better stop. You don't want to give our little secret away, do you?" Richard kept his mouth near my ear.

"I'm doing the best I can. You don't know how bad I want you right now."

"Later tonight. I hope you have been a good boy 'cause I don't want to have to stab your eyes out, sweetie."

"You been watching me all night. If anybody should be disciplined, it should be you. All the damn hugs and kisses you gave away today."

"Cool down, you know the only person I want is you, but if you think I need a spanking tonight, then I can handle that."

"You think so?"

We shared a laugh and fought the feeling of wanting to kiss each other. A good halfway into our slow dance, Dorian came and pulled me away. I really wasn't listening to what he was saying because my attention was on Richard. Damn near everybody was walking to the backyard. Dorian pulled me close to him and covered my eyes. We walked a ways together and I held onto him so I wouldn't fall.

"Veronica, today we celebrate your birth, but before I give you your gift, I want you to know that you're a big asset to this team and today, you have our respect." I pulled away from Dorian and gave him a hug. What he said was the law and I knew, from this point on, I would have no more problems. "And this is a little something extra." Dorian turned me around and I couldn't believe my eyes.

"You got me a Bentley Continental! Oh, my God!" I hugged him one more time. "Thank you! Thank you so much!"

"You deserve it." I ran to the car. It was cherry-red, with twenty-twos, the top was down and there were a whole bunch of white envelopes with my name written on them.

"I have something for you as well." Richard took my hand and pulled me over to this nice-ass, red and black motorcycle.

"Thank you. I love it. Are you going to teach me how to ride?"

"Last I recall, you can do that quite well already."

"Shut up."

The rest of the night we did a little more dancing, but by three, people started clearing out. Richard put the motorcycle in my truck and Pricey drove it home. I drove my new Bentley, flying on the damn freeway. This was a close first in my favorite of all birthdays. When we made it home, I gave Pricey one last hug and told her to be ready 'cause I wanted to leave in about two days. I told Richard that I would meet him around the corner in a minute because I wanted to change. That wasn't the only reason I didn't want him to wait outside for me in front of the apartment complex: Tyrese hadn't come to my party and I had a feeling that he had something up his sleeve. I went upstairs to my apartment and his door was open. He was sitting on his couch watching TV. I didn't say anything to him, just went in and closed the door behind me. I packed something to sleep in and an outfit for the next day, then I changed clothes. As I was getting ready to leave, Tyrese came in and closed the door behind him.

"I'm about to leave. I really don't have time for this."

"Where the fuck are you going?"

"None of your damn business. News flash: We are not together. I don't even like you. Why is this so hard for you to understand?"

"Who the fuck do you think you talking to?" Tyrese rushed me and wrapped his hands around my neck. Here we go again.

"You are something sad Tyrese. Mad 'cause I don't want you? Nigga, get a life or a friend or something. Stop pressing me." I pulled away from Tyrese and he put his hands over his face.

"Who you fucking now?"

"Somebody that's not you. Look, I don't have time to waste. I've moved on and you should do the same."

"You ain't moved on. This just has your attention for the moment. Fine, I won't press the shit. Fuck it, have fun." Tyrese made his way out.

"Oh, before you go . . . I want to have this understanding: I don't want you and I don't need you. Life would be a whole lot better if I never had to deal with you again. I understand our work situation, but you need to know that I am not interested in having a personal relationship with you. Please leave me alone."

I locked my door and made my way downstairs. Tyrese didn't say anything else. That nigga had a lot of nerve. Why did he even think he was worth my time? Richard met me at the corner and we drove to his house. Richard opened the door for me and put my bags up in his room while I sat in the living room. I took off my shoes and watched TV. Richard sat down next to me and pulled me into his arms.

"You look amazing tonight, baby."

"Thank you. You didn't look too bad yourself. Did you miss me today?"

"You know I did, crazy." Richard started to tickle me and I rolled around in his arms so he could stop.

"Quit! You gon' make me pee on myself!"

"You are so beautiful."

"Boy, somebody is laying it on thick tonight. You trying to get in between these legs?"

"I mean we both know that is a given, Veronica. I don't have to butter you up. If anything, you need to be trying to push up on me to get me in the mood."

"Please! You always in the mood."

"True. Did you enjoy your party?"

"It was okay. I mean it was nice of everybody to show me love like that, but you were the only thing on my mind."

"Same here. Do you want to go out and learn how to ride your bike?"

"We can do that. I can't stay that long because I have to start packing."

"Where you going?"

"Me and Pricey going to Jamaica for about a week to do some shopping and bonding."

"Can't be mad at that. I'll miss you. I saw you more when we wasn't together."

"I understand where you're coming from. I don't know how much longer I can do all this sneaky stuff. I actually want to show you off."

"What do you mean you 'actually' want to show me off? You should be honored to be with me. I'm the shit."

"Whatever, dude." I tapped Richard's cheek and he grabbed my hand with his. He started to kiss my hand and suck my fingers.

"You make me so happy, Veronica. I want to take a trip with you since we can't do much here in Chicago."

"We can still go somewhere. I just really want to do this with Pricey. She always with Trip and I'm always working. I haven't really seen her."

"It's cool. I can wait. But are you sure you gon' be up to two trips?"

"If you paying, I'm down for whatever."

"I think I can find some money to take care of my baby. Where you want to go?"

"I don't know, maybe France. Somewhere nice and romantic. I don't usually do all that weak, lovey shit, but I guess I can fuck with it."

"You guess?" Richard said with his perfect smile.

"Yeah. I am wondering why I still have my clothes on."

"I'm just taking you in right now, Veronica. I really don't want you to go, being without you today for a couple of hours was hard enough."

"Awwww, you a punk. My boo is sprung." Richard held me tight in his arms and kissed my cheek.

"Shut up. I want to tell you something, but I don't want you to freak out."

"Alright."

"When I say this, Veronica, I don't want you to reply."

"Okay."

"Come here." I sat on his lap and he held me tight as I lay my head on his chest.

"I want you to know that I love you and I want to be with you forever. Now that isn't a proposal, I just want you to know that I have no attention of going anywhere, so you can relax." I looked up at him and knew Richard was serious. Wow, I was really about to get lost in this man.

"Let's go to bed."

Richard carried me into his bedroom and laid me down. I couldn't help but inhale his smell. His covers were wrapped in his scent. I had to bury my face in one of his pillows. Every time I was in his room I couldn't help but take Richard in. If there was one thing that got me in the mood, this was it. As I lay on my back, he pulled my pants off and helped me out of my clothes. His hands were so warm and soft, I couldn't wait. I had to have him close to me. I pulled Richard into bed with me and started to kiss him. I sat on top of him and started to unbutton his shirt. I could feel his fingertips running up and down my back and the thought that we were about to have sex made me bite down on my lip in anticipation. Richard finally reached my bra and, with almost one touch, it was on the floor. He reached for his stereo remote control and turned on some music. I had told him that I had a passion for dancing, so I started to grind on top of him while I undid his pants. He kissed my neck and went down to my breast. The night was filled with love and, before I left early the next morning while Richard was still sleep—I told him I loved him, too.

I wanted to get all my packing out of the way so I could, at least, spend a full day with him before I left for Jamaica. When I made it home I wasn't shocked to see Tyrese up to something again. His door was wide open and he was with some chick on the couch, kissing her. He heard me opening my door and he smiled my way. I just shook my head and went inside. Tyrese was like a big kid who had too much time on his hands. I was so over him. I packed up a few things and called Pricey.

"What time we leaving tomorrow?"

"Yeah, about that, Veronica . . . we all leaving early."

"Who is 'we all?'"

"I mean my baby didn't want to be without me, so you know Trip has to tag along, and when Tyrese heard that everybody was taking a trip, he wanted to come. You know if Tyrese can't come, then Trip not gon' want to, and he not gon' want me to go."

"When have you ever listened to what Trip say to you? You know what, Pricey? That's some real hoe shit! You know this is my damn birthday getaway! What the fuck will I be getting away from if you invite everybody in Chicago that I don't fucking like?"

"Roni, chill the fuck out. It ain't even all what you trying to make it."

"You know, it sure isn't. Ya'll do what the fuck ya'll want to do. If I see ya'll, I see ya'll. Have a fun fucking time!"

I slammed my cell phone shut and finished packing. This was time for me and Pricey to spend together and she was shitting all over that. How the fuck she gon' play me for Trip weak ass? It was cool, though, 'cause I had one better for all they asses. I put my bags in my truck and went right back to Richard's house. He came to the door with a towel around his waist.

"Did you just get out of the shower?"

"Yeah, come in."

"I forgot to do all that at my place. I was so ready to get the hell out of there." I started to pull off my clothes, heading to the bathroom. I ran a hot shower and jumped in. Richard sat on the closed toilet.

"What's wrong?"

"Nothing. Just a change of plans, that's all."

"What changed?"

"I want us to leave for Jamaica tomorrow so I can enjoy time with you away from fucking Chicago."

"What about Pricey?"

"Pricey has Trip. She will be fine without me. What time do you want to leave?"

"I don't care. Whenever we get up, I guess. So what really happened, Veronica?"

"Nothing. Nothing important. I just don't want to talk about it. Can you hand me a towel, please?"

Richard left the bathroom and I cut off the shower. He came back in and wrapped the towel around me. We laid in bed for a couple of hours before anybody said another word. Richard just understood me in that way. He didn't push me, and he could just read me like that. I lay on his chest, feeling like he was the only one I could depend on at that moment. Our relationship was new, but it was serious and I hoped that this one didn't end in a ball of fire. I fell asleep and Richard woke me later on that night with dinner. I put on a little nightgown and met him in the dining room. He was dressed in blue jeans and a button-up shirt.

"Are you going somewhere tonight?"

"Yeah, I have some runs to make and some lose ends I have to tie up if I'm going to be leaving tomorrow. I think we should let everybody know that we're together. This secret shit isn't helping anything either way."

"Okay." He kept eating his food. "Pricey pissed me off so bad today. Put Trip over me, and this my birthday weekend."

"I figured it was something like that. Your cell phone's been ringing off the hook since you went to sleep. So I'm your backup. Since you can't spend time with Pricey, then you'll settle for me instead?"

"Shut up, Richard, you know it isn't like that." I smiled at him. He was so sweet.

"Sure it isn't. So not only was Pricey trying to get Trip to come along, but Tyrese as well. What I don't understand is what, exactly, are you mad about? Trip crashing you and Pricey's time together or the fact that if you're alone with Tyrese, you might do something you will regret?" I dropped my fork on my plate and looked at Richard.

"Are you serious? You think I still have feelings for Tyrese?"

"I mean with a history like the one you and Tyrese have—on again, off again—who knows when you will be on again?"

"I see." I took a look at him one more time. "You're dressed to impress, but you're about to go make some runs this late at night?" I got up from the table and walked away from Richard.

"Don't try to flip this on me, Veronica. When you found out that Tyrese was coming on this trip, did you not confront him about it? Did you not fuck him before you came over here? That's really why you had to take a shower!"

"Are you really serious? I don't want Tyrese! Remember, I had a choice and I chose you. If I was trying to sneak around with Tyrese, then I wouldn't have invited your ass to come with me. All ya'll can kiss my ass." I put on the clothes that I planned on wearing the next day and grabbed my keys to leave. Richard stood in front of me and pushed me away from the door. "Yes! There is the psycho that we all know and love! What, Richard? What!"

"Don't fucking walk out on me! What the fuck do you expect me to think?"

"Maybe that I'm not a whore, that I can be faithful to the man I love and that there is no comparison to you and Tyrese! Fuck you!"

"You better sit yo ass down. You not going nowhere."

"Try and stop me." It wasn't a good move on my part because, as soon as I came close to Richard, he punched me in my stomach so hard I couldn't help but fold up. At least, I didn't fall on the floor.

"Yeah, you ain't Miss Badass now, are you? Now sit yo fucking ass down!"

"What the fuck is your problem?" I took a breath and sat on the couch.

"Veronica, I will not be made a fool of! I will not be disrespected and there will be no confusion on who is the man in this relationship! Do you understand me?" I took a deep breath and stood up. I walked over to Richard and smacked the shit out of him. His lip was cut from the ring I had on.

"I will not be your punching bag! I have killed two out of the four men who put their hands on me, and you will be no exception to my rules. You don't run me and there is not enough love in the world to make me bow down to you."

I kicked Richard in the stomach and he was on the floor. We spent the whole night, into the early morning, fighting. Any other time, I could appreciate his violent acts of love, but I didn't have it in me to deal with this on that night. Even the hardest bitch wants something gentle in her life, if only for a moment. I thought this was my moment, but nobody seemed to be able to deliver it. I finally gave Richard the one-hitter quitter at around five that morning and left his place. This shouldn't have been a surprise to me, but there weren't a lot of people that I could depend on in this world, and I had to learn to deal with that. I drove myself to the airport and took that good flight out. When I finally stepped off my long flight, that warm Jamaica air hit my face something great. I took a cab to my hotel and called them to let them know I was on my way. I had the best suite in the best hotel in Jamaica and

I was right on the water. I couldn't wait to swim. I went straight to my room and had a shower in time to get my mind set right. I gave Steve, my personal valet while I was on vacation, fifty bucks to let him know what was up. If he took care of me I would take care of him. I went over to my king-size bed and made a call to the spa, so I could get a full-body rubdown. I was going to get rid of all the stress in my body and relax, come hell or high water. I grabbed my purse and headed down to the spa after changing. When this big, black Jamaica laid his hands on my back and got to rubbing, I couldn't even hold back my moans. I mean dude had me sounding like he was giving it to me, which, in a sense, he was, but it wasn't nothing sexual. He was just pleasing the hell out of me. Boy, what an hour-long feel-me-down can do to a girl!

Then I found a nice spot on the beach and laid out in the sun. After being in the sun for an hour I felt myself getting sleepy, so I went back up to my room. Unfortunately, when I stepped into the lobby all I heard was Pricey's loud ass cussing out the desk clerk because she wouldn't give Pricey my room number. I started to back out, slowly, so I wouldn't have to deal with the drama, but I bumped into something on my way out. Before I could turn around to see what it was, I felt hands on my shoulder pushing me to Pricey.

"Chill out! I found her," said the voice that I knew without looking to see who it was.

"Who said I wanted to be found?" I asked Trip, putting my hand on my forehead and closing my eyes. There went my good time.

"Roni, how you gon' leave without me? I know you mad, but damn, it's like that?" I looked at Pricey like she was crazy.

"You made your damn choice! Don't act new!"

"Why is it a problem, all of a sudden, if Trip and Tyrese hang with us? It's always been like that. We have a pretty good time together."

"That's not the fucking point and you know it!"

"Why are you being so damn difficult, Roni? Shit, we just trying to have a good time right now. Just shut the fuck up and go with the flow!"

"Who the hell you think you talking to, Pricey? I should slap the shit out of yo brain-dead ass!"

"Do it then, bitch! I'm older than you! You don't run me!" Just as Pricey was about to step up, Trip came out of nowhere and grabbed her. I didn't care.

I was still about to slap the shit out of her anyway. As my hand stretched into the air and was in the midst of coming down on Pricey's face, someone grabbed my hand.

"Enough of this bullshit! Veronica, calm your ass down!" It was Richard. "You and Pricey are making a spectacle of yourselves. Let's go. Everybody, we will meet down here at six o'clock so we can go to dinner. Right?" He said it with as much force as one man could without actually pushing your ass.

Pricey's mouth dropped open, along with everybody else's. Shit, I wasn't no fool. I knew Richard was ready to make himself felt. I pulled my arm free and walked to the elevator. Richard followed me all the way to my room and closed the door behind him.

"I'm sorry, Veronica."

"That's nice." I wasn't in the mood for this. I took a seat by the window facing the beach. Richard sat down next to me.

"No, I am *really* sorry." He took my hand into his and pulled my face gently in his direction.

"I know you didn't need my bullshit on top of everything that you're dealing with. I know that this vacation of yours is way overdue and what you need right now is for me to take care of you. I was wrong and out of line. It won't happen again." I looked up at Richard and burst into tears.

"I want my sister!" I ran out the room to the elevator and got on. The elevator stopped at the next level and the doors flew open. Pricey was standing right there with her eyes red from crying. I ran out of the elevator and into her arms and we collapsed onto the floor.

"I'm so sorry I was being a asshole! I love you! Please forgive me!"

"No, Pricey. I'm sorry, I know you have a life with Trip and he yo man, I need to respect that. I love you."

"Naw, rule number one is to never put no nigga over yo girl. I fucked up."

"Trip not no regular nigga. I should consider him when we make plans."

"Fuck that nigga. We should be here having a good time, chilling, bonding and shit. Niggas fuck up everything."

"That they do." We finally dried our eyes and burst into laughter.

"I'll meet you in the lobby," Pricey said with a grin

"Cool."

We both ran back to our rooms to get our purses and meet in the lobby. We had a lot of shopping to do. We took a cab to the inner-city and found a mall. In one day, we spent ten-thousand dollars each and then we spent another five-thousand on market jewelry. We flirted with the local men and threw money away like it was nothing. I missed doing this, I missed it just being me and Pricey. When we were together things were better, I didn't have to worry about anything. We sent our bags back to the hotel and decided to go snorkeling to look at the pretty fishes and shit. The water felt so good and it looked so clean. We lay out on the beach and Pricey told me she was going in to get ready for dinner. I told her I would be in, in a minute. I closed my eyes and felt the hot sunrays tan my skin, making me darker then I already was.

"Damn, how did that white boy get so lucky?" I heard Tyrese ask.

"Why did you even come? Nothing better to do?" I asked with my eyes still closed. I really didn't want to address him.

"Being the loyal nigga that Trip is, he invited me and I accepted 'cause I felt like getting away."

"So you saying you didn't know that I would be here?"

"No, sweetheart, that was an extra bonus." Tyrese sat next to me and put his hand in between my legs.

"Don't you fucking touch me!" I pushed his hand away and started to get up so I could go back to my room.

"Don't fucking try to walk away from me." Tyrese pulled me down next to him, twisting my wrist.

"I see that you have this little thing going with the white boy, but don't forget who you belong to, alright?"

"I belong to myself. Now please stop embarrassing yourself." I pulled away from him and finally stood up to walk away. Tyrese got up with me and pulled me into a bear-hug embrace.

"You don't really love Richard. This is just another game you're playing, so why don't we cut the bullshit and go up to my room?"

"Can you please get your fucking hands off me? Damn!"

"I believe Veronica has made a request." I looked over at Richard, who had appeared out of nowhere and smiled.

"Man, fuck you! We handling business over here. I'll give her back when I'm done."

I closed my eyes again 'cause I knew that what Richard was about to do was something I didn't need to see. I felt a force brush past my head and Tyrese let go of the grip he had on me. The fight had begun. Richard gave it to Tyrese, to my surprise, but it didn't take long for Tyrese to recover. When he punched Richard in the mouth and I saw that gush of blood fall from Richard's face I lost it. I saw red and just lost my head. I pulled my blade from my bikini top and ran at Tyrese. I would kill him where he stood and be willing to deal with the aftermath when I had to. Tyrese saw me coming and, instead of punching Richard, he met my face with the back of his hand. I fell down. I won't lie—I fell down *hard*, but I was back up before I could fully recover, which caused me to fall once more. Richard saw that and took the opportunity to punch Tyrese in the stomach and face. They fought like that for ten more minutes until Trip came, trying to break them up, with Pricey holding me back and screaming in my ear about my face. Needless to say, we never made it to dinner and I spent the rest of the night icing Richard down. I was still pretty mad at him because he had planned on going out that night before I left and I knew he was going to cheat on me with somebody. Not to mention the beatdown he handed my ass.

No, I hadn't forgotten a thing. I was just proud of my man for trying to hold his shit down. I put ice on my very swollen right cheek and hoped it didn't bruise the next day. I slept in late the next afternoon. This wasn't much of a vacation and the stress was way worse than back in Chicago. I should've just gone back home, locked myself in my apartment and forgot that I had the life I had. I finally rolled out of bed at two in the afternoon and went straight to the bathroom. I ran me a bath and sat in it. If I could find someone selling peace of mind I would've bought their ass out. I washed up and got out of the tub when, just my luck, Richard walked into the room while I was putting on a white bikini with red strings.

"Good, you're up. What we doing today?"

"Nothing."

"Why not? Don't you want to go out with me?"

"No."

"Veronica, I said I was sorry. What more do you want?"

"I want you to leave me alone, give me some damn space."

"Fine." Richard walked back over to the door in a rush and I beat him there.

"Where you going? Gon' run to another bitch who gon' lick yo wounds and make you feel better about us? Every time we have a problem you gon' go out and be with some bitch!"

I looked at Richard with tears in my eyes. I was so in love with this man that I knew in my heart that if he cheated on me, I had already forgiven him. I let my head fall away from our eye contact and walked away from him. Richard didn't let me get far before he pulled me close from behind and held me tight. I tried to pull away, but I couldn't move.

"I'm sorry. I am really sorry. I was just so mad." I twisted to face him and my eyes widened with fear. Richard couldn't even look me in the face, so he placed his head on my shoulder.

"*Noooooo!* No! Get the fuck off me! Let me go!" My knees felt weak and I was limp in Richard's arms.

"How could you fucking do this to me? How could you?" I started to ball my eyes out and every part of my body hurt.

"Veronica, I am so sorry. Baby, I love you. I just fucked up. Please forgive me. Please.

Richard held me tighter as we slowly dropped to the floor. My eyes were burning, my throat was hurting and my heart was breaking. He just kept saying "sorry" over and over again. The more he said it, the worse I felt; this was so real. The man that I had given my heart to had crushed it. What Richard and I had was serious. We were going at a very fast pace, but it was serious. I shook my head and after a half hour I shed my last tear. I was all cried out for right now. I took a deep breath and calmed down.

"Richard, let me go."

"If I let you go, I'll lose you."

"You have already lost me. Now let me go."

"Veronica, don't do this."

"Don't do what? You did this! You fucked up! Let me go!" I kicked Richard in his balls and stood up. I put on my sunglasses and walked out, found Pricey by the pool downstairs and sat in a chair next to her. I undid the back of my top and lay down to tan.

"You alright?"

"Yeah. Where's Trip?"

"Out getting some of that Jamaican weed so we can smoke that shit later. He left a while ago, so he should be back in a minute."

"Tyrese still here?"

"Yep, anything to piss off you and Richard. You know ya'll getting together was the last thing Tyrese wanted. I say push the knife in deep and twist that shit."

"I hear that."

"Richard alright?"

"He will leave." Speak of the devil, there came Richard, looking pissed as hell. I hurried up and tied my top back on.

"What the fuck is your problem?" Richard grabbed one of my arms and pulled me up to him. I pulled away from him and smacked the shit out of him. Pricey sat up so she could watch. Richard grabbed both my wrists and pulled me close.

"I told your ass I was sorry. What the fuck else do you want me to do? I can't change the fucking past. Get over the shit!"

"Oh, I'm over it. Just remember: A eye for a eye, and what you don't know will hurt you."

"Are you fucking threatening me?" Pricey stood up, ready to ride on his ass, so he calmed down. "Can we go talk about this back in the room?"

"No, I'm spending time with my sister. Please go away."

"Wow, trouble in paradise?" Tyrese asked, approaching us with Trip behind him. Trip grabbed Tyrese and moved in front of him. Now, me and Trip were in the middle of Tyrese and Richard.

"We don't need a re-enactment of yesterday. Can ya'll be grown men about this?"

"I can handle myself, Trip. Yesterday is forgotten. I just wanted to apologize to you, Veronica." I looked over at Tyrese then at Richard; his worst fear was me and Tyrese making a fool of him. I walked away from Richard and right into Tyrese's arms.

"Apologize for what?" Me and Tyrese were one and the same, we had the same goals, we thought in the same way and we were both as cold as ice.

"For hitting you yesterday. I knew you were coming for blood and I just reacted. I'm sorry, I would never want to hurt this pretty face." Tyrese touched my cheek gently and Richard tried to step up, but Trip held him back.

"Richard, chill. She grown. Be easy." Richard took a step back and nodded his head. I smiled and looked back at Tyrese. If he wasn't just waiting to stab me in the back, I would give in to him.

"Thank you for your apology. That means a lot." I gave Tyrese a hug and, just when he was about to go in for the kill, Richard pushed past Trip and ripped me from Tyrese's hand.

"Alright, Veronica, I didn't cheat on you! I wanted to, but I didn't. I just said that 'cause I thought you had already been with Tyrese. I am so sick of you and him. I can't be in a relationship with some immature bitch." Tyrese laughed, happy that he could destroy something else.

"You stupid bitch!" I pulled back my arm and with all my might and punched Richard so hard in his left eye that he flew into the pool.

"Pricey, come on. Let's get something to eat. Tyrese, just because shit is fucked up between me and Richard don't mean you getting in between these legs."

"We shall see."

Pricey gathered her things and we went into the hotel so we could have room service delivered to her room. I knew she was about to run off at the mouth about my situation. Not only did I not want to talk about it, but I didn't know what to say. I didn't know how I would handle this or if this changed anything between me and Richard. When Pricey opened her mouth I gave her that look and she just cut on the TV. We pigged out on food and talked about how we were already over Jamaica. She told me that Trip had planned to go home when we wanted to go to China, and he was taking Tyrese with him. I was happy to hear that. Richard could pack his shit now, with the way I was feeling. Trip came back to the room at twelve, just enough time for me and Pricey to act a fool together. I didn't want to go back to my room, but I knew if I didn't, I would get into even more trouble than I was already in and I didn't think that my relationship could handle any more bullshit. Tyrese passed my elevator just as the doors closed. He had a Jamaican bitch in his arms and a smile on his face. Niggas ain't shit.

When I reached my room a note was on the door. "If you want me to leave, send me off. I'm in the lobby waiting." What was he up to now? I went downstairs with a towel wrapped around my body 'cause I was still rocking the bikini. I found Richard in the lobby, just like he wrote. He was in some shorts and a wifebeater. This fool wasn't going nowhere. I laughed when he turned around and he had on sunglasses.

"Damn, it look like somebody fucked you up."

"Yeah. Ha, ha."

"Don't look like you going nowhere to me."

"I am. I just wanted to show you something first. Hear me out."

"You said all I had to do was come down here to send yo ass off. You asking for too much now."

"Please, Veronica." I rolled my eyes and threw up my hands.

"This better be good." Richard smiled and pulled me down a hallway. We ended up in the indoor pool room and Richard had sat up some champagne with strawberries.

"This is nice but it's not good enough."

"This not for you, this is for me. I wanted to pay you back for earlier today." I turned around to face Richard and he pushed me in the pool. I swam back to the top and I could see Richard jumping in. As I was trying to get out he pulled me back into the water.

"Where you going? You said you would hear me out, so listen."

"You are so the bullshit."

"I fucked up huge. I know this. But I was thinking too much. This love shit is really overwhelming for me. I don't know how to make moves with you. All this weak love shit is making me soft. Any other time, if I had a hint that one of my girls was cheating on me, I would just kill them, but with you . . . even if I could kill you I wouldn't take it that far. I fucking love you and I don't want to hurt you. You my angel. I just didn't know what else to do, so I said I did what you did. I wanted you to feel what I felt. Tyrese is a sneaky motherfucker and I know he don't have no respect for what we have. So when I pissed you off I thought you just gave in to him."

"Richard, if we gon' be together you're going to have to trust me. It's just you and me in this relationship, fuck everybody else. What we had was good when we were sneaking around. Maybe we should go back to that."

"Naw, I don't want to fuck no dumbass up over no misunderstanding. I want everyone to know that I love you and we together. We just need to take this shit one day at a time."

"I feel you. You got me emotional. I'm starting to act like a girl. Shit is stressful." Richard kissed me and pushed me up against the side of the pool. He started to kiss my neck and I fought not to give in. I moved away from him and got out the pool. "You made me cry! I can't let that shit slide!"

Richard got out of the pool and followed me over to the Jacuzzi where the champagne was. I downed a glass and got into the Jacuzzi. Richard got in with me, but sat on the other side.

"Veronica, if I hadn't made you cry, I don't think you would have accepted how you felt about me. Besides, all the people that you loved the most in your life have made you shed many a tear."

"Not Pricey."

"Bullshit! You were just crying about her before we came to Jamaica and when we first got here."

"Oh. Well, not my mom."

"You didn't cry when she killed herself or tried to attempt suicide?"

"I don't remember." I was starting to see his point.

"The only way people can hurt you is if you really care about them and, as sick as it was, I needed to see those tears to know that you was feeling the same as me."

"Shit, when am I going to see your damn tears?"

"I don't know."

"I should punch your ass in the other eye." Richard came over to my side and started to rub my back.

"Why you want to fuck up my pretty face?"

"And yo ass called me a bitch!"

"Don't get mad at that now, you already got me back for that. Hence the fucked-up eye."

"I can do what I want. So far in this relationship I haven't fucked up, not once." Richard poured me another glass of champagne and handed it to me.

"What do I have to do to get back on your good side? I don't want us to be on bad terms anymore. I want to enjoy being with the woman I love, 'cause you're going to be gone with Pricey over in China and I have to wait to I see you again in Paris."

"You're going to feed me some strawberries, promise me that you won't act a fool again until we get back to Chicago and fuck the shit out of me in this Jacuzzi."

"That, I can do. Veronica: I promise I won't act a fool until we get back to Chicago."

Richard fed me a strawberry and started to kiss my neck. I slipped off my bottoms while he stood up. Damn! Them abs! I kissed his chest and pulled down his trunks. I debated on giving him head, but I figured that would be best for Paris. Richard took me in his arms and we kissed for what seemed like forever. His lips were like heaven and his touch was so soft. I felt like I was worth something when he made love to me. We had a quickie in the Jacuzzi. The hot water mixed with sex had me overheated. We spent the whole night making love; Richard whispering how sorry he was to me and how much he loved me. I believed him because I wanted to. I could love him enough for the both of us. I didn't think about it too much. When it's good, you don't question that shit.

15

The next afternoon, Richard woke me up with a slap to the ass.

"Get up, you're going to sleep your vacation away. I want to have lunch with you." I rolled over on my back and covered my very exposed breasts.

"You are so sexy." Richard stood above me and bent over to kiss me on the forehead.

"What is that? I can't have no kiss, Richard?"

"No, stank breath. You can't have nothing from me until you wash yo ass." I looked at him and he had already gotten dressed. I sat up in bed and scratched my head.

"I feel so drained. We can't have lunch in the room?"

"No, because then you will never get out of bed. Come on, Veronica. I'm ready to start this day. I have a surprise for you."

"What is it?" Richard gave me that look that said he wasn't going to tell me anything, so I got in the shower and got dressed like he wanted. I found Richard downstairs in the lobby waiting on me.

"She finally graces me with her pretty face. Come here." I walked over to Richard and he kissed me. I slipped my hand into his and placed my head on his chest.

"Where are we eating?"

"Your choice. Do you feel like going into town?"

"I was thinking maybe we could . . ."

"Roni! Yeah, I knew that was ya'll. Only black and white couple here." Pricey and Trip shared a laugh. "I'm just joking. Were ya'll about to get something to eat? Because me and Trip was about to go sit down to grab a bite."

"And we would love for ya'll to join us, 'cause we just love ya'll so much and all that other soft shit that was about to pop out Pricey mouth," Trip said. I let a laugh slip out while he pulled Pricey away to the hotel restaurant.

"You want to eat with them?" Richard asked me.

"Might as well." He gave me a gentle hug and we followed behind Trip. I kept a smile on my face when we had to seat down at a big table with Tyrese and whoever he was entertaining the night before.

"Good afternoon, Veronica," he said. Richard pulled out my chair and I sat down. I looked at Richard and he gave me a nod.

"Good afternoon, Tyrese."

"Wow, it only took you one whole night to teach her a new trick, Richard. Good job."

"Tyrese, shut up. It is too nice of a day for you to open up your ugly mouth." Pricey was the only one still standing up.

"Pricey, what are you waiting on?" I asked.

"I'm waiting for Trip to get off his ass and pull out my chair, I am a lady, nigga." Trip rolled his eyes and opened up his menu.

"You can keep waiting on that shit. You spoiled as it is. The baby doesn't get anything else. Now sit yo ass down so we can eat." Pricey turned her back to Trip and remained standing. I stood up and pulled out her chair.

"Thank you, Veronica."

"Only the best for the queen. Besides, this is your week isn't it?" She looked at me and grabbed my hand.

"Sorry, niggas just get so comfortable after a while, but that is okay. I have something that will keep his ass on his toes. All these Jamaican men around here, I know somebody need a green card or something." Me and Pricey shared a laugh as we looked over at Tyrese's date, who he still had not introduced.

"Pricey, I would advise you to watch your mouth," Trip said.

"Whatever. So Veronica, did you have a good night?"

"Yeah, it was cool." I smiled and Richard kissed my hand.

"Are we going to order some food or what?" Tyrese asked out of nowhere. I had forgotten he was even at the table. I looked over at Richard and he was looking at me.

"So what are we doing today?" I asked.

"I made some calls and we're going on a hot air balloon ride." I kissed Richard on the lips.

"That is really sweet, I can't wait to do that."

Everybody at the tabled looked at me like I was crazy. What could I say? I was infatuated with this man. We were able to get through a whole meal without anyone saying anything else that was out of the way. I kissed Pricey on the cheek goodbye and told her to behave. I could feel Tyrese's eyes on me and Richard as we walked away. The balloon ride was amazing. I mean being that high in the air looking down on everything was breath-taking. At first I wouldn't let Richard go because I thought that I would fall off, but as I looked down on the sand, water and trees, he couldn't keep me away from the edge. Richard held me tightly from behind and we watched the sun set. I was so ready to have sex with him on that damn balloon, but the African man who was handling the ride was already creeping me out. Just before it got dark we landed back on the ground and headed back to the hotel.

"Did you see that man looking all crazy at us when we were in the air?"

"He wasn't looking at me, Veronica, he was looking at you. Never seen such a fine woman."

"Whatever. The way he was looking at me was freaking me out."

"Why? You know I have you. No harm coming yo way with me around." I kissed his cheek and we sat quietly for the rest of the cab ride to the hotel. When we got out I was heading up to my room, but Richard grabbed me and pulled me back outside.

"What's going on? I'm sleepy. Why we out here?"

"The hotel's having a picnic outside tonight. Come on."

"I'm really not up for that tonight."

"If we go to the room, you not going to sleep anyway." Richard gave me a smile and pulled me toward the picnic. To my surprise, they were honoring me.

"Another birthday party for my doll face." Everyone cheered as we approached. I gave Richard a hug and held onto him for a while.

"You know you didn't have to do this. I just want to spend time with you, nothing big like this."

"It's nothing. I just want to enjoy you tonight, like it should have been for your birthday at Dorian's house. So take off these shoes so we can dance in the sand, and I will whisper freaky shit in your ear all night." Richard got on his knees and took off my shoes. Once my shoes were off I bent over and kissed him.

"You want to get something to eat?"

"Naw, I'm fine. Just dance with me white boy."

"Alright, black girl. Come here."

I closed my eyes as Richard held me. We were barely moving, at first, but it didn't take me long to open up and start moving around. The drums had my body acting a fool. I vibrated all over Richard and got damn near naked. All of a sudden, I was overheated and sex was the only thing I had on my mind. I think that's just the effect Richard had over me. There was nothing sexier than a man who could dance and Richard was keeping up with me. Just as we were getting into the Jamaican grind, looking like we were trying to make a child on the dance floor, here came the peanut gallery.

"Shake yo ass, Roni! Put it on him, girl!" I rolled my eyes and slowed my pace.

"Don't give them your attention, enjoy tonight," Richard said.

"I'm trying. You know you're the sexiest man here tonight?"

"Yeah, until I showed up." I wanted to turn my head 'cause I knew it was Tyrese. But Richard put his hands to my face and held our eye contact steady.

"No, baby, it's just you and me tonight." I couldn't help but let out a laugh. Richard was being so cute.

"Since we have an audience let's give them a show." Richard gave me an evil grin.

"You think you can hang with me?"

"Show me something, white boy."

Richard backed up off me and took off his shirt. The boy had the most perfect upper body. I kept swaying to the music and licked my lips. Richard undid his belt and started walking toward me.

"What you doing? You not trying to have sex right here on the beach?"

"Why not, Veronica? You told me you could hang."

"Boy, beat it. Get back away from me."

I started running away from Richard and he was right on my tail.

"Oh, mommy! I love the chase! Come here!" I couldn't help but scream and laugh.

"Richard, stop playing!"

"Girl, give me that pussy!" I was switching it up on Richard's ass. I was too quick for him. But he finally caught me and I was still trying to fight him off.

"No, Richard, you can't have my goodies! Leave me alone!" Richard pulled me to the ground and sat on top of me, tickling me until tears streamed from my face from laughing so hard.

"Okay, okay! I won't run no more."

"I know, 'cause you don't have nowhere to go. I should spank yo ass for making me run after you." Richard gave me a kiss on the forehead.

"You can do that later on tonight. Come here, I want to tell you something." Richard looked down at me to see if I was playing or not.

"Veronica, if you bite me it's not gon' be nothing good for you." I gave him a smile.

"I'm not. Just come here." Richard placed his ear to my lips and I bit the shit out of his neck.

"Damn, Veronica!"

"What can I say? I'm a liar."

"That's it. Yo ass is going in the water." I held onto Richard.

"No! This is a five-thousand-dollar outfit!" Richard threw me over his shoulder like I hadn't said a word.

"Shoulda thought about that!" He threw me into the warm water and, as I went under, I pulled his feet from under him. We resurfaced together and swam to each other. As we stood there together with the water up to our necks, I started to feel on his package.

"This has been a great day, Richard."

"As long as you're happy, doll face. I love you."

"I love you, too." We kissed in the water for a while, then headed back to the party.

"Are you hungry now?"

"Yeah, a little bit. You want me to make you a plate?"

"I'll fix me something to eat after I get you settled." Richard helped me over to a lounge chair next to Pricey, and kissed my hand. I smiled and finally gave Pricey my attention for the first time since she arrived. She handed me a towel.

"Thank you, girl. Looks like yo ass is blowed out of this world."

"Yeah, man. Me and Trip took a boat out and got fucked up something nice. Then, to top that shit off, we was butt-ass naked on that bitch, making waves and shit. I mean he had me in a handstand on a damn boat. Telling you the nigga is blessed."

"Long as you having a nice time."

"Shit, Roni, me? You seem to be having a alright time yo'self. Richard gon' tear that shit up tonight."

"Girl, he always do."

"Girl, did you hear Tyrese ass? Nigga need to get a hobby or something."

"Ain't nobody thinking about Tyrese, Pricey. He so played."

"Speak of the devil, here he come." Tyrese knelt down next to me, all smiling in my face.

"Yes. Is there something I can help you with?"

"Can you explain to me, Veronica, why you would want to waste time with some white boy when you could be having me cater to that pussy all night long?" Richard sat down in front of me and handed me my plate.

"Because, Tyrese: Richard fills me up to the rim with his huge dick. And what else can I say? I'm addicted." Richard kissed my lips and got back up to fix himself a plate.

"There you go, Roni! Damn, Tyrese, you got hoed! Give it up, nigga. Ain't nobody pressed."

"You might have everybody else fooled, Veronica, but I can see through all that." Tyrese moved in closer and his lips rested on my ear.

"When Richard fucks up and you see him for the bitch he is, I'll be there for you to make more mistakes with. Don't matter who you lay down with, yo pussy is molded to fit my dick." Tyrese stood up and walked away. No lie—that shit got me wet as hell.

"Tyrese so hurt you ain't thinking about his ass. Lord knows I never thought the day would come, but boy, am I happy." Richard came back and we ate together. Pricey left shortly after that and we got on the dance floor one more time.

"I can't wait to get you out those wet clothes, Veronica."

"Let's go. I want you right now."

Richard took his hand in mine and we headed upstairs. Tyrese caught my eye as we went inside. I licked my lips. Tyrese was pure evil, but something about him drove me mad, set my body on fire. But why settle for imitation crab meat when you can have lobster? As soon as the elevator doors closed, I was in Richard's arms, legs wrapped around him and dress pulled up.

"Baby, I can't wait. I need your dick now."

"Veronica, damn." Richard let his pants slip to the floor.

"Damn, fuck. Put it in, Richard."

"Oh shit, you feel so good."

"Pound this pussy, daddy." I grabbed a fist full of Richard's hair and pulled his head to the side. I was going to town on his neck and he had me jumping up and down on his dick. "Oh shit, baby! Fuck me harder!" The elevator doors flew open and this old couple almost had a heart attack. I burst into laughter as Richard frantically hit the "close" door button.

"I thought we was still putting on a show," I said.

"Oh, you think that shit is funny. Well let everybody hear you moan for daddy." Richard started hitting my spot and I got louder.

"Yes! Right there! Fuck, you feel so good. Richard!" Next time the elevator door opened we were on our room's floor and we were up against the door fucking like crazy.

"Veronica, the key is in my pocket and my pants are on the floor." I started to grind on Richard's dick.

"Baby, please don't stop. It feels too good."

"Veronica, it will only take a second. Come on, baby, help me out."

"Nooo, don't pull out. I have a key in my bra. Here." I tried to hand the key to Richard, but he just started to fuck me harder.

"Why don't you pull out the left titty for me, and open the door." I did as my man said and, as soon as his tongue hit my nipple, I came.

"God! Damn!" Richard tossed my ass on that bed and ripped my dress off me.

"Richard . . ."

"Shut up, I don't want to hear it. Open your legs."

"The door is still open." Richard stepped out of his pants and put a crazy look on his face.

"Veronica, open your legs!" As soon as I did what Richard said, he was back inside me going jackrabbit on my ass.

"Whose is this? Who's pussy is this!"

"Yours!"

"You better say my name!" Richard rolled me over on top of him and slapped my ass.

"Richard! Richard!" I started riding his ass as we held hands and I threw my head back so I could scream out his name again in sweet ecstasy.

"*Richard!*"

"Lay on your stomach for me, baby." I wasn't about to question shit. Now he was digging into me. I could feel his pelvic bone pushing up against my ass. As Richard dug in and out, our arms tangled up in each other's and his lips kissed the back of my neck as far down my back as he could.

"Oh God! Oh God!"

"Damn, Veronica, you feel so good. I love you, baby."

"I love you, too." Richard wrapped his arms around my stomach and lifted me off the bed and into his arms. Now we were on the edge of the bed and I was on top of him, my back facing him as I rode my man once more.

"Jump on this dick, ma! Work that shit!" Richard reached around and started squeezing my nipples. Dude was really blowing my mind. I was drenched in sweat and so was he.

"I'm about to come again!" I exploded on top of Richard and slowed down, placing the back of my head on his shoulder.

"It's not over, baby."

He carried me to the bathroom and we went into the shower. Richard stood behind me as he turned on the water. As he adjusted the temp, I ran my hands over my body. I turned to face Richard and pushed him up against the wall. "You damn right it ain't over." I dropped to my knees and, before he could object, my lips were wrapped around the head of his dick. I put my right hand on his shaft and went around the head of it with my tongue, sucking and licking his head. I jacked him off as I did this, then I started to take his whole dick in my mouth, sucking him off. Just as he was about to bust his nut, I relaxed my jaw and deep-throated him. At the last minute, Richard pulled out of my mouth and nutted on the shower floor.

"Shit, Veronica, you trying to kill me."

"Maybe."

I pushed Richard back up against the wall and stood up. I went over to the opposite wall, right underneath the shower head, placed both my hands on the wall and stood to the side.

"Girl, what are you doing?"

"Just wait."

I lifted one of my legs as far in the air as I could and started to maneuver toward Richard. I got about a couple of inches away from him and told him to put it in. As he did that, I moved back, completely, fucking the shit out of Richard while doing the splits. I had never done this position before, but I knew it would become a favorite real quick. We did it like that for a while, then I dropped my leg, allowing Richard to hit it from the back while I touched my toes. He pounded into my pussy for what seemed like forever and then, finally, I felt a burst of hot nut all over my ass. We washed each other up and went to bed. I was so drained the next night, I had slept the whole day away and I wasn't mad about it. I could feel Richard looking at me, but my eyes were still heavy.

"What is it?"

"Nothing." Richard kissed my nose and moved my hair out of my face. "You were wonderful last night, Veronica."

"You weren't too bad yourself, either. Last night was perfect."

"I know. You hungry?"

"Not really. You horny?"

"You know I am." Richard came closer to me and rubbed his dick up against my thigh.

"Come over here and make love to me, then."

"Are you serious, Veronica?" I reached out my arms to him and he got on top of me. I parted my legs and, as we kissed, he moved inside of me, slowly.

"You so tight, baby."

"You're so big." Richard started to stroke me and I moaned in his ear

"Richard, I love you."

"I love you, too, doll face. I love you, too."

We made love until the sun came up and I fell back to sleep on Richard's chest as he held me tightly in his arms. I was finally on vacation. I woke up a couple of hours later and slipped out of bed so I could get something to eat. I found Pricey at a table in the restaurant and joined her. She had on some big-ass sunglasses.

"What the hell is up with the glasses?" She pulled them down so I could see her eyes.

"Whatever kind of Jamaican weed Trip got us still have me blowed. This nigga been out for almost two days and my eyes still bloodshot red."

"That's what ya'll get." I let out a laugh

"So you and Richard the talk of the hotel. Fucking all night and day, on the elevator . . ."

"And it was great, I might add."

"Oh I heard. Everybody in the hotel heard ya'll."

"So when is Trip thinking about leaving?"

"He said this is his last week. He say his body not programmed to sit around for too long."

"I hear that. I'm kinda over the whole vacation thing myself, but I can't wait to go shopping." Pricey gave me five and we laughed.

"Girl, tell the truth! We gon' shut China down."

"Damn right, Pricey." We ate together and then we went over to the spa to get our nails and feet done. Pricey went back to her room and I went and sat on the beach. The water was so pretty and the sun felt so good on my skin.

"Enjoying yourself?" I looked up—and started to gather my things so I could leave.

"Don't leave, Veronica, I just want to talk to you." I stood up, but Tyrese pulled me right back down, making me fall flat on my ass. "I said all I want to do is talk to yo simple ass. Damn! Chill. Richard put fear in yo heart like that now?" I laughed and kept looking forward. "So you not gon' talk to me."

"I'll talk when I have something to say. Being near you is the best you're going to get, for now."

"Damn, like that? How did I go from being number one to not even being on the list? It's cool, Veronica, I still have love for you."

"Nigga, you have no fucking idea what the hell love is, let alone how to have it for somebody else. Don't kid yo'self."

"So you really think Richard the one? You think he gon' do right by you? I mean he wasn't doing right by Karen, talking to you all close. Don't you ever think about who's going to replace you when Richard get bored with you?"

"You are so sad. I'm not worried about a thing. Clearly, whoever I fuck with always ends up coming back."

"You have a point, there. I mean a white boy. I never saw that for you. I mean not on no serious tip. Just keep this in mind, Veronica: People like us don't end up happily ever after. All the things we love end up dead."

"Thanks. I'll keep that in mind. I'll try loving you a little bit harder now." Tyrese looked at me and saw he wasn't getting anywhere, so he got up to leave. I smiled and lay back for a while. Richard came outside and lay down with me.

"You enjoying yourself, doll face?"

"You know I am." I lay on his chest and took in his smell. He had just gotten out of the shower. Richard kissed my lips, but I felt something was wrong.

"What's the problem?" I said, sitting up so I could look at his face.

"I have to leave tonight, doll face. Dorian wants me to come back a little early." My body tensed up. Did Dorian know about us?

"You think it's something bad?"

"I don't think so, but you can never tell with Dorian." I stood up and put my hand on my head.

"Naw, that shit not going down. I'm coming back home with you."

"Veronica, I'm sure it's nothing. I want you to finish your vacation and I'll meet you in Paris." I rolled my eyes.

"What if you don't make it to Paris? You don't know what you about to run into when you go back to Chicago." I put my hands over my face and fought the urge to cry. Richard stood up and took me into his arms.

"Don't do that, Veronica. Like I said, I don't know what will happen, but whatever it is, I don't want you to be there. I don't want you or me to do anything stupid because of one another."

"I'm not ready to let you go."

"I feel the same way, but you know there is not much we can do right now."

We stood on the beach holding each other. We weren't in a position where we could take out Dorian. We didn't even have a plan for all that. Everybody was eating too good with Dorian, and we couldn't offer each other the same lifestyle if he was gone. We had nobody to back us and, knowing Dorian, he would be expecting that. Too many things were stacked against us and if we tried to fight this it would only end in death for both of us. I pulled away from Richard and went inside to start packing. Richard came up to the room just as I got done.

"Veronica, what are you doing? I don't want you to come and I don't want to fight about this. Can you just stay here?"

"No, I can't. I can't just sit here and I don't know what is going on. I have to go. I'm going to have to face the music, just like you, sooner or later. If we go to Dorian together and explain ourselves, he might have respect for that."

“Veronica, you can’t go.” I rolled my eyes and started to put on some jeans. “I mean that shit!”

“You said you didn’t want to fight, so don’t. I’m going and that’s that.”

“If you go and something happens to you, I’ll . . .” I walked over to Richard and put my hand over his mouth.

“Don’t say it, I know. Don’t worry about me.” Richard kissed me and let me walk out the room.

We both wanted to have sex, in case this was the last time we saw each other, but we knew Dorian had somebody watching us. I got on the elevator and it stopped on Tyrese’s floor. Tyrese got on the elevator with a smile.

“Helping Richard with his bags?”

“Naw, these are my bags.” Tyrese’s eyes almost popped out of their sockets and he placed his hands on my shoulders.

“Veronica, on some serious shit—you cannot go back home yet. Dorian is pissed.”

“All the more reason to go home; don’t want to miss out on all the fun.”

“Are you ready to die for Richard’s bitch ass? ’Cause that’s what’s going to happen if you go back. Do you want to see this nigga die?”

“How did you make it this far in the game, bitch-ass nigga?” Tyrese tightened up his grip on my shoulders and tightened his jaw, trying not to hit me.

“I know my place. You need to learn yours, Veronica, or you not gon’ see next year. Richard not even gon’ see tomorrow.” I pushed Tyrese off me and stepped off the elevator. Pricey was downstairs with Trip, saying goodbye.

“Veronica, are those Richard’s bags?”

“No.” Pricey looked at Trip then shook her head.

“I’ll be back.” Trip grabbed her arm.

“Pricey, you not going.”

“I said I wouldn’t go if Veronica stayed. Let me go.”

"No, I don't need you to be in harm's way, just chill here. Veronica is not going." Pricey looked at me and I looked at her.

"Let me go, Trip." Trip looked at Pricey and let her go. When she left, Trip came over to me.

"What are you doing? Why you just won't keep yo ass here? Dorian is not happy right now. The last thing you should be trying to do is prove a point to him. He will kill all of us and not think a thing about it. Do you want to die?"

"Death is promised," I said. Trip threw his hands up in the air and got closer to me.

"Do you want *Pricey* to die? Are you ready for that shit? You don't know what the hell Dorian is going to do! You don't know shit! Why don't you try thinking, for a change?" Trip walked outside, frustrated, and Tyrese walked up again.

"Are you ready to lose everything over Richard? Lose Pricey, lose all this shit you have worked for? We both know Dorian not gon' kill you, but, Veronica, there are a lot worse things than death, and Dorian know all of 'em." Pricey and Richard came into the lobby together. I put my head down.

My sister or Richard?

There was nothing to think about. If a choice had to be made, I wouldn't think twice.

16

"Ya'll ready to go?" I walked outside and the cabs were there. I got in the first one with Pricey, and the guys got in the second one. I knew Tyrese and Trip was getting in Richard's ass.

"Pricey, I fucked up. I didn't think. I don't want to lose Richard, but I don't want to upset Dorian."

"Bitch, cool out. We don't even know where Dorian head at yet. Chill the hell out. We will just have to play that shit by ear. The worst that can happen is you get slapped around and Richard die." I looked at Pricey like she was crazy. "I'm just saying we been through worse. Show no fear. You a bad bitch! Shit, whatever happens, we gon' survive. Don't sweat the little shit." She paused for a minute, then: "All I'm saying is, do this mean we can't go to China no more? 'Cause I had my heart set on that shit." I looked at Pricey and fell out laughing. She gave me a hug and we kept it moving.

"You know Richard back there catching hell."

"He can handle it. He kicked Tyrese ass."

Richard told me about the conversation later on. It was just like I had imagined it would be:

"If anything happens to Veronica or Pricey, I will kill you if Dorian don't," Trip said.

"Trip, chill. You know Dorian is going to kill this fool," Tyrese added. Richard sat in the front of the van that was turned into a cab with Tyrese and Trip in the back seat.

"Death is promised to all. Ya'll don't faze me."

"You know, you and Veronica one in the same. She says the same thing, but the only person on yo side is you. When it all falls down, Veronica is going to pick Pricey over you and you're going to die."

"So be it, it was still worth it. Every stroke, every moan. Tyrese, you know. Not as well as me, but you know. Things like that will keep me comforted."

"You a stupid bitch! Learn your place and you'll make it far in this game, Richard."

"Tyrese, what is the point of being in the game when you not even your own man? Yeah, you been in the game for a while, but past all that other shit, the money and the status, you just Dorian's number one bitch. That's all the streets know you as." Tyrese moved closer to Richard.

"You a funny guy."

"I aim to please."

"Let me make a few things clear. When Dorian tells me to take you out, I won't hesitate. And when you fuck up and Veronica come running back to me, telling me to fuck her, I won't hesitate. You haven't seen the truth of the game yet, but you will. Keep that in mind when Dorian is slapping Veronica around for your bullshit."

Richard closed his eyes while Tyrese sat back in his seat. He tried to get his mind together for what was to come.

When we made it aboard the plane I went to sleep. I didn't want to think about what was going to happen in Chicago. But I had a dream about the day I killed B. Instead of him being in the chair that day, it was Pricey. I couldn't pull the trigger, and Dorian killed me. Then Tyrese killed Pricey. I woke up with tears in my eyes. I shook that shit off as we got off the plane. It was getting dark when we reached home. All I could do was hope Dorian didn't want to make an example out of no one that night. I looked at everybody and wondered how I got there with them. Granted, this love shit was changing me, but I didn't think it would have that much of an effect on my life. And I, for damn sure, didn't think Dorian would freak like this. I thought he had some kind of an idea about me and Richard. I know he said don't hook up, but still. It was too late to try and make sense of the situation, so I debated on going home and changing into something that would make Dorian happy. But I knew it wouldn't make a difference. I had to put on my game face, whatever it took to survive. When we pulled up to Dorian's there was already a shitload of cars parked outside. I shook my head. This was about to be a very fucked-up night. Tyrese smiled to himself and we all got out. I gave myself the once over: jeans, bikini top with a tight, white, see-through top; some Forces and my hair down, curly. I wouldn't be able to sweet-talk this situation. I didn't look good enough. I was the first to go into a room full of niggas surrounding Dorian, who was yelling about something. I told Pricey to wait by the door. I didn't want Dorian to see her and get any ideas. Me and Richard walked into the living room together with Tyrese and Trip behind us. Dorian looked at us and got an even more upset look on his face.

"What are you doing here, Veronica?"

"I wanted to be a part of whatever you were planning."

"Really?" Dorian smiled, slightly, and sat down. "Come here." I couldn't help but smile at him. Dorian was a man; he wasn't the best man, but he was all man. He wouldn't be moved and he wasn't going to let anybody get in his way. There were no exceptions to his rules.

"Come have a seat." Without thinking, I sat in his lap. Dorian was so hot. "Did you have fun in Jamaica?" That woke me up. I looked over at Richard, pissed at the fact that I was in another man's lap.

"It was pretty nice," I answered.

"That's good to hear. Who is your number one man, Veronica?"

"You." Dorian grabbed my chin and looked me in my eyes. Before he could ask me why, my mouth was open and the words were already coming out.

"If it wasn't for you, I wouldn't be living the life that I want. I wouldn't be doing what I love for a living and I wouldn't have my respect. I mean, with you, I'm safe and, with you, I eat very well."

"Good answer. So what is this I hear about you and Richard being together?"

"You know how I am, Dorian. You tell me not to jump off a building and I'll be the first bitch over it, but I didn't think this would upset you. That was not my intention."

"Do I look upset?" I looked at him and smiled.

“No, you don’t look upset.” Dorian smiled because of the sexy tone I put in my voice.

“What do I look like?” he asked. I put my lips to his ear.

“You look good enough to put my mouth on.”

“The point of tonight is a lot of people have gotten comfortable in this group. A lot of you have been doing business with other people. Some of you even have balls enough to talk about taking me out the game, and there are some who want out the game so bad, you involve the police. Then there are others who do little things to piss me off just because you think you can get away with it, or you think it’s not that big of a deal.” Dorian took a moment to look at me. I bit my bottom lip. “I have come to realize that I have gotten too soft or I have been sending out the wrong message. Now since all of you aren’t as eye-pleasing as Veronica, ten of you will die tonight.” All of a sudden, ten men were removed by other workers and taken to the back. Dorian tapped me so I could get up. I did, but he grabbed my arm before I could walk away.

“As for you two, I will not be killing you today, Richard, but know that you were very close to making the list. One more fuck-up and you’re done, Veronica.” I stepped up to Dorian. I knew that wasn’t going to be good for me. As I tried to brace myself, I was punched in my stomach. I don’t know what was wrong with me, but a laugh fell out of my mouth. Dorian looked at me and wrapped his hands around my neck.

“Richard,” he said. “Everybody and everything in this business is mine. You keep that in mind the next time you decide to go against my word. Someone very close to you will not be spared, and neither will you.” Dorian pulled me close. “Pricey better advise her sister to start using her head before she loses hers.” My face went blank and my heart sank. Dorian let me go and kissed me. I kissed him back for so many different reasons. Richard tried to run up, but I pulled away from Dorian and held him back. Richard held my arms and looked at me, then at Dorian. He pushed me back into Dorian’s arms and he left.

“Oh, he is going to get his self killed fucking around with you. Veronica, wait for me in my office while I deal with everybody else.

Damn. Dorian was everything I wanted in a husband. I wanted my husband to be running shit while I stood by his side and handled his light work. Dorian was just hot. I loved everything about him: The way he acted, thought and carried himself. He demanded everything from you. What was I gon’ do about Richard? I knew it was going to get a lot worse before it got better.

Dorian came back into the room and locked the door behind him. I took a deep breath. Technically, me and Richard weren't together at that moment. I mean he didn't say it was over, but that's the way he was acting. Dorian came over to me. I stood up and we started to kiss.

"I didn't hurt you too bad, did I?" he asked.

"Yes. But I liked it." I bit down on his bottom lip and he picked me up, putting me on his desk. We continued to kiss as he started to undo my pants. I undid his shirt and kissed his chest. There was a knock on the door, and Dorian responded, angrily.

"What?"

"Dorian, somebody got away."

"Then go after his ass and finish the job!" I waited for him and we stopped touching. Dorian pulled me to my feet and started to tug at my pants.

"Dorian, I can't do this." He looked at me with a tight jaw and I thought he would hit me again.

"Why? Because of Richard?"

"I know you said not to get involved, and, at first, it wasn't serious. It was just flirting bullshit, but now, I really love him."

"You love him? Veronica, people like us don't love!"

"I know, but I love Richard."

"Fine. But before ya'll hook up again, he needs to come to me man to man. I meant what I said—you are mine."

"I know."

"What if I just kill him?" I smiled, even though I feared the thought.

"Richard would be gone, but my love for him wouldn't. And I would hate you." Dorian took me into his arms and we kissed a while longer.

"You and Pricey go to China. I want you to take care of some business there. Leave right now and stay away from Richard until I talk to him. I saw this bullshit coming."

"Thank you, Dorian."

"If you really wanted to thank me, you would get my dick down."

"I love you, Dorian. Have a great rest of the night."

I walked out of his office. Damn, I didn't want to call a cab and he had made everybody else leave. Ever since I started making my own money, I'd been losing it like crazy. Tyrese had just come back as I reached the bottom of the steps.

"You need a ride home?"

"Yeah." I got in his truck and we pulled off.

"You fucked up with Richard."

"You think? Don't matter. If Dorian don't want it to be, then guess what? It won't be."

"Ready to let the white boy go that easy?"

"I don't even care right now. We will see what happens. I'm about to call Pricey and we are leaving."

"So you must have really put it on Dorian."

"Dorian just likes to be in control. I'm nothing special to him, but boy, is he great in bed." Tyrese looked at me with disgust. "That's what you wanted to hear, right? That's what you keep fishing for. 'I'm not really in love with Richard, I enjoy fucking Dorian, but you will always have my heart.' 'Oh, Tyrese, please take me back. I'm nothing without you.' 'You're the greatest that I have ever had, no one compares to you.' 'Please just give me a second chance; I know I don't deserve it and you could do so much better!' Is that what you wanted to hear? Will that get you off my back?" I started to laugh in his face.

"Don't forget who ride you in. I could easily put your ass out and have your stupid ass walk back home."

"Nigga, please! Shit just isn't right, right now. Every time something good happens, something bad follows it. Why do I even try?"

"You know I can help you out with whatever is bothering you."

"Tyrese, don't start. I really don't feel like going through this with you."

"This is nothing sexual, Veronica. I can really help you." I looked at him and tried to hold in my smile.

"I'm intrigued. Tell me what you're going to do."

"I'm not doing anything if you don't ask me." I finally cracked a smile.

"You said it's nothing sexual, right?" He smiled at me.

"Right."

"So no kissing, no feeling me up and no sex talk. Alright. Give it to me."

"Right now?"

"Yeah, why not, if it's nothing sexual?" Tyrese licked his lips and gave me a smile.

"Alright." Tyrese pulled over on a side street. We were only fifteen minutes away from home. He opened his door and I grabbed his arm.

"Where you going?"

"Get out the car so I can give you what you need."

"Tyrese, we almost home. We can do this there."

"Now you know damn well Richard is going to be there waiting on you. Come on, get out the car." Tyrese got out and came over to my side, pulling me out.

"Tyrese, don't make me regret this."

"Just come here."

Tyrese pulled me into his arms and wrapped his arms around me, tightly. I felt so small in his arms and so safe. I didn't question this; this was what I needed. A moment when someone removed the stress from my body. I lay my head in his chest and put my hands on his back. "You are so wonderful. You are a strong and powerful woman." I looked up at Tyrese and smiled.

"Thank you."

"I'm not done, but we can finish the rest at home."

"If you could always be nice to me like that I might have fucked with you a little longer."

"I'm not for that lovey-dovey shit, I have to be a asshole at all times."

"Most of the time, I can deal with, but not all the time."

"That's why we not together."

We sat silent for the rest of the ride home. I had already seen Richard's car parked down the street, so I wasn't surprised when I found him standing outside my door. I looked at Tyrese when we reached the hallway to our apartments.

"I'll be over there in a minute," he said.

"Tyrese, don't come over here. You will just make things worse." Tyrese didn't say anything, he just went inside. I let Richard in.

"What the fuck was tonight about?"

"What do you think? Dorian wasn't happy about us. Be thankful we're not dead." Richard rushed me and pushed me up against the wall.

"Be thankful that Dorian has all access to my woman? The man can do whatever he wants with you and I have to stand by and let him!"

"What did you want me to do? I can't tell him no in a room full of people! You know Dorian isn't going for that!" Richard backed up a little and hit himself in the head with both hands.

"And you kissed him. You fucking kissed him!" Richard slapped me and I went flying into my glass table. For the first time, I was shocked that I had been struck by a man. Richard came over and sat with me in the shattered glass.

"Veronica, I will not share you. I love you and I can't have some other guy putting his hands on you."

"I talked to Dorian and he said that all you have to do is come to him and ask his permission. Get his blessing."

"What? Are you fucking serious?" Richard got up while I stayed there on the floor. My best bet was that if I stayed down, then I wouldn't get knocked down again.

"I am not handing Dorian my balls on a silver platter. You're my woman and that will not change because Dorian doesn't like it. You are not his property!"

"We are *all* Dorian's property. He has our lives in his hands. The sooner you get that through your head, the easier things will be for us."

"I can't believe I am hearing this. So you saying you don't want to be with me?"

"No, Richard, I'm saying I don't want to die because of you. Just swallow your pride this one time and go to Dorian."

"I'm not doing that!" It was time to wrap this shit up. Dorian didn't want us around each other and I had my own life to think about.

"Then we can't be together. I can't see you anymore. Please leave." I was trying to be strong, but I could feel the tears coming on.

"I'm not going any fucking where." I threw up my hands and started to walk to the bathroom because my arms were cut up. Richard tried to grab me and kiss me, but I pushed him away. He slapped me again and we started fighting.

"Why are you doing this?" he yelled. "I love you! Why are you turning your back on me? You want to be with Dorian, don't you?"

"Richard, get off me! Get off me!" He pushed me over the couch and I fell down hard. He was about to choke me. I tried to get up and run to my room, but he kicked me in my side.

"Don't try to run from me!"

"Richard, stop! Please stop!" He started to choke me and, by this time, tears were rolling down my face. I felt so weak I didn't want to fight back. I didn't want to hurt him anymore. I loved Richard and I wanted us to be happy together.

"Richard, please, I love you." He let go of my neck and pulled me into his arms.

"I can't lose you, I can't let you go. I love you."

"I know, but . . ." He jumped to his feet and roughly pulled me to mine.

"What do you mean, 'but?'" I pushed him off me and went to the door.

"But I will not die for you. I will not put my sister in harm's way for your sweet words and heavy hand."

"I didn't want to hit you, Veronica. I'm sorry."

"But you did. If you really love me, then go to Dorian."

"No. I won't." I opened the door and Tyrese was standing outside.

"Then, Richard, you need to leave." He ran up on me and Tyrese stepped into my apartment.

"This is not over."

"Yes it is." Richard looked at Tyrese and then at me.

"If you fuck him I will kill you."

He looked at me with hate in his eyes and walked out. Tyrese closed the door behind him. He took a look at my face, arms, neck and the broken table. He just shook his head and we went to the bathroom. He cleaned up my wounds and pulled off my shoes. I went to my room and pulled off my clothes. Tyrese pulled back the covers and I got in bed. He sat on the edge about to get in bed with me.

"I think you should leave. Thank you, but I really want to be alone."

"Do you want to be alone or are you just scared of what Richard might do if I stay?"

"Tyrese, please don't." He got out of bed, walked out and slammed the door when he left. I curled up in a little ball and cried my eyes out. I felt depressed and weak. My body ached for Richard; it had been an hour since he left and I missed him so much. I got up five hours later and threw up. I was making myself sick, I felt so bad. I didn't want to go anywhere. I wanted to stay in my room and wait on him to come back. Why couldn't he just go to Dorian? Why couldn't he just do what he needed to do so we could be together? My phone was ringing off the hook for a week straight, but I didn't care.

It wasn't Richard so it didn't matter. My phone rang the following week at three-something in the morning. I hoped it was Richard, but it was Dorian. I had to answer it.

"Hello?"

"How are you?"

"Fine." I was lying through my teeth and wasn't trying to hide it.

"I heard about you and Richard. You're doing the right thing." I let out a loud breath and rolled my eyes. "Look, I know you don't feel like doing much, but I need you to take care of something in China. The jet will be ready at five. Be there."

"Alright. I'll be there."

"Good girl."

Good girl? Oh, what a good little bitch I was being! I was really starting not to like my job or my fucking boss, for that matter. Why did I always have to lose the things I loved? Why the fuck hadn't Richard talked to Dorian yet? Why hadn't he called me? Did he even want to be with me? As I got dressed I started to get pissed off. Fuck, if Richard didn't handle his fucking business I would kick his ass. That's why I really wasn't tripping off what went down between me and Richard. I loved him enough to beat the fuck out of him if he wouldn't be with me. After I got my clothes on I called Pricey on my cell phone.

"You ready to roll, bitch?"

"Damn right, come scoop me, hoe." I cracked a smile and pulled off, heading to her place. When I got there the door was wide open and, before I cut down my radio, I could hear Pricey going at it with Trip.

"How in the fuck you just gon' pick up and leave like this? It's too damn early in the morning for you to be going any damn where!"

"Get the fuck out of my damn way. I'm leaving nigga, shit!"

"Pricey, sit yo ass down. You just gon' have to call Veronica and tell her you can't make this trip." I felt like being bad so I honked the horn.

"Here I come," Pricey yelled. She came back out, but Trip stood in her way and took her bag from her. She just pushed him out of her way and got in. I pulled off.

"Can you believe that nigga?" she asked.

"Yeah." Pricey looked at me crazy.

"What the hell happened to yo face?"

"Me and Richard got into it a couple nights ago."

"The way you kissed Dorian, I'm surprised Richard didn't kill you. I saw that before we left. Did you and Dorian have sex that night?"

"No, I couldn't go through with it. I love Richard and he is who I want to be with, but I will not fuck up my life because of him."

"I hear that. You give them a inch and they want a mile. Damn, ain't it enough that we love they sorry asses? They always want more."

"Tell me about it, and all he has to do is just go to Dorian so he could let him know what's going on between us—just ask Dorian can he be with me."

"Damn. Richard stubborn ass is not going to do that. Not after everybody seen Dorian just disrespected ya'll whole relationship."

"He better! Or this shit is war."

"Oh God. See that's why people never want to see you in no relationship, you crazy."

"If everybody mind they own damn business, then nobody would have to be subjected to what I do in my personal life."

"Right."

We talked some more about our possessive men and how we were suckers for them. As independent and strong as we were, love made us so weak. We made it just in time to board the jet and as soon as we got settled we went to sleep, slept through the whole flight to China. You can imagine how long that was. I don't know what was up with Pricey, but I was exhausted because I hadn't gotten any real sleep in a week. When we got off the plane we were approached by a tall, caramel complexioned, nicely built, kinda handsome man. I didn't think much of him until he extended his hand to me and I shook it.

"Hello, Veronica. Dorian informed me of your stay here and we both agreed that it would be best for you and your sister Pricey to stay with me. China isn't safe for us right now and once you do what you came here to do it will be even more dangerous."

"What? Shopping? Veronica, what is he talking about?"

"I came here for a job."

"Oh."

"Excuse me what's your name?" I asked.

"Dewayne Cleveland." He moved over to a nearby limo and opened the door for us. Pricey started to get in, but I put my hand in front of her.

"Let me call Dorian before we make any moves." I dialed his number and, before I could get a word out, he answered: "Yes, Dewayne is fine. He'll hand you your assignment and you'll be staying with him at his house."

"Okay." Dorian hung up and I gave Pricey the head nod. We got in the limo with Dewayne.

"Women don't pack anymore when they go on trips?" he asked.

"Not these ladies. What do we need with clothes we already have, when we're here to buy all new things?" Pricey gave Dewayne a smile.

"I see. Well, besides all the commotion going on here right now, I hope you enjoy your stay here." Pricey licked her lips and Dewayne tried to hold back his smile.

"I'm sure we will be able to find something to entertain us," Pricey said, putting her arm in mine. I shook my head.

We rode in silence for the rest of the ride and I watched as Pricey fucked the shit out of Dewayne with her eyes. I laughed at her. She was a mess. Dewayne's house was very impressive, very big, and the landscape was wonderful. While Dewayne gave Pricey a tour of the house I stayed outside by the koru pond and looked at all the different fish. This was so pretty. I sat on a bench next to the pound and took a moment to take in the trees, the sky and grass. It was so peaceful. Dewayne came out of nowhere and sat down next to me. I kept staring into space.

"China is really a beautiful place, don't you agree?"

"Yes."

"So you're Veronica Avery? This is really a pleasure. Dorian says you're one of his best."

"Funny. Dorian never mentioned you." I kept looking straight ahead.

"I work on international things. I never come to the States."

"I've been all over the world for Dorian and I still have never heard about you."

"I guess I'm not one of Dorian's best. I'm not in the business you're in. I'm more negations than anything."

"I see." I stood up and Dewayne got up as well. He touched my face.

"Another battle wound?"

"You can say that." I moved his hand away from me and walked into the house. Pricey was just getting out of the shower and I was about to get in.

The shower reminded me of the one in Jamaica. I thought of Richard, then looked at my arms. They were still in slight pain, but my face wasn't bothering me. I had been hit so many times in the face that it didn't faze me now. I looked up and could have sworn that I saw Dewayne's face, but I didn't. I let the water hit my hair and got out of the shower as soon as I did that. I needed to take a bath, so I ran the water and let myself relax. Half-hour into my relaxing bath, Dewayne came into the bathroom and sat on the edge of the tub.

"What do you want?"

"How did you get into this line of work? You are very young. I mean I've heard the stories, but . . ."

"Why don't you tell me my story and I'll correct you as you go along? Can you get my back for me?" I sat up in the tub and handed him a sponge.

"I heard that after your mother killed herself you went crazy."

"Nope, I've always been crazy. My mother's death had nothing to do with that."

"After she died, your father abandoned you and you had to take care of yourself. Then your father came back and he beat on you for a while until Dorian offered you a job. You killed your father, and that was about it."

"You left out how I killed Game, the guy who raped me, that I was tricking with white men and I had sex with Dorian. I had an ongoing relationship with Tyrese, one of the hardest niggas in Chicago. That I'm a punching bag for guys, currently, for my boyfriend Richard. That I'm a woman serial killer—and that I am a evil bitch who values nothing but my sister's life."

"Yeah, that's what I heard." We burst into laughter and I sat back. My boobies where exposed so I covered them up with bubbles.

"So the question is what do you want from me, Dewayne Cleveland?"

"What do you mean?"

"Do you want to fuck? Would you like to get into my head and see where everything went wrong? Do you want to save me from this life? What exactly do you want?"

"Why do you think I want anything?"

"All men want something, considering the fact that I am a very attractive woman who, apparently, doesn't seem to have any respect for herself, to let men use her for sex and beat on her, right?"

"I'm not passing any form of judgment on you, Veronica."

"Sure you're not, Dewayne. It doesn't bother me a bit. My life is what it is and I can't change a thing from my past. I can only press on."

"I agree. Besides, you are a victim of your circumstances. The only thing I want is your friendship and that's the only thing I'm offering."

Dewayne got up and left. "Don't go there, Veronica," I told myself. I finished washing up and got out. I went to my room and there was a dress already laid out for me. I put it on and found Pricey in the living room, looking out the window on the couch. I sat next to her and crossed my legs.

"So you gon' hook up with Dewayne?" she asked. She gave me a smile.

"No, why would you ask me something like that?" I folded my arms and gave her a mean mug.

"I don't know, I feel something between ya'll."

"Girl, please. He a cool dude, but you know where my head at."

"Yeah. Richard. But where the hell is *his* head?"

"Hell if I know."

"Be careful, Veronica. You know Tyrese waiting."

"I'm not thinking about Tyrese. Try as he might, it's not gon' happen while Richard is alive." Pricey slapped my thigh.

"There you go! Stand by your man."

"Don't be hitting on me like that, fool!" Pricey laughed and I laughed with her.

"When we leaving? My hands are ready to pick up expensive things." She pushed her hands in my face and I moved them to the side, laughing.

"I don't know, man. Whenever Dewayne give us the okay, I guess."

"Why do we always have to follow after some man? Every time we try to take a step, what happens?"

"A man get in our way."

"Damn right, Veronica." I couldn't stop laughing at Pricey. She was going off about any and everything." Dewayne came out of nowhere and sat on the couch next to us. We stopped laughing and looked at him.

"What?" I said.

"What?" he said back to me. I put a strange look on my face and looked at Pricey.

"Did you come in here to tell us something?"

“I was just wondering when you ladies were leaving?”

“We was waiting on you,” Pricey said, with attitude.

“Well let’s go.”

We all got up and left. China was one of the most beautiful places in the world. I loved the customs and the fact that they had a history. They were always polite to people, and the greatest thing, in my opinion, was downtown. Everything down there looked like a video game and it kept my attention. We had been to over twenty stores and bought them all up. We had our little fashion shows in the dressing rooms, acting crazy and I would look over at Dewayne. He stood by the entrance, acting like he wasn’t laughing at us. Like he was so focused. But I caught his eye a couple of times. Dewayne said we had to wrap things up for today and if we wanted to go back out tomorrow, we could. Pricey and I paid for our things and got back in the limo. I could tell we were going back to the house, but I wanted to go out to eat that night.

“We can’t stop somewhere?” I asked Dewayne.

“It’s not safe. As soon as we sat down, there would be people coming to kill us.”

“Fine.”

We arrived at the house and we all went our separate ways. I’m sure Pricey was on the phone calling Trip. She couldn’t stay mad at him for too long. I wanted to call Richard, but didn’t. I made my way over to the kitchen and looked in the fridge. I found some chicken and rice, so I decided to make some orange chicken. That was mine and Pricey’s favorite. After dinner, Dewayne disappeared and Pricey was back on the phone. I took it upon myself to look around. I headed upstairs and found Dewayne’s office, where the first thing I noticed was his desk. It was cherry oak with nothing on top of it. His chair was small, almost unbearable to sit in. There were no arm rests and the back rest had a curve in the middle, making it impossible to sit back in. I crossed my legs; this was very interesting. Where was his computer? I looked at his drawers and there were locks on them. I hadn’t brought my lock-picking equipment. I got up and took a moment to stand in every corner of Dewayne’s office: There was something missing. There was nothing in his office but his desk, his chair, and two chairs in front of his desk. Nothing more. I sat back and looked closer, then I put both of the palms of my hands on top of his desk and rubbed the surface. Bingo! I pressed down on the center of the desk and a laptop popped up. Nice. I spent the next hour trying to break codes and going through all his files. And what did I get for all my effort? Not a damn thing. Dewayne was clean, so clean that it gave me an idea of just how dirty he was.

Maybe this wasn't his "business" computer, maybe he deleted everything once he didn't need it anymore. Whatever he had done, I couldn't find a thing. Just as I was about to exit out of his computer's system, a screen popped up and I was looking at a little girl. From my guess, she was eight years old.

"Who are you?" I turned around like somebody was behind me.

"I'm talking to you, nobody else is in the room." I turned my face and started to exit out again.

"It doesn't matter. Look up, please." Just as I did that, a flash went off and the little girl disappeared. I didn't have a good feeling about that.

"Don't worry, Amya. Everything is fine, she's cool." I looked up and Dewayne was standing in the doorway, talking on the phone. I turned off his computer lowered it back into his desk.

"I miss you, too. Yes, I can't wait to come visit, either. Alright, have a good day at school. I love you, too. Bye, honeybee." I started to stand and Dewayne put his hand up, moving closer to me.

"Please, have a seat." Dewayne sat on his desk and looked at me.

"Find what you were looking for?"

"No."

"I hate for you to think that you couldn't come to me and ask me whatever you wanted and expect for me to deliver the truth."

"How old are you?"

"I am twenty-six."

"Is that your daughter?"

"No, Amya is my niece. I don't have any children, I've never been married and I am not involved with anybody."

"Do you think I care about your personal life?"

"I think that it interests you. For your life to be such an open book for the world, I believe that, in order for you to be able to handle that, you need to know just as much about the people who surround you."

"You went to college and majored in law and psychology. You're the middle child of three kids, you have a older brother and a younger sister."

"Very good. How did you figure all that out?"

"I know a few things about psychology myself. Remember, my mother was a psycho. Who do you think took care of her? Your mental tricks don't work on me. My mind was the first thing that I learned to strengthen in this game."

"I see. Then you will last very long."

"So if you're so smart, how did you end up in this line of business?"

"Because smart people get away with shit." I laughed a little. He was shutting down. I stood up and walked over to the door.

"Good night, Dewayne."

"Good night, Veronica."

I went to my room and got ready for bed. I needed to be on my toes around Dewayne. I tossed and turned all night, thinking about Richard. I had a bad feeling. I finally gave up on sleep at four in the morning and went downstairs. I found Dewayne in his gym, stretching, so I sat against the wall and folded my legs.

"Good morning."

"Good morning, Dewayne." He stopped stretching.

"No, please, act like I'm not here. I want to observe you."

"You couldn't sleep, I take it?"

"No."

Dewayne didn't say anything else as I watched him begin his karate. It was like he was fighting an invisible man and, as crazy as it sounds, I could see he was winning. Watching Dewayne kick with such power in the air and move so quickly made me relax. I looked at his form and then at his eyes; he was so focused. I would like to have focus like that someday to be able to separate my life from my work. That was hard to do when my life and my work were intertwined so completely. Just as the sun was about to come up, I got up, leaving Dewayne behind and went outside. I sat in the same spot that I had when I first arrived, pushing my knees into my chest, holding myself tightly. The sun kissed my skin as it rose and I put my head against my knees and let my eyes close. I felt Pricey plop down beside me, and just as she was about to wake me, I lifted my head and opened my eyes.

"Damn! You scared the shit out of me, Roni! Fucking robot." I smiled at her. "Are we going shopping today? 'Cause the day has started and I don't want to be stuck in traffic like we was yesterday. Or are you going to stay sleep all day, Roni?"

"Give me a minute to get in the shower and I'll be ready."

"Alright. I'll wait out here." I went in and found Dewayne in the kitchen. I waved at him and headed to the bathroom.

I took a quick shower and we all left the house. I really wasn't feeling the whole shopping thing so I didn't get as much as Pricey, but it was nice spending time with her anyway. And boy, did she have a surprise for me. I noticed on our way home that we were going in the wrong direction. When we arrived at the airport I looked over at Dewayne, then at Pricey.

"What are we doing here?"

"Girl, I got to go home. All this at peace thing China got going is too boring for me. I got to go to the club, have some sex, smoke some weed or something. Don't get me wrong, the shopping was off the hook. I have a lot of nice things, but it's time for me to go. This is a great place for you to recharge your battery and, while you're doing that, I can keep my eye on Richard. Maybe then you can get a good night's sleep." I folded my arms and looked straight ahead.

"You could have stopped at your first sentence. Nobody is holding you against your will." The limo came to a stop and the door to Dorian's jet opened.

"Look, don't be mad. I love you and as soon as I get home I'll call you."

"Sure." Pricey gave me a hug and kissed my cheek.

"Nice meeting you, Dewayne. Bye, Roni."

We waited until after the plane took off and I looked out the window as the limo headed back to Dewayne's place.

"I didn't realize that you needed to 'recharge,'" he said.

"I don't."

"You and your sister are like day and night."

"Yeah." Dewayne stopped having conversation with me after seeing that I didn't want to participate. We went our separate ways when we made it back to his place. I changed my clothes and went down to his gym. I tried my damn best to work all my frustrations out of my body, but the shit wasn't happening.

"Take it easy," Dewayne said. "You look like you're trying to kill yourself." I got off the treadmill and took the water bottle he had in his hand.

"You're welcome," he said.

I rolled my eyes. "Thank you." Dewayne put a towel on my shoulders.

"Wow. Do I detect a bit of attitude?"

"Maybe." I looked at him, coldly.

"What is this? I know you aren't stressed. You act like you have the whole world on your shoulders.

If you're going to make it in this business, you're going to have to learn how to not mix personal and professional together."

"I don't think I asked you, Dewayne." I finished my water and walked up on him.

"What? You want some?" He smiled and took a step back.

"Maybe I do." Just as Dewayne started to take off his jacket, I rushed him and kicked him in the side. It was like something out of a Jet Li flick. He was the karate master 'cause, after the first hit, I couldn't touch him again. He was blocking everything that I was trying to give him.

"Where did this come from, Veronica?"

"Thought you had everything figured out, did you?"

"Just about. Come on, I know you can do better than that." I dropped down and knocked his feet from under him. He jumped right back up and came at me strong. I couldn't block his shots like he had done me, but I blocked a couple. Dewayne put my hand behind my back, twisting my wrist. I thought he would break it, it was hurting so bad.

"Fine! I give!" Dewayne pushed me away from him and I hit the floor, lying on my back to catch my breath.

"Where did you learn those attacks?" he asked me.

"Here."

"Here?"

"Yeah, Dewayne, I'm a fast learner."

"You didn't learn all that from today, don't lie to me." Dewayne stood on my stomach and I flexed my abs.

"Alright! This guy, Metro, taught me a few things." Dewayne stepped off and sat next to me.

"Where is he now?"

"I don't know. Probably dead. Last I heard, he owed some Russians some money."

"He didn't teach you much. If you really want to learn, I will teach you."

"If you teach me, then I'll really whip yo ass." Dewayne slapped my thigh.

"I find that hard to believe." He got up and left. I sat up and headed for the bathroom. After I got dressed I went looking for Dewayne again. He was in the living room watching TV.

"Wow, the professional has time to relax?"

"Just the news. None of the dumb reality show mess."

"Right. You hungry? I'm about to make something."

"Naw. Let's go out."

"Are you serious?"

"Yeah." Dewayne got up and headed for the door.

"I thought you said that it was too dangerous to go out at night."

"It was too dangerous for you and Pricey to be out at night. I can't keep my eye on both of you and I didn't want to be at fault for any harm that may come to you ladies."

I just shook my head. I didn't have words for him. We went to his garage and I was shocked to see only two rides in there, a truck and a two-door. We took the two-door.

As soon as we got to the restaurant, I could tell they was on some foul shit. The hostess looked like she was going to shit herself when she saw us. Dewayne didn't say anything, so we just walked past her, down a long hall and seated ourselves.

"Thank you for bringing me to a restaurant that I can't even eat in."

"Why wouldn't you be able to eat? The sushi is great here." He placed his napkin in his lap and pulled out his chopsticks.

"Very funny. You know that they're going to do something to our food."

"No, they won't. Don't be paranoid." Just as Dewayne said that, five men dressed in black came into our seating area.

"Yeah, I'm being paranoid, alright." The men just stood there looking at us for about ten minutes and then a Chinese man walked in.

"Dewayne, what are you doing here?"

"Trying to have dinner, but no one has come to serve us yet. We haven't even gotten any tea."

"You know this is going to upset Wong. Everything is fine now!"

"Not from what my boss tells me. Me and Wong are going to have a meeting tomorrow to straighten things out." The Chinese man didn't say another word and the rest of the men that were in the room left when he did.

"So this is what you do?"

"A little piece of what I do."

I put my napkin in my lap and our tea came soon after. We ordered and ate. It was actually good. I wanted to ask Dewayne more questions about himself, but I needed time to prepare for this meeting tomorrow. I looked at my cell phone before I got into bed. Pricey had called me five times. Against my good judgment, I called her back.

"'Bout muthafucking time, Veronica," she answered. "I been blowing your damn phone up."

"I see. What's up?"

"Well I haven't seen Richard. Word is Dorian sent him away on business. Won't nobody tell me where, but I'll find out."

"Did Richard talk to Dorian about us?"

"No, he still being bull-headed. How is my boo, Dewayne?"

"Your *what?*" I could hear Trip saying in the background.

"Damn, Trip! I thought you was sleep." Pricey started to laugh.

"He is fine. We have a meeting to go to tomorrow."

"That's what's up."

"Anything else you have to tell me about Richard?"

"Nope. Trip told me that Richard wouldn't be back to Chicago for a couple of months, but that's it."

"Alright, I'm about to go to sleep."

"Alright. Bye."

"Bye."

17

There was going to be a murder today. Dewayne woke me at eleven and told me to get ready. Our meeting was set for noon. I took a shower and spent a good majority of time trying to figure out what the hell I would wear. Dewayne had put two big-ass machine guns on my bed while I was in the bathroom, and I had to find something to wear that would cover them up. At eleven-thirty, I decided to go balls-to-the-wall and just wear a fly-ass suit with guns on either side of my shoulder. Fuck it. I was sure they knew what was coming. If they wanted a war, I could fuck with that. My hair was pulled back and I had flats on my feet. I made my way outside where Dewayne had pulled the truck to the front. I got in and he smiled at me, pulling off. I know I probably looked like something out of a movie. The next thing I knew, we were in an office full of workers. Wong was behind a desk. I stood by the door while Dewayne stood five feet from Wong.

"What is it going to be, Wong?"

"You tell Dorian that I do not appreciate his threats! He sends this whore to come and kill me. Such disrespect!"

"Wong, watch your mouth. We are just protecting ourselves. Hopefully, this lovely lady doesn't have to pay you another visit."

"Fucking American bastards. Give him the damn money!" For the first time, I noticed all the briefcases in the room, filled with money.

"Good. Too bad things aren't that easy to fix."

"What are you talking about?" Dewayne pulled out his gun so smooth; before anybody realized what was going on, the shot had been fired and Wong was dead. I stepped into the room and held up my guns. Dewayne walked over to me and put up his gun.

"Wait. Before anyone does anything dumb, think about this: Do you want war or do you want money?" Nobody moved. Dewayne picked up two briefcases and walked out the room. I backed up, slowly, and followed him. That shit blew my mind. What had just happened? We got in the truck and headed back home.

"What the hell was that about?"

"Dorian wanted him out. Their partnership was over. I had the shot, so I took it. Don't worry, you'll get paid for helping." Dewayne looked at me and could see confusion painted all over my face.

"What?" I asked. He smiled at me. "You kill people for Dorian?"

"No, sometimes I do it for pleasure." I looked at him crazy.

"I'm joking, Veronica. When negotiation falls through on a case, I handle things."

"So back there I was your muscle?" I finally broke out in laughter, and so did Dewayne.

"I guess so."

"I see I haven't even scratched the surface."

"Veronica, the more you know, the more reason I have to kill you." I sat back in my seat and looked out the window.

"We shall see, Dewayne. We shall see."

"No, we won't. You're going home tomorrow."

"Are you telling me? 'Cause, last I checked, I was still on vacation."

"Okay. What hotel would you like me to take you to?"

"I don't want to go to no hotel. I want you to teach me." Dewayne gave me the once over.

"I'll think about it."

When we got back to his place I started on lunch and Dewayne went off somewhere. I heard the sound of his voice in a back room, so I snuck over to the cordless kitchen phone and slipped it to my ear:

"She wants to stay."

"What?"

"Veronica wants to stay so I can teach her karate."

"Good, she needs to add to her talents."

"Dorian, I don't know about this. I'm not trying to get caught up in the drama that is this little girl."

"Then keep it professional."

"I don't think I can. You know I don't even say things like that, and I'm not some pussy-hungry man, but it's something about her."

"Tell me about it. The more you know about her, the harder you fall. Just keep it professional. Don't worry. She is in love with Richard."

"Dorian, you got to make her go somewhere else. The only reason I agreed to this was because you said she would be in and out."

"Well things have changed. Roll with it and call me in a couple of months to let me know her progress."

"A couple of months?"

"Bye Dewayne."

Dorian hung up and Dewayne realized what a fucked-up situation he was in. How in the hell was he going to deal with me for a couple of months? When Dewayne came back into the kitchen and saw the plate I made for him, he wolfed down his food and disappeared again. I finished eating and went to my room, like I hadn't even heard the conversation. Dorian was right: My thoughts were still consumed by Richard. I still couldn't help but wonder where he was and what he was doing. Did he even miss me? 'Cause I missed the hell out of him. I curled up in the bed with my pillow and fought the feeling of wanting to cry my eyes out. I figured my best bet was to stay with Dewayne so I could get my mind right. I couldn't go back to Chicago and let everybody see me in such a weak state. Maybe if I stayed away long enough,

Richard would miss me, come to his senses and talk to Dorian. I went to sleep early that night and was glad I did when I got up the next morning: Dewayne woke me up at four a.m. and, from that point on, I was in boot camp. This nigga was not holding me up, he worked me so fucking hard that, some days, I didn't think my body could do more. He exercised my mental, physical and emotional, and, at first, the whole thing excited me. I had never been tired like this before, and I was shocked to see that I had weaknesses. But once I found that out, I wanted to get them all out of my system. Every day, Dewayne was pushing on me. We would get up every morning and run with about two-hundred pounds on our backs. For miles, we would run, with little water. Then we would go down to the gym and work out for a couple of hours. I ate so much health crap that I thought I would puke it up, but I didn't. I was in "boot camp" for two months. I had a lot of seafood, raw eggs, fruits and vegetables and stuff in a cup, that tasted like death. Dewayne wanted me to get rid of all my body fat and be nothing but muscle. Boy, this shit was killing me, but I just tried to stay focused on what was going on because Richard was hurting me. I talked to Pricey and she had informed me that, not only was he back in Chicago, but he was running around with numerous women. Pricey assured me that he wasn't fucking any of them, that he was just showing out. She told me that he knew I was in China with some guy and Dorian gave him direct orders not to come anywhere near me. I broke down and called Richard every night, but I never got an answer. I never left a message because I didn't know what to say. I was pissed that he wouldn't take my calls, but I felt something stronger than anger, for the first time in my life—I felt alone. I was going through hell without Richard and he was fine with that. Most nights, I cried myself to sleep and other nights I couldn't sleep at all. I just lay in bed with my eyes open, waiting for Dewayne to come and get me. Every day, Dewayne said that I wouldn't be able to move on until I centered myself. I would never master anything if I let every little thing affect me. I agreed with him, but try as I might, I couldn't control what I felt, to save my life. One morning, my body woke itself at four in the morning and I waited in bed for a couple of minutes. Where was Dewayne? Why hadn't he woke me? I got out of bed and took a quick shower, then went to Dewayne's room. He was still in bed. I walked over to him and couldn't believe that he was actually asleep. I kicked the side of his bed and he popped up.

"What?"

"What do you mean 'what?' What do we do every morning?"

"Sleep in. Boot camp is over. We will have a session at eight at night. Meet me in the gym."

"Alright."

I did my daily workout without Dewayne and, since I finally had free time, took the opportunity to go to some of my favorite hot spots in China. I didn't do much shopping, but I did make it a point to go get a full-body massage. I needed it bad. I went back to the house at five, made something to eat and then took a short nap. I woke up at seven-thirty and went to the gym so I could stretch out and get ready for whatever Dewayne was about to throw at me. He came in at eight o'clock on the dot, and he was dressed in his traditional karate master outfit. I couldn't help but laugh at him. He was looking all serious.

"Why do you have that on?"

"Tonight you get your first real ass-kicking and your first real lesson." Dewayne got into his stance, showing me that he was ready to battle. I threw my hands up before he could make his first move.

"Wait a minute. If this is my first lesson, then what the hell was boot camp? I mean I have been here for two damns months and you're telling me that I haven't learned anything?"

"Boot camp was only supposed to last for a month, but you're so headstrong that you are not willing to separate professional from your personal." I crossed my arms.

"What the hell does that mean?" I asked. Dewayne relaxed and broke his stance.

"It means that you're here to learn, and every night you're on the damn phone making yourself upset over your personal life. I can't teach you if you're not completely focused."

"So what is this about? If you don't think I'm ready to learn, then why did you end boot camp?"

"Because my patience is getting very thin with you. It's time to move forward. You're not ready, but you have potential. If you're not ready after tonight, then you have to go somewhere else."

"Fine. So you think fighting me is going to help me get ready?" Dewayne didn't answer me, he got back into his stance and I got into mine. He came at me quick and fast, trying to punch me in my face. I stepped back so quickly that I fell on the floor.

"You better step it up, Veronica, or you're going to hurt yourself." Dewayne gave me a smile and I got on my feet. I needed to focus. He was not playing with me. I put my hands back up and Dewayne came at me again. I blocked his shot to my stomach and hit him in the mouth. We fought for another half-hour and I was actually holding my own with Mr. Black Belt. I was tired as fuck, but I couldn't stop fighting because, if I did, Dewayne would win. I blocked Dewayne's last five shots, but I didn't have the energy to whip his ass. I wanted him to see I was serious about this, that I wanted to learn.

"Veronica, you are a good fighter, but you have the potential to be great. You just let your emotions get the best of you." Dewayne tried to sweep my feet from under me, but I jumped in time.

"No, I don't! I am focused!" I screamed that at the top of my lungs, trying to show no sign of weakness.

"Your emotions rule your life. Everything you decide is based on how you feel. That's why you didn't pursue dancing, that's why you killed B and Pricey's mom." Dewayne was coming at me and I felt myself getting weaker. "That's why Pricey is going to end up dead. You're a loose cannon!"

"No!" I hit Dewayne in the chest.

"You're going to come up against somebody that you can't beat and they're going to go after Pricey," he said. I started fucking Dewayne up.

"Nobody is going to touch Pricey! I'll kill whoever I have to, in order to keep her safe! You shut your fucking mouth!" I was kicking Dewayne in the chest and punched him in the mouth. He grabbed me from behind and held me tight.

"There is a good way to use that anger, Veronica, but if you can't control, it you will lose." I couldn't move. I couldn't get Dewayne off me. I lifted my right leg and kicked him in the face, causing him to let me go as he hit the ground. That wasn't stopping me. I was still coming at him strong.

"Good, Veronica. Use that anger, don't let it use you." Despite the fact that I was kicking Dewayne's ass, he still got up like it was nothing, like my punches didn't hurt him. He started to block my shots.

"Good, Veronica! So what if Richard is fucking somebody else? You can do much better than him." Without thinking, I let my hands fall to my side and Dewayne hit me square in my left eye. I stepped back and held my face.

"Do you see what I'm talking about? Your emotions." I stood up and pushed those thoughts of Richard out of my mind. Dewayne had hit me. It was time to take him out. I ran at him, wanting to draw more blood. I kicked him in the knee, making him bow and then kicked him in his head. Still, Dewayne got up like it was nothing.

"Better."

"Damn! What will it take for you to stay down?"

"Don't be mad at me, I'm not the one ignoring your phone calls. I'm not the one pushing you to the side. Richard is. I guess he must not be too interested in you. Like he said, men fuck hoes, they don't keep them around." Again, my hands dropped for a second, but before Dewayne could hit me, I blocked his shot.

"You're getting there, Veronica." I couldn't believe that Dewayne was saying all this stuff to me. I knew that it was only to get in my head, but I couldn't look past it.

He was right.

"Ain't that a bitch! Richard fucking you over and you can't even see the shit! How does Dorian's top worker turn into some dick-whipped woman? You give Richard your love and he gives you a hard fist every time you step out of line." I threw my hands down and let Dewayne hit me. I let this man whip my ass, and when I fell down this time, I stayed down. Dewayne stood over me and put out his hand.

"I'm not trying to get you to quit. I'm trying to get you to understand what's stopping you from being great. Are you ready now?" I took Dewayne's hand and he helped me up.

"I'm ready." We went upstairs and helped attend to each other's wounds. Dewayne put ice on my eye and I cleaned up his busted lip.

"How come my hits didn't hurt you?"

"Because, Veronica, pain is a state of mind. You must have control over your mind and body when you go into battle. As long as you have control, both will take care of each other. Trust me. I'm feeling it now."

"Good."

Dewayne smiled at me

"Don't be mad. I'm was just trying to prove my point. I didn't mean any of that." I bit my bottom lip. I felt so naked right then.

"How did you know about my dancing?"

"I know everything. You think I would just let some stranger stay in my house?"

"I didn't say, 'How *much* do you know?' I said, '*How* do you know?'"

"When Dorian moved all of your things out of your father's apartment, he sent them to me."

"I see.

So where do we start?"

"We start with you telling me about all the things that bother you, your fears, what you wish to have in this life, future plans. And I want you to address all those things that are ruling your life." I smiled.

"So you're going to be my physiologist. I guess you're going to be able to get in my head after all."

"Do you trust me?"

I thought about his question and came up with this: "I trust you just as much as I trust myself." Dewayne nodded his head and walked away.

I went to the bathroom and took a long, hot bath. I missed my bathroom back at home, I missed my home, period. From this point forward, Richard was out of my mind. I would deal with him when I got home. I wondered if he would be on the same tip when I was face to face with him again. Richard was not going to fuck this up for me. I didn't realize how big of a hold he had on me, but now my eyes were open. The next morning, I slept in. I would have slept all day, but my stomach was calling out for food. I went downstairs and found Dewayne in the living room eating sea food pasta. I sat next to him.

"The dead has arisen," he said.

"Where's mine?"

"I didn't make you anything." Dewayne smiled at me and I went to the kitchen. I made myself a plate and sat back down.

"So when do we start training?"

"Whenever you're ready."

"When will I be ready?"

"I don't know, Veronica. Are you in a hurry to get started?"

"Yeah, I'm already one month behind. So come on, let's start, 'cause I'm ready."

"You sure?"

"Yes, Dewayne."

"What was it that made you kill your father?"

"I wanted to get into the game. Dorian gave me a shot, so I took it."

"You don't feel bad about what you have done?"

"Naw, he was fucking over Dorian money, so I knew if I didn't do it, somebody else would. Why not kill two birds with one stone? Besides, he had that shit coming."

"How did he have it coming?"

"I mean it's like this: My mom gave that man sixteen years of her life. Yeah, she was fucking nuts, but she loved him and all he did was hurt her. Yes, I'm my father's child but I'm loyal to my mother. His death had been planed way before Dorian presented the opportunity to me."

"Do you hate your father, Veronica?"

"Naw, it wasn't like that. He has taught me a lot. I love him, I just never respected him. When I found out that he was selling me out to Dorian, that was the stick that broke the camel's back. He wasn't looking out for me so why should I look out for him?"

"Are you upset that your mother killed herself?" I pictured my mom in my head and put my head down.

"Nope. I miss her, but I'm not upset. She was feeling so much pain that she couldn't deal with it no more. I'm upset that B pushed her to it. He didn't have to love her, but he could have been clean about his shit. He didn't try to hide the fact that he was fucking around, he just raw-dogged her. All my mom wanted was for B to show that he cared, but he couldn't even give her that."

"What attracted you to Tyrese?" That question took me to a place I wasn't expecting. My natural reaction was to smile.

"Damn if I know. He just seemed to fit into my life better than anybody else. I was attracted to other guys, but Tyrese always seemed to cancel them out."

"How did he fit into your life? You two didn't get along too well, right?"

"No, we didn't, I mean we have our good times, but those are usually covering up a storm that is coming. Tyrese just understood me. He was that flood that came in after the earthquake, after the tornado and everything else. You get what I'm trying to say?"

"Yes. Why do you think he has such a strong hold on you?"

"I admire Tyrese. He is pure evil and, most times, I wish I could just let shit slide, like he do. I respect him."

"Is there anything left between you and Tyrese?"

"There will always be something between me and him. Once I love you, I can't stop."

"Why didn't you go with Franky when he moved to New York. He wanted to marry you, right?"

"Yes, he did. Franky deserved better than me. I wasn't ready to make that kind of commitment. Franky wanted a normal life, he wanted kids, and I didn't want that."

"Why did you stay involved with Franky for so long if you knew it wasn't going anywhere?"

"Franky was my peace of mind, he was my fresh air when the game got too muggy."

"Do you regret killing him?"

"I wish I didn't have to. He was hurt and I felt sorry for him, but he crossed that line, so it had to be done."

"Do you think you deserved to be raped by Game?" I took a deep breath and cleared my head.

"Nobody deserves that. Was I playing with fire? Yes. It was a humbling experience. I've moved on from that."

"Killing him made you feel better?"

"No, it was an impulse thing. He got off way better than I did."

"Would you do anything different?"

"No. As fucked up as most of my decisions were, I wouldn't be who I am, I wouldn't be where I am, without them. I just have to take it in stride. Can't change the past so I have to keep it moving."

"Why do you feel so responsible for Pricey's safety?"

"Because I don't want anything to happen to her. She my sister and I love her. She doesn't deserve to die."

"Who does?"

"Everybody in the game. We all know what will happen to us, we all take that chance. We do wrong and we agree to accept the consequences. Pricey's hands are clean. She hasn't done anything to even be involved. If she was murdered I know that the only reason she would be gone would be to punish me, and I can't have that."

"Didn't she accept the consequences when she got involved with Trip?"

"No!" I slapped my hands on the table.

"Trip is not that important to the game for somebody to go after his loved ones. If Pricey died it would be on me, nobody else, just me. Pricey is the only thing in my life that I can't lose. I can't be in my right mind when it comes to her safety. Nothing is more important than her. I know that it is stupid to have her around, for people to know about her, but I work so hard for my life not to affect hers. I can't just stash her somewhere, I can't ask her to live like that. So I'll do whatever I have to. Yes, she is my weakness, but I can't do nothing about that."

"We will move onto something else."

"Thank you."

"Why do you think you are so accepting of abusive relationships, Veronica?"

"What do you mean?"

"I mean there was never any physical abuse in your household. What made it alright in your head to be physically abused?"

"At first, I couldn't do anything about it. That was the way Dorian dealt with me. He wanted me to be broken, so the punches were coming left and right. I think it was Game who hit me first in a relationship, and when he did it he was upset. He was 'in love with me,' and it hurt him that I didn't feel that way about him. So he hit me. I fought him and that didn't work out in my favor. I accepted it because I deserved it. I feel like that's my punishment for all the things in this world that I have done wrong. I can't go back and I can't move forward, so I just accept it. My life is just one big, fucking punishment, so why should I feel bad about all the fucked-up shit I do?"

"Why was it so easy to stay with Richard, but not Tyrese." I laughed.

"Because when Richard says he loves me, he sounds like he really means it. Richard will make a fool out of his self for me, like I will for him. He shows me that he feels something. Tyrese is cold all the time. I know that Tyrese doesn't have it in him to love anybody but his self. He is smart like that."

"Do you ever see yourself getting married or having kids?"

"Nooooooo. Not at all. Pricey is enough to worry about."

"So how do you feel about your sexual relationship with Dorian? Do you feel obligated to have sex with him because he is the boss?"

"Wow, that came out of left field. So why do you call your niece, honeybee?"

"This isn't about me, Veronica. Please don't change the subject."

"Sure it is about you, Dewayne. You can't get something for nothing."

"It's not about getting anything. I'm trying to help you."

"Well then help me to feel more relaxed with some of these questions, help me to see that I can trust you. I'm putting everything on the line."

"You haven't told me anything that you wouldn't tell a stranger."

"Do you call her that because she is so sweet?"

"Did you fuck Dorian because you were afraid of what he would do to you if you didn't?"

"Maybe you call her that because she is sweet, but she has a little stinger."

"Or maybe you fucked him because that's the only way you know how to deal with men. Maybe Veronica doesn't have as much self-esteem as she thinks. It could be that you're just simply a whore." I smiled at Dewayne, I could see through his mask.

"Maybe you're right on the money, Dewayne. Maybe I don't value myself. But that doesn't change the fact that you're not much different than other men in my life. You think that I can't tell that you want to fuck me? You're just as crazy as I am. If we have to fuck in order to get a better understanding, then that's fine with me. What's flesh amongst friends?"

"This may come as a shock to you, Veronica, but I'm one guy in this world who is not interested in fucking you."

"Then why is your guard up? Why don't you want me to get close? If it's not sex, then it must be love. When you're ready to be real with me, I'll be real with you. Remember, Dewayne, learn how to separate your personal and your professional life."

"That's what I'm trying to do."

I got up and headed to my room. I stayed up for a while before I went to bed. My last thoughts before I closed my eyes were of Dewayne. He was a sweet man, but I could tell that whenever I was around, he was torn. After the way he reacted to my sex comment, I was beginning to figure him out. I blushed a bit. Dewayne was kinda into me, he found me attractive.

I felt special, I felt pretty.

18

I slept in once again, getting up at around ten. I took a shower, made some coffee and sat outside by my pond.

This was becoming my favorite spot in the house. For the first time in a long time, nothing was eating at me. I could sit outside and look at the fish swim around. Dewayne came outside shortly after I finished my cup of coffee. He sat beside me and handed me a blanket.

"Here, it's a little chilly out here."

"Thank you, Dewayne." I wrapped the blanket around me and continued to look at the fish.

"Yesterday I was out of line and I apologize for that, Veronica."

"It's fine. Everything you said was right. You don't have to be sorry for that."

"I shouldn't have spoken to you that way and it won't happen again. You were right the other night as well: She does have a little stinger. She is the strongest person that I know, the smartest, too." I smiled and made eye contact with Dewayne.

"She is your sister's daughter, isn't she?"

"Yes. She is the apple of my eye and my weakness."

"Dorian is the only man that I have ever known. He isn't the best man and he isn't the nicest man, but he has been such a big part of my life. I respect Dorian. For all that he has given me, I am loyal to him and whatever he wants he gets."

"Do you want to die, Veronica?"

"No, I don't want to die. I have just accepted death."

"Do you love yourself?" I giggled a little bit.

"I don't know. Have you ever been in love before, Dewayne?"

"I don't know. What does that feel like?"

"Hell if I know. I'm just winging it."

"You love Richard, don't you?"

"Yes, but it's a different kind of love. I love Richard because I can see inside of him. He is just as sick as I am and I love that. I think that love is accepting everything about one person and loving it."

"Even if they hurt you? Love isn't supposed to hurt, right?"

"I have never experienced a love like that."

We sat there and talked for a couple of hours. We did that every day for three weeks. I had learned a lot about myself and I had found a friend in Dewayne. He was like nobody that I had ever met before, and I respected him. Dewayne said I was ready. He informed me that we would be leaving for Tibet early the next morning. We were to relocate there and stay with a man named Ykio. Dewayne and Ykio were to teach me everything that I needed to know. On some *for real* shit, Ykio scared the shit out of me. Nobody should possess that much skill. He was like a god or something. Ykio was something out of this world. He didn't talk much, but in those two months that I lived in his house with his two daughters and Dewayne, I learned so much. His daughters Mylin and Melon taught me how to be a lady, how to walk, talk and carry myself. I mean the whole experience blew my mind. Every day was peaceful and I found it very easy to center myself. We worked out twice a day and I tightened up on my moves. I learned to move almost as fast as Ykio, but he would always show me up. He wanted me to take this very seriously, and appreciated all that I was being taught. I didn't take the discipline personally and I wasn't even in pain. I spent most of my free time lying in the tall grass at night, listening to the grasshoppers make music. Dewayne would sit with me sometimes and we would talk about whatever popped into our heads. He was the only friend that I had and I was so grateful to have met him.

"Dewayne, do you want to get married one day and have a family?"

"I am satisfied with the family that I have, but I wouldn't mind having one of my own. I'm letting everything play itself out. I try not to plan my personal life."

"I never had the desire to have kids or get married, but if me and my family could live this peacefully, then I would think about it."

"Yeah, it is nice out here."

We fell quiet for a moment, then went inside. Dewayne walked me to my room and stopped me before I could walk in. He pulled me close.

"Tomorrow Ykio is going to tell you that is time for you to go home." I tried to pull away from him, but he held me tight.

"You're not going to question him and you're not going to get emotional. If you do, he will feel as if you have not learned all that you need to and he will be very disappointed." I wrapped my arms around Dewayne and buried my face in his chest. With the most humble tone that I have ever used in my life, I let how I felt slip out my mouth.

"I don't want to go home, I want to stay here."

"Veronica, remember what I told you. Good night." I reached out to Dewayne and he stopped.

"What about you, Dewayne? Will I see you again?"

"I don't know." Dewayne walked away and I went into my room. I lay in bed with my eyes open. I didn't want to go to sleep and bring tomorrow any sooner. The next morning, Ykio came to my door at six o'clock.

"'Ronica . . . pack your things." I didn't say anything. I got of bed and did as I was told. I wanted to break down, but I stayed strong. The last thing I wanted was for Ykio to feel as if he had failed with me. I made my way to the living room and everybody was waiting on me.

"Do you have everything?"

I looked at Ykio. "Yes." He nodded and Mylin and Melon came over to give me a hug. I could see in their eyes that I wasn't the only one holding back tears. I said goodbye to them, then left with Dewayne. We rode in the back of a limo to what I thought was the airport, but before I could realize what was going on, we were outside Dewayne's house. He started to get out and I grabbed his arm, pulling him back.

"You're not going to the airport with me? At least, see me off." Dewayne faced his exit and wouldn't look my way.

"I can't, Veronica. Have a safe trip." Dewayne pulled away from me and closed the door behind him. The limo pulled off.

As we drove closer to the airport I thought about all the things that were waiting for me in Chicago. I had mixed feelings about Richard. It was clear that we didn't have a relationship anymore and I thought about how I would react to seeing him again. What would he say to me? What excuse could he make up for his behavior? Would he even care enough to try and explain it? I shook my head. I was a completely different person and I didn't know how the new me would fit into the life that I had in Chicago. I got on the plane and the whole ride I couldn't help but think of Dewayne. Over the past few months, I'd found myself loving him. He was such a good man and an even better friend. I had love for him, serious love. I loved him like I loved Pricey. If he ever needed me I would be there for him. I smiled just thinking about him and all the time we shared together. When I finally landed in Chicago, Pricey was there to pick me up. She got out of her truck to help me with my bags and we embraced for a while.

"Damn, it seems like it has been years, Roni!" I smiled at her and we got in the truck. "I would have come to see you again, but Dorian said nobody was to come and see you. He said he didn't want anything to get in the way of your progress, all that bullshit. So what's up? Did you and Dewayne get closer?"

"I mean, of course, we did. We had to live together and train together all the time." Pricey rolled her eyes and smacked her lips.

"No, bitch, I mean did ya'll fuck?"

"No! It wasn't like that, he's my friend." A look of shock came over Pricey's face.

"Friend? Wow! Never thought I'd hear that word come out your mouth."

"I know, but Dewayne is cool people."

"So what you gon' do about Richard?"

"Nothing. He is not on my mind. Right now I'll just chalk it up to another mistake." Another shocked look appeared on Pricey's face.

"Damn. Maybe I should spend a couple of months in China and get my head straight."

We laughed and chatted some more about nothing. When we pulled up in front of my apartment building it was kind of surreal. It wasn't like I had forgotten anything, but, in a way, this was all new to me. I had a new mind and a new perception. Pricey parked in back of my truck and I jumped out. I ran over to my truck and gave it a big hug. I had missed my sexy Range Rover. I heard Pricey say, "You a fool," as she started to pull bags out of her truck. I looked up at the entrance of the apartment building because I could hear the door opening. Trip and Tyrese were coming out. I walked slowly over to them and, before any words could be exchanged, Trip pulled me into his arms.

"Hey, Sis! I missed you!" I smiled and hugged Trip back.

"Yeah, man. I missed you, too." He went over to help Pricey with my things. Tyrese moved closer and we stood there looking at each other.

"You alright, Veronica?"

"Yeah, I'm good. You alright?"

"I'm cool." I slapped Tyrese in the arm.

"Good." I walked past him and we all took my things into my apartment. I opened up some windows. "It's stuffy in here," I said.

"Well that's what happens when you're gone for five months." I pushed up against Pricey, playfully.

"Shut up."

"Come on, Roni. We have to get ready for tonight and you know how long you take."

"Get ready for what?" I asked no one in particular.

"Girl, you know Dorian is throwing you a welcome home party." I rolled my eyes and sighed heavily.

"You know we all must celebrate Dorian's number one," Tyrese added. I looked at him, and instead of going there with him, I just gave Pricey a hug.

"See you tonight then."

"Alright, I'll call you later so I can see what you're wearing. Are you going to get your hair done today?" She touched my hair and I smiled.

"I might." I laughed a little bit. "I know I look a mess, Pricey, you don't have to tell me." Pricey hugged me once more and I walked them to the door. I kept it open for Tyrese to leave, but he just sat down so I closed it and went to the kitchen.

"Everything needs to be thrown out." I grabbed a garbage bag from under my sink and started to clean out my fridge. Tyrese came in and stood over me.

"Aren't you going to tell me about your trip?"

"There is nothing to tell. I was there to train and now I'm back."

"What about ole boy you was staying with, what was he like?"

"Dewayne was cool."

"That's it? Just cool?" I looked up at Tyrese and tried to search his face for what he wanted me to say.

"Yeah, he was cool. We trained, we handled some business for Dorian and that's it. That was my stay in China."

"Did you fuck him?"

"I can always count on you, Tyrese, to think crazy things," I said, smiling. "No, we did not have sex. I'm not interested in Dewayne like that."

"What? Is he ugly?" I shook my head and laughed.

"No, he isn't ugly, Tyrese."

"What? That nigga gay, then?"

"No! Why would you say that?"

"So if he not gay, he not ugly and you claim that he is a cool guy, why didn't you hook up with him?"

"Because he is my friend and I don't think about him in a sexual way."

"Get the fuck out of here!" I shook my head again and continued to clean.

"So what about Richard?"

"What about him?"

"Ya'll together?"

"I haven't talked to him since I left, so I'm guessing no."

"You handling this pretty well, seeing how he played you so tough."

"I guess so." I stood up and headed for the door.

"I'm about to go take out my trash. You staying?" Tyrese walked up to me.

"Let me get that for you, we can finish up this conversation later."

"Alright."

I closed the door once Tyrese left and started to laugh my ass off. *That's* who used to have me so open? I couldn't believe that, at one point in my life, I was attracted to him. I ran a bath and watched TV. I soaked in the tub, washed up and slipped on some thin sweats so I could go get my hair and nails done for that night. While I took care of business, stopping at the grocery store so I could refill my fridge, I noticed that I was being followed by Richard. I didn't pay him any mind. He could follow me all he wanted. It would've been easier to just call, though. I made it back home a couple of hours later and put up my groceries. Going to my room, I stood in front of my closet wondering what I should wear. What kind of party would this be? Should I dress casual or formal? I decided my best bet would be just to call Dorian and ask, so I did.

"I see you made it back safe. How was everything?"

"It was fine. I learned a lot, Ykio was great to be around and so was Dewayne. He was very hospitable."

"Good. So I'm sure Pricey told you about the party."

"Yes, that's what I'm calling about. Is this going to be a big or small party? I'm really not sure what I should wear."

"Why didn't you call Pricey for that?" Dorian said, playfully, and I thought about what choice I'd made for a moment.

"Because I wanted your opinion, Dorian. I hope you're not too busy to help me out."

Dorian laughed. "No, I think I can give you a few minutes of my time."

"Thank you." I smiled into the phone. I had to say I missed Dorian.

"You can wear whatever you want, it's your party."

"Thanks, you're a lot of help."

"I try, Veronica." We shared a laugh and I told him I'd see him soon.

Just as I was about to call Pricey, I heard something in the living room. I moved slowly to my closet and pulled out one of my guns. Somebody was in my house. I made my way out of the bedroom, checked the bathroom, then the kitchen. Nothing. As I was walking to the living room, I could feel myself getting closer to my target. I flung my gun to the side of me and dropped it to see Richard's face. I rolled my eyes and went back to my room.

"How did you get into my place?" I asked the question, but didn't care if he gave me an answer. I flipped through some of my clothes.

"I have a key."

"Remind me to get the locks changed." Richard came up behind me.

"Now you know if I couldn't get in, I would just break the door down."

"I'm sure." Richard wrapped his arms around my waist and kissed my neck.

"I know you're a little upset about not hearing from me and I'm sorry. I would have come to see you, but Dorian said it was out of the question." I pulled away from Richard and pulled out a navy-blue suit.

"Richard, I really haven't given you much thought these past months. You don't owe me any kind of apology. If you don't mind, I really have to get ready for my party. I'm sure you can let yourself out." He flung me around to face him and held tightly onto my arms.

"I'm not going nowhere! You can run to Dorian, but you don't want to talk to me?"

"Richard, I really don't have time for this right now, let me go." He took a step back from me and we finally made eye contact.

"Fine. I'll see you later."

When I heard the door close I sat down on my bed. How was I going to do this? How was I going to see Richard and pretend that I didn't care? I thought he loved me, but why didn't he take my calls? How could he just act like nothing happened? Like he hadn't turned his back on me and hurt me. I didn't know how to feel; whether I should be mad or if I should let it go. Should I reconsider a relationship with him or just walk away from him? I loved him, but why was he making this so hard? I took a deep breath. The show must go on. I stood up, went back to my closet and called Pricey.

"I don't know what to wear."

"Roni, me either. Nothing is popping out at me. I want to wear pants, but then I don't."

"I know, I want to wear pants, but I also want to wear a dress."

"I just don't want to be overdressed. I'm not feeling the evening gown and shit like that."

"Okay, Pricey, this what I'm thinking: Maybe we should wear a suit."

"A suit? Girl, I'm trying to be sexy tonight. A suit is not going to do it."

"Then I don't know what to tell you."

"I mean what haven't we wore already?"

"It's not like we not gon' look better than everybody else, no matter what we wear."

"True, true." We laughed on the phone and I told her I would see her soon.

It was down to the wire. I needed to leave, like, five minutes before, so I just decided on a very light-blue, strapless, short dress. It was tight up top, but kinda flowed out at the bottom, and it had a darker blue bow that went around my waist. I was cute. I left my hair down in loose curls and ran out to my truck. I didn't want to be too late. When I arrived, I could see someone was in Dorian's room, but I couldn't tell who it was. If it wasn't Dorian, someone would be in a lot of trouble when I told on them. When I walked into Dorian's house I ran upstairs before anybody could say anything to me. I caught a glimpse of Richard looking at me with evil eyes. I opened the door and saw Dorian sitting at his desk, and another gentlemen sitting down with his back to me. I ran over to Dorian and we embraced in a deep hug.

"How you doing, old man? I missed you!"

"I missed you, too, Veronica. You look great." We pulled away slowly and I was shocked to see that Dewayne was the man that I didn't recognize from behind. He stood to his feet and I damn near tackled him to the ground trying to give him a hug.

"This is a nice surprise for my party. From the way you was talking, I thought I would never see you again." Dewayne pulled us apart.

"We weren't supposed to see each other again. I didn't know Dorian was having a party for you tonight." I took a step back from Dewayne and tried to search his face, but couldn't read a damn thing.

"Well then what is this about?" I looked at Dorian and he looked at Dewayne. Dewayne took my hand.

"Veronica, I had fun with you. I really did, but I think it's best that we don't communicate with each other on a personal level. You told me to keep it professional and that's what I intend to do. I can't allow myself to get caught up in your drama." I pulled my hand away and started for the door. "Veronica, I'm trying to explain." I stopped and turned, facing him, but there was still a lot of space in between us.

"Most people in this business didn't know my name and now that I have met you, it's like a red bull's eye has been placed on me." I folded my arms, signaling that he needed to hurry the hell up. "Please don't call me anymore. You're not welcome at my house when you're in China, and it would be better if we didn't have to do business with each other anymore." Dewayne said that last part in the direction of Dorian. I unfolded my arms and held my head high.

"Thank you for being up front with your feelings. I appreciate your honesty about our past situation and I agree. Keep things professional. You won't ever hear from me again. Sorry for interrupting your meeting." I closed the door behind me and fought the urge to fall and cry out my soul in the process. Instead, I just ran to the nearest bathroom and cried into a rag. The bathroom just happened to have a vent where I could hear the men talking.

"Wow, China did wonders for Veronica. Good job, Dewayne."

"She hates me now."

"Veronica will bounce back, she always does. It's hard for me to walk away from that pussy. How do you do it so well?"

"What? We didn't have sex. Veronica is my friend. That's all."

"Then why would you give your friend the boot? Why be concerned about drama when you're just friends?"

"Because you know how I feel about her!"

"Then maybe you should have told her how you felt and explained where you were coming from. All Veronica knows now is her first friend cast her aside." They stopped talking and then I heard Dorian say, "Come downstairs. There are a few people I want you to meet."

Dewayne got up and headed downstairs with Dorian. How could he face me now? I got off the closed toilet lid and cut on the bathroom light. I didn't even want to look at myself in the mirror. I was sure I looked bad. When I looked at myself, a fresh batch of tears wanted to form, but I closed my eyes and took a deep breath. I quickly washed my face, put some lotion on, did my eyes and my lips. I was good as new; hell, I looked better than I did when I first came in. I unlocked the bathroom and made my way down the stairs. I spotted Pricey and she had a drink in her hand for me. That was my girl. I wasn't going to get too fucked-up, but I needed a buzz right about then, so I took my drink.

"Here you go, Roni."

"Thank you. I love your dress. Is that the one you picked up in China?"

"Yes. I like yours. Blue is your color, baby." We laughed and then Pricey's face went blank. She moved in closer to me.

"Oh no. Here comes psycho, and he looks mad."

"I'll meet you outside by the pool in a minute," I said.

"Alright." As Pricey walked away, Richard grabbed me by the upper arm and pulled me into a close embrace.

"Did you fuck them, Veronica? You were up there for a long time!"

"I think you better let me go before this turns into a ugly thing, Richard. If you would like to speak with me in the hallway, that will be fine." Richard pulled away from me and I followed him into the hallway. I could feel Dewayne looking at me as we walked past him. When we got to the hall, I wasted no time grabbing Richard by the throat and putting my death grip on him. "Let me clear things up for you, white boy. If you put your fucking hands on me again I will break your arm. You don't have the right to question me about anything, because you decided to bitch up and not talk to Dorian. If you continue to disrespect me, we won't have anything to talk about." I could see that Richard's eyes were rolling toward the back of his head, so I let him go, only to take my right arm and put force on his neck, once more. "Get this through your head: I am not your property and I am, for damn sure, not afraid of you. Being in a relationship with me is a blessing. The Lord can giveth and the Lord can taketh away. Remember that shit!" I let Richard go and he reached out to hug me—the only reason I accepted it was because Dewayne had decided to stick his head out into the hall. I moved closer to Richard as he began to cry. "Your tears sicken me. You will get no sympathy from me." I kissed Richard on the cheek and walked away. As I made my way to the pool area to meet Pricey, out of the corner of my eye I could see that Dewayne was following me. I sat next to Pricey and folded my legs, while Pricey passed me another drink. Dewayne stood over us.

"Veronica, I would like to explain myself a little bit better. I think you have taken what I said in the wrong way."

"Dewayne, I am sure I heard you quite well and I understand. I will honor your wishes. Don't worry." Pricey looked at me and started to unravel the secret Dewayne was trying to keep under wraps.

"No, Veronica, there was something else I didn't tell you. Something else that will make you feel better about the situation." I looked up at Dewayne and put my hand on his chest.

"I feel fine about the situation. I'm sorry that you feel bad about it, but that's really not my problem. The only way to honor this little thing is if we both stop talking to one another." I patted his chest, then pulled my hand away and turned, facing Pricey. She was trying to hold in her laugh, but in doing that, she made me laugh. Dewayne just walked away. It served him right.

"What the hell was that about, Veronica?"

"Girl, I'll tell you about it later."

"So what was psycho talking about?"

"He didn't say much of anything, trying to act tough and I had to let him know momma not playing those games anymore." Pricey gave me five.

"Yeah, that's what I'm talking about! Put that ass in place. So you think you gon' get back with him? He was the love of your life not too long ago."

"Girl, what was it—about five months since we were in Jamaica? Seems like a lifetime to me. I don't know why I was stressing him so hard."

"Because he was laying it on thick, girl. What woman doesn't want a man to tell them he loves them, unconditionally? Ya'll had a good thing in Jamaica, Veronica. All you have to do now is figure out if it was real or if it was game."

"I don't think it was game and I don't think it was real. I think that Richard is a different person when he is in a relationship. I think my past has him paranoid and he tries to control me, but that shit ain't gon' fly." Pricey put her glass in the air and looked at me to do the same. I did.

"Here's to a bitch who has her head on straight!"

"Here, here, I'll drink to that, Pricey." We clicked our glasses together.

"Veronica you will drink to anything, you fucking alcoholic." I finished my glass and decided that would be all I would drink that night.

"I know you not talking, Pricey. You drink like a fish."

"Yeah. I drink water." We looked at each other and burst into laughter.

"Let's go dance. I haven't been dancing in a long time."

We went inside and the DJ had just started to kick off the music. Me and Pricey tore the dance floor up. While we danced I had not a care in the world, I let loose and danced all my worries out my body. I looked around the room at Dewayne: Mistake! At Tyrese: *Big* fucking mistake! At Richard: *Good* mistake. And then at Dorian, out near the pool. Before the words could come to my mind, he smiled at me. I smiled back and noticed some chick behind him. She looked so familiar, but I couldn't put my finger on why. I did see her reaching for something in her jacket, and when I saw a small twenty-two in her hands, everything stopped. I was running as fast as I could, drawing my gun from my inner thigh and, just before this mystery woman could pull the trigger, I shot her in the wrist that she was holding her gun in.

Nobody moved when they heard the shot go off, but all eyes were on me as I quickly approached the girl who was behind Dorian. She had dropped her gun, but I could tell she was about to try and pick it up again. Within the blink of an eye, Dorian drew his gun and was pointing it in my direction. That didn't stop me from coming at the girl. She was about to make a move and I needed to stop her. Dewayne tried to grab me as I ran past him, but I hit the floor, sliding through Dorian's legs and kicked the girl in her knees. Shots rang out this time; three, to be exact. I held onto my gun and wondered if I was hit. I looked over at this woman who I was so determined to stop and she was in the pool sinking to the bottom. As I sat up, I could see her face: It was Dawn. Her eyes were still open as she hit the bottom of the pool. I crawled slowly over to the edge of the pool and looked at her. I saw her clothes and the jewelry she had on, then her face one last time. The pool went dark around her and I could see nothing else. I felt people rushing me, pulling me up on my feet, hands going all across my body, and loud voices in my ear.

I couldn't take my eyes off the pool.